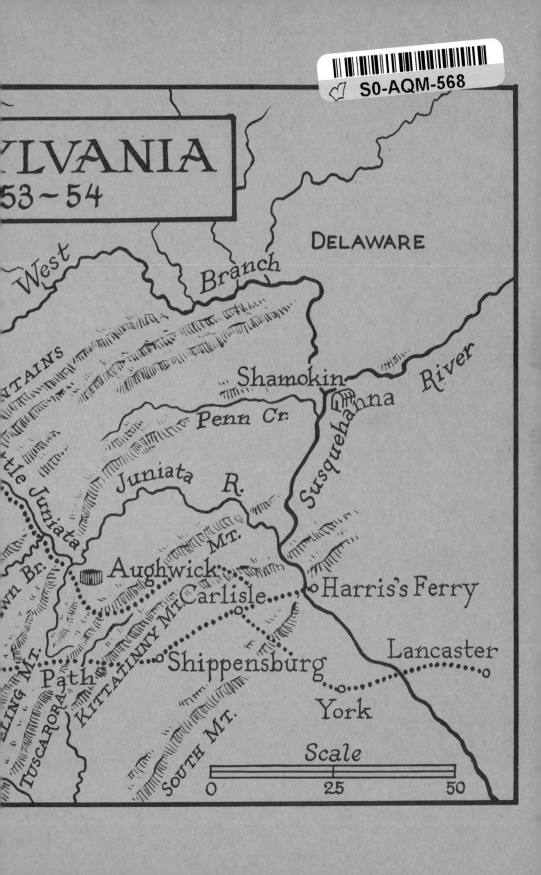

YLVANIA

53 – 54

West

Branch

DELAWARE

TAINS

Shamokin

Penn Cr.

Juniata

R.

tle Juniata

Susquehanna River

wn Br.

MT.

Aughwick

Carlisle

Harris's Ferry

LING MT.

Path

Shippensburg

Lancaster

TUSCARORA

KITTATINNY MT.

York

SOUTH MT.

Scale

0   25   50

Jason McGee

By the same author

Jim Mundy

JASON McGEE

Robert H. Fowler

HARPER & ROW, PUBLISHERS
New York   Hagerstown   San Francisco   London

FIRST EDITION

Designed by C. Linda Dingler

Endpaper map by Charles Dallas

Library of Congress Cataloging in Publication Data

Fowler, Robert H
  Jason McGee.

  1. United States—History—French and Indian War, 1755–1763—Fiction. I. Title.
PZ4.F7867Jas [PS3556.0847] 813'.5'4   78-20203
ISBN 0-06-011382-0

---

79 80 81 82 83 10 9 8 7 6 5 4 3 2 1

To
William A. Hunter

By Way of Explanation

Although most of the characters in this novel are fictional, a few are or were real persons who lived in Pennsylvania in the mid 1700s. I confess to taking some liberties in my characterizations of these people, but have avoided having them do or say anything contradictory to what can be learned about them from the historical record they left. If I have misrepresented them, I ask the pardon of the ghosts of John Harris, Sr., John Harris, Jr., the Reverend John Elder, George Croghan, Benjamin Franklin, Conrad Weiser, Tanacharison (the Half King), Captain Philippe-Thomas de Joncaire, and Ensign Villiers de Jumonville.

I deliberately did not give a speaking part to one important historical figure even though he played a considerable role in the events with which this novel deals. In the winter of 1753–54, the young George Washington was sent by the governor of Virginia to warn the French to clear out of the upper Ohio Valley. I kept Washington off my stage partly out of respect for him as the father of our country, but mainly because he did write a well-known account of his adventures and if he had met my leading characters he hardly could have failed to include them. So my fictional people hear of his visit, but do not encounter him.

From my backyard in a suburb of New Cumberland, Pennsylvania, I can look out over that part of the Susquehanna River where several generations of settlers and countless horseloads of trade goods crossed in one direction, and packs of furs in the other. Raising my eyes, I can see the Blue Mountain range, which at the time of my story marked the boundary between white and Indian country. Thus many of the adventures of Jason McGee occurred, if not in my own backyard, at least in sight of it.

Likewise, much of my research was done in the same local area. My thanks go to the personnel at the New Cumberland Public Library, the Pennsylvania State Library, the Pennsylvania Historical and Museum Commission, the Historical Society of Dauphin County and the Cumberland County Historical Association's Hamilton Library at Carlisle for their assistance.

Away from my backyard, but well within the setting of part of my story, the staffs at the Historical Society of Western Pennsylvania in Pittsburgh, the Laughlin Memorial Library in Ambridge, the Beaver Area Heritage Foundation and the Venango County Historical Society have been helpful.

It would be wearying and pointless to list all the county histories and other books, the pamphlets and manuscripts, my wife and I consulted in researching *Jason McGee,* but I would like to recommend several of our most useful sources:

George Croghan, Wilderness Diplomat, by Nicholas B. Wainwright, Chapel Hill, 1959; *William Trent and the West,* by Sewell E. Slick, Harrisburg, 1947; *Pioneer Life in Western Pennsylvania,* by J. E. Wright and Doris S. Corbett, Pittsburgh, 1940; *Pennsylvania Architecture and Country Life, 1640–1840,* by Stevenson Whitcomb Fletcher, Harrisburg, 1950; *The Wilderness Trail* (two volumes) by Charles A. Hanna, New York, 1911; and *Forts on the Pennsylvania Frontier, 1753–1758,* by William A. Hunter, Harrisburg, 1960.

Finally, let me recommend three books, all by the late Paul A. W. Wallace, who was a distinguished scholar of this period: *Conrad Weiser, Friend of Colonist and Mohawk,* Philadelphia, 1945; *Indians in Pennsylvania,* Harrisburg, 1975; and *Indian Paths of Pennsylvania,* Harrisburg, 1971.

Early in the writing of this novel, I had to choose between clarity and absolute authenticity of dialogue. My wife dutifully reread *Tom Jones* and *Tristram Shandy,* novels published respectively in 1749 and 1761, for examples of how people spoke in that period. But I decided against slavishly imitating Henry Fielding or Laurence Sterne, and, instead, sought to give the flavor of the language only.

To avoid confusion, I have settled arbitrarily on spellings of certain names and places. Delaware Indians called themselves the Lenni Lenape or the "True People." The French referred to them as "Loups." The influential Iroquois tribes were often spoken of as the Six Nations (formerly the Five Nations, until they took the Tuscaroras into junior partnership). Many Pennsylvanians called them Mingoes.

The Indians known as the Shawnee today had several designations in the 1750s. I chose Shawanese.

The people we now call Scotch-Irish were rarely so designated in the 1750s. Then they variously were called Irishers, Ulstermen, Scots or Ulster Scots.

The Cumberland Valley, in which I live, was the Great or North Valley in the 1700s; the Blue Mountain range was the Kittatinny Mountain. There were four different spellings of the Indian group of settlements I call Kuskusky.

As I have intimated, my wife, Beverly Utley Fowler, has helped me with the research. She has accompanied me on several trips over back roads in Pennsylvania following old trading paths, shorthand note pad at hand, and she has suffered through listening to windy first drafts of the book read to her aloud. I am grateful to her, to my literary agent, Victor Chapin, who has read and criticized the book, part by part, as it has been written, and to Harvey Ginsberg, senior editor at Harper & Row, for his patient guidance in polishing the manuscript for publication.

Despite their help, the generosity of libraries and historical societies, and the availability of so much material, this book would have taken an extra year to write had it not been for the advice and guidance of a number of friends and neighbors. Robert G. Crist of Camp Hill, Pennsylvania, a respected local historian, read the manuscript and saved me from some embarrassing errors; Joe Darlington of New Bloomfield directed me to the sites where white squatters lived in the 1740s; the Reverend Morton G. Glise, pastor of Paxton United Presbyterian Church, advised me on the history of his institution; Donald H. Kent, former director of Archives and History of the Pennsylvania Historical and Museum Commission, read portions of the manuscript; Dr. Frederic S. Klein assisted me with the history of Lancaster County; Mrs. Ethel Smith doubled as amanuensis and critic in typing the final drafts of the book; Mrs. Odette Spurgin, a native of France who now lives in New Cumberland, advised me on French as it was spoken in the 1700s; and Mrs. John Curtis, Quaker Bibliographer for the Friends Historical Association at Haverford College, on Quaker speech of the same period.

But of all the people who have offered assistance, I have relied the most on William A. Hunter, retired chief of the Division of Research and Publications at the Pennsylvania Historical and Museum Commission, and the best authority I know on Pennsylvania in the mid-1700s. I have picked his brains and borrowed from his personal library shamelessly. Besides giving me what amounted to a year-long course in the history of the Pennsylvania frontier, he has read behind me chapter by chapter. No one is better qualified as a mentor than Bill Hunter. I am most grateful to him for his instruction and for his generosity. That is why this book is dedicated to him.

Jason McGee

Introduction

On a chilly morning in early October, 1753, a strange procession left the frontier town of Shippensburg, Pennsylvania, following an old Indian path westward toward a gap in the Kittatinny Mountain range. It was headed by a lean, dark-haired man in his mid forties, wearing a deerskin hunting jacket and coonskin hat, and leading a nimble gray pony. Just behind him walked a stocky blond man, somewhat younger. Dressed in a long-skirted black coat and knee breeches and wearing a broad-brimmed black hat and buckled shoes, he led a sleek roan gelding. Bringing up the rear was a tall, red-haired youth wearing a workman's rude smock and a tricorn hat, and carrying an exquisitely crafted flintlock rifle. He led a one-eyed mare, and was followed closely by a large yellow dog.

The man at the head of the column was an Indian trader, and his mission was to obtain furs from the Shawanese and Delawares in the western reaches of the Pennsylvania wilderness in exchange for the rum, combs, pots, blankets and other trade goods packed on the backs of the three horses. The man in black was answering the call of his Quaker inner light to go and save the souls of the Indians with whom his companion meant to trade.

The youth was Jason McGee, aged nineteen, and his purpose was one that cannot be told in a few words and, anyway, should not be disclosed so early in this narrative. Besides, he was not altogether certain at that stage of his exact motives, although he thought he was. The dog was going because he lived to please Jason McGee. The horse, the mare and the pony had no choice.

If any one of the three men had known how the expedition would end, he would have turned back to Shippensburg that very morning. They were not privileged to see the future, however, only the past. And for Jason McGee, this journey really had begun almost exactly nine years before.

PART ONE

1

The adventures of Jason McGee began on one of those flawless days that sometimes grace Pennsylvania's Susquehanna Valley in October. Not a cloud marred the soft blue of the sky arching over the low, close-wooded mountains. The air was calm, caressing the skin like balm. The earth felt as warm as a mother's bosom, and all around the McGee cabin and clearing, the forest of oak and hickory rang with the calls of birds. It was a day that the ten-year-old Jason might have remembered for its sheer beauty. But he would have other reasons to recall that October day in 1744; to bear it like a weight on his memory for the rest of his life.

His mother had sent him to the spring. The two leathern buckets, now full of water, felt as though they would pull his arms from their sockets. He stopped on the knoll overlooking his family's clearing, put the buckets down beside the path and sat against an enormous hickory tree to rest.

He was a skinny lad, tall for his age, with violently red hair and pale blue eyes set amidst a constellation of freckles.

It had been an uneventful day thus far. His father, Abraham, was away on one of his overnight trips to Harris's Ferry and, in his absence, Jason and his older brother, Isaac, had fallen into another of their fights that morning. Isaac had ordered Jason to milk the cow. Jason protested that it was not his turn. Isaac had advanced upon Jason, thinking to overawe him. The brothers stood face to face, glaring at each other: Isaac square-shouldered and dark-haired; Jason nearly as tall, but lighter-framed.

"If you want the cow milked, milk her yourself."

Isaac slapped Jason, and the fight was on. Jason rushed at his brother, trying in vain to throw him down. They struggled in silence so that their mother, Gerta, would not hear. But their little sister, Stella, saw it all and ran to tell her. When Gerta arrived, Isaac was sitting on Jason, barely able to keep him down. Jason did not mind, for he realized he was gaining strength. In time he would be able to win.

Had he been home, Abraham would have settled the row quickly with his belt, but Gerta only chided them in her German accent, saying, "Why do you fight so? Brothers should love one another."

Finally, having shamed them into a truce, she had set them on tasks that would keep them separated.

Even though he had caught his breath and his arms no longer ached, Jason remained sitting on the knoll, staring down at the clearing, where Isaac hacked away with a mattock in the vegetable plot, readying the earth for winter turnips, while Stella played about the cabin door. Gerta was hanging out clothes to dry on a bush. She was still pretty, not yet grown fat or toothless like so many pioneer women, with hair that gleamed as brightly in the October sun as the golden cross about her neck.

Gerta had a favorite saying: "Muessiggang ist aller laster anfang," or "Idleness is the root of all evil." But as Abraham sometimes countered, "Well-earned rest is good for the soul." Jason found it good just now to rest and think.

The McGees had no legal right to be out here north of the mountain, for these lands were reserved for the Indians by the provincial government in Philadelphia, a fact that galled Abraham.

"By God, the land is here and the Indians aren't using it," he had said to Gerta the night before he set out for the Susquehanna.

"We would get better use here if you did not drink so much," Gerta had replied, not so much to rebut him as to remind him not to spend their money on rum at Harris's Ferry. "I don't want you to become a siffler."

"If ye are calling me a drunkard, do it in English," he had retorted. And once started, he had gone on, railing against the Germans now so thickly settled east of the Susquehanna. "Sure, they are a pious lot. They got their land and they don't want others getting theirs."

Stung at last, Gerta had charged "the Irishers" with being lazy and quarrelsome.

"Aye, ye say hard things agin my people now, but ye were ready enough to run off with me with no thought of kirk or pastor."

It was a remark that always stung her. Proud of his new lands in the Pequea Valley and full of Lutheran piety, her father would not consent to her marrying a penniless immigrant from the North of Ireland. So she had simply left in the night to become the woman of Abraham McGee, taking only her clothes and the delicate gold cross and chain left to her by her grandmother. They had moved to a nearby settlement of Presbyterians and there Abraham had worked for eight years as a day laborer, but he had found his countrymen inhospitable to a couple from such different backgrounds. By the time Gerta's nagging had moved him to improve their lot, more enterprising men of his race and religion had crossed the Susquehanna and taken up the richest lands of the North Valley, with or without provincial licenses.

At last, in the spring of 1740, with the boys soon to be old enough to work and with a few shillings laid by through Gerta's thrift, they had loaded tools, kitchen equipment and bedclothing on the backs of a decrepit horse and a young milk cow, crossed the Susquehanna and walked over a gap to settle in the forbidden north shadow of the mountains. A lean-to had sheltered them that first summer, and Abraham had argued for merely patching it up to make do for the winter, but Gerta had persuaded him otherwise. By November, working harder than he knew he could, Abraham had completed a snug fifteen-by-twenty-foot cabin of notched logs. The boys and Gerta had chinked the gaps with mud while Abraham had constructed a crude fireplace and chimney across one end. Later they had helped him build a sleeping loft across the other end and a sound roof of painfully hewn oak shingles.

They were glad Gerta's will had prevailed, for that winter was the most severe in the memory of white settlers. The first of several heavy snows fell in early December, followed by cold so intense that it made the crust hard enough to bear the weight of the cow and horse. Their food came that winter from the frozen carcasses of deer in adjacent woods. Packs of wolves, mad with hunger, sometimes came to the clearing, leaving only when Abraham fired his musket at them. The McGees did not see the bare earth again until mid March.

Then in 1743, acting at the insistence of resentful Indians of the area, colonial authorities had turned many squatters off their clearings and burned their cabins. Only luck and its remote location saved the McGee cabin.

So they had survived. But Gerta was far from satisfied. After four years their cabin floor was still bare earth and Abraham was slow about clearing more land, saying they should wait until the boys were older and stronger.

"We can't starve here. We got the cow. We raise vegetables, and there is plenty of game in the woods."

Gerta reminded him that he long ago had promised her a brass pot.

7

"Ye don't know what they cost. Someday, when I get some extra money."

"When a pig sprouts wings."

After twelve years, Gerta still loved her profane Ulsterman even though his lackadaisical attitude offended her German sense of industry. There were many tender moments between them, but their quarrels were becoming more frequent. Stella could sleep through them, but Isaac and Jason often lay in their shuck bed in the loft, embarrassed and frightened by the bitter words.

Jason put the memory out of his mind. There were many good times, living on the edge of this wilderness. He and Isaac did not always fight. They often wandered down to Sherman's Creek to fish and swim. And occasionally their father would take them to an Indian village along the river to trade for deerskins, which he tanned for resale at the Harris trading post.

In the evenings, the family often sat about the fire and listened to Abraham tell of his hard life in County Antrim and describe his voyage on an overcrowded ship from Belfast to Philadelphia. Or he would sing songs boasting of Orange victories over the Catholics of Ireland. Gerta had the better voice. She sang gentle, soothing songs that made them feel secure, even though they understood few of the German words.

Now, away from Isaac's bullying, lying at ease, Jason looked up into the trees, trying to discern which bird made which sounds, until, as if by a signal, their singing halted. Jason heard the rustle of leaves and saw a doe pick her graceful, nervous way onto the path, followed by a still-awkward half-grown fawn. Jason reached for a stone, but before they came into range, the doe stiffened and suddenly scampered back into the woods.

An enormous hawk, nearly as large as an eagle, glided overhead, turned above the clearing and then swooped back low over the knoll. Its shadow flickered for an instant across Jason's face.

Time to get up. If he delayed his return much longer, Gerta would be calling him.

Jason was bending over to pick up the buckets when he heard her screams.

2

Three Indians with blackened faces, one enormously tall, were racing across the clearing. Two of them flung themselves upon Isaac and subdued him as he was raising his mattock to defend himself.

The giant Indian loped ahead to intercept Gerta and Stella at the cabin door. His tomahawk blade caught the sunlight for an awful instant and then fell again and again.

Jason first thought of running back toward the mountain gap in the hope of encountering his father on his way home. Then he thought of running down the hill and hurling himself upon the Indians. But the massacre was over so quickly that he only watched in horrified silence as the big Indian dragged the bodies of Gerta and Stella into the cabin while the other two bound Isaac's arms and gagged him.

In a few moments, the giant Indian emerged from the cabin holding up an object which Jason knew from its golden glitter to be his mother's cross. He also carried a burning stick taken from the fire that Gerta always kept going. After piling litter around the cabin and on the roof, the three Indians set fire to it and tossed the brand inside as well.

While the flames mounted around the cabin, the big Indian examined Isaac, holding him by the hair as he looked him over. The Indians seemed to be arguing. Finally the tall one nodded and lowered his tomahawk, sparing Isaac. Next they led the cow from the lean-to and cut her throat. Bawling and gushing blood, the beast went down on her knees and fell on her side. The giant unfastened the bloody rope from the cow's neck and put it around Isaac's. The three of them laughed at the boy. Throwing back his head, the big one slipped Gerta's cross about his own neck. Again they laughed. Jason would remember that the giant's profile showed a Roman nose, minus the tip.

All this he observed with frozen limbs and paralyzed voice. He remained beside the hickory tree, watching as the cabin blazed. The Indians stood about until the roof collapsed and then, leading Isaac by the cow's rope and shoving him along, they passed out of Jason's sight, headed west.

Abraham did not return until late that afternoon. He came over the mountain gap leading his old horse and carrying a shiny new brass pot, as fine a pot as Gerta had ever imagined. Jason could hear him lustily singing "Barbara Allen":

> "And from her grave there grew a rose,
> And out of his a brier,
> And they climbed to the steeple top,
> Till they could grow no higher;
> And there they formed a true-lover's knot,
> The red rose and the brier. . . ."

He found Jason standing beside the charred and still-smoking rubble that had been their cabin.

"What happened? Speak up, you fool boy."

At last Jason managed, "Indians . . . th-th-three Indians."

"Your mother. Did they take her away?"

Jason shook his head and Abraham's face showed momentary relief.

"I-I-Isaac. They t-t-took Isaac."

"What about your mother? What about Stella?" Abraham was shouting now. "Damn you, boy. Stop your stuttering and tell me."

"D-d-dead. They k-k-killed her."

"Killed? Killed Gerta?"

When at last it sunk in, Abraham hurled the brass pot into the bushes and went down on his knees, weeping with clenched fists pumping up and down. Then he rose and walked in circles, raging toward heaven, and all the while Jason, unable either to swear or to cry, stood silently, his heart near to bursting.

Just as Jason had been torn between running toward the gap for help, or flinging himself upon the Indians, so Abraham debated whether to cross the mountains to seek aid among the settlers in the valley, or to take Jason and set out after the Indians right away. But it would soon be dark and the Indians would be fifteen miles away, who knew where? Besides, his only weapon, a short-barreled musket, had been in the cabin, hidden under a shuck mattress. And so, like Jason, Abraham did nothing. Using coals from the smoldering rubble, he built a fire in front of the lean-to and he and Jason huddled there, leaning against the sleeping horse, through the longest, bleakest night either of them would ever know.

The next morning Abraham cut a piece of meat from the haunch of the dead cow and charred it over the fire for their breakfast. He and Jason dug two graves beside the bush Gerta had used for drying clothes. Finally, when there was no way to avoid it any longer, they rummaged through the rubble to find the ghastly, roasted things that

10

had been a warm, pretty woman and a golden-haired little girl.

It was afternoon before they completed the burial and recited the Lord's Prayer over the mounds. Abraham was too tired, too drained, to rant anymore. His tone became gentle. "Come, Jason, son. We got to keep living. Let's go back to Harris's and tell them what has happened. They will get up a party to help look for Isaac."

Their story created a sensation along the river. Relations with the Indians of the area generally had been peaceful, the only exception having occurred earlier in the year when some Delawares murdered three white traders in a dispute over a horse. But they had been turned over by their own people to the provincial authorities. The ringleader, named Mushemeelin, had been found guilty and even now awaited execution in Philadelphia.

The first to hear a full account of the McGee massacre was John Harris, the elderly Englishman who owned the ferry and thriving trading post on the eastern shore of the Susquehanna. Abraham spoke at angry length, but when it came Jason's turn, as he was to do for many a month, he began to tremble and his words came out in a stutter.

"Th-three of th-them. One v-very tall with no n-nose."

At the conclusion, the old ferryman trader put his hand on Jason's head. "There, me lad. That's enough. 'Tis a sad, bad thing to see yer mother slaughtered so. I can't understand why they would do such a thing."

Abraham was growing angry at Harris's calm questioning, for he had assumed that the trader would send out calls for an expedition to wreak vengeance on the guilty Indians and recover Isaac.

"They must be punished. All three of them must be killed. I want them dead and I want my son back."

"Aye, I know, but we must follow certain procedures. Remember the crime took place in Indian territory. I mean no offense, Brother McGee, but ye were illegally settled up there."

"I have heard it said ye were an Indian-lover, Mister Harris. Are ye taking their side in this and saying the Indians had a right to murder my wife and little girl, to burn my cabin and take away my son?" Abraham's voice rose to a shout and then broke. "The filthy savages even cut the throat of our milk cow."

But Harris declined to promise to do more than present Abraham's deposition to the county court and to send a report of the incident to Shikellamy, the Oneida chief appointed by the Six Iroquois Nations to oversee the Delawares centered around Shamokin, fifty miles upriver.

11

"What about my son? How will I get him back?"

"That, too, we will lay before the chief. Now let's settle you two down for the night. Tomorrow we send word to Shamokin and Lancaster."

So news of the murders went up to Shamokin to be laid before Shikellamy and his Delaware underlings. While they waited for the Indian reaction, Abraham and Jason occupied a small feed shed beyond the Harris barn.

The third day after the massacre, the pastor of the nearby Paxton Presbyterian Church, the Reverend John Elder, rode down to hear their story. After listening gravely to Abraham's now practiced account, he offered to have his congregation collect clothing and other articles for them.

"We'd be grateful for the clothes," Abraham said. "But I should think yer people first would want to take up arms and help me avenge this crime. Aye, and get my boy back as well."

Elder was a tall man, with calm blue eyes and a cultivated voice with little of the common Ulsterman's brogue in it. He took his time in replying. "It is natural for you to feel so. There was much sentiment in my congregation to do just that last spring when we learned of the murder of poor Jack Armstrong and his two companions. But Mister Harris here and other calmer heads prevailed, and justice was done." Then, ignoring Abraham's glare: "Let me inquire after your spiritual condition, Brother McGee. I assume you are a good Presbyterian."

"I haven't been to the kirk in twenty years, Pastor. Not since I saw whole families turned off their land in Antrim and starving."

"And Mrs. McGee, was she of the faith?"

"My wife was German. Her family was Lutheran."

"I suppose you married in her church."

"We did not marry in any church."

"It may be of cold comfort to you, but it is likely you would have been required to leave your place anyway. The Indians are insisting that white encroachments on their land cease."

"It is cold comfort indeed that I am getting from either you or Mister Harris. You are more interested in my spiritual condition than in helping me get my son back, and he puts his business with the Indians above seeing justice done."

Reverend Elder seemed embarrassed at this outburst. Once again he said he was sorry about the massacre and that he would send clothing. When he had mounted his horse and ridden away, Harris said, "Take no offense, Abraham, but I wish ye had not spoken so bluntly to the pastor. He is in the midst of a difficult time over a dispute between the followers of Whitefield and men like himself, who follow strictly the old teachings of their John Calvin. Half his flock have split away into a New Side congregation. Aye, it makes me glad that I'm Church of England and not Presbyterian."

"It makes me glad I am neither," said Abraham.

On the fourth day after the massacre, two Indians arrived at the trading post in a dugout canoe, accompanied by the half-breed messenger Harris had dispatched to the Delaware capital at Shamokin and bearing a large bale of assorted furs and deerhides. One of them a Delaware, the other a Mohawk, they had been sent by Shikellamy himself to make inquiries and to offer apologies. Both were middle-aged and wore white men's tunics under blankets. Harris explained that while they spoke some English, they preferred to converse in their own language, with him as interpreter.

They sat in a circle beside a large mulberry tree on the bank of the Susquehanna: the two Indians, Harris, Abraham and Jason, and a justice of the peace, with a dozen or so traders, packers and passing farmers standing nearby to eavesdrop. The Indians listened impassively while Abraham, through Harris, told of what had happened. Abraham felt contempt for all Indians and he was irritated at having to explain even to these two official emissaries. Twice Harris had to caution him against making derogatory remarks, reminding him that the two men did understand English.

The Indians remained silent, listening to every word until Abraham had finished and Harris invited them to speak. The Delaware went first, asking for a description of the murderers. It then became necessary for Jason to stammer out descriptions of the three men; all with blackened faces, their hair shaved on the sides, wearing leggings, two of average height, and one, apparently their leader, very tall, the tallest man he had ever seen, white or red, with the tip of his nose missing.

During those long minutes he had stood in shock beside that hickory tree on the knoll overlooking his family's clearing, Jason had formed indelible images of the three Indians. They had raced across his brain a thousand times during the past four days. When he was through stammering out his story, Harris took him by his trembling shoulders and gently led him back to sit beside his father, then addressed the Indians, telling them in Delaware that their white brothers laid this case before them and expected them to apprehend the murderers and bring them in to be tried as they had Mushemeelin. For the first time, one of the Indians spoke to the other, softly. The other,

13

the Delaware, carried the bale of furs over to Abraham and said in broken English, "My chief, Sassoonan, say tell you he sorry. He send you this skins."

Abraham's eyes grew hard and his face reddened. Harris, signaling him to remain silent, spoke in English.

"Our white brother appreciates the generosity of your chief. These furs will give him the means to begin again, for he lost all he owned in the burning of his cabin. But furs will not restore his wife or daughter to life; they will not recover his lost son. He is a good man and I know he will not seek revenge against the brothers of the guilty men, but you must tell Sassoonan and Shikellamy that we all wish the murderers to be captured and brought before our courts. For whom should the warrants be issued?"

The two Indians conferred and then the Mohawk spoke in his own tongue at length. Harris leaned forward during the long discourse, nodding his head in encouragement. He then reported; "He says they know only one of the guilty men. He is a Delaware, a member of the Wolf clan. He is the tall one and his name is Meskikokant. He has long borne a resentment toward both the Iroquois and the white settlers. He resents the way in which the Six Nations dominate and humiliate his people, refusing to let them take the warpath or negotiate on their own behalf with the white colonies at the recent great conference in Lancaster. He feels white men have cheated his people out of much valuable land. He hates traders for selling his people rum. Lost his nose in a fight with a drunken Mingo. He has been going through the Delaware villages and telling them that all Indians should rise up and slaughter the whites. When the other Delawares turned a deaf ear he told them they truly had become women, just as the Iroquois call them. His fellow Delawares fear him because of his great height and strength, and his violent disposition. They say that when the Iroquois delegates to the Lancaster conference came back up the Susquehanna last July with news that they had agreed to secure our borders against the French and sell western lands to Virginia, he swore he would take up the tomahawk himself. Meskikokant is the guilty party, no mistake."

"Where is the evil beast?"

"They do not know. They think he went to the west, far beyond the mountains."

"Will they go and bring him back?"

Harris translated. The reply came in slow and apparently carefully chosen words.

"He says they cannot promise to bring him back. He is beyond

14

their control, but they will inquire of their brothers who have moved out to the Allegheny."

"In other words, they will do nothing. What about my son? How will I get him back?"

"They will send word. And they will ask their uncles, the Iroquois, to help. But it will take time. They ask you to be patient and not to be angry."

Abraham walked over to the two Indians, who were still seated, and spat into the face of the Delaware. The Indian remained sitting, no show of emotion on his face, as the spittle ran down his forehead.

Harris put his hand on Abraham's arm. "Brother McGee, you should not have done that. You will accomplish nothing by insulting these men."

The two Indians looked at each other. The Mohawk nodded and they arose and walked deliberately toward the bank where their dugout was tied up, leaving Abraham shaking his fist and swearing at them.

"By God, I will get a musket and go after them myself. I will not be bought off. I don't want anything from you savages."

But the Indians left their peace offering behind. And after they had paddled out of sight, Abraham got control of himself. He accepted John Harris's offer of two pounds for the furs. That night he got drunk from the rum he purchased with part of the money.

3

Winter came early that year. It caught Abraham and Jason still occupying the feed shed at Harris's, waiting to hear from the Shamokin Indians. By New Year's, 1745, the Susquehanna was frozen and all traffic across and up and down the river halted. John Harris continued to feed and shelter the pair, in exchange for odd jobs around his trading post. Abraham's worn-out old horse died that winter, spoiling his hopes of hauling for traders in the spring.

Late in March, four Indians arrived by canoe bearing a fresh bale of furs and a letter to John Harris from a Moravian missionary who lived at Shamokin. Harris called Abraham and Jason to hear its contents.

"Sassoonan, the old chief of the Delawares up there, and Shikellamy, their watchdog from the Six Nations, both have talked to this missionary and they report that they have sent messengers as far as the Allegheny to speak to Delawares who have settled out there. They say they have not seen Meskikokant or your son. Sassoonan says they have done all they can for the present, but will send word if they learn anything in the future. Meanwhile they ask you to accept this bale of furs as a final peace offering."

The four Indians who delivered the furs and the message were young and strong. Abraham did not spit in their faces or threaten them. He said simply and bitterly: "So there it is. Nothing will be done by whites or Indians."

With the return of spring and the breakup of the ice on the Susquehanna, John Harris resumed his ferry service, giving Abraham a job working on the flat-prowed craft, partly out of pity. Jason worked about the trading post at odd jobs and was beginning to enjoy it until the day Pastor Elder rode down from his farm to enroll him in the school the Paxton Church had started the year before.

"It is held in our former church building. I am the schoolmaster, and instruction will run until June. I know you are no kirkman, Mr. McGee, but we should not let that stand in the way of the lad's education."

Abraham agreed, and on a mild day in April, Jason McGee, clad in deerskin trousers and a filthy smock, walked barefooted the four miles to the new school at Paxton Church. Things went well enough for him at first. He was one of a dozen lads, all bearing Scots names and varying in age from seven to fifteen. The others were dressed in decent, clean woolens and linens, and most wore shoes, in contrast to Jason, with his red hair falling down to his shoulders and his rude backwoodsman garb. The school was conducted in a log building, the original church, in the shadow of a new and larger stone structure. But to Jason it seemed a grand building. The students sat on benches made of split logs, under the eye of Parson Elder. Jason shared a large slate with two seven-year-olds. He quickly mastered his letters and numbers. Soon he could write his name and could make out words in the tattered copy of the short catechism.

The trouble began for Jason after a couple of weeks, when Parson Elder, proud of his progress, asked him to recite the alphabet in class. Jason's stammer grew worse as he went on. The oldest and largest boy in the class, one Angus Cameron, laughed and the others followed suit. Reverend Elder stopped and rebuked them, but the damage had been done. It took Jason ten agonizing minutes to get to "Z" and he sat down in humiliation. Thereafter the parson had him recite in private while the others went out to play. The teasing came soon afterward and it was started by Angus Cameron.

"Hey, Red Top," he called to Jason. "Why don't ye ask the parson to let ye recite in German?"

"Wh-what do you mean?" Jason replied.

"I hear ye mither was a Dutchie. Thought mayhap ye might speak Dutch without stuttering."

The others laughed. Jason let it pass, swallowing the embarrassment he felt. Angus Cameron was large even for fifteen, with dark brown hair and a pudgy face. He had a great store of dirty stories the others liked to hear. Reverend Elder reigned inside the school, but Angus ruled the boys outside.

Jason's schooling lasted exactly six weeks, long enough for him to pick up reading and conquer adding and subtracting and the signing of his name. And long enough for him to form a hatred of Angus Cameron. The bully taught his toadies to call Jason the "red-headed woodpecker," and likened his stuttering to the tapping of that bird on a tree. Actually, Jason did not stammer when reciting in private for the parson, but it overwhelmed him when Angus and the others circled around him on the school grounds to ask sarcastic questions about living in the forest. He would simply hang his head and look down at the ground in humiliation, until one mild day in May, Angus said to him, "My pa says yer mither was a German whore."

Jason raised his eyes to look into the bully's face.

"Wh-what did you say?"

"Aw, now, Angus, that's not fair," another boy said.

"It's the truth, see if he denies it. His mither ran off to live with his pa and they niver got married. She was a whore. . . ."

Angus made the mistake of looking aside to see the effect of this remark on the others. So he was not prepared when Jason piled into him, fists pounding away. Angus fell back several steps before this onslaught, turning his head to avoid the blows.

"Half-German bastard," he said, catching one of Jason's wrists and then, with both hands, twisting his arm behind his back. "I'll teach ye."

He threw Jason to the ground and sat on him until Parson Elder came out and stopped the fight. But Jason's anger did not subside. He sat through the afternoon staring with hatred at the profile of Angus Cameron. In a curious way, it felt good to be angry rather than merely embarrassed.

After school, Jason McGee, who had been accounted the shyest lad in the class, confronted Angus Cameron, saying, "Ye'll take back what ye said about m-my m-mother."

Angus looked down with contempt at the skinny redhead.

"I'll not take back a word. She was a German whore."

Jason drove his fist against the older boy's nose. Angus recovered quickly, and with blood streaming from his nostrils, threw an arm around Jason's neck and squeezed. Just as he was about to go down, Jason bit as hard as he could into the soft flesh inside Angus's upper arm. The bully cried out, trying to pull his arm free, but Jason's teeth were too firmly clenched and so he could only scream in pain. Jason let go, but before his tormentor could retaliate, he leaped on his back and began clawing at his eyes. Angus, half blinded and now crying out in terror rather than anger, flung Jason off his back.

The others were quiet. This wild redhead was no longer a laughingstock. Jason got to his feet, lowered his head and rammed it hard into the belly of Angus, knocking the wind out of him and pitching him off his feet.

Parson Elder had been watching from the school doorway. He had never cared for the Cameron family. Now he had to intervene, he decided. But by the time he reached the pair, Jason was kicking his tormentor on the sides, the genitals, wherever he could find an opening, and Angus Cameron had become a helpless, bawling mass.

Jason strode back to the trading post feeling cleansed, almost exalted, although aching from his exertions. When his father asked how his knuckles had come to be scraped and his fingernails torn, Jason told him that he had been wrestling.

"That's good, son. They're coming to accept ye, then."

The next morning Jason returned to school ready to resume the fight with Angus Cameron if necessary, but his adversary was absent. No one called Jason "woodpecker" that day. Shortly before noon, several men arrived at the school on horseback, among them the father of Angus Cameron. After Parson Elder went out to confer with them, Jason could hear angry voices. The men left and the parson called Jason outside.

"It's a sad thing I must say to you, Jason McGee. You see, I was not supposed to have you in this school, seeing that your father is not a communicant and neither of you comes to our church. The other lads pay a tuition, but I took you in free, as I knew your circumstances. Well, now the fathers of my other students say they will withdraw their sons if you are allowed to remain in the school. You see, Jason, you rather banged up Angus. They say his private parts are bruised and swollen painfully and the lad can hardly see out of one eye. You are lucky you did not kill him."

"I'm not sorry. He called my m-mother a whore."

"You should have reported it to me directly. I would have handled it in a more Christian way. Anyway, it is too late now. Would you tell your father about this and ask him to understand? I can teach you no more."

So ended the formal education of Jason McGee. But he had learned a great deal in those six weeks.

4

Jason's life entered a curiously happy phase, for now that his father had a job on the ferry, the boy could come and go as he pleased.

The shallow Susquehanna River, more than half a mile wide at that point, teemed with fish, and its shores abounded with bird life. Jason often rode to the western shore on the ferry in the morning and spent the day happily roaming over the area, much of which had been reserved by the heirs of William Penn as a special "manor" for Indians in the stubborn hope that they could entice the Shawanese to return from the west.

A large Shawanese village had stood beside the mouth of Yellow Breeches Creek and remnants of their lodges remained, together with arrowheads, broken pottery, bones and shells—all the debris of a generation of this gypsy-like tribe. Jason's happiest discovery came one summer afternoon when, in exploring the banks of the fast-flowing Yellow Breeches, he found a small dugout canoe concealed in a thicket beside an enormous sycamore. His father was amazed when the boy appeared at the ferry landing with this craft.

"Ye didn't steal it, did ye, boy?"

"No. The Indians left it. Can I keep it?"

"Aye. If ye've paddled it this far, keep it."

This canoe opened a new world to Jason, enabling him to explore the Susquehanna and its numerous islands for miles. He got to know every channel so that he could paddle upstream in still water and ride strong currents down again. Often he would beach his canoe on an island and eat his lunch there, feeling like the king of a small secure domain, as long as he did not gaze to the north at the Kittatinny

Mountain range. That low mountain wall loomed like an ugly memory. And when he saw Indians coming down the river, he concealed himself until their boats had passed. Otherwise, Jason was free of school, free of the comforting but restraining discipline of a mother, free of everything but the memory of the massacre. For a while he was nearly as happy as he ever would be.

Jason remained at Harris's Ferry for five years and during that time he grew from a gangling ten-year-old to nearly sixteen, tall and lean. His nightmares about the massacre lessened, although the memory of that awful October day was never far from his mind. His stammer afflicted him only when he was ill at ease or under pressure, or when an occasional party of Indians with painted faces and carrying tomahawks stopped at the post on their way south to make war on the Catawbas and Cherokee, their traditional enemies to the south, seeking revenge in a feud whose original cause could not be remembered.

As for the Delawares, they remained relegated by the Iroquois to the role of "women," and hence were not allowed to take the warpath. The post attracted them, plus remnants of the Shawanese, Nanticokes and Tuscaroras, mostly older Indians so addicted to the white man's rum that they were no longer fit for either the hunting trail or the warpath anyway.

Abraham's hope that the murder of his wife and daughter would be avenged and his older son recovered faded in 1747, when Sassoonan, the chief of the Turkey clan of the Delawares, died. It disappeared entirely the following year, when Shikellamy, the Oneida overlord of the Delawares, died as well. These deaths were followed by an acceleration of the exodus of the Delawares beyond the Allegheny Mountains to the villages already established by tribal members: Kittanning, Logstown, Saucouk and Kuskusky.

Another death occurred near the end of 1748. John Harris, surrounded by the evidence of his hard work and good business sense, died, leaving a widow and six children, the eldest of whom was John Harris, Junior, aged twenty-one. This younger John Harris had inherited his father's shrewdness. He catered more and more to the needs of the growing white population while still continuing as a middleman in the fur trade. And he was not as tolerant of the drunkenness and irresponsibility of Abraham McGee as had been his father.

Soon after the ferry service was resumed in the spring of 1749, when the river was nearly out of its banks, Abraham failed to secure the boat properly and it was carried downriver during the night. It took the young Harris two days to find and recover the craft. Meanwhile dozens of traders and immigrants were kept waiting on the eastern bank, and farmers from the valley on the western. Harris removed Abraham from his job as assistant to the ferryman and relegated him to work around the fur sheds, sorting pelts, repairing harness and caring for the packhorses. For more than a year Abraham endured the humiliation of being little better than a stableboy. It was a hard year for Jason as well, for the boy had to listen to his father's well-practiced complaints against the English, the Quakers and the Germans, plus his hatred for the Indians. And when he was drunk, his maudlin recollections of Gerta.

Jason heard much about Abraham's life in Ulster, of how the English government, having encouraged the Lowland Presbyterians to come over and subdue the Catholic Irish in that corner of Ireland, had turned the screws on their descendants, taxing them cruelly and imposing penalties on them for their nonconformist religion. Abraham told of seeing Presbyterian and Catholic Irishmen alike suffering, even starving, after the great crop failures of 1725.

"Me father died and the landlord turned us off the land. And me mither had to go and live with me older sister, and her and her husband, and I, a lad little older than yerself, ended up begging in the streets of Belfast. Oh, I've had a hard life, Jason, with little luck to help me. I thought I'd find it better in this country, but I see others prospering who came years after I arrived. Your lovely mither was the only luck I iver had, and now that has been taken from me."

For a while after Jason had left school, the Reverend Elder would stop by the post and chat with him, even lending him an occasional book and generally showing an interest in the boy. He did one other thing for Jason, which meant more to him than books. While Jason was helping sort furs one winter afternoon, the parson came riding down from his farm, all bundled against the cold and carrying a large sack in one hand.

"There you are, lad. I've brought you something you might fancy. Here."

Jason set the sack on the ground and knelt beside it, but before he could open it, out wriggled a yellow pup, which immediately sprang up to lick his face. Abraham, who had never forgiven the parson for failing to organize a posse against the Indians and who bore him a further grudge for expelling Jason from school, came up, frowning.

"Ah, Brother McGee. We find ourselves with an extra pup on the farm. I thought it would be good for Jason to have a companion."

"We've no place for a dog here."

Jason listened, his joy fading.

"Ah, but this is a fine dog. We've had his mother for five years. And this is the pick of the litter."

"As I say, we have no place . . ."

The parson smiled. "In fact, we have named this pup already. Given him a fine Quaker name. One that should appeal to an Ulsterman such as yourself."

"What's that?"

"We've named this young dog James Logan, after the provincial secretary himself."

News recently had reached Harris's Ferry that the proprietors of the Penn family in Philadelphia had instructed their agents in newly formed York County to sell no more land to Ulster immigrants, but to encourage them to move on into the North Valley, where, presumably, they would be less troublesome. Feelings among the Presbyterians on the frontier ran high against Logan, even though the secretary himself had come from Ireland.

"James Logan?" Abraham said, then broke into a smile. "Ah, that's rich. James Logan." Then he began laughing. Jason kept his dog.

Logan grew into a splendid animal with a full, well-muscled chest and a massive head. His affection for Jason developed into total devotion. The red-haired lad and the yellow dog became a familiar sight, something about them seeming to excite good humor. Hard-bitten traders slyly would offer Jason extravagant sums for the dog, taking delight in his indignant refusals. Even dour old Indians who had rarely been known to smile, except when drunk, laughed at the pair.

Life became a pleasant adventure for Jason McGee, and the old confidence he had felt when he realized he one day could beat Isaac returned. It swelled on those occasions when Angus Cameron and his father appeared at the post. Even though Angus had grown into a strapping six-footer, he took pains not to look at Jason or to come near him. Jason, now a lithe, strong fifteen-year-old, knew fear only in his nightmares.

5

By 1750 the number of Presbyterians living across the Susquehanna in the North Valley was reckoned at more than three thousand, and these staunch people were prospering. On January 27 their special needs were recognized by the provincial government with the establishment of the county of Cumberland, with its own courts to meet in the thriving settlement at Shippensburg, thirty-five miles down the valley from Harris's Ferry.

Later that year, in May, in response to the urgings of the Indians remaining along the Susquehanna, and eager to keep them from further defections to the west, a large party of justices of the peace, accompanied by representatives of the Indians, crossed the mountains, just as they had in 1743, and descended upon scores of squatter families, evicting and sometimes arresting them, and burning their cabins along Sherman's Creek and the Juniata River. At this news, Abraham cursed the authorities who had yielded so to Indian pressure. The following September, a trader who was at the post to replenish his trade goods overheard his complaints and said in amusement, "You seem unduly bitter about this matter, my friend."

"I have reason to be bitter," Abraham replied, and proceeded to tell the trader about how his wife and daughter had been murdered and his son stolen.

"You say you lost a son? Taken off by the Indians?"

"I did. Six years ago in the terrible month of October, 1744."

"How old was the lad?"

"He was twelve."

"So he would be eighteen now. What sort of boy was he?"

"Ah, he was a bonny lad. Not so tall as me other boy, with hair as black as a raven and a strong, well-set-up form."

"Did he have blue eyes?"

"As blue as a summer sky."

"Well now. I spent the last winter amongst the Delawares at the Kuskuskies and there was a young man passed there with hair as dark as an Indian's but not so coarse, and with skin turned brown from the sun. I was amazed to see up close that he had blue eyes. I tried to speak to him, but he would say nothing to me. The next morning he was gone."

"Jesus Christ! Tell me more."

"I asked the Delawares about him and they said he had been living futher west with another tribe, that his white name had been Isaac."

"Christ be praised! It's me own son. In Kuskusky, ye say. Glory to God. Jason! Come running, boy, and hear this."

Jason had never seen his father rejoicing so. Abraham had the trader tell him over and over the little he could remember of his meeting with the blue-eyed Indian captive. That night he said to Jason, "This is what I've been waiting for. I am going west to bring back your brother."

Abraham did, indeed, head west to look for Isaac, but first, after saying goodbye to the Harrises and hangers-on at the post, he and Jason, accompanied by Logan, walked east for two days, deep into Lancaster County, and there presented themselves at the farm once owned by Gerta's father and now shared by her two brothers.

The Koble brothers were gruff, blond men who barely spoke English and showed no hospitality to their brother-in-law, nor any interest either in their red-haired nephew or in helping Abraham raise money for a horse and musket. Abraham came away fuming at their meanness. He muttered and swore all the way to a blacksmith shop on the road near Lancaster.

"We'll just try our luck here," he said. "Your mither's cousin abides here. Her husband is a good blacksmith and a man of prosperity. Don't be put off by his manner. Let's see if he can find it in his heart to help me."

The blacksmith, one Ernst Koch, was a powerful fellow, standing some five foot ten and possessed of the widest shoulders and bulkiest forearms Jason had ever seen. He looked surly, but he was not so hostile as Gerta's brothers had been.

"Ach, so this is Gerta's son, hey? The eyes are the same. The red hair must be the Irisher in him. I was sorry to hear about Gerta and the baby. And they took your oldest son off across the mountains?"

"Aye, they did that. But now I know where he is and intend to go and bring him back."

"So? You and this redhead?"

"No. I won't take Jason."

This was news to Jason. His father would not look at him and he would have spoken out if the smith first had not asked, "Why not?"

"Well, you see, Ernst, I don't have a musket. I don't fancy going out there with no weapon and I will need a horse to carry blankets and such. I spoke to Gerta's brothers about help, but they still bear me ill will for taking her away. I thought you might help, seeing as how Gerta was your Maria's cousin and the two of them used to play together as bairns."

"A horse and a gun would come to a lot of money, Abraham. I'm not a rich man and I got a wife and two girls to feed and clothe and all the work to be done by myself."

"I know, and that is where Jason comes into it. He is a clever lad. Only went to school a few weeks and he picked up reading and sums right off. He knows how to fix things, aye, and he is wonderful with animals. Well now, Jason soon will be sixteen and I thought I'd give him to you for three years, free labor and all for the price of a horse and maybe a gun."

"Three years ain't so long. Apprentice time usually runs seven years."

"Come now, Ernst. The boy *is* your wife's cousin. You would get three years of free labor from him."

"Even if you come back in a few months?"

"Aye, no matter when or whether."

"He ain't worth a good horse and a new gun. I do have a one-eyed mare that won't breed, but she would be good for what you want. I repair guns on the side and I got a musket that has been unclaimed for two years. I can't shell out no money."

"I'd like to see the goods."

"Ja, and I want to look at the boy closer. Ach, such red hair. What's your name and how old are you?"

"J-Jason. I'm f-fifteen."

"He stutters. I hope he has good sense."

Abraham and the smith stood for a long while in silence, Celt and Teuton, restless ne'er-do-well and stolid, industrious craftsman, each waiting for the other to change his position. At last Koch spoke. "Let's go to the house once and hear what Maria says."

Koch's dwelling was a two-story log house covered with rough-sawn boards. His wife was a small woman with a gentle expression, dressed in a bodice and long skirt, with light brown hair drawn back in a bun.

"So, Abraham McGee. It has been a long time," she said in a soft voice. "And this is your son?"

While Koch explained the situation to her, their two daughters entered the room. One of them was a slender girl, with brown hair, a year or two older than Jason. The other was blond, with a round, saucy face, and a figure well developed for a girl of only fourteen. Mrs. Koch introduced them as Katie and Sallie.

"So there it is, Maria. Abraham needs a horse and a gun to go west and seek his son—"

"And a few shillings and some provisions," Abraham interjected.

"Perhaps. Anyway, he is willing to donate three years of this boy's time. I told him three years ain't much, and the boy would have to be taught. He stutters, besides."

"Aye," Abraham flared up, "but you are only offering me a used musket and a second-rate horse. Blind, you say?"

"In one eye only. And the musket is as good as new. I repaired it myself. Besides, it will cost me to feed this boy. . . ."

"Ernst," his wife said. "Is not this the son of my cousin, Gerta?"

"Ja. You know that."

"Then we got a place for him for three years. We got no son.

Give Abraham the mare and the gun and don't argue all day about it."

The Kochs cleared out a lean-to attached to the smithy. Maria brought out a straw tick and furnished the space with a chair and a table. The blacksmith grudgingly gave Abraham a few shillings, which he took into Lancaster to purchase powder, shot and other provisions. Jason was afraid he would come back drunk, but he returned wearing new shoes and a hat.

After he had arranged two sacks over the withers of the mare, Abraham slung the musket on his shoulder, shook hands with the smith and his wife, then held Jason's face between his hands.

"Ye're a good lad, Jason. Work hard and learn to be a good blacksmith. That way ye'll always have a living and ye won't end up like your father."

Jason, his face wet with tears, threw his arms around Abraham and held him until the man, embarrassed, broke away. The Kochs and Jason watched him ride off toward Harris's Ferry, never once looking back.

6

Jason was miserably unhappy for several days after his father left. He had grown used to eating when he felt like it, and dressing as he pleased, for Abraham had paid little attention to such things. Now he was kept busy from sunup to dusk, doing the bidding of Ernst Koch. The smith was a demanding boss who made no allowances for Jason's lack of skill and became impatient with the boy when his stammer made him slow to answer.

It turned out that Koch had needed a helper for many months, but had been too stingy to hire one. Not only was his shop situated in the midst of a prosperous farming section, but also it stood beside a road that bore heavy traffic moving grain and furs toward Philadelphia in one direction, and trade goods and settlers toward Harris's Ferry in the other. So the smith was kept busy shoeing farm horses, repairing carts, forging plow points, and even mending pots and guns. His hammer rang against the anvil from morning until night, the clanging interspersed with his mutterings in both German and English. Often he and Jason worked right through their midday mealtime, stopping only to wolf down bread and cheese sent out by Maria.

When the sun went down, they would wash and go to the kitchen for supper with Maria and the two girls. Jason came to look forward to these evenings, for he had missed the pleasure of eating at a table presided over by a woman. Even though the Kochs spoke a mixture of German and English that was unintelligible to him at first, it was good just to be with a family, to hear the merry voices of the girls and feel the warmth of the kitchen fire. Maria noted which dishes Jason liked best and began catering to his taste. Without consulting her husband, she made him a smock and a pair of comfortable trousers. At first Jason was too shy to do more than answer the questions put to him at these evening meals, but in time he relaxed around the family so that he could speak without stammering.

The two girls were quite different. Katie, the older, with her brown hair, darker than her mother's, had a serious manner and a fresh, honest way of speaking her mind, sometimes rather too bluntly. Like her mother, she was always busy around the house or yard. Sallie was not as industrious and, while usually more cheerful, was inclined to pout when she did not get her way. She delighted in making Jason blush.

Jason worked so long and hard most days that it was easy for him to fall asleep at night, especially after Maria's good suppers. As for Koch, he rarely rested after supper even though he worked harder than Jason and was middle-aged. Usually he would light his pipe and work with pen and paper by candlelight, making drawings. On those evenings when the day's work had not been so heavy, he would bring a reflecting candleholder out to the smithy and putter away in the corner that held his gun-repair tools, losing himself in this evening work, no longer scowling or muttering to himself.

One day when the smith was outside the shop talking to a wagoner, Jason sneaked a look at the mysterious papers, which he had left on a bench, and saw a design for a flintlock rifle with a long, narrow octagonal barrel and a butt curved to fit the shoulder, a delicate-looking weapon with an intricate trigger guard and patch plate. The guns Koch occasionally repaired, such as the one he had traded to Abraham, were clumsy affairs with fairly short barrels and large, smooth bores, possessing none of the elegance of that now taking form in his plans.

In the little leisure left for Jason, he liked to sit quietly and let his imagination run free, picturing himself back in the family cabin north of the mountains, with his mother and Stella still alive, and Isaac there as well. Abraham did not drink or swear; Gerta never wept and Isaac never bullied. So did time soften Jason's memories.

27

And in his daydreams about the past, those three Indians, led by a painted giant, did not race across the clearing and butcher his mother and sister, nor burn their cabin, nor slaughter their cow and abduct his brother. That occurred only in his nightmares.

Jason daydreamed of the future as well. In a month or so, before winter came, Abraham would return with Isaac, full of accounts of their adventures in the west. It would seem strange between the two brothers for a time; after all, Isaac had been living amongst red savages for five years. But after they became reacquainted, Isaac would regale him with stories of his Indian life.

Jason pictured himself, Isaac and Abraham settling down nearby, perhaps in the fast-growing town of Lancaster, and opening a black-smith shop of their own. No more of the life of a squatter. He would prosper quickly, to the point that he could persuade Sallie Koch to marry him. Jason had fallen in love with the merry blond girl the first day of his apprenticeship. Not only was she prettier than any girl on the frontier, with full hips and bosom accentuated by a tiny waist, but she had a generally bubbling disposition that cheered him up even when she made him blush with her teasing. It did not matter to him that she was a bit spoiled and given to dodging the chores her mother set for her. The very sound of her voice thrilled him.

Within a month after Abraham's departure, Jason had become adjusted to his new life. Maria's cooking was putting weight on him and the hard work was converting that weight into solid muscle. After the first snow fell, he moved his bed into the main room of the smithy, where the charcoal fire in the forge kept him and Logan warm.

Christmas was an especially happy time. Ignoring her husband's complaints about her generosity, Maria gave Jason a pair of boots. Koch not only allowed him the entire day off, but also lent him a fowling piece so that he and Logan could go hunting. They returned with three rabbits, from which Maria and Katie produced what they called a hasenpfeffer, a rabbit stew.

In April, soon after the Pennsylvania countryside had begun to turn green again, a wagoner passing east stopped at the smithy to give Jason a letter from John Harris, Junior. He had never received a letter, and it took a long while for him to make out the message:

Harris's Ferry
5 April, 1751

Dear Jason McGee:

Yr Father, Abraham, passed this way last fall. He told us you are apprenticed to the Blacksmith Ernst Koch & that he was goeing over the Mountains to seek the return of yr Brother.

Abraham crossed the Susquehanna here & we heard no more of him until yesterday when a Tavern Keeper from Shippensburg came here to replenish his Stores. In making conversation, this Man told us a man by the name of McGee had stopped in Shippensburg last September to rest & while there unfortunately fell to Drinking & soon running out of money, had sold his Horse to buy more rum. Because of his rude remarks about Quakers and Indians, he was ejected from the Tavern and told to come there no more. The Tavern Keeper assumed your Father had gone on West afoot but two days later two Tuscarora Indians living near by brought him in deathly sick of a Fever. They found him lying beside the road West of there.

To make a sad, long story short, this Tavern Keeper & his good wife put yr Father to bed & nursed him tenderly for 3 days & nights. During that time he was frequently out of his head, calling the names of Gerta and Isaac. Despite their attentions, he died, I am sorry to tell you, about Oct 1st of last year.

It grieves me to relate this news to you. Yr Father, for all his faults had a good heart.

By the way, the Tavern Keeper & his good wife were put to considerable trouble & expense to care for yr Father in his illness and in burying him. They thought themselves entitled to keep his Musket & few personal effects as compensation.

I wish I had better news. Very truly yrs, Jno. Harris

Jason read this letter seated by the forge in the smithy. Koch came in, ready to berate Jason for letting the fire burn so low, but when he heard his sobbing, he called for Maria to come out and comfort the youth. Although she and the girls could not have been kinder after that, and even Koch himself became more tolerant, those next few months were a bleak, bitter time for Jason McGee. His daydreams, no longer dwelling on a future of prosperity and hope, turned to revenge and regrets. He let the massacre back into his conscious mind, thinking with hatred about the giant renegade, Meskikokant, who had set all this trouble into motion, and wishing that he had gone west with his father immediately upon hearing of Isaac's whereabouts.

He began to wonder if, when his apprenticeship was over, he might accomplish his revenge alone. He could picture himself as a strapping nineteen-year-old, with the help of Isaac, subduing Meskikokant and leading him back across the Susquehanna to be tried. Fantasizing about killing or capturing Meskikokant, he no longer had his nightmares of standing helplessly beside the hickory tree on the hill, of hearing the screams of his mother and doing nothing.

That summer and fall of 1751, Jason had little time for daydreaming, for the rich farms of Lancaster County and those up around Paxton Church produced wheat, rye, oats and maize more abundantly than anyone could remember and there was increased demand for blacksmith work. Great wagons shaped like boats, called Conestogas, were becoming common now, but there was more grain coming off the farms than they could handle. The markets in Philadelphia were glutted. Carts and wagons with grain were lined up outside gristmills. Some farmers fed good wheat to their pigs; others set up stills and began turning their rye and corn into whiskey.

And still the Ulster Scots and German immigrants streamed westward past the blacksmith's door.

7

"Ach, Chason. Look here once what I got."

Jason McGee, now a tall, well-muscled eighteen, nearly nineteen, glanced up from the washbasin, water streaming from his face, to see Koch standing in the back door of his house, holding a long rifle with an elegant maple and walnut stock.

"I finished her last night. Ain't she a beauty?"

It was indeed a beautiful rifle, looking almost delicate in the great paw of the blacksmith.

"Two years I been working on her, and there she is."

During the nearly three years Jason had been with the Kochs, he had never seen the blacksmith so elated. Feigning a polite interest, his daughters came out to see the completed weapon. Sallie, now even prettier, praised her father's craftsmanship until he beamed and ducked his head. Then she made a face over his shoulder at Jason, knowing he dared not smile back at her.

Koch's unaccustomed joviality continued at the breakfast table until Maria protested, saying, "Now, Ernst, you been working on that gun for two years. Are you going to spend the next two talking about it?"

"By God, woman. You don't understand. All day I spend shoeing horses and hammering on that damned anvil, and here I make a beautiful thing like this rifle, and you ain't got sense enough to see."

Katie, who normally maintained a scornful silence, broke in. "He's right, Mama. It is a beautiful gun. Papa should be proud."

"Yes," said Sallie. "Maybe Papa should turn gunsmith and let Jason take over his blacksmithing," then, impishly, "someday when he grows up. How much would somebody pay you for that gun, Papa?"

"Ho, this gun ain't for sale. I ain't ever going to sell this gun!"

After breakfast the smith said, "Hey, Chason. Let's not open the shop this morning. Come with me."

The two of them took the new rifle into a neighbor's woods, set up a target and test-fired the weapon. The rifle, fitting against Jason's shoulder just right, was so well balanced that he could support it easily with his left hand. And with its small bore, it required little powder.

The near-sighted Koch was impressed both with the rifle's accuracy and with Jason's marksmanship. "You got the shooter's eye."

For a while Koch neglected his work, showing off the rifle to his customers, some of whom were amused at his extravagant pride. Others tried to buy the gun. One Indian trader, stopping to get his pack-horse shod, offered Koch ten pounds, pestering him to sell until the smith became angry. "I wouldn't sell this rifle to Chesus Christ himself."

Jason had grown taller than Koch and while not nearly as heavy, had developed good shoulders and a full chest. On summer afternoons, after their day's work, the two of them would remove their sweaty shirts and wash up at the well behind the house. Maria forbade the girls to watch this display of seminudity, but Jason often caught a glimpse of Sallie peeking out a bedroom window as he bathed. Jason had learned to tease the girls as they did him. Often, in the summer after supper, they would sit in the grass beside the house and talk until dark. It annoyed him that Katie would always appear so that he could not be alone with Sallie, but in a way her presence did make it easier for them to talk.

Katie often questioned Jason about his life in the forest. She was a practical girl with a grave way of listening and with strong hands that never seemed to rest, always knitting or fondling Logan's ears. It was the older Koch daughter who fed him, and the dog seemed to adore her almost as much as he did Jason. For all her relative plainness, Katie did not appear jealous that her father doted on Sallie or that Jason obviously was smitten with her. Both she and her mother, whom she most resembled, seemed to regard Sallie as a willful, merry child. Being nearly twenty and a strong lass who liked to work, Katie had an occasional suitor, although she never flirted or gave them much encouragement. A strapping young farmer of twenty-five came to pay court through most of one winter. He sat about, red-faced and tongue-tied, through several evenings while Katie did nothing to put him at his ease. She shrugged when Sallie chided her about this.

"If you like him so well, why don't you ask him to sit about making moon eyes at you?"

Another time, a tavernkeeper from Lancaster, a self-assured wi-

31

dower with four children, a man of means, met Katie and noting her nimble ways and supple, strong figure, began to call. Sallie thought this was hilarious and often pressed Katie to tell about the short-lived courtship as the two girls and Jason lolled in the grass.

"Tell us again what he said to you."

"Well, he asked me about my cooking and my sewing and all that. Then he wanted to know about my health. Found out I am not sick much. Then he wanted to know if I liked children. 'What children?' I said. 'Children in general,' he said. And I told him it depended on what kind of children they are."

"Oh, and what did he say to that?"

"Nothing. It was right after that he brought out all four of his brats. You saw them. One still in diapers. He invited me to come into town and visit his fine tavern. I asked why and he said, 'So you can see how you might like it there.' "

"That's how he finally got to the point?"

"Ja. And he got *so* mad when I said I did not want to marry him and tend to his brats or work in his tavern, even if he was one of the richest men in Lancaster. 'So stay an old maid, then,' he tells me, and I told him I would live and die an old maid before I would marry someone I don't love."

Sallie laughed. "When I marry it has to be someone I can be proud of. I want a man others will look up to."

Katie frowned. "I will wait for a man *I* can look up to. Or else I will never marry."

"At twenty years old, you can't be so choosy, Katie. You will end up an old maid."

"Ja; well, Papa is so choosy about you, maybe you will be an old maid too."

"Ain't it the truth? He says I ain't old enough to do more than talk to boys on Sunday afternoons. He won't let anybody come and visit. It ain't fair, Katie. You know it ain't. After all, I soon will be seventeen. Do you think it is fair, Jason?"

Jason, lying stretched out on the grass, had been worshiping her as she gestured and rattled on, the sun making her hair shine like gold. He looked down at the grass in embarrassment.

"Your pa is just l-looking after you, Sallie. He don't want you seeing j-just anybody."

Katie watched Jason closely as she asked, "What about you? You will soon be a man. Some boys your age are getting married."

"Aw, I ain't even thinking of getting married. I ain't even got a girl."

Sallie laughed. "He don't have a girl because he don't try to get one. My friends at church ask me about the handsome redhead that works for my pa." She giggled. "And I have to tell them I am saving Jason for myself. See there, Katie, I have made him blush again."

That night Jason went to bed thinking again and again of her remark. *I am saving Jason for myself.* If only he could speak to Sallie from his heart and tell her without stammering or blushing just how he felt. Lying on his narrow bed at night, he rehearsed what he might say to her, going over the words until they became as smooth as pebbles on a beach, as familiar and comforting as a litany.

She would be sitting on the grass with her ankles crossed and her hands in her lap, her head tilted, and she would listen to him without laughing, her eyes never leaving his face, as he said to her: "You must know I love you. What you don't know is that I have loved you since I can remember. You or someone like you has existed in my head since I first could talk or walk. There is no other way I can account for the feeling that struck me that day you came into your kitchen to hear our fathers haggling over me as though I were a colt. There I was, sick with disappointment and jealousy because my father was trading a piece of my life for a broken-down mare and a damaged musket, and doing it for the sake of my brother, all without consulting me. I loved him and he was using me like a piece of trade goods. I was ready to burst, to cry out and tell him I would follow him no matter what. The words were forming in my throat when you appeared. It was more like a reunion than a first meeting. And suddenly it did not matter so much what my father was doing. I had found you."

She then would take his hand. "Go on," she would say. "This is beautiful."

"I have heard your mother say that you look like my mother when she was a girl. Maybe that explains it. Whatever it was, something leaped up inside me at my first sight of you, and I have loved you ever since. I love your graceful white neck, the smoothness of your skin, the freckles on your arms, the way you trip about the kitchen when you set the table. I love the sound of your voice, your eyes, your smile; I like the way you talk back to your father and the way you stir up poor Katie. I cannot live without you."

Tears would come into her eyes. He would draw close. "I used to dream of going over the mountains alone to avenge my mother's death and to rescue my brother, to succeed where my father failed. Now I know that you are worth a dozen brothers and, in a curious way, you have taken the place of my mother in my heart. I am yours

33

and I wish you to be mine. I wish us to live together for the rest of our lives. I will labor from morning to night so that you will never want for anything that lies within my power to provide. Please from this day forward let us never be separated."

She would listen gravely and when he was done she would put her arms about his neck and kiss him. "My beloved Jason. I do wish to become your wife."

It was all so easy in his dreams.

8

With the end of his three-year apprenticeship drawing near, Jason debated over whether he should strike out on his own or remain with Koch and work for wages. He knew he would be welcome at any blacksmith shop and he was weary of Koch's slave driving, yet he dreaded the prospect of being separated from Sallie.

The subject of his future came up one afternoon in the late summer as he and the girls sat under the mulberry tree chaffing with each other.

"What will you do?" Katie asked.

"I am not sure."

Sallie frowned. "You won't leave us, will you?"

Just then Maria called from the kitchen. "Katie, come here once and help me move the table."

So they were alone, without the older sister hanging about listening to every word. A soft yellow light lay over the land as the sun began to go down, illuminating Sallie's face and creating an aura about her head.

Jason took a deep breath and stammered, "Sallie. I-I l-love you."

"What?"

"I l-love you. I want to m-marry you."

He was afraid for an instant she would laugh.

"Jason. How sweet of you."

"W-well, you s-see." Damn that stammer. Why did it have to return just now? "Marry m-me, please."

"Marry you? Oh, Jason. I don't know."

His words came out in an awkward rush. He rattled away, promising to work hard, become a rich man and provide her with a fine home.

"What would Papa say if he heard you talk like this?"

"Remember what you said about me t-taking over the shop so he c-could do what he wants—make rifles?"

Now she was blushing, not meeting his eyes.

"D-don't you love me?"

"Oh, Jason. You are so sweet."

Then before he could say more, she kissed him on the lips and ran into the house.

Two days later Jason found her in the kitchen, alone, while her mother and sister were working in the garden. Her back was turned when he came in and she was startled by his touch.

"Jason. You gave me such a fright."

Not trusting his voice, he looked down into her face, serious now. She resisted at first when he put his hands on her waist and then, standing on her tiptoes, she kissed him quickly and drew away.

"That is enough. Mama and Katie will be back any minute."

"I l-love you, S-Sallie."

"I know. But not now."

That night he lay in his rude bed next to the smithy and thought back over those few delicious minutes, remembering the brief feel of her waist and her fresh smell. It made him sweat with pleasure to think about her.

The next day he saw her in the chicken barn gathering eggs, and waited outside where he could not be seen from the house. She came out holding the corners of her apron in one hand to make a pouch for the eggs.

"Careful, Jason. You will break the eggs," she warned when he bent to kiss her. But this time she did not pull away, and responded with parted lips.

"We mustn't," she protested when he pressed himself against her. "What will Mama say if I bring back cracked eggs? We must wait, Jason. There is lots of time."

Still she lingered, kissing him in return until her mother called for her from the kitchen door.

Jason lived for the moments he stole with her during the next few days, storing their memory to be savored at night when he was alone. No longer was she an unattainable dream. She responded to him, each time allowing him to hold her longer and closer, but always breaking away with a warning when he became too ardent.

At mealtimes he talked even less than usual, barely able to eat for love of her, looking at her furtively when he thought the others would not notice, glowing when she rewarded him with a quick smile.

His practiced speeches never came out as he wished; indeed, as he became physically bolder, he grew even more inarticulate. What did it matter whether Sallie became his through pretty words or through actual possession? he thought.

Having so long existed on the fringes of others' lives, he had never had the opportunity to know girls intimately, had never so much as hugged any female besides his mother. His father's maudlin accounts of Gerta and the rough talk he had heard about women at Harris's Ferry had not prepared him for the sweetness of Sallie's kisses or the thrill of feeling her breasts pressed against him.

Why had this marvelous secret been kept from him? Now he understood why his father and mother, so different in background and temperament, had labored together in the wilderness and why the warm-hearted Maria Koch devoted herself to a callous ox like her blacksmith husband. There was a magic between men and women and he would have it with Sallie. He had only to bide his time, so he thought, and yet he yearned to consummate his love. Later, when they were man and wife, there would be a world of time for him to tell why and how he loved her. Meanwhile he would wait for his opportunity to take what he felt already belonged to him. He no longer had any doubt that it would come.

It happened on a Sunday morning when he returned from a tramp in the fields with Logan. He had thought the entire family had gone to church as usual, but there she stood in the doorway.

"Where have you been so long, Jason? I have been waiting."

"I thought you w-would be at ch-church."

"I told them I did not feel so good."

She let him hold her without resisting and when he kissed her she put her arms around him.

"Oh, Sallie."

"It is all right, Jason."

She followed him without protest as he led her upstairs to her little room at the rear of the house. When he fumbled with the buttons, she removed his hands and undid her bodice. At the sight of her plump breasts and her triangle of cornsilk-colored hair he hesitated in confusion until she took his hand and asked teasingly, "Isn't that what you wanted?"

"God, yes."

"Now you."

She looked alarmed at the first sight of him without his trousers, but then half smiled, saying, "I saw Mama and Pa doing it once, when I was little. Here."

They had barely lain down on her small bed when it was over. Her thighs gleamed with his wetness.

"I couldn't hold it."

"That's all right. Maybe it is for the best." They lay together, with her cradling his head against her breasts, smoothing his hair, neither of them speaking until they heard the sound of Koch's cart in the front yard.

"They are home. Get up, Jason. Pa will kill us."

As Jason was slipping on his trousers, he could hear Koch saying, "What's Logan doing out here?"

After tossing his shoes out the window, Jason lowered himself over the sill and dropped to the ground. Several minutes later, when he walked back through the yard, trying to appear nonchalant, Katie looked out the kitchen door at him, frowning.

"You lost your dog," she said.

"He was hungry, I expect. Come on, Logan."

It may have been his imagination, but it seemed to Jason that Katie hovered about more than ever during the next few days, making it impossible for him to see Sallie alone. He could not turn back, though; there was a bond between them now. Sallie belonged to him and he must claim her openly.

Jason screwed up his nerve to talk to Koch, but one day the smith was too busy; another, he was in a foul mood because one of his customers, an Ulsterman, had deserted his small farm and moved over the river into the new county of Cumberland, leaving without paying him for work done on a wagon.

"Verdammt Irisher!" Koch repeated over and over until that evening at supper Maria made him hush, thinking of the offense he might be giving Jason.

On two other days, Koch went into Lancaster to pick up supplies and equipment recently hauled in from Philadelphia. Jason's opportunity came after Koch's second trip to town. He returned with two long pieces of equipment on his wagon.

"There, Chason. I got them at last. I got a boring machine and a rifling bench so I can make rifles better and faster. It won't take me no two years for the next one. I can get rich making rifles for hunters and traders."

"What will you do about the blacksmith business?"

"Ach, I'll keep that. Maybe I'll even get you to run it for me.

You ain't built like a blacksmith, but I can get you a strong Cherman boy to help. How would you like that?"

Jason did not answer at once, waiting for Koch to stop tinkering with the new equipment. He would never forget those next few minutes. The smith's face was more relaxed and his small blue eyes kindlier than Jason had ever seen them. Now was the time. He took a deep breath and gripped the ends of the anvil to steady himself.

"I *would* like to stay here and"—then the stammering began—"and I w-would like to m-marry S-Sallie."

At first he thought Koch had not heard him.

"What?"

"I w-want to m-marry S-Sallie. I l-love her."

"Marry Sallie?"

Koch's face no longer was relaxed, and the kindly light in his eyes had faded. He stepped forward, causing Jason to loosen his grip on the anvil and retreat.

"I l-love her."

"You? You think you could marry her? Where did you get such a crazy idea?"

"I-I-I d-didn't—"

The smith took another step forward, and grasping the anvil by both ends, raised it to chest level. It seemed he would cast it upon Jason, but instead he hurled it down upon its block, splitting the wood.

"Irisher scum. I take you in out of pity and you think you can marry into my family. My Sallie. You think I want grandchildren descended from trash like Abraham McGee? Ha! He didn't have the guts to go bring back his own son. He let the redskins murder my wife's cousin and never did anything about it but talk. I don't want you around here no more. I don't want to see your face here in the morning."

As he continued, the smith's voice grew louder and louder and he began to swear in German. Hearing her husband's swearing, Maria came running from the house, followed by the two girls.

"Ernst! Calm yourself. What is the matter?"

"This redheaded half-Irish bastard says he wants to marry our Sallie. Damn it, woman, I knew we should not have taken him in. Let him eat at our table. Sit about talking to our girls. No wonder he got such a notion."

"Ernst, you mustn't be so angry. Jason is like our son."

Koch's eye now fell on Sallie, standing in the doorway, her mouth open and her face stark white.

"Sallie. Did you say you would marry this half-Irisher?"

"No, Pa. No."

"Then what makes him think . . ."

His rage was mounting again when Katie picked up a dipper and scooped it into a bucket of water beside the forge.

"Papa, you are acting like a child."

With that, she dashed the dipper of water into his face. For a moment it seemed he would strike her, but she did not flinch. "You are saying bad things you will be sorry for. Get control of yourself."

"Yes, Ernst," said Maria. "You are making too much of this. It is only natural for Jason to like our Sallie. We all love her. Now come to the house and shout no more." Then, as Katie led the smith toward the house, Maria turned to Jason.

"I am sorry. You should have spoken to me about her first."

"I'm sorry too."

"Well, you calm yourself. I'll send your supper out here tonight."

Jason sat in humiliated silence, staring at the glowing coals in the forge, comforted only by Logan. Now and then he could hear Koch's voice raging in the house and the tearful denials of Sallie. After a bit, Katie came out carrying a plate of hot food and a glass of milk, then she stood watching him as he ate, no longer the mocking, distant older sister.

"Poor Jason. You really love Sallie so much?"

He nodded.

"What will you do now?"

"I don't know. I didn't think he would get so angry."

"He said bad things to you?"

"He said my pa was a drunkard and a coward."

"He does feel your father should have avenged your mother's murder and recovered your brother from the Indians. But it was not fair to treat you so."

"What about Sallie? He won't hurt her, will he?"

"No, he dotes on her. I doubt she will ever find a man he thinks is good enough for her. Poor Sallie. She is such a goose."

"Now, Katie. Don't you say anything against her."

"I am saying nothing against her. It's just that Sallie still thinks like a spoiled little girl. She ain't ready for marriage, Jason, and neither are you. How would you support a wife?"

"I would find a way."

"Oh, Jason. You have some growing up to do yourself. Finish your supper and stop feeling sorry for yourself."

Unable to sleep, Jason reviewed the smith's remarks again and again. He knew his father had not been respected by others, but he had never heard him spoken of with such contempt. If only Abraham had been able to bring back Isaac and perhaps Meskikokant, in chains, then the McGees would have earned the respect even of stolid Germans such as Ernst Koch. Was he doomed to live in shame for the rest of his life because of his father's failure?

Logan scratched in his sleep and licked his chops. An owl hooted mockingly in a nearby tree as Jason, sleepless and forlorn, wondered if Isaac had felt so cut off from others in his long captivity.

"Jason, oh, Jason."

It was Katie, calling from the smithy door. He stumbled out of his lean-to, to find her standing beside the forge with Sallie. He thought for a moment that Sallie had come to elope with him, just as Gerta had done with Abraham more than twenty years before, but then saw that both girls were in their nightgowns.

"Listen, Jason, you can't stay here. Papa swears he will drive you away in the morning. He has lost his reason. You must go. Here, take this." Katie handed him a bag filled with food. "And this." She put several coins in his hand. "Now Sallie wants to say goodbye to you. I'll wait outside."

By the light from the forge, Jason could see that Sallie's face was puffy from crying.

"Oh, Jason. I am sorry."

Jason held her tightly; he put his face into her hair.

"Please go away with me."

"I can't, Jason. You come back when you can provide for me."

"You'll wait?"

"How could I ever love anyone else?"

They clung together until Katie called in at the door. "Come on, Sallie. If Papa wakes up, he'll kill us both."

Sallie pulled away and Katie stepped back into the smithy.

"Jason, I got something else for you."

She handed him Koch's new rifle.

"Take this. You earned it. Papa cheated your father when he gave him that old musket. I have heard him brag about it. Besides, he can make himself another gun."

"I can't take his rifle."

"I got Mama's permission. And here is powder and shot. Now, Jason, you look after yourself."

With that, she put her arms about his neck and kissed him.

9

Jason and Logan reached Harris's Ferry after sundown. In the faint light of a half moon, he found his old dugout, beginning to rot about the gunwales, tied up beside the ferryboat. Quietly he and Logan got in the craft and Jason paddled them across the river. There they spent the night in a haystack, setting out again just before dawn. By early afternoon they had traveled twenty miles along the rutted valley road to Carlisle.

The new seat of Cumberland County looked like a country fairground. Beyond a log courthouse and a scattering of new houses and taverns, scores of Indian lodges had been set up around a square. The place was thronged with Indians, dressed in various ways, obviously from different tribes, together with many whites, some wearing the garb of frontiersmen and others that of gentlemen.

Jason made his way into a tavern for a mug of ale, which he carried outside to drink with his lunch. A bearded fellow wearing deerskins stood watching the parade of Indians and whites. His eye fell on Jason's rifle.

"Look here, lad, that's a splendid gun ye're carrying," he said in a south-of-Ireland brogue. "Where would ye be after getting such a foine weapon?"

"I earned it," Jason said.

"May I see it?"

Reluctantly Jason let the man examine the rifle.

"What is going on around here?" he asked.

"Big conference with the Indians. Got 'em here from six or seven tribes."

"What is it all about?"

As he inspected the rifle, the man explained how the Indians, who had been powwowing down in Winchester with the Virginians, learned that the Pennsylvania Assembly had voted the previous May to distribute several hundred pounds' worth of condolence gifts to keep their loyalty. They had sent word to Philadelphia that they would not return west and north until they had the goods. "So the Assembly hurried some bigwigs here to confer with them. Benjamin Franklin,

41

the printer, is here. That's him, the portly gentleman with long hair over there talking to Conrad Weiser, Pennsylvania's ambassador to the Iroquois."

He turned the rifle over and examined the trigger guard. "What a splendid rifle. Would ye be selling it?"

"Never."

"Well, thin, where are ye headed with it?"

"West."

"Over the mountains, eh? Hunting, I suppose."

"You might say."

"Ye'll play hell making the trip pay if ye've naught but that yellow dog to carry back yer furs."

"I'm not going after furs."

The man smiled slyly. "I see. I'll not pry into yer affairs, then. By the bye, my name is George Croghan. I'm somewhat involved in the fur trade myself. That's why I am interested."

"Do you live around here?"

"I operate a trading post back at Silver's Spring and I'll soon have another over at Aughwick on the new path out to the Allegheny River. What did ye say yer name was?"

"Jason."

"No last name?"

Jason shook his head.

"None ye care to reveal, eh? I do hope ye're not an apprentice running away from his master. And that ye came by this lovely rifle by honest means."

Jason wanted desperately to get away from the Irishman, but before he could do so the portly gentleman ended his conversation and approached them.

"Ah, Croghan. Weiser and I want to talk to you in private after a bit. Before we confer again with our red friends. We must make it plain they are to have no rum until after our talks. And we may require you to hold the gifts."

"Yes, Mister Franklin."

"Who is this fine-looking lad, and whose is that gun?"

"His name is Jason and he says he is going west." Croghan winked. "But not for furs. Just to hunt something or other. The gun is his."

"Too bad. With a name like that, he might bring back a fleece of gold."

"I don't follow ye, Mister Franklin."

"No matter. It was a bad pun." The Philadelphian turned his bright gaze upon the boy.

"It would appear to me that you are well equipped in both the dog and the gun line, Master Jason."

"Yes, sir, I am." Jason took the gun from Croghan. "Pleased to meet both of you. I must go now."

"Good luck to you, lad."

Away from the Irishman and his probing questions, Jason stopped at a small stream west of Carlisle and bathed his sore feet. Then he pressed on toward Shippensburg.

It was growing dark and chilly when an exhausted Jason McGee came upon a settlement of several dozen houses strung along two intersecting roads. He stopped outside a two-story log house, almost flush on the road, with the sign of a white horse showing in the dim light from the glazed paper windows. He could hear the voice of a woman inside, talking loudly.

"God rue the day ever I married you, Sam Pickering. You wouldn't know the truth if you met it in the road."

Jason, unable to make out the muffled words of the reply, stepped close to the door.

"Don't add lie to lie," the woman continued. "You are a rogue. You chase after everything that walks on two legs and wears a dress. By God, if they were to put a petticoat on a she-bear, you'd be after her too."

"Now, now, Ida."

"Don't now, now, Ida me. I don't know what is to become of us. If I leave you here alone, you drink up the rum and there is none to sell. If I let you out, you go chasing after girls. Lord, why didn't I listen to me father back in London? Don't marry Sam Pickering, he pleaded with me. He tried to warn me, but I believed your promises. Said you would bring me over to America and become rich. What a liar—"

Jason opened the door and walked with Logan into a large room with a brick floor and an enormous fireplace across one end. An enclosed bar occupied an opposite corner and standing behind it was a large woman with bulging breasts and protuberant blue eyes. The only other occupant, a short, stout man with red cheeks, sat at one of several rough tables.

The woman looked up.

"You gave me a start coming in like that. Is it a bit of refreshment you'd like? Here you, now, Mister Pickering, take this young gentleman's sack and draw up a stool for him to rest in front of the fire."

"Yes indeed, lad, right here," the man said. "What would you like my good wife to bring you to drink? Dram of rum, perhaps?"

43

"Just some warm food."

"Food?" the man said. "Well now, Mrs. Pickering . . ."

"I can bring him a pot of fresh stew and some bread baked by myself just this afternoon."

While his wife went to the adjoining kitchen, the tavernkeeper drew his stool close and asked to examine the rifle.

"I'm no hunter myself, being city born and bred, but anyone can see you have an extraordinary weapon there, a most extraordinary weapon indeed."

"I know."

"As I say, I may be a poor judge of firearms, but if you are interested in raising a bit of coin for your journey, I'd be glad to discuss the matter of a loan or purchase."

"N-no. It's not for sale."

"No offense meant. Which way are you headed?"

"I've come from Lancaster County and I'm going over the mountains."

Jason was relieved that the woman returned just then so that he did not have to answer any more questions.

"There you are," she said, setting a bowl of hot stew and a dish of bread and cheese on a table. "If you'll just turn your stool around, you can warm your back and fill your stomach at the same time. I cut you a bit of cheese too. . . . Mister Pickering, the poor dog is hungry also. See how he begs. In the kitchen, my dear, you'll find a bone and some meat scraps. There's a good man."

When he had gone, she folded her hands and watched Jason attack the stew.

"Such an appetite. Have you lodging for the night?"

Jason, his mouth full of boiled venison, shook his head.

"We can find a bed for you upstairs, if I may be so bold. Generally we're full here this time of year, what with traders and packers coming and going, but they are all stopped over at Carlisle. . . . There, Mister Pickering, put the bones on the hearth for the dog. . . . Yes, they say there are hundreds of Indians gathered at Carlisle for a conference."

"Carlisle, that damnable place," her husband interrupted. "When this county was created three years ago, they established Shippensburg as the county seat and rightly so. Mrs. Pickering and I were newly arrived from Philadelphia, looking for the right situation, and when I heard the news about a sixth county coming into being, I says to myself, 'Sam Pickering, I smell an opportunity.' So what do Mrs. Pickering and I do but betake ourselves out here and start this place. No sooner than we get the White Horse saddled and ready to ride

. . ." Here he paused and winked at Jason. "Forgive my little joke. Why, no sooner than do we start building a good trade amongst visiting magistrates, witnesses and such at the court sessions, than they move the county seat east to Carlisle, a place of no significance whatsoever."

"Mister Pickering, this young gentleman can have little interest in our difficulties. By the bye, I have told him he may have lodgings here for the night."

Jason, unused to such effusive attention, ducked his head and continued ladling in mouthfuls of stew. The comments and questions of the Pickerings ceased at the sound of a horse's hoofs on the road outside the tavern. Logan looked up from his bones and growled.

The door opened and in stepped a stocky, blond man with a square face and the kindliest gray eyes Jason had ever seen. Clad in a long black coat and wearing buckled shoes, he did not remove his broad-brimmed hat as he inquired: "Might this be a public house?"

"Indeed it is, sir. Sam Pickering, proprietor, speaking. And this is my good wife. I see by your manner of dress you are a member of the Society of Friends, so I'll not offer you drink, but if it's food and lodging you're after, you've come to the right place."

The man, still wearing his hat, smiled. "I am indeed a Quaker and it is food and lodging that I require, for myself and my horse. There seems to be no place to lay one's head in Carlisle, so I have ridden on through the darkness to your establishment."

"We can put you up for the night."

"Good. I'll just set my bags inside. I wish my steed to be fed before I eat."

Jason got to know the Quaker better that night, for they shared the same bed in a tiny room upstairs, a bed that Sam Pickering assured them had often accommodated as many as four travelers in comfort. His name was Ephraim Haworth. He came from Philadelphia and had felt himself called by God to establish a mission for the Indians on the Ohio. He had spent several months studying with a former Moravian missionary to the Indians so that he could recite the Lord's Prayer, the Twenty-third Psalm, the Beatitudes and certain sayings of George Fox's in the Delaware tongue. Haworth was in his early thirties. He was such an honest, open fellow that Jason felt no restraint in talking to him.

"Why is thee going over the mountains, young friend?" Haworth asked after they had settled themselves in the bed.

Jason, his old nervousness returning, stammered out the story of how his mother and sister had been killed and his brother stolen nine years before. Haworth listened patiently.

"So thee is going to rescue thy brother?"

"Yes."

"And I am going to rescue my red brothers from savagery. Perhaps thee and I should go together. Hast thee a horse?"

"No."

"Let us discuss this again on the morrow. Good night, Brother Jason."

That night Jason dreamed his old nightmare about the attack on his family, but this time no massacre occurred. In his dream he held Ernst Koch's rifle and with it he shot Meskikokant through the head before he could wield that dreadful hatchet. The nightmare was so vivid that Jason awakened with his heart pounding. He calmed himself by thinking of Sallie.

As they dressed the next morning they could hear Mrs. Pickering's voice raised again, this time on a different tack.

"You are lazy and you need not deny it. 'Oh, Ida,' you said, 'let us go and open a tavern. You shall have bar maids and serving girls to do your work. You can live the life of a lady there at Shippensburg.' But see who gets up first and must light the fires herself, and see who lies abed like a lord. And when I think of the chances I had to marry back in London. Fine, upstanding young lads with futures in trade. Even a young vicar. But who did I choose? The man with the smoothest words."

"Our Goodwife Pickering seems to have a sharpish tongue this morning," Haworth remarked to Jason.

"Yes. It was just as sharp last night. She was giving it to him when I arrived."

Mrs. Pickering's tirade ended when she heard them on the narrow stairs leading down to the common room. While her husband and Haworth looked after the Quaker's horse, she set out a good breakfast: hot corn mush, bread and honey, sausages and strong tea. Mr. Pickering came in with Haworth, to watch them eat. When he had finished, Haworth pushed his stool away from the table and addressed the couple.

"My young friend and I both wish to go over the mountains and neither of us has a clear notion of what to expect. Have you any maps or information about the proper routes to the Forks of the Ohio?"

"As I was telling the lad here last night, I am a city man. Never been west more than ten miles of here. But from the tales the traders tell, a man would be foolish to go out there alone, not knowing the Indians or the trails."

"Yes, Mister Pickering is right," his wife said. "You are venturing into the unknown. You'd be well advised to go along with a pack train."

"Mrs. Pickering speaks wisely," her husband said. "Only I don't know of anyone ready to go. Carlisle seems to be attracting the traders as a dead horse draws flies. All trying to get on the right side of the Indians, you know."

"Is there not a trader in town at the moment?"

"There is one, but I don't think he is ready. He lost two horses on his last trip. Drowned they were, in the Allegheny. Swept away with the furs they carried. He has but one horse left and can't return until he has raised the money for replacements."

"If you are speaking of Christopher Cadwell," his wife said, "why, he could raise the money from John Harris or that Jew, Simon, down in Lancaster, if he would tear himself away from that dreadful McGinty woman. She has him so besotted he has lost his sense."

"Now, my love, Maud McGinty is not a dreadful woman."

"No, Mister Pickering, I wouldn't expect you to think her dreadful, her nor any other female."

Haworth, in his benign way, drew from the couple the information that Christopher Cadwell at the moment was residing in the home of a young widow of the community, one Maud McGinty.

"Come, Friend Jason," Haworth said. "Let us go and consult with this Christopher Cadwell."

Jason left his rifle standing against the fireplace.

"Look out for Cadwell, gentlemen," Pickering called to them. "He's a sharp one."

"And look out for that McGinty woman too," his wife said. "She's no fit woman to consort with a missionary or a young lad."

As they closed the door behind them, they could hear her voice rising in some fresh complaint.

10

At the door of Maud McGinty's snug cabin, Haworth knocked gently, and waited. After a bit he knocked again, less gently. Still getting no answer, he pounded so hard it made the roof rattle and he called out, "Halloo. Be Christopher Cadwell within?"

"Who wants him?" A woman's voice, full of sleep.

"Two travelers who have business with him."

They heard the sound of a bolt being drawn back, and the door opened just enough for them to see a pretty woman in her thirties, with a mass of long black curls hanging down to her bare shoulders and a fair, round face with turned-up nose. She put a hand in front of her face against the light.

"What do ye want?" she said in a North Irish accent.

"We have a matter of interest for Christopher Cadwell, who, we are told, may be in residence here."

"In residence. Ha. He is in bed. Sound asleep."

"Would thee mind to awaken him? The business is of some importance."

"He won't like it. Drank a bit too much last night, I fear."

"Please do try."

She closed the door and they could hear her speaking, so softly they could not make out the words. Then louder and louder.

"Christopher, my love. Rise ye up. . . . Christopher, the sun is well up and two gentlemen are here to see ye. . . . Christopher Cadwell, God damn it, get your lazy arse out of that bloody bed."

They could hear no response. The door opened again, wide enough so they could see that the woman had a good figure, with small, firm-looking breasts.

"Hand me that bucket of water there, if ye would, sir. I'm getting nowhere being gentle with the sluggard."

She left the door ajar as she took the pail. They heard the slosh of water and then a sputtering noise and finally the enraged voice of a man.

"Damn you to perdition, you whore's mother."

They heard an object strike the wall. The door opened and the woman darted past them into the road, followed by a half-dressed man of about forty-five, tall, with a tanned face that would have been handsome had the nose been less prominent and had he not had a knife scar running across his face diagonally. He blundered into Haworth, causing him to stumble back against Jason.

Logan growled at the man, who stopped in confusion.

"What's going on out here?"

"We wish to converse with thee, friend."

"What the hell about?"

"Nothing to do with hell, friend. Can we not sit down quietly somewhere to talk? We understand thee is a trader to the Indians and that thee knows the trails to the Ohio well."

"I should. Been going back and forth for over ten years."

"And we hear thee is familiar with the Indians out there as well."

Maud McGinty, who had been hiding behind Haworth, laughed at this. "He is familiar with their squaws, at any rate."

48

Cadwell glared at her. "Maud McGinty, I shall spank your saucy ass when I get my hands on you."

She stuck out her tongue at him. "Ye'll have to catch me first."

Cadwell laughed, then addressed Haworth again. "So what do you want? To go in the trading business? There is enough competition already."

"No, friend. We seek no monetary gain from the Indians. We want to go west in the company of some person who will guide us and instruct us long enough so that we can look after ourselves in the wild. We are told thee is the only trader in town, and we don't want to wait."

"You are out of luck. I lost two of my three ponies just lately. With just one pony, there is no profit in going west. I need at least three or four. Have you got a horse?"

"I do. A good-sized roan gelding."

"What about the redhead?"

Jason shook his head.

"There you are, then. Nothing to talk about. As soon as I have finished my business here"—he winked at Maud McGinty—"why, I'm going east to buy some horses. You'll have to find yourselves·another guide. . . . Get in here, woman. Have you no shame, standing in a public road in naught but your shimmy. What will your neighbors say?"

The woman laughed and stepped inside. Before Haworth could speak again, the door had been closed in his face and bolted. They could hear Cadwell and Maud laughing inside.

When Jason and Haworth returned, dejected, to the White Horse, Sam Pickering was sitting in the common room, holding Jason's rifle.

"We saw Mister Cadwell but got no satisfaction. He needs at least two horses more. And I gather he needs money to buy them, as he lost two loads of furs."

"You have a horse."

"I do, but friend Jason does not."

"Nor do I have money to buy one," Jason said.

"But you have this fine rifle. You could trade it for a horse."

"Then I wouldn't have a gun."

Pickering cleared his throat. "Young man, Mrs. Pickering and I have been talking about what a brave lad you are to be going west with only a dog and a rifle. You would be well advised to go in the company of some older man, someone who knows the country. You need a gun and you need a horse if you are to enlist the help of Christopher Cadwell. You have no horse, but you have a splendid

49

rifle, rather more splendid than your needs require. Mrs. Pickering and I always stand ready to be of help to strangers."

Jason was growing irritated by the man's garrulousness.

"W-what are you g-getting at?"

"It happens that I have a good enough musket for your requirements. And I have a steed which, while not perfect in all details, still would fill your needs. Here, then, is a way you can accomplish your purpose through Christopher Cadwell."

Mrs. Pickering had stopped rattling mugs behind the bar. Haworth was listening, with a look of slight concern.

"L-let me see the other gun."

The tavernkeeper's wife brought a short-barreled musket out and laid it on the bar.

"There you are, son. It's all you really need."

Jason frowned at the sight of the musket. "W-where did you get this?"

"I purchased it."

"Who from?"

"I don't know that it matters. I'm not asking you how you came by your rifle."

Haworth interrupted. "The horse you propose to exchange with this musket for Friend Jason's rifle—would it be the one-eyed mare you have in your stable?"

Jason looked into the shrewd eyes of Sam Pickering. "A one-eyed mare? How long have you had her?"

"Near to three years."

"D-did you get her from a traveler? From the same man who had this old musket?"

"As a matter of fact, I did."

"Was it someone who fell sick here?"

Pickering lost his air of self-assurance. "How did you know that?"

"Did he die in this tavern?"

Mrs. Pickering could not keep silent any longer. "Course he didn't die in here. He died in our barn. . . ."

The tavernkeeper shot her a vicious glance.

"He fell ill, after drinking too much. We tended him as best we could, what with a tavernful of guests and court in session here."

Now Jason was on his feet, his fists clenched, looking down at Pickering. "Was the name of the m-man Abraham McGee?"

Pickering, his mouth hanging open, did not reply. Jason took him by the front of his blouse and hauled him to his feet.

"Abraham McGee. Was that his name?"

Haworth interrupted. "Jason. Thee frightens Mister Pickering. Release him. There. Now, Mister Pickering, thee can answer."

The tavernkeeper backed away from Jason. "I—I am not sure. . . ."

"Yes." His wife spoke up. "His name was Abraham McGee, he said. Used to work on the Harris Ferry."

"That was my father. You let my father die in a barn. And you lied to John Harris about it."

"Here now, young fellow. You want to be careful making such accusations."

"Shut up. D-damn you. You let him die. And you d-didn't buy that mare. Y-you just kept her. And the gun."

He was moving toward Pickering with his fists clenched, when Haworth stepped between them. "Come out to the stable, lad, and let's discuss this in private."

At the sight of the same mare Ernst Koch had traded to Abraham McGee, Jason clenched his fists and swore. Haworth calmed him down enough so that he could relate the full story of his father and his intention to go and recover Isaac.

Haworth thought for a few minutes. Then he said, "Follow me."

They went back into the tavern, where the Pickerings were anxiously whispering to each other.

"Pay careful heed to what I am about to say." Haworth addressed them, standing just inside the door with feet spread apart. "It would appear that thee gave out a false story at Harris's Ferry. It would appear that thee might have traded Abraham McGee rum for his mare. Of course, if thee has some bill of sale or receipt showing a fair sum, Jason and I would be glad to alter our opinion. As for keeping the musket as payment for treatment of the man, I put it to thee that lodging in a barn might not deserve quite such remuneration. If thee has any documents in this matter or if we could find neighbors here to corroborate thy tale, that, too, would put matters in a different light. But failing such evidence, I think we must assume that the mare is the rightful property of the son of Abraham McGee, who stands before thee here. And the musket as well."

"They can keep the musket," Jason said.

"There it is, Sam Pickering." His wife found her voice. "I told you you couldn't get away with it. Always looking for the sly way around things. Then had to go and blab a cock-and-bull story to John Harris. Couldn't pay the fellow a pound or two for his mare and get a receipt. No, had to try it on the cheap with rum."

"Shut up, woman." Pickering shouted at her. "Damn you and

your big mouth." He turned to the Quaker. "This woman has made my life a hell. She nags and nags. Never shows me any tenderness, and then charges me with fornication with all things female. Always going on about who she might have married back in London. Let me tell you, her father was a church sexton and the only man as ever asked to marry her was a fishmonger's half-witted son. She should have married him, for she would have made a natural fishwife. Take the damned mare. She is of little value anyway. I would go west with you myself if I were a younger man. Take her."

Mrs. Pickering put her apron over her face and wailed.

"Wait," Pickering called out as Haworth and Jason started for the door. "You did not pay for your lodging or your meals."

Haworth drew some coins from his vest pocket and tossed them in on the brick floor. "It is a blessing I did not fall ill while a guest in thy establishment. God send thee peace, Friend Pickering. And thee, Goodwife Pickering."

By the time they reached Maud McGinty's cabin again, Christopher Cadwell was drawing water from the community well across the road.

"I thought I was rid of you."

"As thee can see, we now have two horses, or to be more precise, a horse and a mare. We want to accompany thee to the Ohio. We wish to leave as soon as possible."

"You don't understand. You have a saddle on your horse. There would be no riding. The horses would carry trade goods: pots, combs, blankets and rum."

"Rum?" The Quaker frowned.

"Yes, rum. Can't do business without it."

"It goes against my conscience, but I suppose we have no choice."

"Indeed, you do not. And furthermore, the horses would have to come back, with or without you, in the spring. I have to bring back furs and I can't carry them myself. So that would mean walking more than two hundred miles west and then two hundred back again." He looked at Haworth's buckled shoes. "It would mean blistered and bruised feet. There would be cold weather out there. Sleeping in Indian lodges. And Indian food is not meant for tender stomachs. Methinks I'd be well advised to borrow money and buy my own horses."

"We expect hardships. We are prepared for it. I would bear any burden, travel any distance, to bring God's message to the Indians."

"You have to be prepared to defend yourself or you will soon be dead. You have no gun for protection or for hunting."

"I—I have a g-gun," Jason said.

"So you have. Was just admiring it. Gift from your father, I suppose. Pretty thing, but what does a stripling like you know of shooting?"

"I can shoot good."

"Every farm boy that ever shot a rabbit thinks he is a great hunter. Believe me, lad, a pretty gun don't make a good hunter. I'll waste no more time on you two. Be off. Find yourselves a nursemaid elsewhere."

Maud McGinty called from her cabin door. "Christopher, will ye stay all day at the well?"

"Coming, Maud, my love."

As Cadwell picked up the bucket of water and crossed the road, a flock of crows feeding among the shocks of corn in a field behind the cabin cawed, as if taunting them. Jason and Haworth stood holding the reins of their horses, feeling like fools.

"W-wait a minute," Jason said. "L-let me show you something."

Cadwell paused at the cabin door, a look of annoyance on his face.

Jason stood the butt of his rifle on the ground, poured a measure of powder from his powder horn into the muzzle, drew a patch of cloth from his pocket and nested a lead ball in it and inserted the load. Then he removed the ramrod and thrust the ball down against the charge.

"D-don't go away," he said to Cadwell.

He drew back the flintlock and dropped a few grains of fine powder in the pan.

"Now." He raised the rifle to his shoulder.

The sentinel crow for the noisy flock across the road sat high up in a walnut tree some hundred and fifty yards away, enjoying the clear, warm morning air, gossiping to his companions on the ground.

Jason lined up the crow in his sights, made an allowance for the distance, and squeezed the trigger.

Click, spang! The spark ignited the priming powder and the main charge exploded in a flat, loud crack. The sentinel crow's chatter stopped in midsentence and his wings shot out from his sides as he was knocked off his arrogant perch and went cartwheeling down, bouncing from branch to branch until he hit the ground. Logan raced toward the fallen crow.

"Jesus Christ," Cadwell said. "What a shot. Let me see that rifle."

He held it appraisingly in one hand, then tried the fit against his shoulder. "What balance."

Logan returned with the crow in his mouth. Cadwell held it up by its feet.

"You hit it square in the breast." He smiled. "Come inside, the two of you, and let's talk."

They worked out the arrangements with little delay after that. Cadwell had enough trade goods stored in Maud's loft to make a load for three horses, so they could load up the animals in the morning and be off for the Forks of the Ohio.

"The Indians shift about, you know. And I want to go to a village where there are no other traders in residence. Then I have my own ways of enticing them to come to me with their furs."

He questioned them more closely about their reasons for going west.

"So you want to convert them to your Quaker beliefs, and you want to find your brother?"

"Yes, and bring him back."

"Just remember this. I am in command on this trip."

"In matters to do with the horses and the trails," Haworth replied.

"In matters having to do with how we travel, where we sleep, when we get up and where we camp."

"In those matters, yes."

Cadwell looked at the Quaker, appraising the character of this plain-speaking man with the guileless but willful gray eyes. He started to say more, but ended with, "As long as it is understood who is the boss."

After visiting the unmarked grave of Abraham in the community potter's field, Jason, with Haworth, spent the night on pallets spread in front of Maud McGinty's fire. Jason was awakened once during the night by the sounds of the widow's voice coming from her bed in the loft, which she shared with Cadwell. He could not make out her words or the trader's replies, but there was no mistaking the soft weeping or the sounds of love-making that followed. He lay awake thinking of how it would be to lie abed with his Sallie, as man and wife.

Well before dawn, Maud summoned them to a huge breakfast. She hovered with a spatula in hand, watching with pleasure and an air of sadness as they consumed slabs of ham and bowls of oat gruel and johnnycakes.

"Ye had better eat hearty, good fellows. There's none of Christopher's squaws can give ye food like this."

"Go on with you, Maud McGinty," Cadwell said. "A lady wouldn't pay herself such compliments." He slapped her on the rump and she put an arm around his neck, looking at Haworth as she did.

"Look after the rogue for me, sir. I want him brought back to me in one piece."

Cadwell laughed. "Ah, Madam McGinty, there will be many a piece for you when I return, there will." He laughed to see how Haworth blushed.

"A pox on your pieces," Maud said.

"You wouldn't wish that on me, would you, now?"

"Nay, I didn't mean that. That would be biting my nose off to spite me face, wouldn't it?"

Jason joined in the couple's laughter, while Haworth sat in embarrassment at their crude humor.

Maud bent down and kissed Cadwell on the lips. "I shouldn't bother with a scoundrel like you, not when there are so many good, honest men looking for wives."

Cadwell, still sitting, drew her against him. "Perhaps when I come back from this trip, free of debt, you'll consider becoming the wife of a dishonest man."

"Mind yer tongue, now, Christopher, if ye be not serious. I've witnesses here."

"So you have."

Maud pulled away, pretending that her johnnycakes were scorching, but Jason saw the glistening of tears in her eyes.

So it was that as the sun just appeared on a chilly October morning, two men and a boy, each leading a horse loaded with rum and trade goods, followed by a large yellow dog, set out from the frontier town of Shippensburg, headed for the mountains.

PART TWO

1

With the morning sun illuminating the just turned October foliage, they trudged through a pleasant countryside studded with walnuts and oaks, some twelve miles to the base of the low mountain range. There the trail mounted to a high wind gap. They halted on the first slope to eat the lunch Maud had packed and to let their animals rest.

"Your two nags aren't used to such going," Cadwell warned them. "Cut yourselves good strong switches and don't hesitate to use them. They might just as well learn now what being a packhorse is like."

Haworth acted as if he had not heard the suggestion, but Jason complied.

The trail was steeper than he had expected. The horses sometimes missed their footing. When his did, Cadwell would break into a fury of swearing, and once, ran behind the animal and lashed him across the rump. He would not let them halt until they reached the gap.

Jason was strong and fit from having worked around the blacksmith shop for three years, but the long walk from Lancaster County had sapped his strength so that he was bone tired. Although Haworth uttered no complaint, his distress showed on his face, now red and sweaty from exertion.

Jason gazed east across the valley at the town of Shippensburg and surrounding farm clearings.

"Take a long look," Cadwell said. "It's the last time you'll see signs of so many white people for a while. You're in Indian country now."

After a brief rest, they began their descent down the back slope into a narrow valley, and they halted in the late afternoon beside a creek. As their horses drank from the stream, Cadwell explained that he had hoped to reach the other side of the valley before making camp so they could make the next climb while fresh on the following morning. "But I see you are worn out. We'll just camp here for the night, if you've no objections." This last was said with a measure of sarcasm directed toward Haworth.

The Quaker replied, "I will go on if thee wishes."

"No. I expect you do not take such long walks in Philadelphia."

"Generally I am fond of walking, but must confess I am little used to going over such rough trails."

"It might have been easier if you had worn more practical shoes."

"These shoes were made for me by an excellent bootmaker, made of the best leather. And I took care to break them in properly before leaving Philadelphia."

While Jason and Cadwell unburdened their horses and started a cook fire, the Quaker soaked his feet in the creek.

They slept under blankets beside a giant sycamore tree on the creek bank. Jason dreamed no nightmares, and awakened early to the jostling touch of Cadwell's foot and the trader's voice telling him to get up.

As they ate their breakfast of hot tea and cold johnnycakes and cheese, Cadwell suddenly sat up.

"I hear a pack train coming."

It was several minutes before Jason heard the voice of a man first singing and then swearing, and even longer before he could hear the sounds of the hoofs of the horses and their harness bells. Finally, standing up, they saw five pack ponies, their backs piled with furs, led by a bearded, shambling man of about fifty and followed by a younger man with reddish skin.

Cadwell remained standing, an expectant smile on his face, until the bearded man caught sight of him.

"Christopher Cadwell. God damn, is that you? Powas, look who we got here. It's fearful what you meet alongside the trail when you don't have your gun loaded and primed."

The man walked up to Cadwell and swatted him on the shoulder playfully with his hat and then threw his arms around him and lifted him off his feet in a bear hug.

"What in the hell kind of outfit you got here, Christopher? Them ain't proper packhorses. And what kind of helpers you got?"

Then, in only a slightly lower voice, still audible to Haworth and Jason, "Is that a God damned Quaker? And who is the stripling?"

At last Cadwell got the chance to speak. "These gentlemen are going west and they kindly lent me the use of their horses. Master Haworth, Jason, this big, rude bastard is Ezekiel Manning, and that is his son, Powas. Zeke had been trading with the Indians for twenty-five years. He gave me my start in the business."

"Taught him everything he knows, which ain't much."

"How is Mahagpeta, Zeke?"

The smile faded from the trader's broad face. "Did you not hear? She died last winter. Best squaw that ever did live. Powas and I miss her dreadful, don't we, son? Died among her own people whilst Powas and me was away. Now I'm too old to break in another squaw. Her brothers been trying to foist off her younger sister on me, a widow, but she's got a bad temper and would only make me miserable."

"What about your daughter?"

"Necosshebesco is married. To a fine young Seneca sent out by the Six Nations. Likely young buck. Expect he'll be a chief someday."

Jason was fascinated by the men's free-flowing talk, which ranged over their early days in trading to the current mood among the Shawanese and Delawares to the condition of the fur trade.

"Look there, Christopher," said Manning, pointing at his horses with his pipe. "Five ponies and not one of them carrying a full load. God damned Indians aren't bringing in the stuff to English traders like they used to. Started trading with the bloody French up around Venango. When our fellows try to follow them into that country, the French and their Canadian Indians seize their horses and chuck them out. I tell you, Christopher, I'm thinking of giving up the game. Two years ago, with all the Delawares moved out there and me married to one of their women, why, I couldn't get enough horses to carry out all the pelts. Now just look at the scrappy stuff we're hauling to Lancaster."

"Don't fret so, Zeke. It will be good for the market in London. Prices went down when the bumper crop reached there last year. They'll go up again when the supply slacks off a bit. The Pennsylvania Assembly is sending out several hundred pounds' worth of condolence gifts for the Delawares. Much of it powder and shot."

"They had better send soldiers too."

"You know the Quakers would never do that."

"If somebody don't, the French will take over the country out there. They are building a fort on Lake Erie. The Delawares have warned them officially, but unofficially I don't know how much we can count on them."

"Sure, but the Delawares are steady Indians."

"Yes, but the Shawanese are another matter. They are a bad influence on the Delawares. The Mingoes can't keep these two tribes under their thumbs forever."

After this conversation had trailed off, Manning questioned Cadwell about his loss of two horses. Then he asked what the "Quaker fellow" intended doing among the Indians. Cadwell started to answer, but Haworth interrupted.

"I can speak for myself, Friend Cadwell." Then to Manning: "I am going out in answer to a call from the Almighty to establish a mission among the Delawares, a teaching and preaching mission."

Manning snorted. "The Delawares don't need preaching. They have been following the ways of peace for years, and where has it got them? They don't own a scrap of land in this Quaker province anymore. Go and preach to the Iroquois and get them to stop warring on the Cherokee and the Catawba."

"I shall speak to any Indians I encounter about the pitfalls of greed for the trinkets of this world, not to mention the evils of rum."

"Har, har. Listen to that. Here is a Quaker with a fine horse worth ten pounds, wearing the best broadcloth and splendid shoes, going out to preach against worldly possessions for Indians. That is rich."

Haworth's face reddened. "This is the manner of dress we have always worn. It is not ostentatious. We live simply."

"You Quakers are very successful, too, with your plain, simple ways. Truly it has been said, 'A Quaker is the only man alive that can buy from a Jew and sell to a Scot and make a profit.'"

Before Haworth could reply, Cadwell took his friend by the arm. "Enough of that, Zeke. You've forgotten your manners in the wilderness. Come now and show me your pelts and answer me a few more questions about conditions out there."

Jason was amazed at how the Quaker had kept his temper. There he sat, minus his shoes but still wearing his hat, and reading his Testament, while Cadwell and Manning talked on and on, until nearly noon.

"Jesus Christ, Christopher, look at the sun. You're a bastard to keep me here jawing all day. Hey, you, Powas, we got to be on our way, son."

In saying goodbye, Manning paused with Jason. "Watch out for your dog, young fellow. A Delaware wouldn't eat him except in an emergency, but the Shawanese and Iroquois make a ceremony of eating roast dog."

He laughed at the look of dismay on Jason's face. "And beware of the young squaws. They'll go wild over a redhead like you. Damn it, Powas, let's move on before I get started talking again. I'll tell Maud I seen you. Goodbye, Mister Quaker."

Haworth looked up from his Testament and nodded.

They walked on across open meadows to the next mountain range, labored up it, passed diagonally down the shorter back slope into a broad, deep-forested valley and stopped to camp at a spring well before dark. Cadwell took time to make odds and ends of food into a stew that Jason found delicious. After eating, they sat around the fire and Cadwell smoked his pipe.

"Master Haworth," he said, "I do wish to apologize for the remarks Zeke made about your religion today."

Haworth smiled. "Friend Manning's words to me were as an empty wind, soon passed away and forgotten."

"I don't think people like him should get away with insulting you, though," Jason said.

Haworth was quiet for a moment. "His words were mild compared to some that have been directed at me. Three years ago, I learned that a member of our meeting, an elderly merchant much respected for his charities and his piety, owned an interest in a plantation in Georgia that was importing slaves from the Indies and Africa. I went to him and expressed my concern. He tried to put me off in a courteous way. So I stood up in meeting on First Day and I spoke against what he was doing. He was most angry. But I would not be silent. And whilst I was at it, I went round the city asking that Friends who held Africans as house servants release them."

"Did it do any good?" Cadwell asked.

"Yes. Several Quakers gave their slaves their freedom and began paying them wages. Others agreed to change their wills so that the poor blacks would gain their freedom at the death of the owner."

"What about the old man who owned the plantation shares?"

"He left our meeting and went over to the Church of England."

Cadwell seemed amused by all this. "The world is so full of so many things your faith regards as bad, there won't be time for you to correct all of them in one lifetime, will there?"

"Mock me not, Friend Cadwell. And try to understand. When one ignites God's great universal love in the heart of another, not only does he rid that heart of sin, but he turns its owner into yet another instrument of the Almighty."

"I understand what you are saying, but what happens to your own ambitions, your own livelihood, if you devote your life to meddling in the affairs of others? Live and let live, I say."

"And that is what I say too. Live in the glory of the Almighty and help others live in it as well. Live and help—not let—live."

"But everything is a sin to such as yourself."

"Drunkenness, fornication, revenge, greed, envy—these things

63

bring no lasting pleasure to anyone, no matter what he may think. Nay, they do harm because they deny one the infinite joy of receiving God's love."

"I can see little profit in denying yourself the pleasures of a good pipe of tobacco, a dram of rum or a warm bed with a loving wench."

With that, Cadwell arose to go and make sure the horses were properly hobbled for the night.

2

Jason was glad to lie down that night, relatively untired, wrap himself in two blankets with Logan on one side and his rifle on the other, and stare up at the stars. He had had little time to think since leaving the Koch family five days before. Now he let his mind range back and forth over his recent experiences, recalling the new faces he had seen and the voices he had heard. After each retracing of his steps, he would return to the Kochs and think of Sallie.

How sweet his last two weeks there had been, with his love for Sallie openly stated to her and with her responding to him. Over and over he thought of that Sunday morning when they had gone to her bedroom and lain together, close and naked. Surely heaven could offer nothing better. And despite her father's rage, she had promised to wait for him. He could return neither Gerta nor little Stella to life, nor improve the reputation of his father, but he could and would bring back Isaac. That was his mission and his prize would be Sallie Koch as his wife. He fell asleep thinking of her ripe body and her merry, pretty face.

Later, he had a long, troubled dream. He was a small boy again and he was "it" in a game of hide-and-seek played in a dark forest. He was not sure at first of the identity of the other players until one called, "Over here, Jason," and the other, "No, over here." Then he recognized the voices of Isaac and Sallie. When he could not find them, their laughter rang out jeeringly. Soon new voices, first Gerta's and then Katie Koch's, implored him to give up the game and come home.

Logan, hearing him moan in his sleep, thrust his muzzle against Jason's neck, awakening him. It was a cold, cloudy morning. Over a breakfast of tea, cheese and bread, Cadwell warned them about the difficult trail they would take over the Tuscarora Mountain. "It will be a hard climb, but once over it, we'll be glad."

"Thee is in command in such matters."

"I'm glad you said that, Master Haworth. After our first day, I thought you might have forgotten."

"What dost thee mean?"

"I instructed you to cut a strong switch and apply it liberally to your horse when it falters. You ignored me."

"I cannot bring myself to abuse animals."

"Damn it, man, this is not a cobbled street in Philadelphia. Horses have to be driven. If you will not do as I say, turn back now."

For a moment, Haworth looked as though he might refuse. At last, however, he said, "Very well. But my horse is not used to such harsh treatment."

Soon they entered a forest of hemlocks so thick that direct sunlight could penetrate to the level valley floor only in patches near midday. With heavy clouds overhead, they could barely see. The huge trees stood so close that only clumps of fern and deep patches of moss grew between the trunks.

The three travelers moved over an easy path carpeted with needles. Even the songs of birds seemed hushed and reverent in this cathedral-like atmosphere. Jason walked along wishing that Sallie could be with him to share the dark beauty of the forest. By noon they had passed through the area and had stopped at a clearing to eat a cold lunch and let their horses graze.

"We are in for a ball-busting climb this afternoon," Cadwell reminded them. "This is where I will see what stuff you two are made of, going over the great Tuscarora Mountain."

Jason had regarded their first day as an ordeal, but this one would have challenged him even if he had been traveling alone with Logan. Cadwell stormed away, cursing at his pony and shouting back at the others to "give it to them." Logan, excited by all the swearing and the scrambling of hoofs, solved matters by running up and snapping at the fetlocks of the roan, who quickly developed a terror of the dog. First a nip at Haworth's horse, and then back for another at the half-blind mare; soon he had only to bark and feint at their legs for the animals to speed up the climb. It took most of the afternoon to attain the crest, which was covered with chestnut trees. Despite the cool weather, sweat streamed from men and horses.

As he sat down to wipe his face, with Logan sprawled in front of him panting furiously, Cadwell smiled. "McGee, this is quite a trail dog."

Jason did not reply; he was looking toward the west at range after range of thick-forested mountains blocking their way like walls set up to keep the white man out.

It began to rain as they descended the back slope, a cold rain that fell slowly at first but was coming down in sheets by the time they reached the base of the mountain. The trail became so slippery that each of the men fell at least once, Haworth so heavily Jason feared he was injured. Although he was on his feet instantly, waving away offers of help, he limped for a time thereafter.

The horses groaned and lowered their heads as they braced themselves against falling. Logan gave up his sport of snapping at their heels, as though he sympathized with the burdened animals in their discomfort. At the bottom of the trail they gathered under the low branches of an oak to squeeze the water from their coats.

"Never seen such weather in October," Cadwell said. "No use driving ourselves in rain like this. Shortly we'll come to the ruins of some squatters' cabins that got burned out three years ago. We can shelter ourselves there and wait for this miserable stuff to let up."

They slogged ahead over fairly level ground through a forest of mixed oak and pine until they came upon a collection of blackened chimneys standing around a clearing, and there they spent a cheerless night under a lean-to left by traders.

Cadwell roused them early the next morning. The rain had stopped during the night and now a cold wind herded broken clouds across the dull October sky. Far overhead, long lines of geese honked their way south. Cadwell set a brisk, steady pace over hilly, wooded country along a muddy trail which, after generations of use by moccasined feet only, had been deepened and widened in recent years by the boots of traders and the hoofs of their packhorses.

Whether to annoy Haworth or merely to express his exuberance—Jason could not tell—Cadwell began singing one bawdy song after another. The Quaker, now using his switch as a cane, limped along with one hand on his horse's withers, not saying a word.

All along the way, through deep forests, over bare, rocky hills and grass-matted balds, game abounded. A dozen times that morning, Jason, with his keen eye and accurate rifle, could have killed deer. Once an elk looked up from grazing and stood staring at them, within an easy rifle shot. They made good progress until they came to a small creek that had overflowed its banks. The water was cold, coming well above Jason's knees and almost to Haworth's waist. The horses kept their footing easily, however, and joined Logan on the western bank in shaking themselves vigorously.

They slogged on in their wet shoes through the morning until they came to a place Cadwell called the Sugar Cabins. There, in a large clearing of dead and dying trees, a man, a woman and several children, ranging in age from toddler to near adult, looked up from their labors in a turnip patch. The man put down his hoe and walked out to the trail.

"Why, it's old Christopher Cadwell himself. How be ye?"

"As well as if I had good sense, Tom Williams."

"Here now," the squatter shouted at his family. "Don't put them hoes down. You keep grubbing. I'll do the talking."

Williams, although a small man, had large hands much thickened with calluses. "Got anything to trade besides the usual junk the Indians like?"

"The usual. Blankets, combs, vermilion, mirrors and rum. I'm not eager to start trading yet, though. What have you got to exchange?"

"Potatoes, pumpkins, couple of deerhides. And we're up to our arses in maple syrup and sugar. Couldn't haul it all out last spring."

"No money?"

"You ever see a poor fellow like me with money? Last real money I held in my hand was a Spanish dollar when I finished my apprenticeship. I don't want or need that paper stuff the merchants in Shippensburg try to pass. Who needs money out here? We raise everything we eat. Plenty of game about. I put in a still last year so we can trade corn liquor as well as maple syrup for cloth, tools and such. How is your business, Christopher?"

Cadwell told him of the troubles the French were causing in the west and of his loss of two horses.

"Was just saying to the wife last night how we don't see so many traders coming through this fall. The French, eh? I never seen a Frenchman so they don't worry me." He waved his hand at the several acres of girdled trees surrounding a large two-story cabin, as if he were an English lord speaking of an ancestral estate. "If I can keep them lazy boys of mine aworking, we'll have ourselves the finest place in Pennsylvania in a few more years. And no quitrents going into the Penns' pocket. Look ahere, Christopher. The wife has stew left over from last night. Won't you stay and have a bite with us?"

After watering their horses, they entered the dark cabin and Mrs. Williams, a weary-looking snaggle-toothed woman of about forty, served bowls of venison stew while her husband stood in front of the kitchen fire and questioned Haworth about his mission. The Quaker

67

replied with his usual calm good humor until he had an opportunity to inquire how Williams and his family had come to live here, twenty miles within territory forbidden to white settlement.

As Williams explained it, the hills of the area abounded in sugar maple trees. For many years Indians had built temporary lodges in which to dwell while tapping the trees for their sweet sap. The Williamses, who had come over the mountains nearly ten years before, quickly had become self-sufficient. Once or twice a year, Williams and their oldest son drove their two horses over the mountains to Shippensburg with loads of maple syrup or sugar and corn whiskey, which they exchanged for powder and shot, tools, cloth and shoes.

"Everything else we need, we can grow or shoot or make. Yes sir, we are a world unto ourselves out here, safe from all want and danger."

Jason, remembering his childhood anxiety when the authorities had burned squatters' cabins, and having just seen so many charred ruins the day before, asked how the Williamses had escaped the notice of the magistrates.

"For one thing, it is too far out here for their dainty feet. For another, we get on well with the Indians that pass through here. I won't give them strong drink, but they know that if they are hungry or thirsty, the Williamses will give them food and water. And they are welcome to sleep in our barn anytime."

"As long as they behave themselves," Mrs. Williams said. "I don't let them in my house, though."

Her husband frowned at this unaccustomed interruption. "The Indians do not complain of us. We hunt only for our food, not for furs. We are hospitable. So they don't go running over to the authorities in Carlisle."

Cadwell interrupted, with the air of having heard this same story before. "Mrs. Williams, your stew was beyond description."

Mrs. Williams smiled, showing her gums.

Haworth, who had been amused by the family, agreed. "Goodwife Williams, thank thee indeed for thy excellent food and for thy hospitality."

By the time Jason added his thanks, Mrs. Williams was grinning so that her few back teeth, much rotted, were showing.

"It is a good woman I got here," said Williams. "Works hard, cooks good and never complains. Wouldn't trade her for a new cart and pair of oxen, I wouldn't."

Mrs. Williams ducked her head and blushed.

3

Carrying a sack of maple sugar the Williamses had pressed upon them, Cadwell kept them moving briskly westward across the hilly terrain. They saw no other signs of human beings until they came to a trailside shelter at the base of a low mountain Cadwell called Sideling Hill, where they stopped for the night.

Cadwell, in good spirits over their smooth progress, offered to make them a proper squirrel stew if Jason would take his rifle and "provide the wherewithal."

With Logan at his side, Jason went into the woods a few hundred yards and sat quietly until the squirrels began their evening frolics. In a short while he had shot three and brought them back to the lean-to, where Cadwell had a pot of water with corn meal and dried onions already simmering. Adding the squirrels to the mixture, they soon had a thick, rich stew.

They slept well that night, arose early and made their laborious way up and over Sideling Hill, then entered exceedingly rough country, up and down thicketed hills. It was dreary going, and to add to the gloom, rain began to fall again. Cadwell led the way, cursing the weather at every step, his head down and his shoulders hunkered up. Jason drew his collar close around his neck and pulled his hat over his eyes. Only Haworth, hat squared on his head, walked along with shoulders back, seemingly oblivious to the rain. They stopped at midday to chew handfuls of corn meal mixed with maple sugar. The rain became heavier, so that by the time they reached the Raystown Branch of the Juniata River, they were thoroughly soaked. Finding it impossible to start a fire in the rain, they went to bed that night with only another batch of meal and sugar in their stomachs.

"Isn't this rain the damnedest thing ever sent to try man or beast?" Cadwell said as they settled into their blankets under an old lean-to.

"God sends the rain to his purpose," said Haworth.

"Shit."

"Good night, Friend Cadwell. Good night, Jason."

Curiously, Jason was not disheartened by the rain. It seemed to him that every step he took to the west brought him closer to finding a prize and carried him farther from the painful memories of his family's massacre and the humiliating treatment by Ernst Koch. He was a man acting out his own role rather than a little boy doing what others told him. When he returned to Lancaster County, it would be to claim Sallie Koch on his own terms. He went to sleep to the sound of the Juniata rushing nearby and awakened in the morning to an ever louder roar of water and to Cadwell's swearing.

"The God damned river is out of its banks and there is no way in hell for us to cross."

Jason walked to the edge of the stream, whose swirling waters raged from bank to bank, and saw that even a strong swimmer would be carried away.

"Jesus Christ above, it is worse than that bastard of a flood that drowned my two horses last spring. Damn my luck to hell and back." Cadwell was walking back and forth, waving his arms and shaking his head.

"Friend Cadwell," said Haworth. "What shall we do?"

"Do? What in shit's name can we do but wait here?"

"For how long?"

"Until the frigging river goes down. Two or three days, unless it rains some more."

"And will thee occupy those two or three days with constant blasphemy and oaths?"

"What do you mean?"

"I mean Friend Jason and I, not to mention the Almighty, should not be subjected to two days of incessant profanity."

"God damn it, man, I'll swear if I like."

"Having expressed thy dismay about something thee can do nothing to alleviate, what can thee accomplish by pacing about cursing?"

"What the hell do *you* plan to do? Spend the time in prayer?"

"Much of it, yes. And in reading my Testament. And in practicing my Delaware. There are many ways we could spend the time to greater profit than in raging about like a beast."

"I could build a fire if I had just a bit of tinder," Jason said.

Cadwell looked sheepish. "You damned Quakers. All right, let's make the best of it. But I don't see how anybody can build a fire in this drizzle."

"I have some writing paper," Haworth said. "Would that help?"

"It would," Jason replied. "But I'll need other tinder, and some stones for a fireplace."

Caught up in the enterprise, Cadwell rooted about near tree trunks for pockets of dry pine and hemlock needles and dug into fallen trees for dried bark, while Haworth hauled up stones from the edge of the river.

In a corner of the lean-to, Jason arranged the stones skillfully into a U-shaped fireplace about two feet high, leaving air vents along the bottom. He tore the paper into shreds and spilled gunpowder over it. Holding his rifle upside down in one hand so the sparks would fall into the powder and paper, with the other hand he sprinkled dry bark and moss. He had to cock and snap the trigger several times before a spark fell into the powder and produced a flash of flame that ignited the paper. By carefully introducing the other tinder, soon Jason had nursed a small fire into life.

"There," said Haworth cheerfully as the larger bits of tree limbs began to blaze. "That's the way. Don't curse the darkness. Light a candle."

4

Built between two beech trees, with a stout ridgepole resting in convenient forks, the lean-to was larger and better constructed than most such shelters. There was enough room at one end for the three horses; with the completion of Jason's fireplace and the addition of fresh hemlock boughs on the "roof," they were almost as comfortable as they might have been in a frontier cabin.

Leaving Haworth to read his Testament, Cadwell and Jason went into the wet woods to hunt. They picked a spot in a laurel thicket where they were concealed and fairly dry and from which they had a clear view down a hollow to a spring. Once a black sow bear and two half-grown cubs sniffed around the spring, but Cadwell whispered, "We don't want to have to lug her and if you shoot a cub she'll charge us. Just wait." A bit later a magnificent elk walked down the opposite side of the hollow to the spring; again Cadwell shook his head and Jason watched the animal drink and then go his stately way back into the trees. A family of raccoons came and drank, but scampered away at the approach of a large buck deer. Again Cadwell shook his head and Jason lowered his rifle.

Finally a young doe shyly approached the spring, glancing about nervously and twitching her tail. Cadwell nodded and Jason fired just as she began to drink. She sprawled dead with her nose lying in the water. Logan broke his silence to run yelping toward the fallen deer.

"Good shot, McGee. She is just the right size."

As they hung the doe by her rear legs from a corner of the lean-to to disembowel and skin her, Haworth put aside his Testament to build up the fire. They gorged themselves on roasted venison while Logan happily feasted on raw scraps, and afterward, as darkness fell, Cadwell brought out his pipe and seated himself against a packsaddle. "All the comforts of home, eh, gentlemen?" Still later he played for them on his jew's-harp and showed Jason how to juggle and make coins disappear.

"You've no idea how my little tricks put the Indians in a receptive frame of mind."

"How did thee get into trading with the Indians?"

"It is a long story."

"We've lots of time and it is too early to go to sleep."

For a while Jason thought Cadwell either had not heard or was rudely ignoring Haworth. The trader drew the bung from a keg of rum and poured himself a full cup, after which he emptied a cup of water into the container.

"That will keep the keg from sloshing and the Indians will never know the difference."

He tossed more wood on the fire, settled himself in front of it and sipped his rum. Haworth pointedly drew out his Testament, holding it close to the fire to catch the light. Jason sprawled out with his feet toward the fire and his head resting on Logan's flank.

"You asked me how I got into this business," Cadwell said.

Haworth lowered his Testament. "So I did."

"It was after my wife died."

"Thee was married?"

"Yes, and had two children."

"And where might they be?"

"They died too; carried off the same week, all three of them. By typhoid."

He paused to take a swallow of rum.

"That is too bad. When was this?"

"Thirty-three. In Massachusetts. I was a glass blower. Susannah was just seventeen when we married. I was twenty-one. We had four years together."

"Thee was happy, then?"

"Sometimes I break into a sweat remembering how happy we

were. I used to run home from the glassworks at the end of the day. The other men chaffed me about it. Oh, my Susannah. And our babies. Two little girls. One of them three and the other just starting to walk."

"Too bad. And thee came to Indian country right after that—in thirty-three?"

"Not for four years. After burying my family, I sold everything we owned and took the money to Boston. Stayed drunk for three weeks. Woke up aboard a merchantman bound for Liverpool. The bosun worked me like a slave. I slipped ashore in Liverpool, without a penny. Got in with some gypsy entertainers and worked my way to London, stopping at market towns and country fairs. That's where I learned to juggle."

"Did thee like London?"

"I liked it well enough. Didn't always like the English. They think they are better than us. But I might still be there if a young fop had not insulted me in a public house."

"Insulted thee?"

"Yes, he came in with some other swells. They shoved me away from the bar and when I protested, called me an ignorant colonial. I brained him with an ale pot and ran out the door before his friends could set upon me. For all I know, I killed him. Anyway, I hopped a ride on a freight wagon to Southampton. A ship loaded with Germans and bound for Philadelphia had stopped there for cargo. Captain wanted me to sign a seven-year indenture, same as if I was an Irishman or a German. In exchange for my passage, that is. Told him what to do with his indenture, me whose father was born in Massachusetts and his father before him. When I told him that and the fact I had been a seaman, he let me come aboard in exchange for my labor. Stood a helm watch all the way across the Atlantic, four hours on and four off, on a leaky Dutch ship filled with stinking Germans, packed in like hogs going to market. Twelve of them died, and two women gave birth. Anyway, I came ashore in Philadelphia and got down and kissed the good American earth."

He took another swallow of rum.

"What did thee do then?"

"Took a job in New York with a fur shipper. He was a good man. Treated me fairly. But I couldn't quit drinking. I tried, but I couldn't stop thinking about my wife and babies."

He stared into the fire for a long while. When he began again, his speech was thick and the words came slowly.

"Got so I would near break down when I saw a young mother

with children. Drank too much. Finally came to work drunk and my employer turned me off the job. Out on the streets of New York. Reduced to juggling in taverns for rum. That's where Ezekiel Manning found me. Don't know what would have become of me if it hadn't been for good old Zeke."

He drained off the last of the rum and rose unsteadily to go and draw himself another cupful, this time forgetting to pour in water.

He walked out into the darkness, cup of rum in hand; the others could hear him urinating on the leaves. He returned to his place by the fire, took a sip of rum and began again.

"Zeke Manning, blesh his old God damn heart. Treated me like his son, he did. Took me with him. Those days, didn't have to go so far west for furs. Sometimes go up Sus . . . Sushanna to Smokin. Lots Delaware there. Haul fur down Lancaster. Damn Indians move west. Go west too. Zeke saw it coming. One of first traders on Ohio. Married Delaware woman. Mega . . . Mega . . . Shit—Delaware woman. Two children."

He fell silent, staring into the fire again. Noting how the firelight shone on the scar that ran diagonally across Cadwell's face, Jason asked, "Did you get that cut among the Indians?"

Cadwell put his hand to his face. "Nother trader caught me wif his squaw. Slashed me. Gonna kill me, but Zeke stopped him. Wish he hadn't sometimes."

Jason, who had been both entertained and embarrassed by Cadwell's rambling talk, was sorry he had asked.

"Furs. Split up with Zeke. Get rich by myself, I thought. Croghan, Peters, Trent, Simon the Jew. They get rich. Little man nothing. Now God damn French out there."

"You have the chance to bring back three horseloads at little expense. And Mrs. McGinty will be waiting for you."

"Who?"

"Maud McGinty. She wants to marry you when you return from this trip, remember?"

"I'm married to Susannah."

There was a long silence, except for the crackle of the fire and the roaring of the river.

"God damn river. God damn French. God damn Indians. God damn typhoid."

The cup fell from his hand and he sagged to one side until he lay on the ground.

"Come, Friend Jason. Let us put him to bed. I'll take his shoulders if thee will take his feet. Slip off his boots while thee is about it."

5

Jason had roasted more venison and boiled corn mush by the time Cadwell arose, well after daylight, the next morning. The trader sat up on his blankets, holding his head. After silently eating some sweetened gruel, he put on his boots and inspected the river. "The water is down a bit, but we'd be fools to risk a crossing yet."

"How are you?" Jason asked.

"Aside from a head that feels like a tomahawk hit it, well enough. Don't generally drink on the trail. Don't know what got into me."

"Two full cups of rum got into you."

Cadwell winced. "Hope I didn't make a fool of myself."

Haworth and Jason did not reply.

Cadwell scowled at them. "As it appears we'll be stuck here another day at least, I think I'll go afowling." He drew out his short-barreled old smoothbore. Jason rose and reached for his rifle. "No need for you to come along, McGee. I want to be on my own. But I'll borrow old Logan if I may."

When the trader and the dog were gone, Haworth said, "He is a strange man, our Indian trader."

"He is that."

"A good man at heart. But then I think all men basically are good at heart. Some do things harmful to themselves and others, but we should judge no man until we have stood in his shoes. Does thee agree?"

"I'm not sure that I do."

"Really? Hast thee known people who had no redeeming qualities? I know no such persons."

"I do. I know a blacksmith who is stingy and bad-tempered and cruel. And you saw how that tavernkeeper and his wife back in Shippensburg tried to cheat me, just as they robbed my father. What is good about people like that?"

"But thee should not be bitter about such persons when thee knows their circumstances."

Jason was annoyed at the Quaker's earnest innocence. "You have your opinion on that and I have mine."

"Quite so. Tell me, Jason, canst thee read and write?"

"Yes. I went to Paxton Church School for a few weeks. I can do sums as well."

"Dost thee know any Indian languages?"

"Only a few words I picked up around Harris's Ferry."

"As thee knows, I studied the Delaware language with a Moravian missionary in Philadelphia before setting out. Would thee like to learn some of it? We should not waste this time."

Patiently Haworth recited the Lord's Prayer in a dialect of the Lenni Lenape or Delaware Indians, and within half an hour Jason had it letter perfect.

"Why, Jason, thee has a good mind."

By the time Cadwell returned with a bagful of passenger pigeons, Jason had learned the Twenty-third Psalm and was working on the Beatitudes. The trader listened with amusement as he stripped the feathers from the birds. When Jason finished his recitation, Cadwell corrected his pronunciation of several words.

"You realize that you are speaking the dialect of the upriver clan, but the others will understand you well enough. They are pretty much mixed up on the Ohio anyway. By the bye, they prefer their own name for themselves. Lenni Lenape. Delaware is the name the whites gave them years ago."

"Lenni Lenape. I know that is the correct name, but did not realize they were so sensitive about it," Haworth said.

"They are. They are a proud people. My favorite Indians, they are. More trustworthy than the Shawanese. Not as arrogant or crafty as the Mingoes. Come to think of it, mayhap they should send missionaries to Philadelphia."

He laughed at his joke, and before Haworth could reply, commanded Jason to help him with the pigeons. Weary of hearing Haworth's voice, Jason chatted with Cadwell as they gutted the pigeons. "I tell you, McGee, there is no need for anyone to starve in this province. Not if he has a gun and a good dog like yours."

After feasting on pigeon meat that night, Cadwell sat smoking his pipe while Haworth had Jason run through his recitations of the Delaware tongue.

"McGee learned all that in so short a time?"

"Our friend Jason is an apt pupil."

"I am beginning to think he would make a good trader. If I were to remain in this business I might take him on as an assistant."

"Thee means to give up the trade, then?"

"It is going to hell anyway. Maud McGinty, bless her generous heart, owns her house and has money enough set by to support the two of us in our old age, I reckon. If I bring out three horseloads of good furs this trip, with no expenses to speak of, we'd have aplenty to make her house into a tavern. My Maudie would make a grand tavernkeeper, she would."

"Mrs. McGinty would be a fine wife for you," Jason said. "I hope the two of you would put those damned Pickerings out of business."

Cadwell, who had not heard the full story of the death of Abraham McGee, asked what Jason meant.

"What a pair of rogues. I wouldn't trust them as far as I could throw them. And Master Haworth here forced them to give up the mare? I have noted he is a stubborn fellow, but he is a hard bargainer as well. How came a man of such fiber, such talent, to want to spend his time setting free blackamoors and preaching to our red-skinned brethren?"

"If thee is mocking me, I should prefer to devote my time to meditation."

"Seriously, Master Haworth, 'tis evident you are a man of means and education. If I had your advantages, I would not be out here in a wilderness, wet and cold. Would you, McGee?"

"I would, but I have special reasons."

"And I have special reasons. There is something I must do out here as well," said Haworth, rising to stand with his back to the fire, feet widespread and hands clasped behind him. "Is thee familiar with the parable of the rich young man?"

"About how a rich man cannot go to heaven?"

"Yes, and I am that rich young man. Like him, I have kept the commandments from childhood. And since the time I was a tiny lad, before I had yet learned to read and write, I have felt the absolute reality of God. It came to me one day as I played in our garden in Philadelphia. I was in a pensive mood, when I saw a stark white pebble, the size of one's thumb, lying in the grass. I picked up that little stone, beautiful and smooth, and suddenly it came to me: the marvel of our Creator who made that pebble, the earth, the sun, the breeze and me. Since then I have never doubted God's existence for a moment. I still carry that pebble. See?"

He held up a white stone of a sort Jason had seen a thousand times.

"Seems to me you were easily persuaded," said Cadwell.

"Perhaps. I *was* raised in a pious family. Like thine, my grandfather came from England, and he became prosperous in shipping. He is still alive. My father went into the business young and turned that prosperity into great wealth."

"Which you have inherited, or will, I take it."

"Perhaps not. Dost thee know the story of Job, the servant of God who kept his faith despite plagues and disasters to his crops and flocks, attacks of boils and even the deaths of his sons?"

"Not only have I heard of this Job; at times I have felt like him."

"God has tested me—not as he did Job, through trials and sickness, but in a more subtle way. He has heaped his favors upon me from my birth. Born into a happy, wealthy family. Did well in school. Many friends as a boy. Having money and being in the shipping business, my family have sent me on travels. My wife, like me a Quaker, is one of the most beautiful women in Philadelphia, and we have two sons and a daughter upon whom we dote."

"Why are you complaining?"

"I do not complain, Friend Cadwell. I am trying to explain how God has pursued me with his blessings. Upon my marriage, I entered business with my father so that Grandfather could retire. I became skillful at bargaining and the firm grew even more prosperous. Yet in the midst of all these blessings, I was not easy in my mind. Turned my head so as not to see black slaves being sold at auction in Philadelphia, or the way German and Irish immigrants are cheated when they arrive. Or the way we have pushed the Indians off the best land—yes, and I must say this, permitted traders to go among them with rum and corrupt them with trade goods so that they kill animals wholesale for their furs alone."

Cadwell snorted at this. "You Quakers are in the wholesaling and shipping of furs in rather a big way, my friend."

"I do not defend my fellow Quakers who traffic in rum or furs or slaves. Far from it."

"What are you driving at, then?"

"On my thirtieth birthday, my dear wife had a grand dinner for me, with childhood friends and family present. As he left that night, my grandfather said to me, 'Ephraim, the world is thy oyster. Thee has fifty years ahead of thee if thee takes after me. Think of all thee can accomplish in that time.' He meant that he expected me to create even more wealth, and this troubled me. That night before retiring I read that parable of the rich young man and could not sleep. Just before dawn, I rose and went into our library to pray. And the inner light spoke to me, telling me I should give up the accumulation of wealth and devote myself and my means to helping the unfortunate."

"This pleased your father, I suppose?"

"Nay, it made him most unhappy. He would not turn over his wealth to me. My actions regarding that fellow Quaker who owned plantation shares caused my father and grandfather much embarrassment. I saw that God tested me with wealth. I often emptied my pockets to poor immigrants. I neglected my work at the office, so that my grandfather returned to the business and gave me menial tasks that would keep me from speaking too frankly to customers. My friends became uncomfortable around me."

"Why choose the Indians for your mission? Why not go to the southern colonies where there are so many African slaves, some owned by Quakers?"

"It came to me as I knelt in prayer one evening. Pennsylvania is a Quaker colony. The Delawares trusted William Penn and we have betrayed their trust. I will go among them and establish a mission, a school, as an atonement. How, exactly, I do not know, but God will show me how."

Haworth became agitated as he said this, striking his Testament against the palm of one hand to give emphasis to his words.

Cadwell lit his pipe and looked at him with amusement.

"Next time you talk to your God, pray tell him you know a rough fellow in the Indian trade who is ready for some of the trials and tribulations he has put in your way. Ain't that right, McGee? Wouldn't you like to be tempted with a beautiful young wife, fine children, a rich family and a splendid house?"

Jason laughed. "Maybe Mister Haworth doesn't appreciate all he has because he did not have to work for it. I mean to have everything this world has to offer, but I don't expect it to come to me on a silver platter. And when I get it, I sure ain't going to give it away. But right now all I got is this rifle and old Logan and the promise of a girl to marry me."

"You got something else, McGee. You have good health and youth. Mayhap you are more fortunate even than Master Haworth. You aren't burdened with a nagging Quaker conscience to take all the enjoyment out of your life."

"Ah, Friend Cadwell. I perceive that thee mocks me still. Thee does not understand what greater joy there is in doing the will of the Almighty."

"Let's leave it at that, then, Master Haworth. I do not understand."

As it was still early and none of them was sleepy, they sat in silence, staring into the fire and listening to the contrapuntal serenade of two whippoorwills. Jason was lost in a reverie about Sallie Koch when Cadwell said, "McGee, you are an odd young fellow. Heading off to the west with naught but a gun and a dog. What are you after?"

"It's a long story. I'd just as soon not talk about it. Not now."

6

"Wake up, you lazy louts. Logan and I been up and about since dawn."

Cadwell stood beside the fire, roasting strips of venison. Jason squinted at the unaccustomed sunlight sparkling upon the trees around the lean-to.

"It's a beautiful day. The river is going down. Time's awasting."

After breakfast, the three of them went to the bank of the river. The water level was indeed down, but to Jason's eyes, it looked still too deep and swift.

Haworth shook his head. "I must question thy judgment in crossing while the water is yet so high. We are not in such haste that we cannot wait yet another day."

"Tomorrow may bring more rain or cold. We must make it across this very morning while the weather is clear and mild enough for us to dry out quickly."

It took half the morning for them to load the horses securely enough to satisfy the trader. Finally Cadwell tied a line to a tree stump and stripped off his clothes down to a pair of underdrawers. He stood before them with goose pimples dotting his white, lean-muscled torso.

"If I drown, give Maudie a kiss for me."

With that, he waded into the river and began fighting his way across. Twice he had to swim for it, but each time he regained his footing. On reaching the other shore downstream, he walked along the bank until he could secure the end of the line. After he caught his breath, he recrossed by holding on to the line. Packing his shoes and clothing atop his pony's load, he tied a line between his animal's tail and the bridle of Haworth's horse, then connected Jason's mare in the same way.

"For Christ's sake, don't just stand there with your fingers up your arses. Strip down."

Soon Jason and Haworth stood shivering in the mild sunshine. "In we go. Follow me."

Cadwell took his pony's head, and with Logan barking excitedly at their heels, the two horses followed the pony into the river, the men upstream goading them on. Jason would not have believed the water could be so cold, and when Haworth turned to look back at him, the Quaker's usual expression of benign composure had given way to one of distress.

It was easy going until Jason's mare lost her footing and was swept down against the line. This pulled Haworth's horse off his feet, throwing the weight of both animals against the rope. They floundered there until Jason feared the line would break and the current would carry them away, and the pony in the lead as well.

"Take their bridles, damn it to hell," Cadwell screamed. "Make the bastards swim."

At last Haworth's horse got a foothold and was able to drag the mare after him. They reached the other side with barely enough strength to climb the bank. Cadwell leaned against his pony, shivering and cursing.

"I'm too old for this business. I must give it up."

"What shall we do about the line? Leave it here?"

"Hell, I can't leave it. Paid two shillings for the damn thing. We may need it farther on. But Christ, I am too tired to cross back to untie it."

His teeth chattering, Jason said, "I'll go."

Before Cadwell could reply, Jason had plunged back into the river, followed by Logan, and begun hauling himself along the rope toward the other shore. There he untied the line from the stump.

"Fasten it about your waist," Cadwell shouted.

Jason complied and reentered the stream. Without a taut line, he was borne along by the current, swimming desperately and hanging on to Logan. It seemed he would be washed against the rocks downstream. But then the line tightened, checking his progress.

"Hang on to the dog," Cadwell shouted. "We'll pull you in."

Grunting and straining, Cadwell and Haworth dragged Jason and Logan to shallow water. They stood over the youth as he lay on the bank, too weary to speak.

"Don't do anything else like that, McGee, without my permission. Understand?"

Cadwell's air of irritation did not last long. The trail now ran smooth and easy, paralleling the left bank of the river through a gorgeous little valley of meadows and groves. With the sun warming their backs and bringing out the brilliance of the trees, the trader began swinging his shoulders and singing in a light, pleasant baritone. It was a sea chanty and, to Jason's surprise, Haworth joined in with a clear tenor. The two men sang the last two verses in good harmony.

Cadwell laughed. "Wherever did you learn my song, Master Haworth?"

"I did not know it was thine, but I learned it on a voyage to Barbados when I was a youth."

"Good for you. How about yourself, McGee—do you know any songs?"

" 'Barbara Allen.' "

"I know the tune well. Give us the lines."

For the next mile, the three of them marched along singing so lustily that the horses seemed to catch their mood and smartened their pace, carrying their heads high. Previously Cadwell had spoken little on the trail, trudging along as if absorbed in his own thoughts. Now he chattered away, commenting on the terrain, the trees and the wildlife, and telling of old experiences on the trail. They followed the river for about five miles to a gap in a mountain range, halted there to eat beside the still-swollen stream, and then passed on into the next valley. They camped that night in a gap on the other side of the valley, building their campfire on the riverbank.

"Sleep well, my friends, and pray the river will go down tonight, for I would like to cross it here in the morning. It would save us much time to do so."

Morning found the river nearly normal and they crossed it after removing no more than their trousers. The trail cut across a loop of the river so that they had to make another crossing in a few miles, and then they passed into open country swarming with bird life. The weather was good, the trail easy and the mood among the three men entirely pleasant.

They spent that night in an Indian lodge that, according to Cadwell, had recently been occupied by a family of Shawanese. "Old Catahecassa lived here last time I was through. He was ailing. I reckon he died and they moved west."

The trader warned them of the obstacle Allegheny Mountain presented, but Jason still was awed by the sight of the enormous forested mass that blocked out the western horizon as they pressed on the next morning. For mile after mile, this forbidding bulwark loomed. Cadwell talked about it as they neared the first slope.

"Takes three or four hours of hard climbing. More in rain or snow. At the top is a plateau, five or six miles across. And you know rain falling on the front slope drains east into the Atlantic. On the back side it runs the other way into the Ohio. We got a long, hard climb ahead of us this afternoon, gentlemen."

They stopped for their midday meal just as the ascent up the main slope began. Throughout the rest of the afternoon, they followed the path diagonally up the face of the mountain, then around a fold and a cove tucked into the ridge, then again toward the crest, stopping frequently to catch their breath. Near the top they paused to gaze back across the wide valley they had crossed and beyond to range after range of smaller mountains to the east.

"How magnificent is the handiwork of the Almighty," Haworth said.

"What you see is nothing compared to the mountains farther south, down in the Cherokee country of the Carolinas. They are twice as high."

Haworth looked at the trader. "Oh?"

"Yes. Your Almighty God worked twice as hard down there, you might say."

They camped that night halfway across the broad top of the mountain. After eating, the trader played on his jew's-harp and then cajoled Haworth and Jason into singing "Lord Darnell," then "When Ye Gang Awa', Jaimie," a Scots song Jason had heard his father sing.

Cadwell complimented his voice. "I know the Quakers don't hold much with singing, so I'll not ask Master Haworth, but how about you, McGee? Do you know any songs besides 'Barbara Allen'?"

" 'Des Bucklich Mennli.' "

"What?"

" 'The Little Humpback.' It's German. My mother used to sing it."

Jason hummed the melody and gave them the lines both in German and in English. Cadwell clamored for more and Jason taught him "Der Guchgu"—"The Cuckoo."

They retired in good humor, arose early the next morning and descended the shorter back slope of Allegheny Mountain into a broad, high valley rimmed on the western side by Laurel Mountain. The weather, while still clear, had turned colder during the night, but the brisk air stimulated them, so they made excellent time through the thick oak forests of this new valley. By the end of the afternoon they had reached the foot of Laurel Ridge. Cadwell was full of praise as they made camp.

"By God, we must have covered near twenty miles. The two of you are turning into good trail hands. One more ridge to climb over and another to cross through a gap, and we will be out of the mountains. No reason I can see why we can't reach Loyalhanning in plenty of time for a sociable visit with the Delawares there tomorrow night."

In response to Haworth's question, Cadwell explained that the Delawares had established a village on the bank of Loyalhanna Creek twenty-odd years earlier. "Wait until you see it. A grand place for a town. Good soil for gardens. Good fishing. And the great Catawba path crosses this trail there."

Haworth brightened at the news that they were nearing a Delaware village. "I can try out my Lenni Lenape on them."

"You can indeed, Master Haworth. In fact, we may want to stay over more than one night. We've come well over a hundred miles from Shippensburg in ten days, with three of those spent waiting for the Juniata to go down. We could use a rest. Also I see that your Quaker shoes may soon need replacement. Signs of wear on your right shoe, especially."

Haworth looked down at the worn, loosened sole.

Cadwell chuckled. " 'Twould be a pity if you came to save the Delawares' souls and lost your own."

To Jason's surprise, Haworth joined him in laughing.

Up early again the next morning, they climbed two and a half miles to the broad top of Laurel Mountain, crossed that plateau and descended into a valley lush with brilliantly turned trees. They saw numerous deer and bear and, once, the yellow flash of a mountain lion across the trail far ahead.

About midafternoon, after following Loyalhanna Creek's western course for a time, Cadwell said, "There she is. Loyalhanning village. Let's stop and load our guns, McGee."

"Do you expect trouble?" Jason asked.

"No. I want to give them a two-gun salute. That's all."

Fifteen or twenty lodges were grouped in a rectangle about a long central shed, in front of which stood a stout pole, about seven feet high, and a fire pit. Vegetable patches dotted the surrounding woods.

The reports of the two guns brought Indians of all ages pouring out from the lodges and in from the vegetable patches, until some fifty were standing in front of the central lodge to greet them. Cadwell stepped forward and made a speech, to which a fat old woman with thick lips and kinky hair responded, ending her discourse by pointing toward the door of the central lodge.

"Her name is Tschoquali. She is a person of much authority. You find this sometimes among the Delaware and even the Mingoes. Some old hen is so strong-minded she can dominate village life."

"She doesn't look like the others," Jason said.

"I expect her father was a Negro. Probably a slave who took refuge

84

among the Delawares. Her name means Black Bird; that's another clue. Anyway, she extends to us the hospitality of the village as long as we keep our rum to ourselves."

After unpacking their horses and placing the loads inside the great lodge, with Logan standing guard, Jason and Haworth strolled around the perimeter of the village, their collars turned up against the growing chill. Haworth was ebullient, expressing admiration for the Indian character and deploring the corrupting effect of contact with the white man.

"Ah, Friend Jason, thee cannot know how it grieves me to see a supposedly Christian race, our own, debauch and debase another, more innocent people."

"I don't think they are all that innocent. They can do some dreadful things."

"Ah, but from my observations, they are simple and direct and guileless."

Jason was trying to rebut Haworth when Cadwell came away from talking to Tschoquali to join them. He laughed at Haworth's continued defense of the Indians.

"Take no offense, Master Haworth, but 'tis you who are the innocent if you think them so simple and pure. They can be more cruel to their enemies than you might imagine. And the way they carry a grudge is beyond belief. I tell you an Indian may wait a lifetime, but he will never give up his determination to take revenge. They will travel hundreds of miles to strike back. I deal fairly with them and I never offend their dignity, for I know revenge is the most powerful instinct among them."

"But they are so open, so hospitable. See how generous they are to each other; how exceedingly kind they are to their aged."

"They are all that, but I warn the both of you. Never think they are just like you or me, only with red skins. They are quite different. They see things different from us. And they can be dangerous."

As they walked around the village, Jason noted there were few men of his age. He asked Cadwell about this.

The trader grinned. "Don't discuss this in front of them, but you see, the Mingoes forbid the Delawares to take the warpath. The Mingoes themselves like nothing better than to take scalps and prisoners from the Catawbas or the Cherokee, but the crafty devils protect their southern flank by forcing the Delawares to stick to hunting, fishing and raising crops. They call the Delawares women, meaning they are stable in their habits and reliable, like the fair sex. That is supposed to be a compliment, for the Indians generally honor women, but the younger Delawares see no honor in the name. The main path to the Catawba country crosses here, as I told you. When a Mingo party that is a little under strength comes through, they find willing recruits among the young Delaware braves. Half a dozen of them joined a Seneca war party passing through a month ago."

"How does thee know all this?"

"Tschoquali told me. Men are fools, she says, but she could not stop them. By the bye, we are invited to a bear roast this evening."

It was the biggest feast Jason had ever attended. The Indians roasted a half-grown bear over a huge fire and served slivers of the sweetish meat with baked potatoes and corn pudding, which they washed down with a mixture of apple juice and honey. Jason ate until he became logy and sleepy.

As darkness deepened, Cadwell played his jew's-harp for the villagers. He persuaded Jason and Haworth to sing "The Cuckoo" and then he reached into his bag and drew out three small wooden balls, which he began to juggle, slowly at first, and then faster and faster until they became blurred. Jason had seen a street juggler in Lancaster the year before; Cadwell was his equal. He tossed the balls high and pretended to drop one, recovering it just before it hit the ground.

The Indians, delighted, laughed loudly and clapped their hands. Then Cadwell concealed one ball and appeared amazed that suddenly he was juggling only two. He stopped and went in a circle, searching for the "missing" ball. He glowered at his audience as if accusing them of having taken it. The Indians now sat with open mouths, half persuaded by the charade. Cadwell asked several if they had the ball and when they shook their heads he pretended to become angry.

"Have you got my ball?" he asked Jason.

"It is up your sleeve."

"Shut up. Don't spoil my show."

He pointed a finger at Haworth. The Quaker, amused at the performance despite his disapproval of what he regarded as a vanity, shook his head.

Jason paid no attention to Logan when the dog first began growling at something beyond the circle of the firelight. Again Cadwell pointed his finger at Haworth. Now Logan arose and with his fur bristling, barked at something in the darkness. "Hush," Jason said. "Sit down, Logan."

At last Cadwell removed Haworth's hat, and when he drew out the ball, the Indians howled. Old men wrapped in blankets bent double in their mirth; little children danced about, clapping their hands; Tschoquali's vast bulk shook and tears ran down her dark face. Cadwell paused for effect, holding the ball aloft and pointing at Haworth, then said something in Delaware that set his audience to laughing louder than ever. And Logan began barking even louder, wriggling and trying to break free of Jason's grasp.

The laughter of the older Indians stopped as if by command. Suddenly the lighted circle was entered by more than a dozen young Indians, all wearing leggings and loincloths and bearskin capes. Each had painted his face black and red and most carried war axes.

The leader, a tall, lithe man of about thirty, held up his hand and waited as the children were hushed by their parents. Others now entered the circle leading two youths, whom Jason judged to be about fifteen; their hands were bound behind them and their necks circled by nooses. One had a barely closed gash on one arm, the other a swollen eye and ear. They stood with heads bowed.

The leader made another signal and a brave stepped forward bearing a stick about six feet long, from which hung five scalps. The Delawares gasped at the sight. The leader raised his hand and spoke slowly, with an authoritative ring in his voice. Cadwell, his juggling act upstaged by the intruder, came and sat beside Jason to whisper a translation.

"He is speaking their tongue, but he is a Seneca named Kiasutha. This is the war party that recruited some of the young men of this village. They had a successful raid against a Catawba village in the Carolinas, for as you can see, they have brought back scalps and prisoners."

The Seneca said something else and one of the Delaware women wailed.

"He says one of the Delaware boys was killed. He is telling the boy's mother to dry her tears, that her son died with honor and she should rejoice, not mourn. He says that two of his Seneca braves were killed and others were wounded. One of the slain Senecas was the son of his own sister, and yet he does not grieve."

The woman's lament grew louder. The leader irritably gestured for her to be led away.

"Now Kiasutha says his braves are hungry. He wants to know why they sit about laughing like fools at a white man's trick. He orders them to feed him and his party. They will tell the story of the raid after they have eaten."

The two Catawba prisoners were kicked and slapped over to the post in front of the central lodge and then tied to it. Haworth walked over and tried to speak to them, but the leader waved the Quaker away. While the Senecas gorged themselves on bear meat and potatoes, the families of the Delaware raiders stood about listening to their accounts and murmuring over their bruises and cuts.

The three white men were forgotten, spectators now at a purely Indian celebration. The twenty-odd Senecas and the five returning Delaware braves ate the roasted bear right down to the skeleton and snatched sweet potatoes from the hot ashes raw, before they had time to bake properly. Once the food had been devoured, Kiasutha walked over to the two Catawba prisoners and cuffed them on the head, then clapped his hands and shouted. In response, the villagers gathered in a circle about the center post to watch a sinister kind of pantomime, interspersed with commentary by the leader. Cadwell huddled with Haworth and Jason, apologizing for his inability to follow the rapid narration precisely.

"There. He tells how he collected braves from several villages to take the warpath south. He tells how he and his Seneca recruits allowed six braves from this village to join their party."

Now several of the Indians began to march about in single file, simulating their long journey over the mountains.

"They draw near to a Catawba village. They find a place to hide beside the trail. Now two of them go out at night to scout. They return. Half of the party will attack at dawn with bow and arrow, while the others hide out in ambush with muskets."

Bending low, tomahawks and bows in hand, several of the braves pretended to sneak up on the two cowering prisoners. With a shout, they charged in to strike at the post with their axes.

Jason felt like screaming at this vivid reminder of his mother's massacre. He threw his arms around Logan and put his face against the dog's fur to control the dreadful trembling that shook him.

The attacking Senecas fell back from the post, pretending to be driven away by the villagers. They showed exaggerated fear until they had drawn the defenders away from the village.

"See. They are ready to spring the trap."

The leader and the rest of his band leaped to their feet with loud whoops, discharging their muskets. Jason now shook so that it drew Haworth's attention from the reenactment, and when the Senecas all ran around the center post, shouting and slashing away just above the heads of the prisoners, he arose and bolted for the lodge. Haworth followed him shortly and found him trying to load his rifle. The Quaker took the weapon from him.

"G-God damned s-savages. Like beasts. W-worse than w-wolves."

"Nay, nay. Calm thyself, Friend Jason. This is not like thee."

"G-give me back my rifle. I'll kill them."

"Thee will do no such thing. That would solve nothing. That is no way to save the poor prisoners."

"I d-don't care about the p-prisoners." Jason drew a deep breath and became calmer. "I hate Indians who sneak up for no reason and kill."

"Calm thyself. Thee will feel better in the morning."

Haworth went out to see the end of the reenactment. Jason was spared the sight of the leader pretending to slash the heads of fallen Catawbas and rip away their scalps, and when his companions returned to the lodge he feigned sleep.

"So McGee is upset. Do you think a powerful tribe like the Senecas will change their customs because of one red-headed runaway's feelings?"

"I am upset as well, Friend Cadwell. I do not expect a leopard to change his spots overnight; that will require years of Christian teaching. But what about those two poor lads they have taken from their families? They are terrified. I shudder to think of their fates. Could we not purchase their freedom from the Senecas and send them back south?"

"This war party cares nothing for your Quaker merchant's gold. Those prisoners and that stick of scalps represent something of greater value to them than anything you possess. They are proofs of their courage, their manhood. I would not dream of interfering in this matter. It is none of our business."

"It is the business of a true Christian to prevent cruelty to other humans—in fact, to any of God's creatures."

"You do not understand. After they have had a bit of amusement at the expense of those two boys, the Senecas will adopt them as their own sons. Very likely, within a few years, they will be married to Seneca girls, speaking their tongue and all that."

Momentarily the Quaker had no response. Then, quietly: "Still, they are miserable now. Their families will mourn them always."

"Be that as it may, we shall not interfere. I am in command, remember. We shall do nothing and we shall speak no more of this matter."

As he took off his boots to go to bed, Cadwell said in a kindlier tone, "The Senecas plan to press on north tomorrow. If you would like to remain here another day or so, you could practice your Delaware. I could find you some comfortable moccasins to replace those shoes. Tschoquali says her son knows where there are some beaver dams up in the hills. Now that he is back from the raid, I may be able to strike a bargain with him for skins."

"The Senecas will depart early, I would think. Before dawn, perhaps?"

"Probably not until midmorning. They generally sleep late. Anyway, I want to stay out of their way. Let them clear out. I don't want McGee to go to pieces again. And don't you go near those Catawba prisoners."

"I pray thee sleeps well tonight, Friend Cadwell."

Again that night Jason dreamed that he was standing beside the hickory tree looking down at his family's clearing. His mother and sister were tied to a post in front of the cabin, while a crowd of Indians danced around them, brandishing tomahawks.

In this nightmare, Jason was grown and had Logan at his side. He ran shouting down the hill with the dog and charged into the midst of the savages, who, strangely, stopped their mad dance and fell back into a semicircle and then, stranger still, turned out to be white as well as Indians. There was the leader of the Seneca war party, Kiasutha, and Ernst Koch, the blacksmith, also the school bully, Angus Cameron, and Sam and Ida Pickering. They all stared at him, his mother as well as the others, as if he were guilty of discourtesy in interrupting a performance.

At that point, as he was about to speak, he felt a hand over his mouth, and twisting about, looked into the noseless face of Meskikokant. As he struggled, the grip of the giant Indian tightened and Jason felt himself being strangled.

"Jason, Jason . . . be quiet."

It was Haworth, kneeling over him, one hand over his mouth.

"Where am I? Who . . ."

"Thee must be quiet. Thee was moaning and talking in thy sleep. Thee will awaken the Senecas."

Jason's heart stopped pounding and his breathing became easier. He could just make out the shape of the Quaker's familiar hat. It did not occur to him at the time to wonder at his wearing a hat in the middle of the night.

Jason turned on his side and wrapped his arms around Logan's neck. He wondered if, when Sallie was his own true wife, he still would suffer these damned nightmares. At least, he would have her to comfort him. He went back to sleep, imagining his face resting in the curve of her neck.

Jason awoke to a hubbub outside the lodge. Voices of the Senecas called out. There were cries of astonishment and the sound of running feet. Cadwell drew on his trousers and went outside barefooted to investigate, but Haworth lay quietly on his side, his face turned toward the side of the lodge.

Now Jason could hear the voice of Kiasutha, apparently shouting commands, and in lower tones, Cadwell and Tschoquali talking. He drew on his trousers and was starting out the door when Cadwell shoved him back inside.

"The two Catawbas got away last night. That Seneca is furious. We must stay inside."

After putting on his boots and donning his coat, Cadwell loaded his pistol, stuck it in his belt and went outside to talk to the Seneca leader. Jason jostled Haworth awake and told him what had happened.

The Quaker took the news calmly. "My prayers have been answered."

Cadwell returned and seeing that Haworth was awake, told him of the escape.

"I know."

"You know? How do you know?"

"Jason just told me."

"Oh. Well, that Seneca is ready to kill about it."

Jason spoke up. "Kill? It is his own fault if he did not tie them properly."

"They did not free themselves. Their bindings were cut."

"Why are you so upset?" Jason asked.

"I will explain later. Now shut up and load and prime your rifle. We are clearing out of here. We will not stop for breakfast."

"Won't the Seneca think it was one of us if we rush off?"

"I just told him we are on important business. I told him Haworth is a representative of Brother Onas himself, sent out from Philadelphia on an important mission to the Delawares on the Allegheny. I told him you are the best marksman in Pennsylvania, sent along with a fierce dog to guard him. Now don't waste time. Before he verifies my story with the Delawares, let's load our horses and get moving."

As they said their hurried goodbyes to Tschoquali, Kiasutha stood watching them coldly, his arms folded across his chest.

To Jason's amazement, Cadwell took the smallest of his rum kegs off his pony and carried it to the Seneca leader. He talked rapidly in Delaware until the brave's expression softened a bit and he unfolded his arms to receive the keg.

Tschoquali watched this take place with a look of indignation on her face.

Cadwell spoke no more than he had to as they moved away from the village, and when they were out of sight, he whipped his pony into a trot. He did not speak when they entered the narrow gorge through which Loyalhanna Creek flows west to find its way into the Allegheny River. The trader flogged his pony whenever its pace slackened and Haworth, to Jason's surprise, made no protest. Jason was puzzled by the abrupt departure and disappointed too, for he had been looking forward to resting in the pleasant village. He had thought this would be a good place to begin inquiring about Isaac, just as Haworth had thought it a good place to start practicing his Lenni Lenape and Cadwell to begin his trading. The camaraderie that had prevailed since they crossed the swollen Juniata was entirely absent, replaced by a tension between Cadwell and Haworth that even the animals seemed to sense. Cadwell would not stop for food until well past noon, when they were clear of the gorge. Chestnut Ridge, the last of the mountains, now lay behind them. Ahead swept mile after mile of gullied hill country, covered with scrubby trees and dotted with swamps.

Cadwell held up his hand. "We can stop here. No danger of an ambush anymore. McGee, you hobble the horses and let them graze. Then break out something for us to eat. Mister Quaker and I must have a talk."

Jason could not hear them at first. He could only see that Cadwell, his hat drawn low over his eyes and the corners of his mouth turned down, was making angry gestures in the direction of the village. Haworth stood before him, his face lifted and his shoulders back, listening and saying little.

Cadwell took off his hat and flung it on the ground.

"God damn you for a fool," he shouted. "You could have got us killed."

The Quaker turned away. Cadwell followed him.

"I'll say it again and again. You are a fool. You bloody well can go. I wish you would."

"Wh-what's the matter?" Jason asked.

"Matter? The matter is that this utter damned fool of a Quaker sneaked out last night and cut the bonds of those Catawba boys. The matter is that if I had not lied like hell and left behind a keg of my precious rum, those Senecas would have cut our throats. The matter is . . ." Cadwell's voice choked. Jason feared he was about to assault Haworth. But the Quaker showed no concern, merely gazed at Cadwell as though he were witnessing the tantrum of a small boy.

The trader recovered his voice. "All right. With McGee as a witness, do you swear you had nothing to do with the escape of those two prisoners?"

"Friend Cadwell, thee should know a Quaker never takes an oath."

"Oath or no oath, do you deny it?"

"I cannot be compelled to say anything. I simply affirm that I have done nothing that weighs on my conscience."

"To hell with your stupid conscience. What right have you to endanger my life and that of McGee to satisfy *your* conscience?"

"I can only repeat that I regret nothing I have done. The Senecas did *not* cut our throats. We *are* safely away. Even though I do not approve of thee leaving that rum behind, if that bothers thee so much I am willing to compensate thee in gold." Haworth paused and added, "For the price thee paid for it in Shippensburg, not for what thee expected to receive for it from the Indians."

Instead of pacifying Cadwell, this reply seemed to infuriate him even more.

"You don't understand. That Seneca, that Kiasutha, spent weeks recruiting that raiding party. More weeks on the trail. You have no notion of how much it meant for him to awe those Delawares and to impress the old men and women of his tribe. You robbed him of the fruits of his raid and, worse, you have made him appear foolish. God help you if your paths ever cross again."

"But I thought you told him Mister Haworth was . . ." Jason began.

Cadwell shook his head impatiently. "That story won't satisfy him for long. The Delawares know he is not an official of the government, for he *would* tell Tschoquali he came to save their souls. They will tell him. That is why I left the rum. To buy us time. By now they are most likely drunk. When they sober up, I want to be out of their reach."

Haworth took the reins of his horse in one hand and with the other loosened its hobble.

"What shall I do with thy trade goods?" he said to Cadwell.

"What do you mean?"

"Thee has said thee wishes me to depart from thy presence."

"Depart? You mean dump my stuff here beside the trail? Leave me and McGee in the lurch?"

Jason thought he saw a glint of humor in the Quaker's eye although the tone of his voice was as earnest as ever.

"But thee bade me depart."

"I God damn well don't want you to depart before we get to the

Forks of the Ohio. You bloody well know I need your horse."

"Then I am to remain until we reach that point and then depart? Or just what is it thee does wish me to do?"

"I want you to stop acting like a damned fool. I want you to promise me never to do another damned fool thing like releasing those prisoners."

"I have not said I did release them."

"No, but you know you did. And you know that I know you did."

"I cannot promise thee I will not follow my conscience."

"Then, by God, take your bloody horse and go."

"W-wait a minute," Jason said. "If you make him go away, I am going with him."

The trader put his hand on his pistol butt. "Don't either one of you make a move. I will take your horses from you if you persist in this game."

"It's not a g-game," Jason said. "If Mister Haworth goes, I go too. I'll go back there and tell those Senecas *you* freed the prisoners, if you take our horses."

Cadwell shook his head. "This is not fair. I can't believe you would turn on me, McGee."

"Don't send Mister Haworth away and everything will be all right."

"But he won't promise not to put our lives in danger again."

"Suppose he promises to consult us before he does such a thing?"

Haworth broke the impasse. "That seems a reasonable request."

"You heard what he said, McGee."

"I heard. It is all right for him to stay with us, then?"

"Yes, damn it. I need your horses. But I am out the value of my keg of rum."

"Wouldst thee be satisfied if I give thee a draft to cover the value of the rum in furs?"

Cadwell's voice softened. "Yes."

The Quaker smiled. "That was the little keg from which thee drank so copiously back at the Juniata crossing, was it not?"

"The smallest of the kegs. I did draw a drink from it. Why?"

"It was two large cupfuls. Now, in reckoning the value, we must remember that thee had already taken out that amount for thine own consumption."

Jason sensed that the trader wanted to laugh but would not let himself.

"Zeke Manning was right about you Quakers. We'll speak no more of the matter. We can reach the Forks of the Ohio by day after tomorrow evening if we don't dawdle further."

He took the reins of his pony. "Wipe that grin off your face, McGee. You look like a village idiot."

7

A fragile truce prevailed among the three travelers as they slogged around the swamps and over the monotonous wooded hills west of the mountains. Jason missed the good fellowship they had enjoyed so briefly, but he was relieved that Cadwell and Haworth at least tenuously had patched up their quarrel. It took them three days to reach the western base of a great hill just east of the Forks of the Ohio. Early the next day they arose and made their way up the long slope and then halted at the crest to gaze down at a hilly peninsula dotted with ponds glistening in the morning sun, and beyond to a rampart of high bluffs stretching along the left bank of the Monongahela and the Ohio rivers. The scene would have been spectacular in any season, but especially so now, with vast splotches of yellow, red and gold foliage spread before them.

Jason felt about the Forks of the Ohio as an ancient Viking might have regarded Ultima Thule. He had thought of it as the place where the earth ended, or at least the habitable portion of it. Now it struck him that, on the contrary, a new world began out here nearly three hundred miles west of Philadelphia, where the Allegheny merged with the Monongahela to form the Ohio River.

"How glorious is the handiwork of our Father," Haworth murmured.

"It is a grand sight," Jason replied.

Cadwell looked at them with an air of contempt. "It is more than a grand sight. It is a grand place for a city. The question is whether the inhabitants will speak French or English."

"There is no one there now, though, is there?"

"Only an Indian village just up the Allegheny. Shannopin's Town. If the Assembly in Philadelphia had any damned sense, they would hurry out a thousand or so militiamen and throw up a fort before the French get here. George Croghan and the Mingoes have been urging that this be done for several years."

Even Jason's one-eyed mare acted elated as they descended the slope toward the Forks of the Ohio. By noon the party stood on the tip of the peninsula, watching the swirl where the two rain-swollen rivers merged.

"How are we going to get across? Can we swim it?" Haworth asked.

"You can if you want to drown," Cadwell snorted. "We must make ourselves a raft. Any fool should know that."

Cadwell led them well upstream from the point and set them to their tasks. As the afternoon wore on, he became more and more the martinet, snarling commands at his two companions and criticizing them for their lack of skill with the hatchet, especially Haworth, who, although he turned red at one outburst, kept his silence.

"What's got into him?" Jason asked when Cadwell walked away to scout for suitable trees. "He has never been so mean before."

"Don't mind him, Friend Jason. It is his way of reasserting his authority over us. He knows we have to follow his instructions in this project and he is taking a bit of revenge on us for defying him back on the trail."

Cadwell yelled, "All right, you lazy asses. Stop your gossiping and bring your hatchets."

They spent the night beside the Allegheny and arose early the next day to complete work on the raft. Cadwell had a wide-bladed ax, with which he felled several straight young poplar trees, leaving it to Haworth and Jason to hatchet off the tops and branches and drag the trunks to the riverbank. It was hard work; they were weary by noon, but Cadwell gave them little time to eat their lunches.

By midafternoon they had enough tree lengths to satisfy Cadwell, who then set them to chopping out eight-foot logs to be lashed together. The trader seemed pleased with their work by day's end.

"Someday, mark my words, there will be a regular ferry plying this water. Maybe that is what Maud and I should do: settle out here and operate a ferry as well as a tavern. I could be as rich as old John Harris back on the Susquehanna."

Haworth looked skeptically at the raft. "It doesn't appear large enough to hold even one horse, much less three, plus their packs, not to mention three men and a dog."

"The horses will swim. Just the three of us and the goods will be on the raft."

"Could we not ferry over one horse and its load at a time, lest the animals drown?" Haworth inquired.

"You don't realize what hard work lies ahead of us. We'd have to tow the raft back upstream and pole it across each time. That way you would make five crossings instead of one. And you'd play hell getting the horses to stay on the raft."

As Cadwell had warned, it was hard work getting across the Allegheny even once the next morning. After tying his pony's rope to the raft, and linking him with the other two horses, the trader secured their packs on the center of the raft while Jason cut and trimmed three strong saplings for poles.

Cautioning Jason and Haworth to remain in one place on the raft, Cadwell, with Logan's help, herded the three reluctant horses into the water and leaped aboard with the dog. The three of them poled the raft away from the shore until the current caught it. The pony's line tightened, holding the raft back until the water became too deep and first he, then the mare, and finally Haworth's horse had to start swimming. Now the men were straining to keep the raft moving across the current. Cursing and sweating, Cadwell thrust his pole into the riverbed and pushed.

"Like this, damn it. Set the pole and walk us along."

Soon the three of them established a rhythm, taking turns poling in such a way that there was no pause in the raft's progress across the current. Even so, it took them half an hour of toil to work their way across, landing well downstream on the other side. After leading their horses out of the water and moving the trade goods ashore, they lay down to catch their breath.

Here, on the west bank of the Allegheny, Jason stared across at the point where the rivers joined and beyond to the great hill east of the Forks, then to his right at the line of bluffs, which, seen from here, down on the riverbank, loomed even higher. He was in the fabled west now, in country far from the influence of the Quaker government, beyond the petty theological quarrels of the Ulster Presbyterians and the enmities between them and their German neighbors. He vaguely understood that this territory was involved in a larger controversy between the British and French Crowns, but like the squatter back at the Sugar Cabins, he had never seen a Frenchman, and for that matter, few Englishmen, so how did that concern him? His problem now was to locate Isaac somewhere in this wilderness and bring him back to the shores of the Susquehanna. It had seemed an easy matter in his daydreams. He had not appreciated the difficulties of finding one person in so vast an area.

Cadwell's mood became more pleasant once they had recovered from their laborious crossing. "By God, we did it in good order. We can soon get down to business."

Jason was relieved to hear this remark. With relations so strained over the incident of the freed captives, he had been concerned as to how each of the three could accomplish his aims at the same time: Cadwell to lay in three horseloads of furs; Haworth to establish his mission among the Indians; and he to rescue his brother.

"We'll begin at Logstown. It's about eighteen miles down the Ohio, on this bank. There is a big trading post there, and Indians of all tribes drift in and out, not to mention traders. We can begin inquiring about McGee's brother, and I will nose about to discover where there is a new Delaware village that other traders haven't descended upon. With so many of them back at that Carlisle meeting, we will have the jump on them. I can buy the Indians' furs as fast as they bring them in from winter hunting, and we can clear out by spring. But we have to start at Logstown."

"Yes, and I might begin my missionary work there," said Haworth.

Cadwell laughed. "Wait until you see Logstown before you commit yourself. Here, I'm chilled to the bone. Hand me a blanket, McGee. And could you not make us a fire? The Allegheny is between us and those Senecas now."

The trader wrapped himself in the blanket and sat shivering while Jason started a blaze. As Cadwell lit his pipe with trembling hands, it struck Jason how drawn and weary he looked. Haworth paced back and forth, impatient to move on, but Cadwell would not be hurried.

"What about Logstown?" Jason prompted him.

"Well, it's the nearest thing to a capital the fur region has. Started out about 1726 as a Shawanese village. Then some French traders came and built cabins there. After more Shawanese and some Delawares moved out this way, the Mingoes got worried that the two tribes would slip from under their thumbs, so they sent old Tanacharison, a Seneca chief, down to oversee things. The Half King, some call him. And about that same time, George Croghan, his greedy eye ever on the main chance, moved in and established a storehouse there. And the other English traders poured in."

"Such as thyself?" Haworth stopped pacing to ask.

"Such as myself, Master Haworth, but compared to Croghan, Trent and others of that ilk, I am small beer indeed. Those fellows run in pack trains of twenty horses at a time. They borrow vast sums in Lancaster or Philadelphia to finance their operations and they have agents to do their work out here."

"I know Croghan. I met him when I passed through Carlisle," Jason said.

"I expect you did. Probably had his nose right up the asses of the Assembly representatives there. Oh, he is a very big man, is that bloody Irishman. Charms the Indians with his blarney. I reckon he and his agents haul a quarter of all the pelts that come out of the west. He's come a cropper of late, however. The French have chased his men off the Sciato. Couldn't meet his debts and he must move out of Cumberland County, where he has been a magistrate, to keep from being jailed. Setting up a post over on Aughwick Creek in Indian territory, last I heard."

"Is that not against the law?" Haworth asked.

"The Indians invited him to come there. They like the grasping son of a bitch. Damn his eyes, old Tanacharison has promised him an enormous tract out here as well."

"He must truly enjoy the trust of the Indians if they invite him to move among them and give him land so freely," Haworth said. "Is he not the trader who has carried on so many negotiations with the Indians on behalf of the Assembly?"

"He and Conrad Weiser and Andrew Montour, the half-breed, they spend half their time powwowing with the Indians. And getting rich into the bargain."

"I have heard it said in Philadelphia, however, that he has done much to offset the influence of the French out here."

Cadwell laughed through chattering teeth. "Give him credit for that. The French have good reason to hate the guts of George Croghan. He turned the Miamis against them. His life wouldn't be worth a farthing if he fell into French hands."

"What right have the French to do such as that?" asked Jason.

"Might makes right," Cadwell replied.

"I don't agree with thee that might makes right. I think it is the other way around."

"For Christ's sake, save your preaching for the Indians. Let's go and let you see Logstown for yourself."

The country between the Forks of the Ohio and Logstown was rougher than Jason expected, being much interrupted by ravines and grown up in underbrush. The going was so slow that dark and a cold wind overtook them before they reached Logstown. They slept in a thicket on the bank of the Ohio River Awakened early by the sound of Cadwell's coughing, Jason was surprised at the film of powdery snow on their blankets. Two hours later, they saw smoke ahead and soon came in sight of a collection of some fifty cabins on a grassy bank well above the Ohio.

99

PART THREE

1

Jason would remember Logstown for the rest of his life with a mixture of amusement and revulsion, for this capital of the western fur trade was both a Gomorrah and a frontier carnival town.

Some of the Indians who thronged the muddy paths between the cabins were hard-eyed braves, erect and sober, but many were in various states of intoxication, ranging from exuberance to vomit-smeared unconsciousness. Most of the traders Jason saw were coarse, bearded men with calculating manners, but their numbers were leavened by a few acting in a calm way, talking in easy voices with each other or with Indians. Several traders greeted Cadwell, asking him for the latest news from the east. One shrewd-looking little man drew him aside and offered him a fifty percent profit on his three loads of trade goods, and at Cadwell's indignant refusal, shrugged. "It's a sorry lot of stuff you have anyway."

Cadwell found them a place in a large cabin already occupied by a party of Virginians, explaining that if so many traders had not gone back to Carlisle for the meetings there, they would be lucky to find any place at all.

There were three Virginians in the cabin: two white men and a Negro. The younger of the white men, clad in a well-cut woolen jacket, watched them unpack with an amused look on his face. He introduced himself in a genteel drawl as Geoffry Goodspeed from near Williamsburg, adding, "And this is John Pratt from Winchester, up in the Shenandoah."

Cadwell introduced his party.

"You gentlemen are traders, I take it," Goodspeed said.

"I am a trader. My friends are here on other business."

"Might that other business be the purchase of land?"

"We are not here to buy or sell anything," Haworth replied. "What is thy business?"

103

"I am a shareholder in the Ohio Land Company, which you may have heard of."

"The Virginia land speculation enterprise. Your friends represent that company as well?"

The other white man, Pratt, was a large fellow with thick shoulders and a bull neck; he was dressed in deerskin and wore a long knife at his belt. He stared at Haworth with curiously yellow eyes, like those of a hostile panther. The Negro, slightly built and of a bluish-black complexion, did not look up from the boots he was cleaning.

Goodspeed replied, "No. Mister Pratt is in my personal employ."

"And he." Haworth pointed to the Negro. "Is he also in your employ?"

"That is Cicero. You might say he is in my employ. I own him."

Before Haworth could say more, Cadwell sent him outside to secure their horses.

"For God's sake, McGee," Cadwell whispered as they hauled their goods up to the cabin loft. "Don't let him get started about slavery or rum with those two. Pratt is not to be meddled with. I have seen his sort before."

After securing their trade goods, Cadwell went out to renew friendships in the village and Jason invited Haworth to accompany him in a turn around the town. An Indian lay across the path outside their door, apparently passed out, while across the way a trader had a laughing young squaw pinned against a cabin wall as he fumbled with her garments. Haworth walked away from the village, toward the river, with Jason and Logan following; he did not stop until they reached the steep bank of the Ohio.

"That place back there reeks of greed and drunkenness. Did thee see that poor Indian rendered senseless by rum? And the others, reeling about like mad creatures?"

"I have eyes, Mister Haworth."

"And those foul traders. How disgusting. Why, Jason, that fellow had his hand up the skirt of that Indian woman. Right out in the open."

"Well, at least we share a cabin with two gentlemen who are not rowdy. They are not traders."

"They may be worse than traders. Those men are here to speculate in land. The traders are only interested in furs. Those men would take the land right from under the feet of the Indians and sell it at vast profits. And that Goodspeed is a slave owner."

"I meant that they will make better cabinmates than some loud, drunken traders."

"We shall see. But oh, I am all the more convinced of the need for a mission among the Delawares. To teach them to read and write so they will not be cheated by unscrupulous whites. Not cheated of furs, or land, or virtue. Yes, and acquaint them with the Scriptures."

When they returned to the cabin, Goodspeed and Pratt were gone, but the Negro was dozing on a stool in front of the fire. He jumped to his feet at the sound of their voices and busied himself at brushing his master's coat. Jason had seen a few Negroes around Harris's Ferry and in Lancaster, but they were still a novelty to him. He could not help staring at the man and wondering at the woolliness of his hair and the thickness of his lips. It did not occur to him to speak to the Negro, but Haworth, without hesitating, went over and took his hand.

"Thy name is Cicero. Mine is Ephraim Haworth and this is my young friend Jason McGee."

Cicero seemed embarrassed, and withdrew his hand awkwardly.

"Yas suh."

"Thee is from Williamsburg?"

"Near there. Yas suh."

"And thee is held in bondage?"

"What is that?"

"Thee is a slave."

"Yas suh. I belongs to Mister Geoffry Goodspeed."

"It must be very hard to be denied thy freedom."

"I gets plenty to eat. My wife and me and our children sleeps right next to the kitchen. We eats same as the white folks. I got no complaints."

"But surely thee would prefer to be free?"

"Nigger ain't supposed to be free."

"No man, whate'er his race, is *supposed* to be a slave. Out here on the frontier there is no slavery except to sin and greed—yes, and superstition." Haworth lowered his voice. "Dost thee know, Cicero, that some slaves take refuge among the Indians? They are accepted as brothers."

Cicero frowned. "Mister Geoffry say they eat niggers. Besides, I got a wife and children back home. Now look, Massa Haworth, I got work to do. Massa Geoffry take a strap to me if he come back and find I let us get out of water. Excuse me, please, suh."

Before Haworth could say more, Cicero had picked up an empty pail and left the cabin.

"I hope you haven't forgotten what you promised back on the trail," Jason said. "You promised Cadwell and me that you would not put our lives in danger again without first consulting us."

"I remember that, but why dost thee remind me of it now?"

"If those two Virginians thought you were encouraging that slave to run away, they wouldn't like it very much."

"How would that put your lives in danger? Thee has said Goodspeed and Pratt were gentlemen."

"Shall we ask Cadwell what he thinks about that?"

"Let us not unsettle Master Cadwell just now. I am concerned about his health. His cough is very worrying."

"It would not help his health or yours if you talk anymore to that black man about freedom."

Haworth, drawing his Testament from his pocket, sat down to read, as though he had not heard Jason.

2

Later in the afternoon Cadwell came back, coughing so hard he had to stand in the doorway to recover before he spoke.

"Build up the fire, gentlemen. I can't seem to get warm. Some of my friends are bringing round some victuals." He thrust his hands over the fire. "Ah, it is good to be back out here after all. It makes me feel alive."

Three of Cadwell's friends appeared at the cabin door in the midafternoon, bearing a leg of venison, two ducks, a bag of coarse corn meal, a pumpkin, and jugs of cider and corn whiskey.

Cadwell introduced them.

"This Jew here"—he pointed to a short man with wise, dark eyes—"is Levy. He is a supplier out of Lancaster. And him"—pointing to a tall, red-faced man with sandy hair—"that's MacDonald. He's an independent trader. Don't ask him if he has an official license to trade unless you want to hear him lie.

"And as for this overgrown bastard"—indicating an enormous smiling man with bad teeth and a bald pate—"he is Tiny Little, who is one of George Croghan's innumerable cat's-paws out here."

Jason and Haworth shook hands all the way around.

"Whose dog is this?" Tiny asked as they removed their outer garments.

"He belongs to McGee here."

"Mean-looking son of a bitch. Does he bite?"

"Only dishonest traders such as yourself."

"I am surprised you dare sleep in the same cabin with him."

As they spread their provisions on the only table in the cabin, Cicero returned with the bucket of water he had set out for two hours before.

"Ho," said Tiny. "There's Goodspeed's blackamoor. Where's your master, Cicero?"

"Him and Mister Pratt gone across the river to see is old Shingas there. They be back tomorrow."

"Look what all we got here. Think you could make us a proper meal from that?"

"I don't know. . . ."

"Don't know? Suppose I was to give you an English shilling?"

Cicero looked up into the giant's face. "Well, Mister Geoffry don't hold with his niggers working for hire."

"He don't have to know. Besides the shilling you can have two drams of corn liquor. One now and the other when the meal is ready. Plus all you can eat, right along with the rest of us."

"I reckon I could do that."

So while the four friends stood about the fire, good-humoredly chaffing each other, Cicero worked away at the table, slicing the venison and picking the ducks. Jason, feeling out of place amongst the boisterous group, offered to help the Negro. Cicero seemed surprised, but accepted.

Discerning that Levy, MacDonald and Tiny were a cut above the ordinary traders he had seen in Logstown, and eager to learn from them, Haworth planted himself in their midst, standing squarely with his hands braced against the small of his back. Jason was amused at his incongruous appearance, earnestly peering out from under his Quaker hat into the faces of the traders. MacDonald lamented the laziness of Indians in general and the way they were being spoiled by gifts from the Pennsylvania government and the Virginians. "And now the French are showering them with wine and such. Wine, mind you."

"Ah, the French," Levy spoke up. "You know they would be here in Logstown at this moment had they not suffered so much sickness last summer. They were ready to sweep right down the Allegheny."

"Aye," said MacDonald. "But I hear their old commander, Marin himself, is deathly sick up at Le Boeuf. Not expected to live, so the Indians say."

"It does not matter whether Marin lives or dies," Levy replied. "The French will send another commander and far more men in the spring. They mean to enforce their claim to the upper Ohio all the way east to the main Allegheny Ridge. Mark my words, they will come in force."

Unlike his companions, Levy drank sparingly and did not seem to be annoyed by Haworth's naïve questions. The inquisitive Quaker gravitated to the patient Jew and soon the two of them were squatting at a corner of the hearth, with Levy drawing a map on the earthern floor.

"I show you, Mister . . . Haywood, was it?"

"Haworth."

Jason, too, watched as Levy scratched out the locations of Lake Erie some one hundred miles north, and to the east, about ninety, the main Allegheny Ridge, then eighteen miles southeast of Logstown, the Forks of the Ohio. "There are thousands of square miles involved, and the question is: Who does it belong to?"

"Surely this is part of Pennsylvania. Why would the French think otherwise?"

"They claim that because La Salle traced the course of the Mississippi seventy-five years ago, they have dominion over all the lands drained by that river and its tributaries, which would place the boundary between French and British America along the Allegheny Ridge."

"In Philadelphia we think of this area as part of Pennsylvania, but reserved to the Indians."

"I am aware of that. But in Williamsburg, the Virginia government also takes the position that the Penn grants stop at Allegheny Mountain. And unlike their northern Quaker friends, they want to see this country settled by white people. At the Lancaster conference in 1744 they persuaded the Mingoes to sell their land all the way to the setting sun. And in '47 they formed the Ohio Land Company, which got a royal license for some half a million acres south of the Ohio on the condition that it brings in one hundred settlers by 1755 and establishes a garrison up here."

"But this land belongs to the Indians."

"Which Indians? Just a generation ago the Shawanese and the Delaware were all settled east of the Alleghenies and the country out here had no permanent Indian settlements. The Senecas and their Mingo brothers thought they were clever selling it to the Virginians."

"But the Delaware and Shawanese have no other place to live. We crowded them off their land in the east."

"So you did. First the Shawanese came out and then the Delaware. And then the Iroquois sent out overlords lest their subject tribes slip away from them."

"All this is immaterial to one who wants only to serve his God."

"Well, sir, the French believe in God too, a Catholic God. And

108

the possession of this rich and beautiful country is not immaterial to them. Tanacharison went up to where the French are building a fort on the headwaters of French Creek, and he warned the commander there he was trespassing on Indian territory. That was old Marin, and he told Tanacharison that the Indians meant no more to him than a swarm of flies or mosquitoes. What's more, he said if the English tried to block him, he would take them by the hair and toss them over the mountains."

"That is strong language."

"It is, and it is backed up by considerable force. Up on Lake Erie at Presque Isle, a grand natural harbor, the French have a new fort. Then here, at the head of French or Venango Creek, another, connected by a road fifteen miles long. From there, except in dry spells, they can float down French Creek to where it joins the Allegheny at Venango and thence down the Allegheny to the Ohio."

"That would be an ambitious undertaking, however."

"It is. But have you seen anything out here that will stop them?"

"The Pennsylvania government is sending out a quantity of powder and lead to the Indians."

"The Indians?" Levy laughed. "Ah, my friend, I have a great affection for them, but—well, you will see for yourself."

"Levy, don't squat there gossiping like a worn-out old squaw," Tiny interrupted. "Come and eat. You too, Mister Quaker."

Jason was sorry for the interruption, for, fascinated by Levy's explanation, he had been waiting to ask questions of his own.

Cicero earned his shilling. Not only had he, with Jason's help, prepared a large, delicious meal, he served it with style, standing about with an ever-ready cider jug as though he were a footman in an elegant plantation dining room on the James River. Except for Haworth, the diners around the rude table showed none of the manners that normally go with such service. Tiny Little sat at one end of the table waving a duck leg in one hand and holding a chunk of corn bread in the other as he shouted insults at Cadwell, who presided at the other end. Levy and MacDonald sat with their backs to the fire, with Jason and Haworth on the other side of the table and Logan sitting at attention nearby, ready to grab morsels tossed to him before they hit the earthen floor.

"Say, Red Top," Tiny said, "I'd trade you a bale of furs for that splendid dog."

"Pay no attention to this oaf, McGee," Cadwell said. "If anybody gets Logan it will be me. Or maybe I'll hire the two of you to work for me."

Tiny stared at Jason. "I understand that Mister Haworth has

come out to establish a mission among the Delawares, but what about you, McGee? Are you here to have sport with the Indian lasses, or what?"

Jason had a mouthful of venison, and before he could answer, Cadwell spoke. "McGee lost his mother and sister to an Indian attack back on the Susquehanna in '44. The Indians carried off his brother and he wants to find him."

"Ah. I remember now the Delawares speaking of that. One of their renegades done it. Ran off to one of the French tribes, so the word was, and the Delawares couldn't get to him."

Jason swallowed his food, his heart pounding. "Which tribe?"

"Seems to me it was the Ottawas."

"Who was the Indian?" MacDonald asked.

"His name is Meskikokant," Jason replied. "He is a g-giant. T-taller than Mr. Little, even."

"Wait," spoke up MacDonald. "Is part of his nose missing?"

"Y-yes. It was b-bitten off in a f-fight."

"Meskikokant. Is that his name? Why, he took part in the French-Indian attack on Pixawillany. Well, I know that whore's son."

"Pixawillany?" Jason leaned across the table in his eagerness.

"Miami village two hundred miles west of here. In June of last year, the French came down from Detroit with about two hundred Indians, mostly Ottawas, and wiped out that town. There was a giant with a missing nose among them. I saw him. They slew the Miami chief, Old Briton. Killed and ate him."

"Ate him?" Haworth exclaimed. "Surely thee jest."

"Nay, I jest not. They cut his body up and boiled the pieces and ate them."

"Why?"

"They were hungry." Tiny laughed.

MacDonald, his face growing even redder at the flippant interruption, warmed to his story.

"The French did not like the way the Miamis stuck to the English traders. They tried to make them move away and Old Briton told them to go to hell. He was a staunch friend, was that one."

"Don't get him started talking about Pixawillany, or he'll never shut up," Tiny said. "Besides, I don't want to be reminded of how George Croghan was near ruined out there. Lost hundreds of pounds' worth of trade goods."

"To hell with George Croghan's trade goods," MacDonald replied. "I was there during the attack and I was lucky to get away with my scalp. If my Miami friends had not hidden me, I would have suffered the same fate as poor Old Briton."

"Ah, there was no danger of that happening. Not to you," Tiny persisted.

MacDonald flared up. "What do ye mean, there was no danger?"

"Some Ottawas assured me they never ever would eat a Scotchman."

Levy, catching on to the joke and enjoying MacDonald's growing indignation, asked, "Why not, Tiny? Why would not they eat the flesh of a Scot?"

Tiny paused, darting his eyes around the table until all were quiet.

"Because, so the savages said to me, they are too God damned much trouble to clean."

Cadwell, who held his cup to his lips, laughed explosively, spraying cider over the table, and then bent over to slap his leg with mirth; Levy threw back his head and laughed so hard he fell backward, nearly into the fire.

MacDonald rose to his feet. "Ye've no call to go insulting me and my race like that. Ye've no fear of being scalped. Your great fat bald head hasn't enough hair on it to make a decent scalp. The other Indians would think it was the skin off the arse of some white bairn, they would."

This set even Haworth and Cicero to laughing. Only Jason kept quiet, impatiently waiting for the noise to subside so he could ask more about Meskikokant.

MacDonald seemed at the point of stomping out of the cabin, until Cadwell began coughing again, this time so violently that the others gathered around him in their concern.

"I don't like the sound of that cough, Christopher," Tiny said. "It calls for strong medicine. MacDonald, stop parading about like a turkey tom and hand over the whiskey jug."

Cadwell choked down a drink. Tiny wiped the mouth of the jug, drank, and passed it on to Levy, who took a small swallow, and then to MacDonald.

"I'm not sure I want to drink with men who show me such disrespect."

"Oh, shut up and drink. We meant no harm; just a bit of fun."

The Scot, settling for this as the nearest to an apology he would get, drank and offered the jug to Haworth, who put his hands behind his back.

"I never touch strong drink."

"Here," said Jason on impulse. "I'd like a drink of that."

Haworth and Cadwell looked at him in surprise.

The whiskey assailed his throat and nose, making him gag, but

Jason drank deeply nonetheless. He had to press questions to these men, and to do that he would have to tell about his family's massacre. He thought the liquor might make him less nervous.

"My goodness, lad. You'd think you were in hell perishing of thirst. Leave a bit for Cicero. I did promise him another dram for after the meal, you know."

While the Negro cleared away the remnants of the food, they drew their stools and benches around the fire and Cadwell brought out his jew's-harp.

"You wouldn't think it to look at them, but my friends here have voices like angels." He twanged away at the jew's-harp to get the melody. "Now, gentlemen, let's give them 'Barbara Allen.' "

By the third stanza, MacDonald was humming along with them, and midway through the lengthy song he joined in with a lusty baritone, his grievance against his companions forgotten. He wiped tears from his eyes at the conclusion and called for the whiskey jug.

"Ah, McGee, ye may be only an Ulsterman, but I can tell ye have the heart of a true Scot in ye. Do ye know any more?"

"Enough of this Scotch singing," Tiny said. "Do you know 'King William'?"

Cadwell wiped the sweat from his face and gave his vocalists the pitch.

"King William was King James' son,
From the royal house he sprung,
He wore a star upon his breast . . ."

Tiny grabbed Levy's hand and dragged him to the center of the cabin.

"Look to the East and look to the West."

The two of them began dancing clumsily, like two bears, and then Tiny shot out his giant paw and drew first MacDonald and then, against his will, Cicero in to form a square.

"Go look ye East and look ye West,
Choose the one that ye love the best."

At the conclusion of the old country dance, Tiny shouted, "By God, that was all right. You've brought a fine pair out here, Christopher. Let's break out that other jug, lads."

Again Jason drank deeply. With the liquor warming his blood, he joined the circle around the fire, but Haworth excused himself, saying, "I feel the need of fresh air."

112

"You'll have to pardon my Quaker friend," Cadwell said when Haworth was gone. "He has yet to learn the joys of rum."

"He's an odd one, all right," Tiny said. "But it's his loss if he chooses not to drink."

"Aye," said MacDonald. "Means that much more for the rest of us."

Jason cleared his throat.

"Meskikokant." He forced out the word.

The others looked at him in puzzlement.

"You were telling me about the giant with the missing nose. I want to hear more about him."

"First, McGee, perhaps you ought to explain about your family," Cadwell said.

"Yes," said Tiny. "This happened soon after the murder of Jack Armstrong. And not too far away, is my recollection. Your family were squatters, near Sherman's Creek, right?"

"We moved over the mountain in 1740, when I was only six. Moved there from across the Susquehanna, from Donegal in Lancaster County. . . ." Jason's words were slurred from the whiskey, but he felt a lift as he realized that at least he was not stuttering. He continued telling them of seeing his mother and sister slain, but left out the details.

"And ye witnessed all that?" MacDonald asked.

"I did."

"I was not yet come from Scotland at the time. Surely the authorities did something about it."

Jason went on to explain how the Delawares had been notified and of how they reported that Meskikokant was out of their reach and of their Iroquoian overlords' as well.

"If he has gone over to the Ottawas, there is a naught you can do about this yourself, lad," Tiny said. "That tribe is in bed with the French. It would be madness for a defenseless lad such as yourself to go among that lot."

Cadwell laughed. "McGee is far from being a defenseless lad. He is one of the best shots I ever saw."

"Too bad he was not with me at Pixawillany," said MacDonald. "There he would have had his chance to avenge his mother. I saw that evil beast raging about the stockade like a bull moose. McGee could have killed him then and there."

"What about your brother?" Levy asked, before Jason could respond to MacDonald.

Jason told them, again without stuttering, about Isaac and of how he had been reported at Kuskusky three years earlier.

"He could be anywhere now," said Levy. "I've never heard of a white captive named Isaac. Have any of you?" They shook their heads.

"It's a difficult task you've taken upon yourself, lad. Perhaps an impossible one now that the French have turned so hostile," Tiny said. "Two years ago you might have gone among the Ottawas without risk to your scalp, but no more. Your best bet would be to wait until old Tanacharison returns from the big conference in Carlisle. Besides being the Mingo overseer of the Delawares out here, he is a Seneca chief. And he's a shrewd old Indian in the bargain. Get on the right side of Tanacharison and he may be able to help. Hey, MacDonald, stop nursing that jug and hand it over here. Give us another song, Christopher. Here, Levy, you miserable little Hebrew. Put more wood on the fire. Let's keep this party going."

The party continued until Tiny passed out and nearly fell into the fire. With much difficulty, MacDonald and Levy got him to his feet and half carried him to the door. MacDonald paused to say to Jason, "Remember, lad, lay yer case before Tanacharison. He's yer only hope to find your brother in these times. But ye must waste no time. By spring this entire frontier could be in flames."

Jason, his senses fogged by the unaccustomed drink, climbed up to bed feeling both encouraged and downcast by what he had learned that night. Meskikokant was, or recently had been, among the Ottawas. But the Ottawas were practically at war against English-speaking whites. On the other hand, the Half King, Tanacharison, might help him. Jason fell asleep nursing that hope. Later the sound of Cadwell's coughing awakened him and he lay in the loft thinking of all that had happened in the past three weeks. It seemed as though it had been three years since his confrontation with Ernst Koch.

He put himself back to sleep by repeating over and over: "Tanacharison."

3

Finding Cadwell abed the next morning, huddled in his blanket and cursing his poor health, Haworth put his hand on the trader's forehead.

"Thee is so hot. Jason and I will make thee some broth. Thee must rest."

Cadwell swore that he could not spare the time. "We must hie ourselves first up beyond Kuskusky to find a new village and settle ourselves before the Indians begin their winter hunting. Otherwise all the ass-kissing traders will be back from Carlisle and we will lose our jump on them."

"I did think we might tarry long enough for Jason to talk to the Half King. And for that matter, I would like to speak to him as well. Perhaps he would give me some sign of his approval to carry to that new village."

Cadwell got up and, dragging his blanket, made his way to the fire. "I don't need his blessing for *my* mission, which is to get three horseloads of the best furs I can as fast as I can. As for Tanacharison's advice, there will be other Indians up there who can *advise* McGee what to do. Now God damn it, the two of you are not going to gang up on me again, are you?"

Jason spoke up. "Mister Haworth has got a point. The Half King's blessing would make things easier for him."

"Old Tanacharison won't give a shit for a white man's religion. He'd probably prefer Haworth to take his Quaker talk back to Philadelphia. I am in charge of this party. You both agreed to that. And I say we will leave first thing in the morning and head straight for Kuskusky." He stopped to cough. "All I need is a day's rest and I'll be ready to move on."

Rather than excite him further, Haworth and Jason fell silent. With Cicero's help, Haworth rescued enough duck meat from the previous night's feast to prepare a broth. Without being asked, Cicero dug into his master's cache and found some tea.

"Don't tell Massa Goodspeed I done this."

Cadwell, barely touching either the broth or the hot tea, returned to his bed and offered no resistance when Haworth added his own blanket to his covers.

"Go on, both of you, get out and let me rest. I can't bear to have you mooning about me."

Outside the cabin, Haworth shook his head. "I do wish he would bide here for a few days, for his sake and ours."

"He can take my mare, if that's all he cares about. I could stay here and wait until Tanacharison returns. Then join you at Kuskusky or wherever . . ."

"I dislike the idea of separating. Not when we have come so far together. Look thee, Jason, go walk about if thee wish, but I think I should stay here to look after Friend Cadwell this morning."

Jason, fuming at Cadwell's selfishness and still excited by what

115

MacDonald had told him the night before, was relieved to get away from both the Quaker and the trader. Even when they were not openly at odds, it seemed there was a tension between them, and it was getting on Jason's nerves. So he took his rifle and, with Logan at his side, picked his way around the log cabins that made up the center of the village and then past the bark lodges and wigwams of Indians around the edges. Few people, white or Indian, were stirring so early in the morning, for which Jason was grateful. He needed to think.

The leaves on the bluff-lined western shore of the Ohio glowed orange and red under a clear October sun. The air was just brisk enough to make walking an almost sensuous pleasure.

Logan maintained a deceptive dignity as several scrawny Indian dogs followed him threateningly past a clump of wigwams. They whined after him, but he acted as if they did not exist until he and Jason were well clear of the village, when he suddenly turned and raged among them, sending them yelping back to their masters.

While Logan went foraging along the riverbank, Jason thought of how someday he would describe this scene to Sallie.

"It's a big river," he would say. "Not as wide as the Susquehanna, of course, but much deeper and the current swifter. It flows past a long stretch of cliffs along the left bank. Ah, Sallie," he would say as they lay in each other's arms as man and wife. "It's such beautiful country out there. I'd like to show it to you."

Jason spent most of the morning roaming along the shore of the Ohio. He saw little game worth shooting, but he marveled at the abundance of birds, especially waterfowl. At last he and Logan hid themselves in a thicket and waited for half an hour, until a turkey hen appeared. Jason laughed at the difficulty Logan had in dragging the turkey back to him.

As he walked toward the village with the turkey in one hand and his rifle in the other, and Logan cavorting about like a puppy, Jason felt better. Whether they left before or after Tanacharison returned, he would find Isaac.

He halted just below Logstown to watch a canoe cross the Ohio, smoothly handled by one man while another sat in the front, without a paddle. When the canoe drew closer he saw that it carried Goodspeed and Pratt. They waved to him and he waited while they tied up.

"How is our young cabinmate this morning?" Goodspeed asked in his slightly condescending manner. "And his dog?"

"I am well, but Mister Cadwell is in bed with chills and fever."

"How unfortunate. I see you have been hunting. My, what an extraordinary rifle. Look you, Pratt, how delicate are its lines."

Pratt, who carried a large sack of provisions, looked appraisingly at the rifle.

"It is that."

They walked together toward the village, where now both Indians and whites were going about their daily pursuits.

"We have been across the river, hoping to see Shingas, the chief of the Shawanese, but he has not yet returned from Carlisle. Neither he nor his Oneida overseer, Scaroyada."

"We had been hoping to see the Half King of the Delawares, Tanacharison, ourselves."

Goodspeed chatted away in his languid, superior manner, acting slightly amused by Jason's rough speech. He paused at a bark lodge in the doorway of which a young Indian woman stood looking out.

"McGee, would you like to put your turkey to good use?"

"How?"

"I must stop off here to discuss a certain matter, but I thought a fine meal tonight might be in order. My slave, Cicero, is a superb cook. You provide the turkey and we'll provide the labor and the side dishes. How about it?"

"That is agreeable with me."

"Very well. Pratt, please do give Cicero his instructions." He paused to nod at the smiling squaw. "Tell him to give us a proper meal."

Looking back over his shoulder, Jason saw Goodspeed enter the squaw's lodge and heard her laugh.

Jason was amused at the way the Indian dogs now stood aside as Logan passed their lodges. Following behind Pratt, Jason noted how the Virginian placed one foot directly in front of the other rather than walking in the splay-footed way of so many whites. The frontiersman strode toward their cabin without deigning to talk to Jason or show any notice of the people he passed.

When they entered the cabin, Pratt took the turkey from Jason and flung it on the table in front of Cicero, who was seated, talking to Haworth.

"Here, you worthless nigger. Mister Goodspeed wants a turkey dinner for this evening. And here." He thrust the bag of provisions into his hands. "There's squash and corn and pumpkins in there. Now you'll hop to it if you know what's good for you."

Haworth interrupted. "Cicero and I were having a conversation. I would like to complete it before he starts work. After all, it is some time off before supper."

Pratt ignored the Quaker. "You heard me, Cicero. Get moving."

117

Haworth was ready to protest, but Jason, catching his eye, gave him a warning frown as the Negro carried the turkey outside to pluck it.

"How is Mister Cadwell?" Jason asked.

"Asleep now."

"Does he still want to leave tomorrow?"

"He says he is determined to go," Haworth said in a low voice.

Pratt, after rummaging among his belongings, left carrying a nearly empty bottle of rum.

"That man is sinister," Haworth said. "He treats poor Cicero like a cur dog rather than a human being."

"Well, he is a slave."

"Ah, Jason, no man is a slave in the eyes of God. Cicero is a man, like thee or me. A good man too. He has been telling me of his wife and their two children. He loves them dearly. And his mother came direct from Africa on a slave ship. Imagine. She taught him some of her old language and told him stories of her girlhood on the Guinea coast."

"What about his father?"

"That is sad. His mother was pregnant with Cicero when she arrived in Virginia. The father was another slave, who was sold elsewhere. Oh, Jason, how badly we treat the people of his race. Worse in many ways than we do the Indians. Imagine, that Goodspeed could sell him as thee or I might sell a horse."

"I hope you were not talking to Cicero again about freedom."

"Only of his soul, Friend Jason. Tell me about thy hunting."

Cadwell awoke in the afternoon and accepted some of the duck broth Haworth had kept warming over the fire. Jason told him of his hunting, but the trader showed little interest except to smile at the story of how Logan had put the pack of Indian dogs to flight. Jason went outside to help Cicero gut the turkey.

"You shot this thing yourself?" the Negro asked.

"Yes."

"I heard your boss bragging last night about what a good shot you are."

"He is not my boss, but he did mention it, yes."

"And the Indians killed your mother?"

"And my sister and even our milk cow."

"They take your brother away too?"

"That is right."

"You gonna try to get him back?"

"That is why I have come out here."

"Hmm. Wish somebody from Africa come and take me back." Cicero thought about what he had just said and laughed. "If they take my wife and children too."

"Black people from Africa? They wouldn't know how to cross the ocean. They would play hell getting you back."

"You gonna play hell getting your brother back too, I spect."

Jason did not understand the anger the Negro's remark caused him to feel.

"You want me to help you fix this meal?"

"Sho. I appreciate it."

"Then shut up with that kind of talk. I am going to get my brother back, come what may. I can't go home without him."

4

That night's supper was even better than the previous one. To Jason's surprise, Cicero set the table with pewter goblets. "Massa Goodspeed like to have his wine," he explained. And Goodspeed, dressed in a clean ruffled shirt and velvet jacket, sat at the head of the table, with Haworth on his right, Jason on the left and Pratt at the other end. Cadwell excused himself from sitting at the table.

Jason had said nothing to Haworth about Goodspeed's visit to the squaw, but even so, the Quaker's manner at first was disapproving. Not at all put off, the Virginian, apparently determined to charm Haworth, asked him many polite questions about his family and its business as well as about his proposed mission to the Indians. Haworth unloosened to the extent of sipping his wine and proclaiming it of good quality.

"Madeira," Goodspeed replied. "My father buys a lot each year, right off the ship."

"My father likes Madeira above other wines," Haworth said. "I despise strong spirits such as rum or whiskey, but at home I do allow myself an occasional glass of wine."

As the two chatted on about their families, it struck Jason how much they had in common. Both were from rich homes, both were educated and well-mannered and dressed in good clothing. Both had an air of assurance and, as it turned out, a strong sense of purpose in coming to the frontier. Whereas the previous evening Cicero had stood about laughing at the crude jokes passing across the table, tonight his face was a black mask. Logan sat looking disappointed that no scraps were being tossed to him. Jason and Pratt ate in silence. Jason wondered if the surly frontiersman felt as out of place as he in the presence of such refined conversation. By the time second portions of turkey, corn meal dressing and stewed squash had been consumed, Haworth was thoroughly relaxed. He began to question Goodspeed about his land project.

"My purpose is grand but simple. Once the Ohio Land Company has settled one hundred families out here and has built a fort, it will receive two hundred thousand acres free of royal taxes or quitrents for ten years, and later may have an additional three hundred thousand acres. Well, sir, I mean to establish an early claim to several thousand of those acres."

"What about the poor Indians?"

"If you refer to the Iroquois who claim to have owned these lands, the government of Virginia purchased that part of their domain lying south of the Ohio as far as the setting sun in 1744. As for the Indians being poor, I would point out the gifts they have received from both Virginia and Pennsylvania to keep their good will. They do precious little labor for their wages."

"Our policy in Pennsylvania has been to purchase land from the Indians in small lots and to prohibit white settlements among them. Nothing upsets them worse than to have squatters disturbing their pattern of life."

"I am glad, Mister Haworth, that you said policy and not practice. We hear much about your white squatters in Pennsylvania. Seems to me your purchase treaties generally come after the fact of settlement. Virginians were the first colonists to explore this country and they found it uninhabited. The Delaware and Shawanese are the interlopers. Not us Virginians."

Seeing that Haworth was momentarily lacking for an answer, Jason spoke up. "What about the French? We hear that they may be coming down here in the spring."

"When I left Williamsburg there was much talk that Governor Dinwiddie would send an expedition to build a fort early next year, probably at the Forks of the Ohio. Once that spot is secure, we'll have the French bottled up."

Haworth found his tongue again. "Traders out here say that the Indians are so upset by thy settlement plans that it makes it easier for the French to alienate them from the English."

"What does it matter what the Delaware or Shawanese think?

120

We have bought off their Iroquois overlords. Look you, Mister Haworth: there are more people living in your city of Philadelphia than there are Indians of all tribes out here. Are we to halt the expansion of white, English-speaking civilization because of the doubtful claims of a handful of ignorant Indian squatters? Are we to let this rich country go unsettled because a French colony to the north makes pretentious claims to the land or because a few score Pennsylvania traders, the very scum of the earth, desire to continue their game of cheating the Indians out of their furs? No sir, we shall expand our colony into this area and neither Indian, nor French, nor trader shall stop us."

Jason, growing annoyed at Goodspeed's air of superiority, thought what a row Tiny Little or MacDonald would have made at being called scum.

"I think it wrong to speculate in land."

"Wrong, Mister Haworth? My, you are pure-minded. Land is why we white men are here. Land is what drew our grandfathers across the sea. Land is what has encouraged the spread of our settlements. Thousands upon thousands of acres of rich soil stretching beyond the imagination to the west. Why, sir, one could set the princedom of Wales down in this land drained by the upper Ohio. Think of what it will be someday when it is properly settled and developed."

"I think of what it is today: the home—nay, the refuge—of the people who used to own this entire continent. And of what it used to be: free of rival claims by foreign governments and free of the evil influence of strong drink and uncorrupted by trinkets. Unspoiled."

"You paint a pretty picture, but you should also include scenes of warfare among themselves far more cruel than that of civilized countries. Include their shivering in the cold without the white man's blankets. Make your picture show the way in which one tribe cannot communicate with another. There was not one people inhabiting this continent any more than there is one now. And they do not *use* the land. They let it lie idle."

"Well, sir, it does seem to me that thee puts thy interests above that of all others. The Indians, be they Iroquois or Delaware or Shawanese, do not wish white settlements out here; the French do not wish English-speaking settlements; our provincial government in Pennsylvania does not wish Virginia to send in white families."

"If human beings yielded to the wishes of others, my grandfather would never have come to Virginia nor, I suspect, yours to Pennsylvania. Nor would our common ancestors, the Anglo-Saxons, have crossed the North Sea if they had consulted the ancient Celts. No, the strong must press on in their strength or they will lose it. This land *will* be settled. It is inevitable. Here, you and I have been talking away as though McGee and Pratt do not exist. What think you on these questions, McGee?"

"The Indians have got to live somewhere, I suppose."

"What about you, Mister Pratt?"

"I don't fret about what wolves or panthers think. The Indians are just in the way. They do no good for anyone."

"What a dreadful thing to say," Haworth exclaimed. "They are human beings like thee and me."

"Maybe thee. Not me," Pratt replied.

Haworth sat up straight, his mouth open in indignation.

"Calm yourself, Mister Haworth. Do not let Mister Pratt's blunt talk upset you. He has not had the most pleasant of experiences with the Indians. His father was slain by them when he was a youth and, I fear, he thinks the only good Indian is a dead one, as the saying goes."

"Jason witnessed his mother and sister slain ten years ago—yes, and his brother taken away to the west. But he does not hate all Indians, does thee, Jason?"

"I don't hate them, not all of them. I just want my brother back."

Jason was relieved that Haworth answered Goodspeed's further questions about the massacre for him. Meanwhile Pratt poured rum into his goblet. After draining it off, he said, "If it had been my mother and sister, I would not be sitting here at Logstown. I would go and kill the Indian that done it."

Goodspeed laughed. "Mister Pratt is not making idle talk. He crossed the mountains while still a boy and lived among the Indians for two years, until he got his opportunity, and then he slew two of the Indians that had murdered his father. The Shawanese dread Mister Pratt as the devil does holy water. That is why I employ him, eh, Mister Pratt?"

"If you say so, Mister Goodspeed."

Haworth sat up stiffly. "All this talk of murder and revenge. It is appalling. It only leads to more bloodshed and disorder. Revenge breeds revenge."

"On the contrary. The Indians respect revenge. They understand it. Look you, Mister Haworth, I do apologize for the turn in our conversation. I meant this to be a pleasant evening and now I see that you are agitated. Everything will turn out happily. I do wish you success in your mission to bring Christianity to the Delawares. Here, have another glass of wine."

122

"I have drunk quite enough."

"I shall have another, if no one objects. And a pipe. Cicero, look lively."

As the Virginian filled his pipe and lit it, Jason wished they could get the talk back to less controversial subjects. Goodspeed took a swallow of wine and continued.

"It will turn out well, I am confident. In ten years, you will see the progress that will come to our lands south of the Ohio. I have my eye on a lovely spread of land. Several thousand acres. In ten years or less, if you will do me the honor of visiting me you will find a strong house for my wife and our children, with fields all cleared and under cultivation by my slaves. You will wonder that you ever objected to settlement."

"Thee proposes to introduce slavery out here?" Haworth was frowning.

"Of course. My older brother stands to inherit our family lands on the James. Our supply of land there is fixed, but our slaves do multiply. My father has promised to give me several Negro families to move up here. Furthermore, he says he'll buy some strong Guinea bucks fresh off a slave ship and let me break them in myself."

"I do not hold with slavery."

"Really? Why ever not?"

"It is wrong. It is worse than wrong. It is wicked to buy and sell human flesh."

"But, my dear sir, you really are naïve. It is so much better for the African to be over here in an invigorating climate, under benign Christian influence. Here, ask Cicero. Cicero, would you like to be back in Africa where your mother came from?"

"I don't know nothing about no Africa, Massa Geoffry."

Goodspeed closed his eyes in satisfaction as he blew smoke toward the roof. He did not see the glance that passed between Cicero and Haworth.

The Quaker rose. "I am a sworn enemy of slavery. It pains me that it still exists, albeit on a limited scale, in my native province. I speak against it in Philadelphia, and I will speak against it here. It is wrong, sir."

"You are upset."

"I am more than upset. I am outraged that thee intends to bring plantation slavery to Pennsylvania. I regret that we must share the same cabin. I regret that I broke bread with one so callous toward other human beings as to refer to them like farm animals."

Pratt snickered, but Goodspeed motioned for him to be silent.

When he spoke again, it was in a cold, flat voice, with no pretense of courtesy. "I took you for an educated man of good sense. I did not take you for a fool. I see I was mistaken."

"I am a fool," replied Haworth. "A fool for my Lord."

"You have said it. You are a fool."

The Quaker turned and stamped from the cabin. Jason sat woodenly, not knowing what to say or do.

"Well, Pratt, it is just as well that we are leaving the day after tomorrow. Our Quaker friend won't have to put up with our obnoxious presence very long, will he?"

"We plan to leave in the morning ourselves," Jason said.

"Really?" The Virginian stared at Jason for a long while, then added, "You want some advice, young man?"

"What is that?"

"Go kill that Indian that slew your mother and sister, if you want to be a man."

Jason did not reply.

"And I'll give you another piece of advice. Shed the companionship of your Quaker friend. He is a dangerous fool. He will bring you to grief."

"He is my friend," Jason said quietly.

Jason lay awake a long while that night, thinking about the conversation between Haworth and Goodspeed. He forgot his earlier embarrassment as he reflected on what Goodspeed had said about the opportunities out here. There was an empire waiting to be created. He did not have slaves or family wealth, but perhaps this was where his future lay too. He could go back to Lancaster County, marry Sallie, help Isaac find a wife also, and return to take up land. Two strong brothers with fine young wives, working together, they could hack out a grand farm. He went to sleep thinking of the possibilities.

5

It was cold the next morning, with skims of ice on the mud puddles. Jason shivered as he went outside to urinate and let Logan exercise. When he went back in he found Haworth leaning over Cadwell.

"Then thee has changed thy mind about leaving today?"

Jason could barely hear the trader. "Yes. I'm sick. Dreadful sick."

Haworth stood up. "We must stay here, then. As long as it may take for thee to recover." He looked with contempt to where the two Virginians still slept. "I wonder, though, if we might move to another cabin."

"Mister Goodspeed and Pratt plan to leave tomorrow," Jason said.

"In that case, we may as well stay put. He will require much care."

Cadwell lay with glazed eyes, as if he had not heard.

When Goodspeed arose to dine on the breakfast prepared by Cicero, he did not speak to Haworth, but upon learning from Jason that Cadwell was worse, gave him a small flask of brandy and a vial of laudanum. He excused himself, saying, "I have business about the village that will occupy me until this afternoon. Be sure you pack up properly, Cicero. And, Mr. Pratt, pray have our horses shod today and arrange with someone to raft us across the river in the morning. I don't want to swim our horses this time. It is too cold."

Jason borrowed Cadwell's smoothbore musket and went hunting with Logan, heading away from the river into the hills overlooking Logstown. He killed several passenger pigeons and, while he was at it, dug up some sassafras roots, remembering how his mother used them as a medicine.

Upon his return in the early afternoon, he tied Logan to the doorway and entered the cabin, to find Haworth sitting at the table with his Testament in hand. Pratt was standing in front of the fire holding a half-empty bottle of rum. Cicero, a strained look on his face, whispered to Jason, "Please get Massa Haworth out of here," but before he could say more, Pratt said, "Well, it's our young redhead. Your God damned friend thinks he is too good to drink with me. You'll drink, though, won't you?"

He held out the bottle. Jason took it and pretended to drink.

"Jason." Haworth looked up. "Thee should not."

"Should not? He'll drink if I say so and you will too."

Haworth made no reply.

"You heard me. I say you shall drink with us."

"Take no offense. I do not drink strong spirits. I have told thee that already."

"Thee, thee, thee," Pratt mocked him. "You God damned Indian-lover. I'l give *thee* one more chance. Have a drink."

Haworth looked down at his open Testament. Pratt lifted the Quaker's hat and poured rum over his head, laughing as he did so. Without thinking, Jason dashed the bottle from Pratt's hand and it broke upon the hearth.

The frontiersman, weaving on his feet, turned to face Jason. "You'll pay for that."

"Why don't you leave him alone? He is doing you no harm."

Cicero said, "Jason, tell Mister Pratt you didn't mean to break his bottle. Tell him you are sorry. Please." The Negro's voice was pleading.

"Shut up, you woolly-head. It is too late for him to apologize. The stripling will have to take his medicine."

"I am not afraid of you," Jason said.

Haworth rose. "Jason, do not give offense—" Pratt shoved him back upon the bench.

Later Jason would not remember exactly what happened during the next few minutes. He would recall Cicero and Haworth both pleading with him to remain calm, and Pratt methodically removing his coonskin cap and deerskin shirt, and Logan at the cabin door, and finally standing outside in the cold in the midst of a circle of traders and Indians clamoring to see the fight. For a moment he had the feeling of being back at the Paxton School confronting Angus Cameron, but then he saw that he was facing a powerful, mature frontiersman with arms as hairy and thick as a bear's forelegs, just standing there on the balls of his feet, smiling. This time there was no kindly Parson Elder to interfere, but Jason did hear with relief Tiny Little's booming voice saying, "All right, Pratt. This is going to be a fair fight. No gouging and no knifeplay. You hear?"

Without taking his yellow panther's eyes from Jason, Pratt said, "Mind your own business, Little."

Jason's anger had fled. He wished there were some way he could avoid this fight, but seeing that there was not, he resolved to end it quickly. Remembering how he had vanquished Angus Cameron, he lowered his head and hurled himself toward Pratt, aiming for his stomach. The frontiersman turned and brought his knee up with such force that Jason was flung over upon his back, stunned.

"No kicking either, Pratt," Little shouted.

Jason's head cleared. Pratt stood with his hands by his sides, laughing with the crowd. Jason welcomed the return of his anger. He arose and began to circle the frontiersman, who turned slowly to face him. Jason, counting on his own speed and sobriety, halted and swung his right fist hard toward Pratt's head. The man caught the blow on his left forearm and then slapped Jason hard across the mouth with the back of his hand.

Instead of retreating, Jason swung his left fist against Pratt's head. The frontiersman grunted and reached out for Jason's throat, but missing, grabbed the front of his blouse, ripping it half off him. Jason struck again, his fist this time landing on Pratt's chin, but the Virginian shook off the blow, lunged ahead and caught him around the waist. In an instant Jason was lifted off his feet and locked in a bear hug. Writhing back and forth in the crushing grip, he finally escaped by banging his forehead against Pratt's nose. The frontiersman dropped him to put his hands to his face. Blood appeared on his upper lip.

"So you want to play rough."

Pratt moved quickly toward Jason, who dodged the lunge and slammed a fist hard against his ribs. It was like hitting an oak tree. Pratt swept Jason off his feet with an open-handed slap that sent him reeling in the dirt.

Sensing a quick end to the fight, the crowd closed the circle. But Jason was angered more than injured. He rose and charged into the frontiersman, forgetting his own safety as he pumped away with blows that, even when they slipped past Pratt's guard, did little damage. Again, *Whap!* An open-handed slap sat Jason on his butt. He got to his feet, marveling at Pratt's speed and strength even when nearly drunk. Jason, beginning to tire now, wondered how he could ever get out of this predicament without showing cowardice. He feinted as if to strike at Pratt's face and then sank his fist into the Virginian's stomach, causing him to bend over as if in pain.

"Now, McGee, go for him," Little shouted.

Jason's next blow ended in midair, with his wrist caught in Pratt's right hand. In an instant two hands were around his neck and he felt himself being shaken like a rag doll and his brain near to bursting.

Tiny Little later told Jason and scores of others just what happened in the next few minutes. In fact, he would repeat the story for the rest of his life.

"There the fellow from Virginia stood, choking the red-headed lad. Actually raising him off his feet. The lad had put up a brave fight, but the Virginian was too much for him. Looked like he would kill him. One of my dearest friends, old Bruce MacDonald, and I looks at each other and moves in to stop this Virginian, but we didn't have to. You see, this lad had a huge yellow dog. Splendid brute, and that dog worshiped him. The dog was tied up outside the cabin and all through the fight he had been barking and straining to get free. Well, somebody must have untied him, for suddenly this dog came charging in. He actually leaped over the shoulders of two Indians and landed in the circle. And then he lit into that Virginian. First jumped up and bit his arm, which made the fellow let go his grip on the boy's

127

throat. Then the dog sinks his teeth into the fellow's ankle and wouldn't let go. The lad stood there trying to collect his wits. I thinks to myself: Now whup the son of a bitch good. Everybody around Logstown was afraid of that Virginian, including me. But the lad was nearly unconscious from the choking. Well, the Virginian pulled out his knife and seemed ready to stab the dog. That is when MacDonald and I finally stepped in."

What Jason would remember was Little saying, "That's enough, Pratt. You beat him. Put that knife away."

Logan released his hold on the Virginian's leg to go and stand between him and the still groggy Jason. Pratt, knife in hand, glared.

"This fight ain't over. Little bastard kneed me. I'm gonna take his scalp. This is no concern of yours, Little. Or yours, MacDonald. Stay out of it."

His senses restored now, Jason stood unsteadily, wishing desperately he had never heard of Pratt or Logstown.

"Mister Pratt! What goes on here? Put that knife away!"

It was Goodspeed, thrusting his way through the crowd.

"Here, give me that."

He took the knife from Pratt's hand. "I am shocked at you. Brawling right out in open daylight and you in the employ of the Ohio Land Company. Get inside, sir. You may explain this behavior to me in private."

As meekly as a guilty schoolboy, Pratt followed Goodspeed into the cabin, protesting that Jason had started the altercation. With Pratt gone, Little, Levy and MacDonald shook Jason's hand and praised his courage.

"Ye stood up to him like a true Scot," said MacDonald.

Others in the crowd stepped up and asked to be introduced to the lad who had held his own briefly with the dreaded frontiersman. Jason began to feel like a hero, albeit a bruised and weary one.

"I hope thee has learned a lesson about fighting, Jason," Haworth said. "Thee looks a fright. Thy left eye is nearly closed and thee should see the bruises on thy throat."

"My throat. I thought I was going to die. He had me. Where did Logan come from? I left him tied to the cabin door."

"Ask Cicero," the Quaker said with a mischievous smile.

Jason did draw Cicero aside and ask him if he had untied Logan. The Negro pretended not to understand, but finally burst out laughing. "Don't you never tell another soul I done that. Old Pratt would kill me."

"I'll never tell. But why did you wait so long?"

"I thought maybe you would give him a whipping without any help."

"Anyway, thanks."

"Thank *you,* white boy. I been waiting to see somebody stand up to that man. But I *was* skeered for you. I seen him kill two men. One was a white man. He done it with a knife. The other was an Indian and he killed him with his bare hands. And when he gets drunk he beats me if Massa Geoffry ain't there to stop him." The Negro laughed again. "Law, I wouldn't take ten pounds for the sight of that big dog lighting into old Pratt. Nearly tore his britches off him."

Cadwell, although he had been too weak to intervene in the altercation, had summoned the strength to rise and watch the fight from the loft window. The effort had exhausted him so that he had to go back to bed, but he asked Haworth to send Jason up to see him.

"You were stupid to tangle with that one. Lucky he didn't kill you. But I admire your pluck. Is it true they are leaving tomorrow?"

"So Mister Goodspeed says."

"Tonight move your blankets over to the corner and sleep with my pistol and knife beside you. And tie Logan in place at your feet. I don't want anything to happen to you before you find your brother. Give me another day or so and we'll start looking for him."

6

The two white Virginians and Cicero were up early the next morning. Awakened by their bustling about outside, Jason lay in bed listening to Goodspeed's instructions for securing their gear on their two horses.

Jason put his fingertips to his face and winced. His lips were puffed and cracked, and he could barely see out of one eye. His neck and his ribs were so sore he found it painful to swallow or breathe. He thought again of how Cicero had freed Logan just in time, and decided to bid the Negro farewell.

"Ah, McGee, there you are," Goodspeed greeted him. Then in a lower voice, so that Pratt, who was leading a horse toward the river, would not hear: "I do want to apologize for my employee's behavior. I did warn you that your Quaker friend would bring you to grief, remember. Even so, there was no excuse for Mister Pratt to be so rough. Try some bear's grease on that eye."

He excused himself to go to the young squaw who was standing nearby watching him.

"Thanks again, Cicero," Jason said when they were alone.

"You are welcome. Hope you find your brother."

They were chatting when Pratt returned from the river to tell Goodspeed their raft was ready. At his approach, Logan growled so that Jason looped a rope around his neck. Pratt's face bore a bruise on the chin and a slightly swollen nose as the only marks of their fight. He looked at Jason's battered visage and smiled.

"You want to have another go at me sometime when I ain't been drinking?"

"I ain't afraid of you," Jason lied.

"What about that Indian that killed your mother? You afraid of him?"

"No," Jason lied again.

"You want to kill him?"

"That's my business, not yours."

"I'd go kill him for you for ten pounds."

"I ain't got ten pounds."

"Give me that pretty rifle, then. It would take me a month, but I'd kill him and keep the rifle as my payment."

"How would that help me get back my brother?"

Pratt did not reply to that. "Mister Goodspeed gave you good advice. I'll give you some more. Don't fight out in the open with people watching if you can avoid it. I was just playing with you yesterday. I could have killed you with my hands. Go for the eyes or the throat or the balls. Don't swing so wide. Hit short, straight blows. When you have the advantage, pour it on; don't fall back and let him recover. And don't start a fight you don't mean to finish. Make the other man fear you."

Not quite knowing how to take this cold-blooded advice, Jason merely said, "Thank you, Pratt."

"Wish I'd had somebody tell me that when I was young. Had to learn it myself. Wouldn't have took me so long to get even for my pa's murder. . . . All right, Cicero, you black ape, let's get out of here."

Haworth was wringing his hands when Jason reentered the cabin.

"Poor Cadwell. He is so feverish, and now he has trouble breathing."

With the cabin to themselves, they moved Cadwell down to a bed of fresh hemlock boughs in front of the fire. While Haworth was out drawing water from the river, Cadwell motioned for Jason to come near.

130

"I'll be all right in a day or so, McGee," he whispered.

"I know you will."

"You won't leave me, will you?"

"Of course not."

"I heard Haworth talking the other night. Goodspeed is right about him, you know. He is a fool."

"I still like him."

"So do I, but that don't stop him from being a fool."

Cadwell grew worse during the night, coughing so hard that neither Jason nor Haworth could sleep. Near dawn the trader began talking as if to someone in the cabin.

"I'll come with you, yes. . . . Wait, I must collect my furs. . . . We can be happy again. . . . Wait for me. . . . Don't go away again. . . . Susannah."

They found him up on one elbow, staring into the fire.

Haworth shook him. "Friend Cadwell. What is the matter?"

"You frightened her away, damn it."

"Try this." Haworth gave him a draught of the medicine Goodspeed had left and soon the trader was asleep again.

Because Haworth insisted that Cadwell have fresh meat, Jason went hunting again the next morning. As he passed through Logstown carrying his rifle and accompanied by Logan, every white person in the village spoke to him, congratulating him on his standing up to Pratt. Those Indians not entirely drunk pointed at him.

At the bark lodge where Goodspeed had visited, the same young squaw looked at him with sad eyes and beckoned, saying, "You come in see me."

Jason stepped into the lodge, straining to see amidst a darkness slightly relieved by a smoky fire in the center of the floor and its exit hole in the top of the structure. The lodge stank of burnt bear fat, body odors and smoke. He could make out the image of an ancient woman with iron-gray hair huddled in a blanket and when she turned her face toward him he saw that it was crisscrossed with deep wrinkles.

The young squaw pointed to a bed in the corner. "Give me something. I lie with you. Make feel good."

Jason, confused, backed out of the doorway, shaking his head. "I have to go hunting. Must go."

She followed him outside. Fragile and small-waisted, she was prettier than most squaws. "You come back by and by. Bring me food, I lie with you."

At first Jason was glad to have escaped into the fresh air. With trembling knees and sweating palms, he climbed toward the hills, but looking back, he saw the squaw still standing in front of her lodge, and he wondered what it would have been like if he had stayed.

The country around Logstown having been heavily hunted over for several years, the deer and bear so common in most of Pennsylvania had long since been killed or moved away. But bird life abounded. Jason paused at the crest of the main hill to watch a flight of geese glide down toward the river, jabbering like a crowd of gossipy women entering a church. Across the river, along the bluffs, a swarm of passenger pigeons a half mile long wheeled to rest. Closer at hand, flocks of blackbirds and mobs of jays chattered.

It was well past noon before he heard the sound of a pig's grunting. He had to restrain Logan until he caught a glimpse of a half-grown shoat, the descendant of some porcine escapee from Logstown. Jason had seen wild pigs like this near the Susquehanna, but he was surprised to find one so far west.

His first shot only wounded the pig, but Logan was able to corner it until Jason could reload. The pig ignored the dog, and confronted Jason with eyes both defiant and resigned. This time the rifle ball found the brain. Jason disemboweled the animal on the spot, rewarding Logan with half the liver.

It was tiresome hauling the pig's carcass, heart and liver down the hillside, but he welcomed the prospect of eating fresh pork. Again the young squaw smiled at him and invited him to enter her lodge. He stopped and presented her with the remainder of the liver and the pig's heart, but to her obvious surprise, declined her invitation to visit.

At the cabin he found Tiny Little, MacDonald and Levy all gathered around Cadwell's bed. "We can't rouse him," Haworth explained. "He is in a coma."

7

Toward sundown, at the suggestion of Tiny, they sent for Logstown's nearest thing to a doctor, a wiry little cross-eyed gunsmith who doubled as barber and "surgeon." He arrived with a worn copy of a book titled *Every Man His Own Doctor* under his arm, and a surgeon's kit in his hand.

He made a great show of feeling Cadwell's pulse, lifting up his eyelids, putting an ear to his chest and asking questions about his recent bowel movements and food intake, after which he announced what they had known already, that Cadwell had "lung congestion."

The little man laboriously read aloud a passage from his book to buttress his diagnosis. They nodded at the wisdom of the author and the reading skill of the barber-gunsmith, agreeing with him that Cadwell should be bled, the sooner the better. He called for a bowl and rags. Drawing a scalpel from his kit, he whetted the blade on his shoe sole, opened a vein in Cadwell's arm and drew off a pint of blood.

"There. You must keep him warm. You ought to put out those stinking pipes and use only dry wood on the fire. He's got trouble enough breathing already without all this smoke. He'll be going through the crisis in a few hours. I've done all for him that the science of medicine can accomplish. He is in the hands of a greater physician now." He rolled his eyes skyward. "Who's to pay my fee?"

The three companions looked at each other, then at Haworth and Jason. The barber held out his hand to Tiny.

"You're the one sent for me. I can't work for nothing. It costs a shilling to bleed a patient."

MacDonald broke the silence. "I don't think you should ask for payment until we see if he pulls through."

"I feel the same," said Levy. "You don't collect for repairing a gun until you're sure it is back in working order."

"It is not the same thing at all. If you don't pay, I won't come back to see him in the morning. And don't none of you ever expect my services, no matter how desperately you may need them." The little man was heatedly explaining how much his medical handbook and surgical kit had cost him, when Haworth interrupted. "Here is thy shilling, my good man."

He thanked Haworth and, pointedly ignoring the others, bade the Quaker and Jason good night.

"Alas, poor old Christopher, he is in a bad way," said Tiny. "We must drink to his recovery. Here is a shilling, MacDonald. I'll pay if you'll fetch the whiskey."

The three companions, Levy as well as the others, drank generously from the jug when MacDonald returned. Jason declined and when he did, they fell to teasing him about his performance in the fight.

"Aye, it is the yellow dog we should offer the drink anyway," MacDonald said. "He was the winner of that affair."

They laughed until Haworth shushed them. As they drank more

133

they forgot about their sick friend, letting their talk range over the subject of furs, women, fighting and profit. Jason was torn between concern for Cadwell and amusement at the free-flowing conversation of Little, MacDonald and Levy.

Little told of growing up across the Delaware River from Philadelphia and how he had run away to escape marrying the pregnant daughter of a farmer and had ended up as an agent for the legendary George Croghan. MacDonald gave them an imaginative description of the battle of Culloden and how he had escaped English retribution by fleeing first to Ireland and then to America. Levy recollected his boyhood in a Polish village, relating how his people were harassed by the czarist police and how he had resolved he never again would suffer such oppression and poverty.

After a bit, Haworth quit acting as though he wanted them to leave, and as they were tending toward sentimentality rather than rowdiness, he joined the talk, telling them of his voyage to Barbados as a youth and harking back to his grandfather's stories of growing up as a despised Quaker in England.

"And here is Friend Jason, come out to recover his brother. Look at us, gentlemen," he said. "All of us are refugees of one sort or another. All come out here to the frontier of a new world to escape persecution or to fulfill our missions in life."

This sentiment appealed to them and they applauded it by taking a fresh drink.

Their talk died down after midnight, but out of loyalty to the unconscious man, they stayed on. All dropped off to sleep except Haworth, who hovered over Cadwell like a mother with a sick child.

Jason, his head pillowed on Logan's flank, fell asleep to the sound of the trader's labored breathing. He was awakened near dawn by Haworth's hand on his shoulder.

"Jason. I fear he is gone."

"Gone?" Jason sat up.

"His breathing sounded easier and then he gave a great sigh and now he is still."

Jason felt for a pulse in Cadwell's wrist and found none. No longer did the trader's chest heave. He lay there with one half-open eye glistening in the firelight.

Jason put his head in his hands. He had not realized how fond he had become of this sour, determined man.

Little awoke. "What's up?"

"Friend Cadwell has gone to rejoin his Maker," Haworth replied.

"Poor, poor old Christopher."

The others awakened and joined in a general lamentation.

"Alas, my noble friend." Tiny's voice broke and he sobbed. MacDonald and Levy caught the infection of his grief and all three of them stood with tears coursing down their cheeks.

At Haworth's urging, they knelt and recited what they knew of the Lord's Prayer, all except Levy. Then the Quaker tenderly closed the trader's half-open eye and drew the blanket over his face. This act set MacDonald to sobbing beyond control, but he recovered when Tiny started to pass the whiskey jug. Upon Haworth's protest at their lack of respect, Tiny set the jug aside.

"We should not have let that little butcher bleed him," Tiny said.

MacDonald agreed, adding, "I think Mr. Haworth should have his shilling back."

"Poor, poor old Christopher," said Tiny. "He was very near my best friend. How I shall miss him."

"Where shall we bury him?" Levy asked.

"I should think Christopher would be happy to lie on the hill above us here, looking out over the Ohio River."

No one could think of a better gravesite, and they were at the point of going to get shovels when Jason noticed that Logan was wagging his tail and sniffing at the blanket covering Cadwell. Jason thought at first the dog had barked and was about to scold him for his disrespect to the dead when he heard the sound repeated and recognized it as a cough.

Everyone now was looking at the form and so they all later could corroborate the fact that suddenly the blanket covering Cadwell's face was thrown back.

"Damn it. Who is trying to smother me?"

They drew away as if from a ghost. MacDonald started for the door.

Cadwell's eyes were wide open. "What is going on here? Where am I?"

Haworth was the first to recover. Kneeling beside the bed, he took Cadwell's hand. "It is a miracle. Thee hast come back from the dead."

Tiny Little burst into tears. They all began talking at once.

"Shut up, God damn it. Get out of here and give me some peace. This ain't a bloody public house."

Not knowing what else to do, and fearful of further exciting the sick man, they left to spread the word of how Christopher Cadwell had arisen from the dead. As for the trader, he demanded food, and Haworth hastened to prepare a sweetened corn meal gruel, which Cadwell pronounced lumpy and undercooked. But he ate it nonetheless.

8

News of Cadwell's miraculous recovery spread quickly through Logstown, bringing so many people, both white and Indian, to the door to stare at the trader that Haworth persuaded Jason to tie Logan outside to keep them away.

Cadwell lay in a querulous half stupor for several days. He spent his waking hours coughing up phlegm and spitting it into the fire and complaining to Haworth.

Jason marveled at the Quaker's patience. The youth found the sickroom atmosphere depressing and took every opportunity to go outside with Logan. Truth was, too, he enjoyed the attention he attracted. One of the blacksmiths in the village, a merry Irishman named Kelly, welcomed his visits, especially after he learned Jason had worked in a smithy. He put Jason to work for wages, a half day at a time, leaving him free to hunt and roam about the countryside the rest of the day.

By the time Cadwell could sit up and walk a bit about the cabin, Jason had become friends with half the population of Logstown. He took pains to avoid passing the lodge of the young squaw who had invited him to "lie with me," but he could not shut her out of his thoughts entirely.

All the attention he received, and the fact that he was working at his old trade like a man, gave Jason a sense of confidence he had never possessed. He found that he could discuss his mission to recover his brother without stammering, as long as he did not dwell on the massacre. He got no specific information about Isaac in this way, but he did learn much about Indian life in the upper Ohio Valley.

Cadwell noted the change in Jason's bearing, saying sarcastically, "Well, our redhead is getting pretty cocky these days. You'd think it was him that won the fight with Pratt, from the way he struts about."

Later, as Cadwell grew stronger, he became less demanding and critical toward his two companions. It appeared to Jason that Haworth's kindness and patience were rubbing off on the trader. Cadwell did not object when Haworth insisted on their bowing their heads in silence before they ate. And he did not mock the Quaker when he read his Testament or talked of his plans to build a preaching and teaching mission for the Delawares.

Jason could hardly believe it when the two men began calling each other "Christopher" and "Ephraim." He was even more surprised when the trader ordered Tiny Little to stop telling of an amorous adventure with a squaw, lest it offend Haworth.

By the second week of November, Cadwell was able to walk about the town. He followed Jason to Kelly's blacksmith shop and sat beside the forge watching the boy work and listening to the rough language of the hangers-on. He, too, was a celebrity, regarded with awe as one returned from the dead. But he remained close-mouthed about the experience, growing snappish when anyone questioned him too closely.

"I wasn't dead. Those fools only took me for dead. I came to, and they had covered me with a blanket and were talking about where to dig a hole for me."

His companions who had witnessed his "resurrection" had no such reticence or doubt. MacDonald in particular was convinced he had been present at a miracle. In telling the story, he made it appear that only his earnest prayers had been responsible for Cadwell's recovery. He was indignant when he heard that the barber who had bled Cadwell not only disputed the story that the trader had died but took credit for his restoration to health.

He became even angrier after an abscessed tooth drove him to the man's shop in desperation.

"The grasping little cross-eyed opportunist. He wouldna pull the tooth until I forked over a shilling. And then he insulted me by biting the coin. As if a MacDonald wasna good for his debts or ever would pass a bogus coin."

9

The second week of November, another light snow fell, followed by bitter cold; the third week brought the return to Logstown of Tanacharison, the Seneca Half King for the Ohio Indians.

Tanacharison had taken a leisurely course in returning from Carlisle, finally stopping just east of the Forks of the Ohio to hunt. He and his retinue of Iroquois arrived at Logstown laden with part of the gifts doled out to them by the government of Pennsylvania. Logstown became a madhouse with the return of the Half King and the introduction of several hundred pounds' worth of gunpowder, lead, blankets, mirrors, vermilion, pots and combs. There was so much noise in the village Cadwell could not sleep, nor could the others for his complaining.

Tiny Little had warned them to be at home the next night. They were sitting by their fire eating a stew when the bald giant entered and announced, "I have a distinguished visitor for you."

Tanacharison was about fifty and rather stout for an Indian. His face bore no expression, but his eyes were those of a man used to being deferred to by members of his own race and listened to with respect by all men. He accepted their greetings and, wrapping a new red blanket closer about his shoulders, sat on the floor in front of the fire. Clasping his hands in front of his vast belly and hunching up his shoulders like an obsequious deacon, Tiny made a flowery speech of introduction, which he ended by explaining that Tanacharison understood English but preferred to express himself in his own tongue.

Through Little, the Half King asked several questions. Jason caught the aroma of rum when the Indian spoke, but there was no sign of intoxication in the shining black eyes. In the Indian manner, he listened to their replies patiently, not interrupting, only nodding to show that he understood.

"There you are, O Great Tanacharison," Tiny Little said. "I have told them of your vast influence, how your name is respected to the shores of Lake Erie and westward to the Miami River and beyond. I have assured them that if you but say the word, any Delaware village would open its arms to this good friend of Brother Onas so that he may build his school and preach his message. And I have told this young man that if anyone in the west can help him find his brother, it will be the great Seneca protector of the Lenni Lenape, Tanacharison."

Appearing to take no notice of all this flattery, Tanacharison spoke first to Haworth. When he was through, Little translated:

"He says he does not know what the Delaware need with your God. He cannot see what any Indian needs with him. They have their own Great Spirit and he loves the red man. He says see how abundantly he cares for them, yet they do not labor like oxen as do the white men. The white man goes about looking worried, for he does not trust his God as the Indians do their Great Spirit. As for teaching the Delawares to follow the ways of peace, there is no need for that. The Six Nations have made them a tribe of women. They do not take the warpath. They have no land to sell anymore. The Iroquois are their uncles and they look after them. The white man should not interfere

138

between the Iroquois and either the Delaware or the Shawanese."

Again Tanacharison spoke and Little translated.

"He says he can see that you are a man of good will. He has heard that you have great wealth and that to make yourself feel better you wish to share your goods with the Delaware. He says he cannot understand why you would want to do this, but that is your concern. It cannot do the Delaware any harm, he supposes. He says if you will give him a jug of rum he will give you a string of wampum to present as a sign that you have his blessings."

Haworth seemed confused. "Rum? I do not deal in rum."

"Shut up," Cadwell muttered. "I'll sell you a jugful."

Tiny Little pressed on before Haworth could say more. "O Great Tanacharison, our friend from Philadelphia is so overcome by your generosity that he can scarcely express his joy. You shall have your rum. It is little enough to ask for your support in this undertaking."

Tanacharison turned his gaze upon Jason. He spoke in English.

"You are the man who fought the Long Knife?"

"Y-yes sir."

"This is the dog who overcame the Long Knife?"

"Y-yes sir. His name is L-Logan. I raised him from a pup."

Tanacharison smiled. "You seek your brother?"

"Yes sir. He w-was t-t-taken away many y-years ago."

"By Meskikokant?"

"Yes."

"A tall Delaware with no nose?"

"That is correct."

Tanacharison frowned and when he spoke it was in Seneca.

"He says he has heard of Meskikokant and knows that he is a very bad man. He has heard that he has been taken in by the Ottawas and the French. He wants to know if you intend to kill him."

"N-no. I just want to take back my brother. We h-heard three years ago he had been s-s-seen in Kuskusky."

Resuming his English, Tanacharison asked other questions and when he was through spoke rapidly in Seneca to Little.

"He will inquire of his Senecas what they may know about your brother. And he will instruct them to spread the word throughout the west that you wish to take him back to the Susquehanna. Now he wants his rum."

Before the Quaker could protest, Cadwell carried a jug to his cache and filled it from one of his kegs.

"Here, O Tanacharison, is your rum, courtesy of our pious friend from Philadelphia."

The Half King took the jug and left without saying more. Haworth sat in front of the fire with a look of distress on his face.

"There you are, Ephraim. You have what you wanted from him," Cadwell said.

"Rum. He only wanted rum."

"So he did, and he got it."

"And he thinks I have come out here to benefit myself in some way. To make myself feel better."

"Well, haven't you? The Delaware haven't invited you."

"I am aghast. To think that I must use rum to accomplish God's purpose. I am speechless."

Cadwell snorted. "That would be a welcome change."

"What dost thee mean?"

Cadwell hurled his clay bowl into the fire. "For three weeks I have been listening to you prate about serving the God damned Indians. Now you get the blessing of the most influential Indian in the west and you quibble because he doesn't take you seriously and because it cost you a jug of rum. What's the matter? Afraid I'll charge you too much for it?"

"Now, Mister Cadwell, that's not fair," Jason said.

"Not fair? Look, McGee, you haven't been shut up in this miserable cabin with him. You have been roaming about the country. You have not grown as weary as I of the sound of his self-righteous voice."

Seeing that Haworth's eyes brimmed with tears, Jason said, "He doesn't mean it, Mister Haworth. He's just got raw nerves from being sick and confined here. As for the rum, let me pay for that. I have wages coming from Kelly."

The Quaker smiled. "That is kind of thee, Jason. Thee is a good-hearted young man. I will speak no more of the rum. It was just that I was shocked that a man of authority would sell his favors for rum."

"Look at the bright side. You don't like strong drink. We'll have just that much less to carry to our wintering place."

During this conversation, Cadwell had sat with folded arms, glaring into the fire.

"And don't let Mister Cadwell's hard words bother you. He didn't mean them, I am sure."

As embarrassed as if he had stumbled into a bitter family row, Tiny joined in with, "Sure. Christopher meant no harm. Why, you nursed him as faithful and tender as if he had been a sick child. He'd be dead and buried now if it weren't for you, Mister Haworth. Just take his outburst as a sign he is getting well. He is beginning to act like his usual bastardly self."

Haworth's face regained its customary calm. "Make no apologies for Christopher. It is all right. I forgive him."

"I never asked for your God damned forgiveness," Cadwell finally said. "Now that the two of you have got what you wanted from the Half King, and now that I am very nearly as good as ever, we should be thinking of moving on to Kuskusky."

10

They remained at Logstown for another week and during that time Cadwell walked farther each day, finally taking his smoothbore and accompanying Jason and Logan up into the hills overlooking the village.

They stopped at the crest so that Cadwell could catch his breath.

"It is good to be outside. I feel alive again. For a while there I reckon I looked like a goner."

"You sure did. Do you know I couldn't find a pulse and it appeared you had stopped breathing?"

Cadwell sat down on a fallen tree trunk. "Maybe I was dead. Maybe I did come back from the beyond. I couldn't say this to Ephraim. Right away he'd be after me with his Bible and his prayers. But, Jason, it was like I was walking down a narrow path with darkness all around me and at the end of the path a brilliant light that drew me toward it. As I got near to that light, there stood Susannah, her face all shining, and she held up her hand as I drew near. She told me I must go back, but that she would be there waiting for me later."

The trader looked at Jason for signs of scorn or disbelief, and seeing none, continued. "Then she and the light faded and the bushes on either side of the path closed in, covering my face, and I thought somebody was trying to smother me."

"That must have been when you threw back the blanket."

"I suppose so. I could hear talk of burying me."

"Yes, and this would have been the place, right up here. We thought you would enjoy the view out over the river."

"That was thoughtful of you, but I reckon I ain't ready for the grave yet. Look now, Jason, don't you never repeat what I just told you."

Jason hoped that the young squaw who had been so forward with him would not be at her lodge when they passed, but there she was with the old woman.

"Mocquasaka, you come see me this time?"

Cadwell stopped and chatted with the woman in Delaware. He grinned as he told Jason, "She says she fancies red hair. That's what Mocquasaka means. Says she has been dreaming every night that you come into her lodge."

"Aw, there you go teasing me again. I ain't interested in no squaw." Jason turned and walked away to hide his embarrassment.

The trader followed him. "Don't know what you're missing, lad."

Tiny Little hailed them from the porch of the large Croghan store-house where he had his headquarters.

"Hold up there. Tanacharison wants to see McGee. I am to take you to him."

They found the Half King sitting on a bearskin before a fire, smoking his pipe in a lodge that smelled richly of Indian odors. Two plump squaws hovered about him. On the walls hung strings of wampum, a rusty smoothbore musket, furs, and pots and pans.

He motioned for them to sit.

Little translated. "He has made inquiries. His braves tell him they heard that a white youth with blue eyes has been seen with an Ottawa hunting party up near Lake Erie."

"Where exactly?"

"They are not sure. They heard it from some Senecas to the north."

"I heard that he was in Kuskusky three years ago."

Tanacharison spoke rapidly.

"In that case he says you should go first to Kuskusky and tell them Tanacharison sends his greetings and instructs them to give you assistance. However, he warns you not to go into French or Ottawa territory without a Seneca accompanying you. It is not safe."

Tanacharison spoke to him again, this time smiling.

"He says your yellow dog cannot protect you from Meskikokant or the Ottawas."

Haworth was elated when he heard that Tanacharison had given this report and when he saw that Cadwell was strong enough to travel again.

"Oh, can we press on, then?"

"Nothing to stop us. I may not be able to hit my old stride right off, but we will leave in the morning if you like."

"Ah, Christopher," said Little. "We shall miss you. Look ahere, let us have a send-off party tonight. Come on to Kelly's blacksmith shop and we'll have a grand time. Maybe a few squaws there, who knows?"

142

Haworth frowned. "Christopher should get a good night's sleep. We all should."

"You can stay here if you like, but I'll be at Kelly's tonight," Cadwell said. "You too, Jason?"

"I reckon so. For a little while anyway."

11

After a supper prepared and served by a disapproving Haworth, Jason and Cadwell picked their way around mud puddles to the smithy, where Kelly had moved tools and equipment back against the log walls and had his forge well fired up for warmth against the cold night.

Tiny Little, MacDonald and Levy were already there. Several other traders soon came in, some of whom they had got to know during the past month and others who had only recently returned west from the Carlisle conference.

They began by drinking cider and talking politics. Generally they were full of complaints about the inaction of the Quaker-dominated Pennsylvania Assembly.

"I say, 'Thank God for the Virginians,'" one trader declared. "I don't want them settling out here any more than anyone else, but at least they are supposed to be sending a force up this winter to build a fort."

Levy, scowling and looking doubtful, said, "This talk of Virginian intervention is all well and good, but it is only talk so far. I must decide soon whether to haul my company's goods back across the mountains, out of danger."

"What will ye do with them there?" MacDonald asked sarcastically. "Sell them to settlers' wives at half price?"

"Enough of this dismal talk," Tiny Little said. "Our dear friend Christopher Cadwell, Saint Christopher the resurrected, will be leaving us tomorrow to go and risk his scalp to the north—he and this red-headed rapscallion who calls himself Jason McGee. And we shall miss them. We must not send them away cheerless. Who has the rum?"

Out came a jug and the twenty-odd guests made quick work of it.

While they were pulling at the jug, Little left the smithy, to return

143

shortly with four Indian women, who appeared well known to most of the men, judging from their raucous greetings. They were sturdily built females with an eloquent vocabulary of obscene gestures which set the crowd to laughing.

"Here are the women, Christopher. Where is yer jew's-harp?"

Cadwell began twanging away at the instrument. Within a minute or two he had them stamping their feet, and in another, the squaws had been positioned about the smithy floor and there were four lines of men clamoring to dance with them. At the close of the dance, Jason took a second swig of rum. He had barely stopped gagging when Cadwell struck up a new tune and the largest of the squaws seized him, nearly sweeping him from his feet. With the assemblage clapping their hands, he went through a clumsy dance and was relieved when Mac-Donald cut in to show the group "how a proper Scot can dance."

Two of the rougher sort of traders fell into a fistfight over whose turn it was to dance with the most attractive of the squaws, and Tiny Little rushed over to slap them apart and threaten them with a dunking in the Ohio River if they committed another such breach of etiquette at his leave-taking party for his dear friend Christopher Cadwell. When one of them told him to go to hell, he would dance and fight with whomever he please, Little offered to "cut off your balls and stuff them in your disrespectful mouth" and MacDonald stepped forward to offer his knife. At this, the two combatants fell into a sullen truce.

The noise of the merrymaking drew fresh, uninvited faces to the doors and windows of the smithy. Both Indians and whites began dancing and singing out on the hard-packed space around the smithy, where there was no Tiny Little to enforce standards of decorum.

After his third or fourth dram of rum, he forgot which, Jason found himself standing in front of the forge with MacDonald, the two of them with their arms about each other's shoulders and bawling out all twenty-four verses of "Barbara Allen."

Tears were shed by a few in the audience within the smithy, but outside there were many rude noises and insulting remarks made against the Celtic race. Suddenly MacDonald loosened his embrace of Jason and hurled himself through the open doorway and into the rabble outside, with fists flailing.

Tiny Little had to go outside and rescue MacDonald, and in the process, he may have swung his own great hammy fists too zealously, and that most likely did create fresh animosity among the already resentful outsiders, who had been denied entrance to the party. At any rate, it was not long after Little came back in with a bruised but still pugnacious MacDonald, and with his own knuckles considerably scraped, that someone on the outside lit fire to the straw accumulated on the windowless side of the smithy. The party and dance were going full tilt again when Kelly, already beginning to wish he had not agreed to host the occasion, smelled smoke and saw flames inside the roof. He began screaming at his guests, some of whom had passed out in the corner. There was a general commotion first to save themselves by trying to cram through the doorway all at once, and then there ensued a smaller rush, to return and bring out the unconscious, and finally, and too late, an attempt to save Kelly's smithy from the fire.

There were enough willing if drunken hands, but the buckets were too few, the river too far away, the structure too combustible and the fire too advanced. In a few minutes half the building was in flames, illuminating the entire village. A great social and business institution of Logstown was beyond saving.

Jason stood back, watching the flames. The rum had dulled his normal feelings of self-consciousness. The knowledge that he had been the life of the party filled him with tremendous cheerfulness. And in a way that he could not understand, the sight of the fire produced a new level of excitement in him.

He was watching how the flames lit up the scores of white and red faces, his emotions already in a pleasurable turmoil, when someone took his hand and said quietly, "Mocquasaka. Now you come with me?"

12

This time as he entered the little squaw's lodge, the odor of bear's fat did not affect Jason. The sound of snoring from a corner told him the old woman was asleep.

Beyond greeting him, the little squaw had not spoken, and he stood awkwardly, facing her in front of a barely glowing fire, not knowing quite what was expected of him and half wishing he were back in his own cabin. But her hands were quick and skillful. It took her but a few seconds to loosen his belt and guide him in shedding his trousers, and only a few more to draw him down to her bed of hemlock boughs and to pull a buffalo robe over them.

Jason marveled at her tiny body with its delicate bones and small, pointed breasts, so unlike Sallie's full figure. The rum and her closeness made his brain reel. He tried to convince himself that he was not in bed with an Indian woman, that she did not reek of bear's fat, and that she had a clean, fresh-scrubbed Lancaster County smell. Her hair was not coarse and black as a crow's feathers; it was a corn-silk blond. And she was not a frontier demi-prostitute but rather the daughter of an honest German blacksmith.

"My darling," he murmured as he felt himself quivering almost out of control.

She guided him into her and suddenly Jason felt like a godling, full of power and grace. When he was done, she would not release him, but held him in place while she murmured and caressed his back.

He recovered as only a nineteen-year-old could, and this time— a lingering time of confident ecstasy—her writhing caused him no alarm. Nor did her sharp cry, as if she were in pain.

Jason fell into a sleep deeper than he had ever known. He awoke shortly before dawn and lay there, his head still befuddled by the rum, trying to remember who he was and where. The little squaw lay against him, one frail arm across his chest. The old woman groaned in her sleep, broke wind loudly and thrashed about in her corner.

Jason's stomach was queasy and the stench in the lodge suddenly became more than he could endure. He separated himself from the squaw's childlike body and arose, shivering, to draw on his trousers.

"Mocquasaka," she called to him as he slipped out the doorway, but he did not reply.

His stomach churning, he ran to a large tree whose shape loomed against the sky, leaned his head against its trunk and threw up the rum and, with it, Haworth's supper. Then he went back to his own cabin, where he was greeted so enthusiastically by Logan that he had to shush the dog lest he awaken Cadwell and Haworth.

13

Haworth awoke early that morning, brimming with a good cheer that Cadwell and Jason found hateful, to prepare them a bracing breakfast. He was perplexed at their reluctance to arise and eat. Cadwell swore at him. Jason pleaded for a few moments more of sleep.

The Quaker stood over them like a determined parent, his hands on his hips. "You should not lie abed so. The sun is well up and we have a long way to go. I have prepared a delicious gruel and have even cooked venison. Now please rise up and let us make ready for our journey."

Jason, avoiding the Quaker's reproachful eyes, made his way shakily to the fire and sat before it, wrapped in his blanket, trying to sort out his recollections of the night before.

It was nearly noon before the increasingly frustrated Haworth was able to nag them into loading their horses and departing. Most of the men who had been at the party were still asleep, but Tiny and Levy did rouse themselves to say goodbye and walk with them as far as the ruins of Kelly's blacksmith shop.

Kelly himself was standing beside the still-smoking rubble. Cadwell apologized for having been the innocent cause of the destruction of his shop.

"It's all right, Christopher," the Irishman said. "The business couldn't have gone on much longer anyway, not here at Logstown. If the French come in the spring, as everyone says, they'd close me down just as they did old John Fraser up at Venango. Maybe knock me in the head as well. And if the Virginians build their fort first, it won't be at Logstown anyway, which means I would have to move to the Forks of the Ohio or wherever to have a decent trade. When the ashes cool, I'll be able to salvage most of me stuff. Anyway, it was a great party now, was it not?"

Jason shook his hand and thanked him for employing him.

"Look ye, lad, once ye've found yer brother, come back out here and go into business with me. 'Kelly and McGee, Blacksmith Shop.' Can't ye see it? The Green and the Orange."

They left the smith, Tiny and Levy all laughing as they started north toward Kuskusky. There was no sign of the little squaw as they passed her lodge and Jason was not sure whether he was sorry or relieved.

The elation Jason had felt six weeks before, when he and his companions had departed Shippensburg, was missing as they set out this time. He was tired; the sky was ominously overcast, and his mind kept running back to the party, the fire and the little squaw.

Cadwell, too, looked tired, and he spoke little. Only Haworth and Logan seemed eager for this journey. The Quaker, clad in new moccasins, walked with a full stride, his broad shoulders well back and his earnest face lifted. He offered several times to take the lead, but

147

Cadwell refused to relinquish that spot and their progress accordingly was slow, although the path they followed along the riverbank was smooth.

The trader called a halt at the mouth of Beaver Creek before dark and they appropriated a shed near the trading post. Snow began falling as they built their fire. By the time they had cooked strips of venison, the ground was covered.

Jason could hardly wait to wrap himself in his blankets and draw Logan close for warmth. They had made only ten miles that day, but every step of the way he had been yearning to sleep. Now, out here in the open on the bank of the Ohio, with the snow falling, he recalled not the squalor and fetid atmosphere of the little squaw's lodge, but the wonder of her fragile body. It stirred him to think of holding her in the dark. How pleasant it would be to go back to Logstown to possess her again. To hell with what Haworth would think or how Cadwell would mock him. He suppressed the chilling thought of Sallie Koch's possible reaction and went to sleep reliving what he could remember of the previous night.

The next morning, the snow lay ankle deep on the ground and still it fell. They had to take Cadwell's word for it that on a clear day one could see ahead to the place where the Ohio's mighty current turned to flow west. And they took Cadwell's word that he could find their way to Kuskusky blindfolded if only they would stop questioning his judgment.

"A little snow never hurt anybody. It's only twenty miles and if we stop jawing and get moving, we'll be there by dark."

They did not reach Kuskusky by dark, however. They waited nearly an hour before the operator of the trading post ferried them and their goods over Beaver Creek.

The snow slacked off by noon, but it lay deep enough to make walking laborious. They found a bare spot under an enormous hemlock, where they spent the night, without a fire, cold and miserable.

They set out again at dawn, but had gone only a little way before it began to snow again, so heavily now that it blotted out their view. Jason did not know how Cadwell could possibly recognize any landmarks in such weather, but he was afraid to question him. Even Logan was beginning to have difficulty walking. The horses plodded along with lowered heads as if resigned to their misery. When Haworth asked how much longer before they arrived at Kuskusky, Cadwell swore at him and told him to mind his own business.

They did not reach the settlement that second night either, and the trader admitted that they might have made a wrong turning several miles back. "Not to worry, though," he said. "All trails hereabouts lead to Kuskusky."

The snow turned into a freezing rain during a night they spent on evergreen branches atop the snow. Toward morning the temperature dropped and a bitter wind came up. By morning the snow was covered with a slick glaze. As they ate the last of their rations for breakfast, Cadwell assured them they would have a marvelous feast prepared by lovely Indian maidens that afternoon. "See, the sun is out now. It can't be much farther."

At first Jason welcomed the clearing skies, but after a morning of slow progress, the glare on the snow became a torture to his eyes. They stopped to rest at noon, and the horses, whinnying in their hunger, desperately chewed on pine needles.

"I can't understand this," Cadwell said. "We should have seen some signs of Kuskusky by now."

"We are lost, aren't we, Christopher?" Haworth said as he looked at Cadwell closely. "Thee must tell us the truth."

The trader's face sagged with fatigue. "Yes, damn it to hell. We are lost. Are you satisfied? I just don't know which way to head now. This damned snow makes everything look different. And my eyes hurt. I can't bear the glare."

"Me neither," said Jason. "I can hardly see anymore."

"Christopher, 'tis plain that thee is near exhaustion," Haworth said. "Why not allow me to break the trail while thee walks behind with my horse?"

To Jason's surprise, the trader agreed. So they set off again, the Quaker leading Cadwell's pony while the trader stumbled along, clinging to the horse for support, and Jason walked in the rear with his eyes shut against the glare, holding to the tail of his mare. Logan followed Jason, keeping his paws in the tracks of the men and the horses.

In midafternoon they halted, too tired to go farther. Cadwell sat down in the snow and put his hands over his face. "This is terrible. Never been in such a fix. We're going to kill our horses, driving them through this stuff. They can't go on. I can't go on."

"Nonsense," the Quaker said. "We cannot give up. Too much depends on us."

"Nothing depends on me," Cadwell replied. "Nobody needs me. I should have died back there in Logstown anyway. Oh, God, I am weary. Let me sleep."

"Nay. I have heard that it is dangerous to give in to sleep when one is so cold and hungry. We would freeze."

"What can we do?" Jason asked. "We can't build a fire in this stuff. We can't hunt. I'm tired too, Mister Haworth. Can't we rest until tomorrow morning?"

"No; we must go forward."

"But you don't know where you are going. You are only making us more lost by moving on."

"We will lose more than our bearings if we halt. We must not sleep in this cold. We must move."

The Quaker's will seemed to grow as that of his companions lagged, and he led them forward again slowly into the night under a bright half moon that turned the snow-laden trees into strange and threatening shapes. The wind died down, but the cold intensified.

Haworth talked to them, urging them to keep up their spirits, until Jason came to hate the sound of his voice. Once when Cadwell stopped and sat down in the snow, Haworth spoke to him as to a recalcitrant child, scolding him for his lack of will until the trader lost his temper and cursed him. But he did get up and they kept moving.

At times Jason fell asleep on his feet, clutching the mare's tail and dreaming first that he was following his father and his old horse over the Kittatinny Mountain to Harris's Ferry to report his mother's massacre, and then that he and Sallie, now man and wife, were on the trail west to take up a homestead.

They were passing a cleared area when a pack of wolves began howling off to their right, and soon another pack could be heard ahead, in a new patch of woods. Logan growled and drew closer to Jason. Again Cadwell sat down, and Haworth came back and hauled him to his feet, then tied one arm to his horse's packsaddle, ignoring the trader's uttered curses.

"With wolves about, we dare not stop, Jason. Thee must help me keep us moving. Do not despair. The Almighty will see us through."

"All the same, should I not have my rifle primed and ready?"

"That would be prudent. And I think I best should be prepared with Christopher's pistol."

The voices of the wolves came closer, continuing to taunt them until Logan began to bark in return. Haworth halted as the howls came closer. "There, Jason, I can see them moving. Stand ready with thy rifle. I shall fire this pistol."

Holding the weapon as far away as he could, with both hands, the Quaker shut his eyes and pulled the trigger. The howling stopped at the report of the pistol and they pressed on. At last the sky reddened, and a new dawn broke over the frozen, glistening landscape. As they passed into a ravine with rocks all around them, Cadwell gave a moan and collapsed, hanging by his arm. The horse, too weary to drag him, halted.

They went to the trader. His eyes were closed and he was muttering. "Susannah. I will join you. Don't leave me this time. Don't make me go back."

"Can't we rest now that the sun is up?" Jason asked. "I may be able to build a fire here where there is some protection."

They untied the trader's arm and sat him against a rock with his blanket wrapped around him. Without consulting Haworth, Jason drew off a cup of rum and poured half of it down Cadwell's throat, then drank the rest himself.

"We must pray," Haworth said. "We must thank the Almighty for bringing us through that awful night and we must ask him to send us succor."

He lowered himself to his knees, motioning to Jason to do the same. As they knelt, Jason heard a familiar rustle and looked up to see the flash of a squirrel's tail high up in the crotch of a hickory tree. Very quickly, without disturbing the Quaker's prayer, he arose and took up his rifle, resting it on the back of the little mare and waiting for the squirrel to stop flitting about.

Haworth, still unaware of what Jason was doing, knelt with his hands clasped and his head bowed. Cadwell sprawled against the rock. The squirrel chattered as it moved behind the tree trunk and then reappeared. Now, sitting up on a limb, it was silhouetted against the sky.

Haworth was right, Jason thought as he lined up his sights. The Almighty did provide. He squeezed the trigger, the rifle cracked, and the horses shied as the noise echoed in the forest. The squirrel scampered to the end of the limb, unhurt, and leaped to another tree and disappeared.

"Jason. What is the matter?"

"Can't you see what is the matter? I missed an easy shot. Tell your stupid God that. We are going to die out here in this cold. We are going to die and all you can do is flop down on your knees."

"Jason, I am shocked. We cannot starve. We could slaughter my horse. We *were* in danger last night with the wolves about, but we are past that. Now pull thyself together and do not blaspheme."

Before Jason had time to retort, they heard the crack of first one and then another musket far away, followed by a faint "Halloo."

151

PART FOUR

From the Journal of Ephraim Haworth

ELEVENTH MONTH 17, 1753

God does guide those who do his bidding. Never again shall I doubt that. He has brought me and my two companions through the valley of the shadow of death to this new village of Delaware Indians. Christopher Cadwell says it was "just d——d luck," but I see it was the will of God, for we ourselves could not have found a better place to establish a mission. I will not dwell on the hardships we endured to get here, how closely we came to death from starvation or freezing, for I know now how the Almighty was with us at every step. . . .

We have been lying quietly here for three days, recovering from our ordeal. Poor Christopher is so weak he still cannot sit up and I fear he may lose the small toe of his left foot from frostbite. Jason complains of continuing numbness in his left hand but he, being young and strong, is up and around. Except for a frostbitten ear lobe and a lingering case of snow blindness, I am little the worse for wear. I would have written in my journal earlier, but only today have recovered my eyesight sufficiently to allow such close work.

This is a new village of seven lodges, established last year by several families of the so-called Wolf clan of the Delaware or Lenni Lenape Indians. They chose this spot because it lies on a sheltered southern slope near a dependable spring, and there is much game hereabouts.

Normally there would be about forty-five persons here, but eight or ten of the men are away hunting, leaving only three men above the age of eighteen or so. They are Woapink, a stout fellow of about forty who is handicapped by a clubfoot; Nanwaquepo, a young man not yet twenty, who appears half-witted; and old Tallema, a kind of chief, who is advanced in years and feeble, but is much respected.

There also is a woman, Menumheck, the widowed daughter of

Tallema, who seems to exercise authority over the members of the tribe. At any rate, she is a great talker, and the others obey her commands.

These people, whom some dare call savages, have shown us nothing but the kindest hospitality. Sadly lacking fresh meat because of the snows and the absence of their men, they have generously shared their store of corn with us. They have placed us in the long house in which burns their council fire and which serves them as a general place of meeting. Old Tallema sleeps here, attended by Menumheck and her daughter, Awilshahuak, who would be counted a brunette beauty were she taken to Philadelphia and properly dressed. Awilshahuak may be married in the spring to a brave from another tribe.

As far as I can ascertain, we are about a full day's march from Kuskusky. I judge that we turned away from the Beaver River in the snow and wandered to the west and eventually north of our destination.

The Almighty had his own destination for us. I am content.

ELEVENTH MONTH 25, 1753

Praise God! My prayers are answered. Christopher is nearly himself again, irascible and restless, although not yet strong enough to leave the council lodge. He will not lose his toe after all.

He was made well by yet another miracle, this time at the hand of Menumheck. Without warning she prepared a potion of herbs and mysterious juices which she practically forced upon him. Christopher spat and swore so that Jason and I could not help laughing, which made him all the more angry.

By afternoon he was able to walk about. Now that his strength and spirits are renewing, he says he intends to entertain our kind hosts with his sleight-of-hand feats. This location is ideal for his purposes as well as mine. Menumheck has told him that after their hunters have laid in a supply of meat they intend to get otter, beaver, wildcat and fox furs to sell in Logstown. Christopher sees a great opportunity to purchase these valuable pelts and haul them directly back east. I do not approve of this fur trade, for it encourages the Indians to hunt in an unnatural way, killing animals just to provide themselves with many useless and vain items. The direct sale of rum to the Indians is prohibited, of course, but who can enforce the rule out here so far from magistrates? I keep my silence on these subjects

156

for the present. Until my school is established, I shall be "as wise as a serpent and gentle as a dove."

Christopher is often bad tempered and he uses the most shocking language, but I can see beneath all his rough talk and harsh manner to an inner man of good will. His hard words do not offend me. He is an instrument of God's will as much as I.

As I write, some of the children are gathered to gaze on me with wonder, for they do not understand writing. I must stop and talk to them. That is the way to perfect my knowledge of their language, to become a child myself. Later I shall use what they have taught me as a tool to instruct them about God. They are such winsome children, much better behaved than our white offspring. They make me miss my own young ones back in Philadelphia. And Awilshahuak puts me much in mind of my own dear wife. By the bye, I have learned that Awilshahuak means "Always in Joy." The name doth suit her.

TALLEMA'S VILLAGE
TWELFTH MONTH 1, 1753

The extreme cold has alleviated. With only two rusty old fowling pieces for hunting and shut in by the extreme cold and so much snow, these poor Indians had eaten no fresh meat since their able-bodied men departed. That has changed through yet another miracle.

Jason and Christopher went out ahunting early this morning, taking the yellow dog with them. They returned, dragging a full-grown bear behind them. The people of the village are beside themselves with joy. Already they have skinned the animal and laid a great fire outside to roast the carcass.

Young Jason has become a hero here. The Indians marvel at the redness of his hair and they are impressed by the rifle he carries. Christopher says that Jason killed the bear with a single shot. They were restricted by the snow in their hunting and were beginning to despair when the dog, Logan, ranging ahead of them some distance, began barking. Apparently the bear had broken his long winter's nap to browse in the sunlight and Logan happened upon him. The bear was standing on his hind legs at a great distance, ready to attack Logan, when Jason fired.

Jason seems a different young man since we sojourned at Logstown. He was an extraordinarily quiet, even backward fellow when we met in Shippensburg. Now he bears himself with confidence. He

157

laughs and jokes with Christopher. He teases the Indian children, to their delight, and he even pays the women of the village compliments on their cooking. Awilshahuak beams upon him in a way that would be considered forward for a young affianced woman in Philadelphia. Of course, I am pleased to see him become more sure of himself, but I do pray that he will not allow his head to be turned by all this attention, first at Logstown and now out here. He does have a fine mind and a good heart. I do hope he will find his brother and that he will take him back to the Susquehanna.

Jason has told me of his feelings for the daughter of his former master back in Lancaster County. He is persuaded that they will be married once he has recovered his brother. I have counseled him that it is his own soul he must find and bring back to God, that one can become truly happy in no other way, but I fear he does not heed me. Also I have cautioned him that he must not submit to carnal instincts out here amongst a people who lack the moral restraints of true Christian folk.

Every day I learn more of the dialect of these Indians. My little teachers enjoy instructing me in the practical use of the language. I miscall the names of ordinary objects just to hear their merry laughter.

They now call me Wulilissu, which means "He is good." I love these gracious, simple people. The time nears when I shall discuss my school with old Tallema.

Our bear will soon be ready for the eating. I lay aside my pen for the feast.

TALLEMA'S VILLAGE
TWELFTH MONTH 5, 1753

My heart is heavy and my mind confused. How prone we are to count our chicks ere they hatch.

The night of our bear roast, fortune seemed to smile upon us. It began as such a joyous occasion. Everyone gorged himself on bear meat outside in the cold air and then crowded into the council lodge.

The Indians showed their appreciation for the bear meat by dancing and singing. Their women have a most graceful way of gliding around in a circle about the fire with arms held tightly beside them, turning this way and that and all the while chanting in singsong keys quite unfamiliar to my ears, but nonetheless appealing. As Christopher explained it, this was a special hunting celebration dance. Then they drew him and Jason into their circle and began to bow and chant, praising Jason the bear killer and finally raising their hands above their heads to thank their own spirits for providing them with food. Pagan festival that it was, I must say it was a stirring spectacle.

Christopher reciprocated by playing on his jew's -harp, after which Jason and I sang several songs. Finally Christopher performed various sleight-of-hand feats.

One of his favorite juggling tricks is to pretend to lose one of his balls and to accuse me of having taken it. Then he "finds" it in my hat. When first he did this, I was somewhat offended by being made the butt of a joke, but I have learned to enter into the good humor of the thing and now enjoy it as much as the spectators.

Our Indian benefactors were delighted. Normally old Tallema acts with great dignity, as becomes a village chief, but he laughed as loudly as any. Even Woapink, the rather sardonic clubfooted brave, was seen to smile.

Christopher concluded his program with a speech in which he thanked the villagers for their hospitality, told them of Jason's desire to find his brother, and of mine to build for them a school, and lastly but far from leastly, of how he stood prepared to save their braves a great deal of trouble in the spring by purchasing their furs right here on the spot. He went on at unseemly length, describing to them the objects our horses had borne into their midst.

We already owed our lives to these hospitable people, and it showed a lack of courtesy for him to run on at such length about a business matter in the midst of a celebration, but the Indians gave no sign of annoyance, listening attentively as they usually do. Old Tallema nodded several times as if in agreement.

Christopher would have been well advised to stop and hear what old Tallema had to say, but instead he went to his pile of trade goods and to my chagrin drew out a flask of his wicked rum, poured a cupful and presented it to the chief. The old man held up his hand and shook his head vigorously. Christopher then turned to Woapink, who accepted the cup and drained it down in two gulps. When he turned back toward Tallema, the old man had risen to his feet. He pointed to the doorway, speaking in a voice that cracked like a whip. In a matter of seconds, all the villagers except his daughter and grand-daughter had fled, leaving Jason, Christopher and me standing there.

Tallema turned to us without speaking and pointed to the door. His mouth was hard and I saw that it was not a time to apologize for Christopher's faux pas. We gathered up Christopher's trade goods and left the lodge like whipped dogs. Yes, Tallema turned us out into

159

the snow at night. He hates the white man's rum that much.

Woapink, who loves rum as much as his chief abhors it, took us into his lodge with his wife and three children. We have been here for two days and there is barely room enough for us to stretch out to sleep. I would have protested when Christopher traded him rum for our lodgings, but had he not done so, we would have had to move on, and I am convinced that here is my place to do God's work, besides which the weather has turned so cold again that we would perish if we tried to leave.

Tallema refuses to allow us to enter his lodge to apologize. And Awilshahuak has given us to understand that the old man wishes us to depart his village as soon as the weather lets up. She says that if we refuse to do so, he will set his warriors upon us when they return.

Christopher is in a foul mood, all the fouler because he has no one to blame but himself. I cannot discuss the difficulty with him yet. And he dares not leave the lodge for long lest Woapink break into his rum.

Strong spirits? Nay, rather they should be called evil spirits. Satan does not need to stray from Hell to accomplish his purposes; rum does his work for him.

TALLEMA'S VILLAGE
TWELFTH MONTH 25, 1753

This is the day designated as the birthday of our Saviour. Although the Society of Friends does not celebrate it as do our Popish brethren, still I thank our Father in Heaven that He chose to reveal Himself to man in the person of His very own Son. Amen.

I give thanks as well that our difficulty over Christopher's rum appears to have been resolved, albeit not without much turmoil and expense. Yes, I am ashamed to confess that I was beginning to despair. Woapink sat about in a disgusting state, drunk from the rum with which Christopher had to ply him. The other villagers, fearing Tallema's wrath and Menumheck's sharp tongue, virtually shunned us, all except dear Awilshahuak. During Tallema's naps, she has been darting out to advise us of her grandfather's feelings.

With the return of milder weather, there was no excuse for us to remain and any day might see the return of the village's men. My very soul became weary of waiting, shut up in that little bark lodge with a drunkard and his wife and children, not to mention a companion who sulked like a thwarted child.

Thank the Almighty for Jason. What a splendid young man he is. I have been helping him with his penmanship and instructing him in arithmetic. He grasps things so quickly. I wonder at what he might have become by now had he been given *my* opportunities of education. His unfortunate stutter has become less troublesome since our sojourn at Logstown, bothering him only when he is embarrassed or tired.

Beyond his quickness of mind, he has demonstrated a knack for diplomacy. It was he who broke the impasse brought about by Christopher's thoughtless offer of rum to Tallema; he and Awilsha-huak. Without the two of them, we very likely would be on our way to Kuskusky, our opportunity at this place lost.

I was getting nowhere reasoning with Christopher about his rum. Every time I tried to discuss it, he would cut me off. During these episodes, Jason remained silent, but yesterday he asked me, in Christopher's presence, just how we Quakers settle our differences. I explained how we discuss the question calmly, openly, without rancor, always striving for agreement and avoiding the taking of a vote until the clerk of the session feels there is a sense of the meeting or consensus.

Then, in a sly way, Jason inquired how a Quaker meeting might approach our situation.

Christopher straightway began railing against the stubbornness of Tallema. He took great offense when I barely mentioned the fact that the laws of the province prohibit the sale of rum to Indians, saying heatedly that there is no law against treating anyone to a friendly drink to generate good feeling.

Jason suggested that there would be better feelings on Tallema's part had we left the rum in Logstown, at which Christopher called him an "empty-pated yearling" who did not understand how business is conducted with Indians. Trying as best he could to control his stammer in the face of Christopher's hard words, Jason pointed out that in our present case the rum, far from facilitating our business with these Indians, was hindering us. At this, Christopher declared, "By God, we will go to another place, where they do not have a d——d old fool for a chief."

Jason reminded him that if his purpose was to obtain the best furs without competition from other traders, he should hardly find a better place than this, and that his business would run smoother here if the rum was poured out.

Christopher flew into a rage. Woapink's wife, a fat and slovenly woman, sat holding an infant, her mouth open in surprise at the tone of his voice. He told poor Jason that he had paid several pounds for his supply of rum, and that he would not pour it out at the whim of a feeble-minded old Indian.

Jason held to his course. "But what if you were paid full value and more for the rum and at the same time were assured of getting first chance at the furs?" he asked.

By now Woapink had awakened from his drunken slumber and his baby had begun squalling. Christopher invited us to step out into the sunlight and there asked Jason what he was getting at. "Who would pay me and how much? How could I then be sure of getting back into the good graces of the old fool chief?"

Then did that clever lad turn to me and say, "I merely meant that all of us must make sacrifices if we are to attain our ends, do not you agree, Mister Haworth?"

To which remark, in all innocence, I assented, naturally. He pressed his point by saying, "Even though that sacrifice might be something precious to yourself?"

Again I agreed that this seemed reasonable.

"Your horse, for instance, Mister Haworth. How much did you pay for it?"

"That horse was born to my father's favorite mare and was given to me for my thirtieth birthday," I replied. "I raised it from a colt. It hath a value far beyond any monetary consideration."

That clever lad, standing there with the sunlight gleaming on his fiery red hair, might have been an angel.

"Yet," said he, "would you not give up even your horse if by doing so you could assure that Tallema would allow us all to stay and would assist you in building your school here?"

"If I were convinced that would accomplish my mission, that would hardly be too great a sacrifice, although I cannot see what such a feeble old man would want with a horse," I replied.

Christopher, who had been listening to this with a look of suspicion, said, "I would not allow Ephraim to give his horse to old Tallema or anyone else. I need him to haul my furs back."

Jason persisted. "But Mister Haworth has no real interest in your furs. Tallema would allow him to stay here without us if he were to give him his horse."

At this Christopher became angry again, reminding Jason that we had made a bargain with him for the use of our steeds and accusing the lad of trying to create a division among us. Jason denied this, and Christopher demanded that he come right out and say plainly what he was getting at.

"Why don't Mister Haworth give *you* his horse to keep and you pour out every drop of your rum right out where Tallema can see it?"

I must confess that this suggestion set poorly with me. I protested that the horse was almost like a member of my family, that I regretted having agreed to pay even for the small keg Christopher had given to the Seneca back at Loyalhanning and that it was presumptuous of him to propose that I sacrifice a prized animal to pay for a commodity I hated, all for the furtherance of trafficking in furs, of which I did not approve either.

I should not have said this, for it caused Christopher to flare up again, saying that neither of us would be here without him. It was all I could do not to remind him of how we cared for him when he was so grievously ill.

All this might appear humorous to one reading these lines, but it was not so for the three of us. It was especially painful for Jason. Stammering pitifully, he said that he might just proceed on his own with his dog and rifle, leaving us to stay and quarrel. He said he was tired of our working at cross purposes, that he would be better off in finding his brother without us.

This outburst shocked both Christopher and me, for each of us has become fond of Jason. I think of him as a younger brother and I suspect that Christopher sees in him what his son might have been.

Straightway I took Jason's hand, apologizing and asking him for his solution. He proposed that we summon Tallema and let him see us pouring out the rum. He then would have Awilshahuak let the chief know that I had sacrificed my horse because I hate rum as much as he. Then, with Tallema's permission, he and Christopher would build a strong log building to serve as my mission school and as a council lodge for the tribe.

"Look at it this way, Mister Haworth," he said. "You could say your horse is paying for Mister Cadwell's labor on the cabin, not for his rum."

At first Christopher grumbled about the amount of hard work required to erect a cabin in the dead of winter with only one ax and two hatchets among us, but after thinking it over, he agreed that Jason's suggestion did indeed make much sense. His resolve was strengthened when he entered Woapink's lodge, to find the miserable wretch trying to remove the bung from a rum keg.

Later Awilshahuak came over with a bowl of boiled squash, and we told her what we proposed. As she and Jason sat side by side, it struck me what attractive young people they are. Awilshahuak is

163

slender and graceful. Her hair, which she grooms with bear's fat, as do most Indian women, is gathered at the back of her well-shaped head with a leather thong and it hangs far down her back like the lustrous tail of a lovely mare. She has a pretty, oval face, lacking the prominent cheekbones of so many Indians. Her lips are full; she is quick to smile, revealing extraordinarily white, even teeth. Her eyes are a remarkable shade of dark brown, set in clear white. Truly she is a rare young woman, and as good and cheerful as she is beautiful. I know nothing of her fiancé except that he is called Hopiquon, or "He Is Broad-Shouldered." He is a most fortunate man.

Her mother, the dictatorial Menumheck, speaks to her in a softer manner than she employs with the other women. Her grandfather, Tallema, dotes on her. No one else could have persuaded the old man to come out of his lodge to hear our entreaties as did she. We waited for him in the cold, clear air, with Christopher's two kegs of rum sitting before us on the frozen ground. Led by Awilshahuak, he stood in front of us, as still as a marble statue and as dignified.

Christopher, much embarrassed and wearing a strangely fixed expression, spoke softly, apologizing to Tallema for offending him, saying he had not known of his objections to the drinking of rum in his village, adding that he did not like to carry rum and only did so because many chiefs, not as honest as Tallema, seemed to expect, even demand it of him. He cited the example of Tanacharison, obliquely mentioning that he had given us his blessings for our missions.

Tallema, standing with a buffalo robe wrapped around him and with Awilshahuak at his elbow, did not reply or change his stern expression as Christopher delivered this hypocritical and self-serving speech.

Christopher went on to say that, unlike most white traders, he never cheated Indians and regretted having to burden his horses with rum when he might carry in its place items of more real value for his Indian friends.

While Christopher spoke, the people of the village came out and stood in a semicircle, Woapink among them.

Christopher is not used to humbling himself before an Indian, but such is the bearing of Tallema and such is the extremity of our situation and, I suppose, so great is the attraction of my fine horse that he sacrificed his own dignity. In fact, as he warmed to his task, he became more eloquent, praising the Wolf people as the best of the Lenni Lenape clans and them the best of all Indians. He went on to praise the Indian race in general, pointing out that he chose to come and dwell among them in preference to his own people in the east. He said not a word about this being his last trip among them or of his intention to settle down as a tavernkeeper in Shippensburg with his paramour, Mrs. McGinty. Nay, butter would not have melted in his mouth. One might have thought him the missionary, and not myself.

Christopher thanked Tallema for saving us from starvation and freezing. He praised the old man for choosing so desirable a spot to locate his village. He congratulated the villagers for their good fortune in having so wise and good a chief.

Through all this fulsome speaking, Tallema did not change his expression, but simply stood with his arms folded across his chest. At last, when Christopher ran out of talk, Tallema raised his hand, signifying that he was ready to reply.

"You have many pretty words. Words cost nothing. Liars can speak them as well as honest men. Drunkards often speak better than sober men. Your words mean nothing to me. You say you do not give Indians enough rum to make them drunk, yet I see Woapink hardly able to stand. He looks as witless as poor Nanwaquepo. Who gave him so much rum if not you? Your actions give the lie to your smooth words. You are good at tricks. You make balls disappear. If my braves were here, I would make you disappear."

Christopher, much discomfited by this speech, turned to me and said, "Look, I will not pour out my rum if he intends to chase us off anyway. We will just move on to another place."

I held up my hand and haltingly said in Delaware, "He does not utter empty words, O wise Tallema. See."

With that I drew out my hatchet and struck it against the end of the larger of the two kegs, causing the stinking liquid to gush out onto the ground. Christopher glared at me, but he dared not interfere.

"There, Tallema. Thee sees we are sincere. Now thee will see my friend do the same with the other keg."

"D—— you," Christopher said. "Did you have to ruin the keg?"

He drew the bung from the other keg and Jason tilted it so that the rum poured forth.

"There, O great Tallema," Christopher said. "My rum that I paid twenty deerskins to purchase is no more. Please do not send us away."

Tallema would not look at him. Instead he said to me, "Come into my lodge."

Although I had some difficulty understanding the old chief at

165

first, it soon became plain to me that he was hungry for someone other than women and children to talk to. And the longer he spoke, the more I could make out his words.

We sat on either side of his lodge fire, with sweet Awilshahuak hovering about pretending to prepare supper. Tallema talked to me of many things and spoke with much bitterness of the so-called Walking Purchase of 1737, when the Indians were cheated of land they had not intended to sell. Now that most of the Lenni Lenape had given up residence in eastern Pennsylvania, he feels they should be granted a perpetual homeland out here, west of the Allegheny Ridge. He viewed with regret the way in which the Delawares have surrendered their sovereignty to the Iroquois. He said some of his younger braves resented the fact that their tribe had been denied the right to take the warpath. He said his father had met William Penn himself, and that he, Tallema, had grown up hearing praise for the famous Brother Onas and his fairness to the Indians. He regrets that later generations of white men have been different. He said he understands that I am of the same faith as Brother Onas and that he knows I have not come to buy furs or take up land or traffic in rum or debauch their women, but to teach the Indians. What did I have to teach his people? he asked.

Awilshahuak came to my rescue as I explained my plans, adding her smooth words to my awkward ones.

I told him of my love for the Father of all mankind and the Creator of this world. I told him my heart was sad when I thought how my people had cheated and misused the Lenni Lenape. I told him I felt it would help his people if they learned to read and write the white man's language so they could understand the treaties they agreed upon. I told him that they were God's children as much as the white man and that I thought it would make them happier if they claimed their right to the Father's love.

Tallema watched me closely as I said all this. When I finished, he spoke.

"You are right when you say the white man has cheated my people. We have been like trusting children. We have thought all white men as worthy as your Brother Onas. See where our trust has brought us. Perhaps you are right when you say we should learn to write words on paper and read from books. Yes, and do sums as I see your traders do. Or that might be bad. It might make us as crafty as your people. I think you are wrong when you try to teach the Indian your religion. We do not need it. Already we love the Great Spirit. We know we are his children. He loves us better than he does

166

his white children. See how well we live and with what little effort. Do you see Indians going about looking worried? Do you see us slaving away at the same tasks day after day? Do you hear us tell lies or see us steal from others? We run free in the Great Spirit's world. You white people carry your wisdom about in books and express it with your lips only; we Indians carry ours in our hearts and express it in our deeds. We do not go among your people to cheat them or render them drunk or take their women. Mark my words, Wulilissu"— how my heart leapt to hear him call me by that name—"someday we Lenni Lenape may cast off our women's skirts and go among your people again to take revenge for the wrongs you have done us. Nay, teach us no more of your empty words. Teach us with deeds. We do not need your religion or your school."

I was not sure what to say. I did not wish to argue with him and risk making him angry again. Yet having poured out Christopher's rum and pledged my horse, I could not accept his refusal as final.

Bless Awilshahuak for coming to my rescue.

"Grandfather," she said sweetly, "Wulilissu is not like other white men. Nor is the red-haired youth. They have not come only to teach us; they wish to learn about our ways. They wish you to teach them."

How adroitly she handled the old man!

"I could teach the white man much," he muttered.

"You could indeed. They would have to listen carefully. You could tell them of our legends. They would like to hear stories of your youth. You could teach them your religion."

The old man shook his head. "White men do not like to listen. They have no patience."

"These white men are different. They will listen. And they wish to build us a strong council house of logs."

"Like the cabins they build for themselves? Warm and strong?"

"With a fireplace and chimney and a wooden door and windows," I replied.

The old man pondered for a long time, his eyes shut. I thought he had fallen asleep. Awilshahuak held her fingers to her lips and smiled at me. At last he opened his eyes and said, "Will it have a roof with shingles?"

"Yes, O Tallema."

"And you will listen to my teachings?"

How joyously I replied, "I will listen, Tallema. I am eager to learn all thee has to teach."

"We shall see."

Glory be to the Father. I can say no more.

167

I take pen in hand on this last day of the year with more to write about than I have time, ink or paper to relate. I have spent the past six days being instructed by Tallema in the history and the religion of the Delawares in general, and the Wolf clan in particular; also their ways of marriage and governing themselves. He is a good and patient teacher, if at times tedious, as old men grow to be. It doth try my patience to remain silent when he speaks of pagan beliefs and expresses faith in imaginary spirits, yet I know that for me to contradict him would be to destroy his trust.

He does love the sound of his own voice. But he teaches me much. Perhaps someday I shall write a proper history of the Delaware people.

Christopher thinks all this is foolishness. He makes sardonic remarks about my time spent listening to an old man's endless talk. He may be envious that Tallema likes me so well. He dare not show his feelings too openly, however, lest he fall again into Tallema's disfavor.

Tallema now treats Christopher with mild disdain, largely ignoring him. He tolerates his presence, I suspect, partly because of his respect for my wishes and partly because he is opposed to his braves' traveling to Logstown to trade their furs. Through the presence of Christopher he hopes to offer them an alternative to returning to that pit of iniquity and greed.

Tallema treats Jason in a peculiar way. He has not spoken a dozen words to him in the several weeks we have been here. He does not meet Jason's gaze, and then stares at the lad when he thinks he will not be observed. During our early conversations he asked just why this slender young man with the flaming hair had come out here if he was neither a trader nor a missionary. When I told him, he became much agitated. I assume this is because Jason's mother and sister were slain by one of his own tribesmen. At any rate, he abruptly, almost rudely, changed the subject after I described the perpetrator of the crime as a giant with a missing nose, called Meskikokant, and inquired if he, Tallema, had any knowledge of his whereabouts or of the fate of Jason's brother, Isaac. He replied brusquely that he recalled some such talk of the incident many years ago when he dwelt to the east, then began speaking of other things. I judge he feels shame that a fellow Delaware would have committed such an atrocity.

I let him ramble as much as he likes. And I am learning so much. For instance, I had not appreciated the Indians' notions of family or kinship or marriage. Girls are expected to be married by age fourteen or fifteen, and boys two or three years later.

I asked him why, then, Awilshahuak, nearly sixteen, has waited so long. Apparently this question was too personal, for Tallema ignored it, instead telling me how the parents help in the selection of mates, although they do not dictate the choice.

There is no wedding ceremony beyond a formal exchange of gifts and yet most of their marriages endure to death, even though, if either husband or wife wishes, the relationship may be ended.

The women do most of the labor of gardening, making clothes, etc., but they are by no means slaves. In fact, Indians hold their women in honor, listening carefully to their advice both privately and in formal councils. And, curiously, they trace their lineage through their mothers rather than their fathers.

So it is that Indians feel a special closeness to the brothers of their mothers. Only they are called "uncle," a term of great respect. The brothers of their fathers are called "little father" and they call the sisters of both their mothers and fathers "little mother." Cousins are referred to as "stepbrother" or "stepsister." Thus when the Delawares speak of the Iroquois as their "uncles" it is a term of special respect.

The young Delaware braves usually marry outside their villages or even their own branch of their tribe, and take up residence with the families of their brides. They make up for this loss by the grooms their daughters marry. Thus when Awilshahuak marries, Tallema's village will gain yet another brave for hunting and trading.

A chief is not as powerful as I had thought. He leads by persuasion. He must hunt and fish to support his family, just as any other brave. Once he loses the respect of his people, his power is gone. And the older women of the village have much to say in the selection of chiefs.

The Indians have no laws as we understand them. They govern themselves through a set of commonly held beliefs handed down from generation to generation. The respect and good will of their families and tribesmen mean everything to them. But I fear it is true what Christopher said to me on the trail coming out here: Revenge *is* a most powerful motive among them. Several of Tallema's stories deal with the extravagant length to which some legendary Indians have gone to avenge wrongs done them or a member of their family. Otherwise I am discovering there is much Christopher does not know about these so-called savages.

I long to tell Tallema how wrong it is to repay evil with evil, but force myself to be quiet. I shall wait until I have their children under my instruction.

Yea, it is hard, too, to keep my silence when Tallema relates stories of how he thinks the earth was created and man came to live here. He thinks that once all men lived in the heavens as a kind of "sky people" until one day one of their women, who was pregnant, fell through a "hole in the sky" and landed on the back of a huge turtle swimming in a vast ocean. To this woman were born twin boys, one of her sons growing up to become a creator who gave life to plants and animals, and the other to become a destroyer of life. The two sons fought for domination and the life-giver won.

As for the formation of this earth, Tallema tells a far-fetched story of how a giant muskrat dove to the bottom of the great sea and brought up mud in his paws, which he piled upon the turtle's shell and which in time became the earth. He has rambled on at great length about other legends which I must remember for my book someday, but to get at the essence of his religion, these Indians feel that every object and every creature, indeed every substance, hath its own special spirit. Not just man, but everything hath a soul, it would seem. Besides these spirits on earth, they believe, there are eleven major spirits dwelling in as many heavens who control certain aspects of life below while the Great Spirit himself—their Supreme Being—resides in a Twelfth Heaven, whence he supervises the other eleven spirits.

These eleven spirits respectively have dominion over the four directions, the sun, moon, earth, water, fire, houses and, of all things, corn. They regard the Great Spirit somewhat as we Christians do our God, as a good and kindly father in heaven.

And the number 12 has special significance for them. I must, when I begin teaching here, make much of the fact that our Christ had twelve disciples.

When I walk through the forest, although I do so with adoration for God in my heart, I see trees and water and animals as that and nothing more. The Indian sees these same things, but he also feels each of them is a spirit in itself; they surround him and sustain him.

He trusts in his Great Spirit to supply his wants, yet he expects that life often will be an ordeal and accepts its hard knocks without complaint. He refuses to show fear, believing that after his life on this earth he will pass on to a state of everlasting existence, free of pain and sorrow. In his natural state, respecting the spirits of other living things, he disturbs nature as little as he can, taking only what he needs (at least, he did before the infiltration of the infernal fur traders). He shares what he has freely with family and visitor alike. The white man's idea of land ownership is repugnant to him. Tallema thinks a man might as well own the water and the air as land. I have taken pains to assure him that I agree with him on this point.

Nay, these people would be better Christians than many of us who call ourselves by that name if only they were not so unforgiving of their enemies; if only they were not so remorseless in seeking revenge, so tolerant of cruelty. I long to tell them of Jesus's teachings on this.

There is much more I could write about Tallema's instruction. Now I must set down my good news.

Tallema hath talked past bedtime night after night. This morning on awakening, he found that he had lost his voice from so much use of it. So it was that I, after commiserating with him in his predicament, found an opportunity to speak my piece. I told Tallema of a vivid dream I had last night. I told him that I dreamed that Christopher, Jason and I had worked very hard and that we had built a council lodge of logs for his village, far superior to their usual bark and pole affairs, and that in it I taught all his children, and such adults as wished to learn, how to read and write. I told him that I dreamed the fame of this school spread and other families built lodges nearby so their children also could learn, and that all these people paid homage to the great and good Tallema, the wise chief who had brought the white teachers here.

Christopher and Jason, who sat behind Tallema, on overhearing this made rude gestures, thinking to discomfit me, but they did not succeed. Tallema smiled and told me to go on.

So I told him what I have in fact been dreaming of in my heart. I told him that after the school is built I intend to return to Philadelphia and buy many books and much writing material. And that I might persuade my good wife and others to come out to assist. I told him, too, of my dream of writing a book about his people. It would be his story and it would carry his fame to the city of Brother Onas so that the white people would pay him honor as well as the red. He smiled again.

I told him that tomorrow begins a new year, as the white man counts time, and that there could not be a more propitious day on which to begin our building. At this, I drew out the string of wampum Tanacharison had given me at Logstown and gave it to him, as I related how the Half King thought it would be good to have a school out here. Old Tallema sat holding the wampum, his head bowed as if in prayer. When he raised his face, tears ran down his cheeks. He took my hand and managed a hoarse whisper. "Build your school, Wulilissu."

Praise our Victorious God. I greet the New Year with joy in my heart. My work is ready to go forward.

This is the First Day (or Sunday) of the First Month of the New Year. I write with difficulty because my hands are so blistered and torn from my unaccustomed labor. But Praise the Lord; we are begun.

During the past week we felled four hickory trees, trimmed them out and brought them down to our school site for foundation logs. I have never known such toilsome labor, handicapped as we are with only one ax and two hatchets, yet I dare not murmur. Christopher curses me for promising Tallema such a large, secure building. If I let him know of my weariness, it would encourage him and Jason to do less than their best.

It would have been easier to use pine or another soft wood. Hickory is like iron, and the logs are so heavy our poor weak horses can barely drag them to the site. Tallema is too feeble to assist us. He ordered Woapink and Nanwaquepo to help. Woapink is strong enough, but his heart is not in the work and his clubfoot prevents his getting about. Poor Nanwaquepo is eager to please the strange white men, but he cannot remember instructions. How I wish Christopher had brought along two more axes in place of his kegs of rum.

It is pleasant this day to sit before the council house fire, reading my Bible, jotting down these random thoughts, and chatting easily with Awilshahuak. I miss my own dear wife when I observe Awilshahuak going about her household tasks. I marvel at her grace of movement. Tallema has not yet fully recovered the use of his voice and he sleeps through much of the day. Jason and Christopher, with Logan, have gone ahunting, leaving me here to write and chat with Awilshahuak as she works on a deerskin tunic.

I must not come out here again without my wife. It is not good to be so long separated from her. My dreams disturb me. The memory of them the next morning is an embarrassment to me. When the mind and will sleepeth, what carnal instincts come forward. Now I better understand the debased behavior of fur traders too long away from their mates and without the restraints of religion.

Speaking of separations, the women of the village complain that their men have not yet returned from their hunting. They suppose that the recent snows have delayed them.

I wish that Tallema hated tobacco as much as he does rum. I think one reason he lost his voice is that while he talks hour upon hour, he keeps his long clay pipe going incessantly. I do not like having to breathe the fumes. Please, dear God, let me show no irritation at the old man's habits.

This morning, delighted that I was not working, he brought out his collection of wampum. I do not fully understand the value of these strings and bands of black and white bits of shells, arranged either to tell a story or to transmit a message. Several have intricate designs of people and animals. The more recent strings are made of tiny glass beads brought over from England, yet another evidence of the debasement of these people by the fur trade. Tallema uses his wampum as a Roman Catholic might his rosary beads, as an aid to his memory and almost as objects of reverence.

He is proud of the fact that other tribes call the Lenni Lenape their "grandfathers." He hath a remarkable memory for the legends and history of his people, taking special pleasure in harking back to the time some 150 years ago, before the then powerful Susquehannocks drove the Lenni Lenape eastward across the Delaware River. He enjoys, too, telling how the Iroquois destroyed the Susquehannocks in bloody battle a generation later, but indignantly refutes the story that the victorious Iroquois defeated the Lenni Lenape in the same way, insisting that they negotiated an agreement to give his people protection so as to allow them to continue their civilized ways as "women."

When he was a young man, he says, he made this reply to a Mingo brave who teasingly called him "woman." "If you think I am a woman, why do you not bring your wife and let her sleep in my lodge for a time? She can tell you whether I am a man or a woman quick enough."

He laughed at his joke, which I found disgusting.

The Delawares think one of their eleven lesser heavens is occupied by a Corn God. I have been much impressed by the many uses these people make of corn. Truly it is the staple of their lives. Their women spend much time growing it. It doth require little cultivation. And it is ideal for storage around the year.

Awilshahuak tells me there are twelve ways in which she has been taught to prepare the sacred grain.

What a clever young woman she is. She knows many games, which she plays with Jason in the evening. It is pleasing to hear their merry laughter. She teases Jason to see his face turn crimson and she grows angry when others refer to Jason as Nenachgallit, or "One Who Stammers." She calls him Mocquasaka, or "Red Hair." I cannot tell what Tallema thinks about the friendship that has grown between his granddaughter and Jason. He appears to ignore it.

Jason and Christopher have returned with a small deer. There is much rejoicing. I pray they will not want to celebrate with another feast. I long for my bed. Oh, that I might occupy it for this one night with my dear wife.

Again it is First Day and I may rest. We have made much progress in the past week. I am becoming hardened to the labor. Christopher has become caught up in the work, assuming its direction. He enjoys ordering Jason, Woapink and me about. He may be as dictatorial as he likes, as long as he gets the building up. The four walls now stand waist high. Good stout hickory, notched together so closely it will take but little clay to chink the cracks.

Tallema misses having me about during the day, so eager is he to talk. If I look up from writing, he will take that as his signal to speak and then I dare not interrupt him, lest he think I am like other white men.

This morning he talked at length about his youth. Soon after they begin to grow hair on their private parts and their voices deepen, their young men must endure what they call the "youth vigil." Each youth must go into the woods alone without food or blanket, to wait in solitude for the appearance of his special guardian spirit or "manito." The Great Spirit, it is believed, sends this manito to look over the boy for the rest of his life.

Tallema says that when he was about fourteen, without warning one morning, his father and mother berated him for acting like a child and ordered him from their lodge and village. They told him he no longer was welcome there.

Hurt and confused, he took refuge in the forest, to wander about without food except for berries and roots until he became so weak and disheartened that he sat down to die.

He lost track of the time until one night he was awakened by someone calling his name. A tall, robed figure, its face shining like the full moon, told him to fear not, that he would not die until he was an old man, that it had been sent by the Great Spirit himself to guide and protect him through his life. This was his manito. Then did Tallema fall into a trance, during which various animals came up to him and called him brother. Even the nearby trees whispered his name and wished him well.

Tears ran down the old man's cheeks as he told me of his joy when suddenly he saw how he fitted into nature and was supported by it. He says he slept and again was awakened by his manito, who told him that one day he, Tallema, would lead his people toward the setting sun, far beyond the reach of the white man, and there would establish a new and different settlement.

He slept again and was awakened by his own father, who gave him meat and drink and who, after apologizing for driving him away, led him gently home to his mother. Thereafter he was treated and acted like a man.

Tallema says the things I said to him about attracting new families with my school reminded him of what his manito had said to him so long ago. He said it was this and this alone that persuaded him to allow me to build our school; that through it he might attract other tribesmen here where, also, they could learn skills that would help them preserve themselves. He had despaired of fulfilling his manito's prophecy until then. Now he wonders if I might be his manito returned in disguise.

I was touched by these remarks, paganistic though they were; then in the next breath Tallema suggested something that shocked and disgusted me. He said he felt sad that so young and robust a man as I should go so long without a woman. There is a youngish widow in the village named Wecolis, or "Whippoorwill." Her husband died two years ago, leaving her with two small children. She is a pleasant-faced woman, somewhat too heavy. She needs a man, Tallema said. Why did I not dwell with her during my sojourn here?

I know he means this kindly. Yet it upset me so that I went outside, saying it was to answer a call of nature, but in fact to collect myself. What a dreadful thing to say to me. There is much to teach these people when it comes my turn to do the instructing. Oh, let my school be built quickly so that I may return to my family.

TALLEMA'S VILLAGE
FIRST MONTH 20, 1754

Again it is First Day and my soul is deep in turmoil.

First, I must say that the erection of our school cabin goes well. All four walls are up and we expect to place the ridgepoles tomorrow and soon thereafter to split shingles and build a chimney. I cannot complain of our progress.

No, it is the shameful behavior of Christopher that has upset me. I made the mistake of telling him of Tallema's suggestion that I

175

cohabit with Wecolis and of my shock at the thought. He laughed, which angered me, I must confess. Yet did I swallow my anger, for without Christopher I cannot finish the cabin.

Later I observed him talking with Wecolis and the next day he moved his blankets to her lodge. When I remonstrated with him, he told me to go to h——l and said other insulting things which I shall not honor by recording. Then did I go to Tallema to apologize for the behavior of my traveling companion. Tallema shrugged and said, "Wecolis is lonely. She needs a man. Memhalamund [for that is what they call Christopher] is only a white man and not so young, but he is better than no man at all." Then he looked at me with a smile. "What is this to you, Wulilissu? I offered her to you and you did not accept. Let Memhalamund enjoy her. It will keep him away from the women whose husbands would be jealous if they returned to find their wives with a white man."

So I must accept, or at least ignore, a scandalous matter. I suppose I should have expected such behavior from Christopher, yet had I hoped that I might, through example if not persuasion, help him become a Godly man.

I think Tallema looks upon my school as a doctor might a vaccination against the pox. He thinks that with some education, his people will be able to protect themselves against further harassment by the white race. So we are allies, this wise but vain old man and I. It is amusing when he walks out to see our work on the school. He stands there in his buffalo robe, leaning on Awilshahuak's arm, as though he were a Roman emperor watching a temple of stone going up. He and I rely on each other to realize our dreams, much as Christopher, Jason and I need each other.

Fearful lest he follow Christopher's example, I have spoken to Jason about avoiding involvement with Indian women. Jason says he never could love any woman other than the daughter of his former master. He seemed hurt that I suggested he might do as Christopher did, adding that Awilshahuak was like a sister to him. I had not mentioned her name, but anyway apologized for my remark.

I am baffled by the effect of self-interest. When my horse was my own, Christopher regarded him only as a means of carrying goods out here and furs back. He did not care whether the animal was groomed or well fed. Now that my horse is to be his, he has taken to wiping his coat and cleaning his hoofs. He even gathers dried grass and rushes for the animal. I overheard him telling Jason that he looks forward to returning to Shippensburg and buying himself a broadcloth coat and fine boots. He wants to ride my horse over to Lancaster to show himself off as a gentleman to the suppliers there who have treated him with little respect. He said he might seek the post of magistrate in Cumberland County as well. And this is the same man who sleeps with an Indian woman here and a tavernkeeping bawd in Shippensburg.

Perhaps I expect too much from human beings. I must rest my mind and body for next week's labors.

TALLEMA'S VILLAGE
FIRST MONTH 27, 1754

Another week passed and another week of progress on our school building. My admiration for these people increases as I learn more and more of their ways.

I have noticed that they do not strike their children or shout at them. Yesterday I witnessed how they achieve discipline. One of my little future students, a lad of eight or nine, flew into a tantrum because his mother would not allow him to take a mirror from his younger sister. She brought him under her control by dashing a gourdful of water into his face. Then, when he was quiet, she spoke softly, telling him that he made her feel ashamed to behave so.

Tallema tells me that is the Indian way. They think whites who beat their children are brutal. "Children behave as they see their elders behave," he said. "They must learn never to lose their tempers over matters of little importance. Otherwise they will destroy themselves."

My wife will be glad to hear of this method of discipline.

TALLEMA'S VILLAGE
SECOND MONTH 3, 1754

Our work continues to go well. If the weather permits, we may complete our task in another week. All the people of the village appear elated by our progress.

Even the sharp-tongued Menumheck gives her approval. Hitherto she has remained aloof toward us. Perhaps it is because she scorns all males except her father. I had thought her to be a widow, but from scraps of comments have learned that her husband abandoned both her and Awilshahuak some ten years ago, and she bears him great hatred for doing so. (Perhaps that explains why the daughter

177

has been slower than most Indian maidens to marry, despite her extraordinary beauty. Were I an Indian brave, certainly she would no longer go unmarried. I should not say such things. It is unworthy of me even to think them.) Not only is this formidable woman showing an interest in our school building; she has begun to talk to me in those few portions of my free time when her father is not commanding my attention. And she appears most curious in a guarded way about Jason, perhaps because she can see that Awilshahuak likes the lad.

TALLEMA'S VILLAGE
SECOND MONTH 10, 1754

All praise to our Heavenly Father. Our cabin is completed. The work went splendidly last week, with good weather smiling down upon our efforts. Christopher and I, with Woapink's help, split out long slats of cedar and with them made an acceptable roof, while Jason with Nanwaquepo hauled up stones from the creek nearby and laid a crude but serviceable fireplace and chimney. It was backbreaking labor for us all, but it is completed. Tonight, having rested from our toil, we shall dedicate the structure with dancing and singing; this at Tallema's insistence.

Meanwhile I sit in the cabin alone, cross-legged upon the earthen floor in the Indian manner, trying to visualize what it will be like in a few months when we have chinked the cracks properly and when we have bladders or shaved horns in the open window spaces. Yes, and a properly hinged wooden door where two sewn deerskins now hang.

Did the men who devoted their lives to constructing the great cathedrals of Europe feel any greater elation upon the completion of their work than I now that my rude cabin is so nearly finished?

I only hope that I can persuade Christopher and Jason to continue working. I would like to split several logs and fashion them into benches. Christopher says Indians don't like benches, and besides, he would require iron wedges, heavy hammers, saws and augers to do such work. I think he would change his mind if I were to offer him the fine riding saddle now stored at Mrs. McGinty's in Shippensburg. Jason thinks he can find some wedge-shaped hard stones capable of splitting the logs. He and Awilshahuak are out looking for such material now. As for Christopher, he lies abed with Wecolis, I suppose.

At any rate, my conscience is clear and my soul content as I sit here in the cabin and dream of how it will be a year hence. I can

178

see a dozen or more Indian children sitting on log benches, each with his own slate and his own primer, each able to read and write in English and do sums. I can hear their voices reciting the Beatitudes in their own tongue.

One task, the physical one, is completed. Now must I begin my larger work, that of turning these people toward the true God whilst helping preserve that about them that already is good. May I be equal to the task.

Upon my return to Philadelphia, I shall ask my father to sell my interest in our family business to my cousins and use the proceeds to purchase whatever is needed to provide these people with school supplies and to support teachers amongst them. There should be enough, as well, to hire some scholar from an English university to reduce the Delaware tongue into an alphabet and give them a written language of their own. It would be well for them to learn English, of course, but I wish to preserve and strengthen, not extinguish, their own language.

It seems that five years, rather than only five months, have passed since I took leave of my dear wife and sweet children and turned my horse west from Philadelphia on what my own father called a "fool's errand." We shall see who is the fool.

SECOND MONTH 11, 1754

We had our first day of school today, following a night of dancing and singing and speech-making. Fifteen children, from ages seven to fourteen, attended. Tallema insisted on delivering a long, hortatory address, to which the children listened blankly. Then he remained to hear my lesson. I meant to tell the children the story of our Redeemer, but thought it unwise to do so in the presence of Tallema. So I began by teaching them the English words for everyday things.

Now that I will not exhaust myself each day at physical toil, perhaps I may write more often in my journal. The weather has turned warmer.

SECOND MONTH 12, 1754

How quickly my pupils learn. I am so pleased with their progress. And with the weather. The snow begins to melt.

A curious thing happened in the village today. After noon a tall lad of nearly twenty returned from the hunting party. The villagers flocked around the exhausted youth, pressing him with questions about their fathers and husbands, but he would give his news only to Tallema and that in private.

The youth's name is Apauko. He looked strangely at the three white men he found in his village. Especially at Jason. I do hope that Tallema soon will share his news with me.

SECOND MONTH 13, 1754

Apauko, the lad sent back here from the hunting party, was gone when I arose this morning. Tallema has not yet told me of Apauko's message, but Jason, through Awilshahuak, has learned that the lad told Tallema the men have established a camp about three days north of here where they discovered many beaver dams and otter slides. They wish to remain there for a while to harvest these valuable furs. The snows prevented their returning earlier. They sent the long-legged Apauko, who is a swift runner, home to see whether their women and children have enough to eat. Tallema has instructed him to tell the hunters that the people here have plenty of meat and, further, a trader with valuable goods is waiting here to purchase their furs.

I imparted this news to Christopher, who, naturally, is delighted to learn that a large supply of otter and beaver skins soon will arrive. He was getting worried lest the prime fur season should pass and he would have wasted his time here.

School went well today. Some of my students have learned to connect a few English words into sentences. I am encouraged.

With more warm weather, spots of bare earth now show again.

SECOND MONTH 14, 1754

I mislike to set such thoughts on paper, but now that our labors on the school cabin are completed, and Tallema is so often in my class, Jason spends more time than is right alone with Awilshahuak. He hunts every day and brings the game directly to her, as though he were her husband. This troubles me and yet I am reluctant to

180

speak my mind truly to Jason, lest the relationship be innocent. Tallema must notice the way they whisper and smile. Surely if he thought Jason were taking any advantage here, he would banish him as he did Christopher in the matter of the rum. I might unburden myself to Christopher, but his hands are scarcely clean. So I must keep my own counsel and pray that my feelings are wrong.

How I love my little students. How eager they are to learn the white man's words. How quickly they have learned the Ten Commandments.

Today Tallema did not attend our class. He does not feel well. Without him I made better progress. He is given to joining in the instruction, which can be most disconcerting. I must stop writing and go and talk to him or he will be offended.

SECOND MONTH 15, 1754

Tallema stayed abed this morning. He can barely raise his head. He is well beyond the Biblical three score and ten years, and so does not recover from his illness as would a younger man.

I dismissed our class at noon today. I could not be more pleased by our progress. Praise be to the Almighty for His guidance.

SECOND MONTH 16, 1754

My hand doth tremble so I scarce can hold my pen as I write these words, such is the nature of something Tallema has revealed to me.

He is growing weaker so rapidly that he is convinced he will not recover from his illness, although I think he exaggerates its seriousness. He says this belief was strengthened last night by a dream in which his manito told him that with the completion of this school cabin, his life's mission has been accomplished and that it soon will be time for him to depart for the great hunting ground in the sky. This does not sadden him, but he is troubled by something of which he felt compelled to speak.

I thought I knew the heart and mind of this old man. It doth wonder me that he could have spoken hour after hour of other things, many touching on personal matters, and yet so deviously avoided tell-

181

ing me this one thing. Yes, Tallema did open his heart to me in many ways. I am certain he feels a brotherly affection for me, as I do for him.

Some time ago, early in our sojourn here, when I told Tallema of the circumstances of the massacre of Jason's mother and sister and of the abduction of his brother, Isaac, by a Delaware named Meskikokant, he replied that he recalled some talk of the incident many years ago when he dwelt on the upper Susquehanna, and then quickly excused himself from further speaking. I noted, however, that his voice wavered when he told me this, and his limbs trembled. Nor would he look at me as he spoke.

Now I understand why poor Tallema has acted so strangely toward Jason, never speaking to him and looking at him only when he thought he was not being observed; as though he feared the lad. I understand, too, why Awilshahuak seems so much attracted to Jason.

Oh, how tangled do our human affairs become. What I have learned will bring both joy and consternation to Jason. His search will soon be over and I only hope he will not be dismayed by its outcome. He need only remain here, where I now am all the more convinced God directed us, and avoid involvement with Awilshahuak. I must decide when and how to break this amazing news to him.

Awilshahuak says her grandfather calls for me. I must close.

SECOND MONTH 17, 1754

This is a dismal Sabbath afternoon. I am desolate.

My old friend, the wise and good Tallema, died during the night. He asked for me to come to him just before I retired, and he clung to my hand as he told me he considered me closer to him than any brother. He said if all white men were as I, he would gladly become a Christian.

I was much moved by his speech, but thought it only another evidence of his superstition that he told me again he expected to expire soon. In truth, his voice was stronger than it had been earlier in the day, and I had observed him eating a generous portion of stew at supper. I expected to find him much better this morning, but when Menumheck went to awaken him he was quite dead, lying on his side with a curiously peaceful expression, as though experiencing a pleasant dream.

A great lamentation arose in the village at the news of his death.

All through the morning the women have been sitting about his body, rocking back and forth and chanting death songs.

Menumheck and Awilshahuak are too much overcome to talk rationally, but Woapink has explained to me that the villagers will all gather tonight to sit in complete silence, much like a Quaker meeting. They will bury him in the morning, together with an assortment of his possessions, but there will be in all twelve days of mourning, concluding with a grand feast. Food will be placed on the grave during each day so that his soul may not have to seek sustenance in the lodges of the living. They think a man has a spiritual soul which departs for another world upon the completion of the mourning rites, but has also a soul of the blood which lingers on earth and will haunt those who fail to mourn properly.

So while the women lament and prepare the body of Tallema, I have come to my school to pray for his real soul. Even though he did not come through our Christ, still I feel in my heart that he is as much with the Father as ever I will be. He was my brother, and I mourn him.

Christopher has not known what to do with himself this day. His paramour, Wecolis, early joined the circle of mourners. He left an hour ago, taking the three horses to a field of haylike grass that lies on a south slope two miles away. It is a bright, clear day, and he says he feels the horses must be allowed to graze, but I suspect he merely wants to get away from the constant sound of mourning. He has borrowed Jason's dog, Logan, and taken along his musket to shoot pigeons. I remonstrated with him for going hunting on the Sabbath, but he rather sarcastically replied that there would be a great need for food for the funeral feasts that are to come. He intends to bring back three horseloads of pigeons, he says. And he has left Jason under orders to gather much fuel and lay a great fire outside over which to roast the birds.

It is better to have him away than for him to be languishing about impatiently waiting for the day when the village braves come in with their furs. Life is a simple matter of getting and spending, eating, drinking and sleeping to Christopher Cadwell, I fear. He might as well be a beast.

I have not yet decided when to tell Jason what Tallema revealed to me about Meskikokant and his brother, Isaac. I fear that if he knew, he might take some rash action.

I must close. Someone has just fired a musket and shouted a halloo from the woods. Surely Christopher could not so soon return from his hunting. The horses hardly have had time to graze. . . .

183

PART FIVE

1

Jason was cleaning his rifle when he heard the shot and halloo. He went to the door and looked out just as six men, each bearing a musket, emerged from the woods. Haworth put his journal aside and joined him. Four of the men obviously were Indians; they had scalp locks and were dressed in leggings with deerskin tunics showing beneath buffalo robes. The other two, who were bearded, wore fur caps and an unfamiliar type of long jacket. They approached the lodges, spread out like skirmishers, with muskets carried at the ready.

Jason began to load his rifle, but Haworth restrained him.

"Let us see what they want."

The men halted as he stepped out into the winter sunlight and raised his hand. At that moment a fresh wail arose from the women in the old council lodge, and Jason could see the men glancing at each other in puzzlement. Two of them walked forward warily until they were face to face with the Quaker. One of the bearded men spoke.

"You Anglais. English?"

"I speak English, yes. But I am a Pennsylvanian."

"Him English too?" the man asked, pointing to Jason as his Indian companions stared at the rifle.

"He, too, is a Pennsylvanian."

"What do you do here?"

"We have built this school. We have been here for nearly three months."

Now Jason could tell that the spokesman was a half-breed.

"Where Indians?"

"Away . . . Hunting."

"What make women cry?"

"Their chief died last night. They are mourning him."

The man turned to his Indian companion and said something

Jason could not understand. Then he motioned to the others of his party to advance. As they came forward, the Indian moved behind Jason to stand between him and the school door.

"Give me the gun," the leader said, drawing a pistol from his jacket and pointing to Jason's rifle.

The Indians took the rifle and they passed it around, murmuring at its beauty.

"In there." The man with the pistol motioned them toward the door of the cabin. Inside, blinking in the dim light, the leader gave an order which Jason did not understand until two Indians seized him and tied his wrists behind him with thongs and then placed rawhide nooses around his neck and that of Haworth.

"What does thee mean to do?" the Quaker demanded. "We are here in peace. Thee has no right—"

The leader slapped Haworth across the face so hard that he staggered and almost fell.

"English keep quiet. You come with us."

Jason bolted for the door and was halfway through it when the thong about his neck tightened and he was jerked back into the cabin, flat on his back.

The leader kicked him in the ribs, and before the pain had passed, one of the Indians knelt and tied a gag across his mouth while another did the same to Haworth. They looked about the cabin, gathering up the blankets and other possessions, including Haworth's journal and Testament. Thinking of Cadwell's trade goods, which were stored in Tallema's lodge, Jason was relieved that they did not search elsewhere. Holding Jason's rifle, shot pouch and powder horns, the leader said:

"Now you come with us."

They shoved and kicked Jason and Haworth outside and led them rapidly away from the village, looking nervously over their shoulders at the council lodge. Jason could hear the cries of the women long after they were out of sight, as if they were lamenting his departure rather than the death of their old chief. Their abductors hastened them over the frozen ground until nearly dusk, allowing them only two brief rests and giving them no food. Only when they stopped beside a stream to camp did they remove the gags and give them some cold jerky to eat.

"We are in a hell of a fix," Jason whispered. "Awilshahuak will think we ran away. Who are these people? I can't understand what they say, can you?"

"Yes, but do not let them know. They are Canadians. They are speaking French."

"Where are they taking us?"

"I can't tell yet. Give them no cause for anger, Jason. We are in their power, temporarily. But all will be well. . . ."

That night, with ankles bound as well as wrists, Jason and Haworth slept back to back under their own blankets, under the same shelter as their captors. Since the leader ordered them to keep quiet under threat of replacing their gags, Jason was left to his own thoughts. Weary as he was from the long walk, his mind would not let him sleep. What would Awilshahuak think when she discovered he was gone?

Had anyone asked Jason if he was in love with Awilshahuak, he would have denied it. Certainly she was winsome. And beneath a beauty rare in a young woman of any race, there lay a deep femininity that was at once cunning and solicitous of others. It had struck Jason one day as they bent over a game of jacks, played with deer bones, just what it was that he found so appealing about this granddaughter of Tallema. She combined the teasing surface personality of Sallie Koch with the industriousness and basic seriousness of the older sister, Katie. Like Sallie, she enjoyed making him blush, but like Katie, she was curious about him and concerned; she mended his moccasins, for instance. Even so, what he felt for Awilshahuak was not to be compared with his devotion to Sallie. To return to the blacksmith's blond daughter with honor and to make her his wife remained his goal. He still dreamed of her arms about him, of her as his wife and the mother of his children. Yet such was the natural sensuality of Awilshahuak that he was stirred almost against his will. She knew no English, and although he had picked up many Delaware words, they still were too few to permit an extended conversation.

Jason had never meant for there to be anything more than a sister-brother relationship, just as he had told Haworth, until the previous Sunday, when they had gone into the forest to search for wedge-shaped stones with which to split logs for benches. Until then either Haworth, Menumheck or old Tallema had always been nearby. On that Sunday afternoon, much bundled against the cold and carrying a basket for the stones, they had been accompanied only by Logan. The woods had been unnaturally quiet, with hardly any birds calling and not even a squirrel rustling about. Only the sound of their feet breaking through the snowy crust and of Logan's energetic lunging about through the underbrush broke the silence. Awilshahuak wore

189

leggings under her skirt and, besides her grandfather's buffalo robe, a woolen blanket caped over her head and wrapped about her body. When Jason laughed at the sight of her comely brown face peering out, she impishly wrinkled her nose and stuck out her tongue.

Jason would never forget the exuberance he felt at being alone in the woods with this warm, exquisite Indian girl, away from the observation of the other villagers, free of the hard work on the school and out of the close atmosphere of the small lodges. Once they were within the enclosure of the forest, well out of sight of the village, he had taken her hand and led her squealing and laughing at a lurching run along a snow-covered path. Twice she lost her footing and had to be hauled upright again. Logan, caught up in their antics, loped about them in circles, barking madly.

At last, exhausted, they had come to the bottom of the wooded slope, to the small creek on whose banks Jason had noted the stones they sought. They were weary from their wild run through the snow. Laughing and fighting to recover her breath, Awilshahuak at first leaned against the trunk of an enormous sycamore, while Jason stood in front of her, grinning at her merriment. They stood there laughing at each other until Logan, growing bored, had gone crashing away on business of his own.

Jason put the basket over Awilshahuak's head, drawing fresh, now muffled, laughter. She cast off the basket and slid her back down along the sycamore trunk until she sat on her blanket. She motioned for Jason to sit beside her, spreading out the blanket as she did so. Instead he knelt before her, and taking her hands in his, blew his breath on them and chafed them with his own until they gleamed red.

It might have stopped there. They might have rested for a few moments and then searched for the stones Cadwell would need, had Awilshahuak not put her now warm hands on Jason's nose. The tenderness of the gesture touched him; without thinking, he cupped her small brown face in his hands. There was a moment there in which he intended to withdraw his hands and pull her to her feet. He would have done so had she not murmured, "Ktahoallel, Mocquasaka." His Delaware was not good enough for him to understand exactly what she was saying, but something in the expression of her eyes caused him to put his face against hers and then his arms around her. In yet another moment they were lying on the blanket. And then there was no turning back.

He had learned enough from the woman in Logstown to know how to proceed and to take his time in doing so. She was a virgin.

Jason had to force himself into her and when he did, she cried in pain. This alarmed him so that he started to withdraw, but she pressed her hands on the small of his back to keep him in place. Nothing Jason had ever experienced could compare with this. That Sunday morning with Sallie in her room had been incomplete, only a promise of what he might expect when they were married, and that night at Logstown he had been too drunk to enjoy fully the ecstasy of possessing a woman. This was as natural as the mating of two healthy young animals, without the intoxication of either long-suppressed desire or alcohol and devoid of any feelings of guilt or fear of being discovered.

They lay together for a long time with half of the blanket folded over them, oblivious to the cold, not speaking, until Logan splashed across the creek and shook icy water over them. On their way back to the village, they had walked slowly, arms about each other, no longer laughing, strangely become one.

He had reported to Haworth that they had failed to locate the stones but that Awilshahuak thought she knew another place where they might look, and he had accepted the explanation. All week long, Jason and Awilshahuak had communicated with glances and sad smiles, waiting for another such opportunity to be alone again. But of course Tallema's illness and death had intervened. Now he lay tied up like a pig trussed for market, the captive of four strange Indians and two half-breeds, who had not given him the chance to say goodbye to Awilshahuak.

And the exasperating Haworth dared say it would turn out for the best. How could he have so quickly fallen asleep when they were in such a predicament? He jostled him awake with his elbow.

"What dost thee want?"

" 'Ktahoallel.' What does it mean?"

"That is Delaware for 'I love thee.' Why?"

"I just wondered."

Their captors stirred them awake with their feet the next morning and drove them rapidly throughout a long day under the sky whose grayness would have been depressing even in good circumstances. As they marched relentlessly over low hills separated by ravines, all covered with scrubby trees, Jason could tell from the occasional outline of the sun that they moved in a northeasterly direction. The half-breeds talked to each other in what Jason knew now to be French. Otherwise their captors spoke an Indian tongue quite unlike Delaware.

They slept the dreamless sleep of the exhausted again that night. The next morning the terrain became flatter and after their midday break for food, the trail made a long descent through a heavier forest to a level flood plain and finally to the cleared bank of a small river. After they had followed a well-worn trail along the bank a short way, past a dozen or so Indian lodges, the two half-breeds fired their muskets into the air, shouted, then waited until they heard an answering shot. They proceeded to where the stream joined a wide river and at that point there could be seen a stout log house with several outbuildings and a flag bearing three fleurs-de-lis flying from a long sapling pole. Outside the house there stood a white man wearing the uniform of a French captain.

2

It was jet dark in the little unheated root cellar where, after questioning them separately in his broken English, the French captain caused Jason and Haworth to be locked up. Despite the dark and the cold, it felt delicious to have their hands and feet free and no longer to wear the humiliating noose about their necks. The Frenchman's interrogation of Jason had been brief, but he had kept Haworth for a long while.

"Who is that man?" Jason asked after the Quaker had been shoved into their prison pit.

"His name is Joncaire. And this place is called Venango."

"I remember they spoke of it back at Logstown. This is where John Fraser had his trading post and blacksmith shop."

"Yes, the French chased him away last summer and they intend to build a fort here. Joncaire does not try to hide it. They can portage their supplies from Lake Erie to the headwaters of French Creek, and then float down here on the Allegheny and go all the way down the Ohio and Mississippi."

"Don't look to me like they have enough men to build a proper fort."

"From what I have overheard, they have a thousand men ready or on their way to the shore of Lake Erie. In the spring they intend to build a fort, either at the Forks or at Logstown. They would have done that last summer, but the creek dropped too low."

"Why is Joncaire treating us like this?"

"He thinks we are English agents. The governor of Virginia sent a young militia officer out here just a few weeks ago to warn the French to stop their fortifications and leave. He thinks I may be out here on a similar mission from the government of Philadelphia or the Crown itself, to stir up the Indians against the French. He refuses to believe my story about our school."

"And you did not tell him you speak his language?"

"I did not and thee must be cautious not to reveal that I studied French in school. We may learn much they might otherwise conceal from us. We must be as gentle as doves and as wise as serpents."

The next morning Joncaire had Jason brought out into the large common room of John Fraser's old house for more questioning. The captain was a lean man with dark hair and a large nose that made his hazel eyes look even smaller and more suspicious. Most of his questions concerned Haworth. How had they met? What was the purpose of his companion's trip? Was he in the employ of the Pennsylvania government? Jason had some difficulty understanding the accent, but he answered the questions honestly. The Frenchman seemed not to believe him, and he acted impatient when Jason stammered.

"You, then. Why do you come here?"

"I t-told you l-last n-night. I w-w-want to find m-my brother."

"I think you lie. You have come with your rifle as a guard for your Quaker spy friend."

"I d-don't care what you are d-doing. I just w-want to find m-my brother."

"I will lock you up until you tell me the truth."

They remained in their dark little cellar for three days and nights, allowed out only in the morning and just before dark, one at a time, always guarded by two French soldiers. They were permitted no light in their room, and so they spent their time shivering in the cold under their blankets and talking.

Haworth waited until Jason seemed ready to surrender to his despair before he told him what Tallema had related on his deathbed. The lad had just railed out against the injustice of their fates, when the Quaker said, "Pray do be silent and listen to what I have to tell thee. Then thee will see that God works in a wondrous way which man doth not always divine." The Quaker spoke so softly that Jason had to cup his ear to hear.

"Thee may have noted, Jason, that Tallema acted rather strangely toward thee."

"Yes. He wouldn't look at me."

"He was afraid of thee, Jason."

"Why?"

"Tallema became convinced two days before he died that his time had come and he told me what he had been afraid to confess earlier.

To make a short tale of it, Tallema knows both Meskikokant and Isaac. Knows them very well, in fact. In short, Meskikokant is, or was, what we would call his son-in-law. He was married to Menumheck."

Jason was too incredulous to reply coherently. "M-married . . . but Awilshahuak . . ."

"She is the daughter of Meskikokant."

"That is not possible."

"Wait. Thee has not heard it all. There is more."

"You mean they let us stay there all that time and kept this from me?"

"From us both. Tallema was terrified. He thought thee had come to avenge thy mother's murder and fancied that thee might vent thy wrath upon him or Awilshahuak if thee had known."

"Never. I would never . . ."

"I know. And I told him so."

"Isaac. What of Isaac?"

"Thee knows that Awilshahuak is spoken for."

"She never said she was."

"She *was* spoken for, but Tallema had not given his consent. Oh, Jason, it grieves me to tell thee this and yet thee must know the truth. Indeed, it may bring thee a measure of relief."

Jason felt ready to strangle the Quaker for his deliberate way of speaking. "For God's sake, will you get to the point? What about Isaac?"

"Thee surely heard that a young brave from another village sought her hand."

"Yes. They call him Hopiquon. But she says she has not promised herself to him. Not yet. He is to return in the spring for her answer."

"Hopiquon means 'He Is Broad-Shouldered.' "

Jason raised his voice. "I don't give a damn what Hopiquon means. What about my brother?"

"Hopiquon is the name Meskikokant gave Isaac."

It took a moment for Jason to understand. He arose, straining to see Haworth's expression.

"Isaac? He was at the village?"

"Yes, just a few months ago. And he is to return in the spring."

"But where is he now?"

"At an Ottawa camp near Lake Erie."

"And Meskikokant. Where is he?"

"That is why I have been reluctant to tell thee. It is a story thee may not wish to hear."

Jason fumbled in the dark for the Quaker's lapels, and finding them, hauled him to his feet.

"Please, Jason. Restrain thyself."

"Out with it. Stop beating around the bush and tell me."

Haworth removed his hands with a surprisingly strong grasp and pushed him away.

"Meskikokant regards Isaac as his son. He wants to see him properly married. Tallema, Menumheck and the others despise Meskikokant so that he does not dare return himself. He sent Isaac to the village alone to court Awilshahuak. Tallema said Awilshahuak was much taken with him but that he was outraged at the presumptuousness of Meskikokant. He told the lad he must go away but that he may return in the spring with buffalo robes and iron pots as gifts. He promised he would give Awilshahuak to no other meanwhile."

"I don't understand all this."

"Tallema is ashamed of what Meskikokant did. He says he has always been ruled by evil spirits. He is bitter toward him for bringing shame to his lodge and for abandoning poor Menumheck and Awilshahuak. He thought Awilshahuak should have time to consider carefully whether she should marry a white man and, more important, one who had so long been under the influence of her own faithless father, Meskikokant."

Jason sat on the ground and put his head in his hands. "Why did you wait so long to tell me?"

"When first I learned it, I thought we had merely to wait for Isaac to appear in the spring. How was I to know that we would be taken away like this?"

"I'll be damned. Isaac wants to marry Awilshahuak?"

"Not only does Isaac, but Apauko as well."

"Apauko?"

"The Indian youth who came in from the villagers' winter hunting camp. Tallema says he is much smitten with her, but by Indian custom he is supposed to seek his wife elsewhere. Thee can understand why he finds her so desirable, surely. I can, certainly."

"And so can I. What of Isaac? Is he well?"

"Tallema says he is a splendid young man, very strong and likely to be a good provider. The Indians are not prejudiced as to race in matters of marriage so long as the husband, be he red, white or black, intends to remain as one of them, accepting their ways."

"And Isaac would do that?"

"Yes, Jason. You must realize that Isaac may not want to return with thee."

195

"I don't believe it. Oh, if I could get out of here and find him. I would convince him to go back with me."

"Perhaps thee can. Trust God, Jason. He will make all this come out right in the end."

Jason thought of Awilshahuak lying beneath him under the sycamore tree, joined to him as one flesh. And she was Isaac's intended wife. Why had no one told him in time to prevent it? He wished he could express his feelings to Haworth. Cadwell would have understood, but not this pious Quaker.

"We must return to the village."

"We must indeed. All that we most desire is there. I must go back and be sure that the new chief will honor Tallema's pledge of support for my school. Thee must be on hand to greet thy brother upon his return from the wild, for Tallema sent Apauko to summon him."

"Really? What about Mister Cadwell. Won't he search for us?"

"Alas, Jason. We were taken so stealthily, how would he know where to look?"

"I suppose you are right. And even if he knew, he wouldn't risk the chance the braves might return and take their furs down to Logstown while he is gone. Or plunder his trade goods."

"Yes, I fear that Christopher puts those things and his selfish pleasures above all other considerations. I was disgusted when he began cohabiting with Wecolis, was thee not, Jason?"

"He is not married as you are, Mister Haworth."

"Aye, but we both heard him promise Mrs. McGinty he would marry her upon his return to Shippensburg. He is being unfaithful. Surely thee must see that."

Jason, thinking of his own unfaithfulness to Sallie Koch, and of Awilshahuak's to his brother Isaac, changed the subject.

3

He lay awake all that night, brooding over the astounding news that Haworth had given him. Jason hated the Quaker for sleeping soundly when he had so many questions to put to him, questions that he had been too shocked to think of at first.

What was the relationship of Isaac to Meskikokant now? Why

would his brother have any connection with that murderous beast unless he was compelled? Yet if Isaac was free to come and seek a bride, what prevented his returning to white civilization?

And Awilshahuak. Had the interlude under the sycamore tree that Sunday been just a matter of passion getting out of hand or was it because she so much preferred him to Isaac? He felt guilty that he enjoyed reflecting on the possibility that this lovely Indian girl liked him better than she had his brother. No man had ever penetrated her before. And she had said, "I love thee." What might Isaac do if he learned that his brother had possessed his fiancée before him; or Sallie Koch, if she knew of his unfaithfulness?

Jason lay with seething brain, staring into the dark until daylight appeared through the cracks around the cellar door and he saw that Haworth, too, was awake.

He began asking the questions that had tormented him through the night, until the Quaker protested, saying, "Really, Jason, I have told thee all I know. Pray calm thyself and trust in God."

Later in the day, after they had been allowed to walk about outside and had eaten their miserable breakfast, Jason accused Haworth of being smug and unsympathetic.

"You keep telling me to trust. You have a family with wealth back in Philadelphia. You have an education. You could return to Philadelphia and live the rest of your life in comfort. But I have to go back and find my brother. I can never marry and have a family until that is settled. You keep telling me not to despair. You don't know what despair is."

The Quaker lost his customary expression of calm understanding at this tirade.

"Ah, Jason, thee knowest not what thee sayest. I have experienced the deepest despair in the midst of wealth and position. I have reflected in the depths of my soul on the vanity of riches over the headlong passage of our few days upon this earth."

"Yes, but you have had it drilled into your head that you will go to heaven and live there forever. You really believe that and I don't."

"I do believe it most of the time, Jason. I do. But there are other times, when I doubt, and that is when my soul descends into the pit, when despair blots out the sun like a fog."

"When? I never have seen you when you weren't as cheerful as a hog eating slops."

Haworth smiled at the simile.

"When? When I see white men cheating and corrupting Indians.

When I see men of both races drinking rum and roaring about like demented beasts. When I see Christopher succumb to his carnal instincts and cohabit with an Indian woman. Yea, and to tell the truth, when I feel these same instincts stirring in myself. I feel despair when I see the black man bought and sold like an animal, when I hear Indians express a lust for revenge as if it were a virtue. Ah, Jason, at such times it seems to me that we delude ourselves thinking we have anything of the divine in us. At those dark times in my heart, I fear that we are beasts like any other creature, only cursed, not blessed, with greater intelligence and therefore possessed of greater craft and power to do evil. And then I fear that I delude myself in believing that in the end anything, good or bad, faces us beyond the grave and the ever-waiting worms."

Now it was Jason's turn to be shocked. Unconsciously he had hoped the Quaker might respond with something that would buoy his own hopes.

"Maybe that is all there is," he said. "I just intend to do the best I can until then."

Haworth mistook his meaning. "I am cheered to hear thee say that. I, too, seek to do all the good I can, and trust in God's promises. That is how I overcome my despair. My faith always returns in time. God is patient and timeless. He never leaves me long in my doubts, and when it returns, my faith seems all the sweeter for its brief absence."

4

Jason looked forward to those periods when they were allowed out of their cellar as eagerly as a starving man to a meal. They were given only a quarter hour in which to walk about in the stockaded yard of the trading post, one at a time, and Jason savored every second, even though he was under close guard. Occasionally, when the stockade gates were open, he would stop and stare out at the two steep, conical hills between which the Allegheny curved down from the northeast. This made his guards nervous, however, and they would shove him along with their musket butts.

Joncaire ignored them for a while. Apparently he concluded that even if they had been sent by the Pennsylvanians to stir up the Delaware against the French, they had not yet accomplished their purpose. Besides this, much of his time was taken up with the Indians who came and went at the old Fraser post. Jason could not understand either the Indians or the Frenchmen, but it struck him that this captain treated the Indians with greater courtesy than had the English-speaking traders of Logstown.

Several days later, just when Jason thought he was ready to go mad from being shut up in the cellar, Joncaire ordered the two of them brought before him. He sat at a table in the large common room with his back to a hearty fire whose warmth they were not allowed to enjoy.

"Sit." The captain pointed to a bench on the other side of the table. As Jason's eyes grew accustomed to the light, he was shocked by the drawn appearance of Haworth, whose face he had not seen clearly since their imprisonment. The normally clean-shaven Quaker now had a ragged blond beard and his hands and clothing were filthy. But the gray eyes still shone with the same spirit Jason had noted at Shippensburg.

Joncaire glowered at them as if they were two pupils hauled before a schoolmaster.

"You have told me the truth."

Haworth thought it was a question. "We have told thee the truth. Thee does not choose to believe it."

"You come here to build the school."

"We did build a school building. Surely your friends who abducted us told you they seized us in a new log building. That was my school."

"Why did you build school in French lands? You do not have the permission."

"We did have permission. From Tanacharison, the Iroquois Half King, and from the chief of the village, Tallema."

Joncaire frowned at mention of Tanacharison's name. "They say it is all right to make the school?"

Haworth leaned forward to press his point. "Yes. Doesn't thee see I am *not* here with the permission of the Pennsylvania government or the king of England, or the government of Virginia. Despite what thee seems to think, no one of those principalities knows we are here."

The Frenchman did not follow him. "Tanacharison know you are here?"

Jason spoke up. "Tanacharison is his friend. Good friend. He gave him wampum to give to the village chief. He is a friend of the Indians."

"Friend of Tanacharison?"

"Yes, and if you harm him, the Delawares will be angry with you. They love this man."

Now Haworth was frowning at Jason. But he kept silent.

"I do not harm you. You must leave French land. You cannot stay. Listen, English. Tomorrow I go to Le Boeuf to see new commander. I free you in morning. You go back to Philadelphia. No more school here. Seneca friends take you to Kittanning in boat. You take trail east. I let you go. Eh bien?"

Without giving them a chance to reply, Joncaire rose and called in two guards. He spoke rapidly in French, and the guard took Haworth and Jason back to their room.

Jason danced a jig in the dark. "We will be free. Thank God, he will let us go. Isn't it wonderful?"

"He means us to leave. To return to the east."

"I know what he means us to do. What we actually do is something else. His Indian friends will take us to Kittanning, but we can double back and return to the village in a few days. It is simple."

"That would be simple. We shall see."

The next morning, they were roused early and were taken again to the common room, where this time they were served a huge, hot breakfast by one of the half-breeds who had captured them. After so many weeks of Indian fare, Jason found the meal delicious. As they ate, they could hear Joncaire's voice outside shouting orders. They had finished their meal and were roasting their backsides before the fire when the Frenchman came in, wearing a beaver hat with flaps over his ears and a heavy woolen greatcoat. He was accompanied by a Seneca brave dressed in leggings, a long deerskin tunic and a buffalo cape.

"This is Guyasu. He and his party are waiting at the river with a boat. They will take you down the Allegheny to Kittanning. There you go ashore and never return to French land. Comprehend?"

Jason nodded, but Haworth stood with his arms folded in front. Joncaire looked into the Quaker's face.

"You must swear you go back to Philadelphia. You swear you not go back to your school."

"I cannot swear. My faith does not permit me to take an oath."

Jason began to grow alarmed. "He is a Quaker. They do not take oaths. They can only affirm."

"Affirm?" The Frenchman looked confused.

"That means promise."

"You promise, then."

"No. I do not promise. I will go back to my school. My work there is not done."

"You refuse?" The Frenchman was incredulous.

"I refuse to swear, affirm or promise that I will not go back. I am under the control of no government, the king of England's or thine. I am only under the control of Almighty God and He commands me to return to my mission."

The Frenchman's face began to darken. "You want to go back to that cellar?"

"I want to return to my school."

"You are the fool."

Jason could no longer contain his exasperation. "You *are* a fool," he shouted at Haworth. "You are the biggest damned fool I have ever known. That Virginian told me you were a fool. He said you would bring me to grief. Christopher said you were a fool too. Don't you see? All you have to do is *say* you promise and he will let you go." His voice lowered, became pleading. "Just *say* you promise. Please."

Jason turned to the Frenchman. "I promise for him. I will swear that I will take him back east. Just let us go."

"You do swear you will go and not come back?"

"I swear it."

"And you." He turned to Haworth. "I give you the chance again. You promise—affirm—you not go back to that village?"

"No. I cannot in good conscience promise thee that."

Joncaire spat into the fire. After looking coldly into Haworth's face for some sign of weakening and seeing none, he shouted in French. Two guards came and took the Quaker away so quickly that Jason had no time to protest. When he was gone, Joncaire turned back to him.

"You ready to go?"

"Not quite. You have my rifle. I want it back."

"Rifle?" The Frenchman acted as though he did not understand.

Jason became angry. "My rifle. Gun." He pretended to raise a rifle to his shoulder. "I m-must have it back. Your men t-took it."

"We keep it."

"No. If you do, I take back my promise. You keep my rifle, you k-keep me."

Joncaire smiled at this display of spirit. "You want back the rifle."

"You're damned right I w-want it back."

Joncaire shrugged. At a glance from him, the half-breed stepped into the kitchen and returned with the weapon.

"I give it to Guyasu and he keep it until you get to Kittanning."

He spoke rapidly in Seneca and then placed the rifle in the waiting Indian's hands.

Then to Jason: "Don't forget. You promise. You come back and we scalp you."

"You h-harm my f-friend and I will c-come back and scalp y-you."

The Frenchman pretended not to hear.

Jason followed the Seneca from the house and through the stockade gate. He was elated at escaping from close confinement, but at the same time felt both a sense of guilt at leaving Haworth behind and anger toward the Quaker for his refusal to make a promise that could so easily be broken. He was troubled, too, by what he feared Haworth was thinking back in that dreadful little cellar. He must be downcast, Jason thought, to have been in one moment eating breakfast in a warm room and in the next to be shut away again, with no one to talk to anymore. Somehow Jason would secure his release; meanwhile let the fool suffer for his stubbornness. He had brought it on himself.

On the bank of the Allegheny, just below where French Creek joined the larger stream, two more Indians stood waiting beside a large canoe. Like the man who led him down the path from the stockade, one of them wore a scalp lock and was armed with a musket as well. The other man stood watching their approach with a long blanket draped over his head and shoulders in such a way that it obscured most of his face. Their canoe was large, built with a frame of peeled ash saplings lashed together with rawhide and covered with large sheets of elm bark; both bow and stern curved high so that the craft could breast rapids at either end. It was much larger than the occasional birch bark canoe Jason had seen on the Susquehanna, and sturdier as well. It easily could carry him, the three Indians and the bale of furs already secured amidships.

Jason knew that Kittanning, although it lay only fifty miles south as the crow flies, was an overnight voyage as the cold, clear waters of the Allegheny flowed. He did not mind. It was a sunny morning, made to seem all the brighter by the patches of snow on the adjacent hills and the chill of the water. The air had never smelled sweeter and the sun had never shone brighter for him as he settled himself in the canoe, just forward of the bale of furs. He was free again!

He was impatient at the Indians, who remained standing on the bank talking. The one with the blanket protecting his head pointed at the stockade, speaking rapidly, as though in anger. Jason, in his euphoria, was only half conscious of the familiarity of the tone. The

202

Indian who held Jason's rifle was replying in a whining voice. At last the one armed with the musket settled himself in the stern, then the blanket-clad man sat just behind Jason, leaving only the Indian with the rifle and its accouterments on the bank to untie the rope on the bow.

Jason turned his head and looked directly, for the first time, into the face of the leader, whose blanket now lay over his shoulders. He looked squarely into the glistening black eyes of Kiasutha, the leader of the Seneca war party they had encountered at Loyalhanning, the one whose two Catawba prisoners Haworth had freed.

Had Jason waited even ten seconds more, it would have been too late. Without thought, he moved from a sitting position to a crouch and then into a leap for the shore, all in one unbroken motion. The thrust of his legs shoved the stern of the canoe away from the bank and into the river current, so that the Indian on shore had to strain to hold the tightened line. With a high yipping yell such as his father's Celtic ancestors might have shouted to panic their enemies, Jason swept his rifle from the Indian's hand and then, before the brave could recover, shoved the butt against his chest so that he staggered sideways and pitched across the bow of the canoe and thence into the water.

Jason scooped up his powder horns and shot bag and bolted for the only sanctuary he knew, the stockade. He did not stop to think that he was fleeing back to the place from which, only a few hours before, he would have sold his soul to escape. He had seen the worse fate that threatened him when he looked for that instant into the eyes of the Seneca.

The Indian in the rear of the canoe brought his musket up and fired, sending a ball so close to Jason's head that he felt its passage. The Seneca leader kept his presence of mind enough to seize his paddle and guide the canoe back to where he and the Indian with the musket could leap ashore. Leaving the third man to struggle out of the water on his own, they raced after Jason.

Joncaire was about to mount his horse when he heard the musket shot. He and two soldiers stood at the stockade gate and watched Jason dart up the path, trying to load his rifle as he ran. By the time he reached the gate he had spilled enough powder into the muzzle to make a sufficient charge. It took only a few more seconds for him to ram home a ball, cock the piece and aim it at the advancing Senecas. They stood only thirty yards away. The one with the musket began to reload, but when Jason swung his muzzle toward him, he stopped and looked at his leader.

Joncaire stepped outside the gate.

"If you kill a Seneca, I must turn you over to them."

"I d-don't care. K-keep them back or I will fire."

"That would be a miracle. The rifle is not primed, n'est-ce pas?"

Jason glanced down and saw that Joncaire was right. He had put no powder in the sparking pan. But he kept the gun at his shoulder until Joncaire began slowly walking toward the two Indians with his hand held up in the universal gesture of peace. He called out in French as he did so and the two soldiers stepped forward to take Jason's rifle. They led him, trembling and weary, back to the common room.

It was half an hour before Joncaire joined him there. Jason could not interpret the expression with which the Frenchman regarded him. He could not tell whether it was amusement or disgust.

"You are lucky, mon jeune ami. Those Senecas bear you the grudge. They say you let go their prisoners."

"It was not me. Mister Haworth let them go."

"Foolish man. They want you both. They don't like it I don't give you to them."

"You tried to give us both to them, remember? You tried to trick us."

"That is not so. The Seneca trick me. They did not tell me they know you until now. Now I see why they offer to haul you to Kittanning."

"You can let us go on our own, then. Later."

"Not so fast. They tell me something else just now. They say you tell them your friend sent here by Pennsylvania government. You come to guard him. You lie to me."

"We did not tell that lie. We had another friend. He told those Senecas Mister Haworth was an official of the Pennsylvania government so they would not harm us for freeing their prisoners. Look, Captain, you see what a fool my friend is. Let me take him away. Please."

"I cannot do that. Not now. I must tell all this to my commander at Le Boeuf. You stay here until I return. Don't worry, we don't let the Seneca take your scalp."

Joncaire stopped at the doorway. "By the way, what happen to your other friend?"

"I don't know. He went off to trade with the Indians."

Joncaire called in the guards as he left. Only much later did Jason recall that he carried with him the pouch in which Haworth kept his writing papers and journal.

5

Jason dreaded returning to the little prison room, not so much because of the cold and dark, or even the close confinement—all that was preferable to torture or enslavement by the Senecas—but rather the embarrassment of facing Haworth after having seemed to abandon him.

But the Quaker greeted him joyously, saying, "Ah, Jason, thee changed thy mind. Thee gave up thy freedom rather than make a promise thee did not mean to keep."

"Go to hell," Jason replied, deliberately to shock him. And then he told him what had happened.

"There," Haworth said after he had finished. "What would our fates have been had we both made a false promise?"

"I'd sooner like to think what my fate would have been if you had not freed those Catawbas back at Loyalhanning. Mister Cadwell had good reason to be angry at you. He knew you had made an enemy for life."

"Thee is distraught and I have no wish to contradict thee, but I must say that I would rather think of those two lads back in the bosoms of their families in the south. If I incurred enmity in their oppressors, so be it."

"Well, I very nearly paid for your good deed."

"Do not be bitter, Jason. I am so happy to be rejoined with thee. Come, let us have no more hard words. All will yet come right in this."

Although Jason and Haworth continued to be locked in their cellar at night, the soldiers, apparently following Joncaire's last-minute instructions, permitted them longer periods of freedom within the stockaded yard and, to their amazement, fed them hot food twice a day in the common room before the fire. Thus they passed the remainder of March, while Joncaire was absent, in relative comfort. At night, when they were locked up, Haworth would relay to Jason the information he had picked up from overhearing the talk of the French soldiers and the half-breeds.

"They have received word that a body of Virginia militia have taken possession of the Forks of the Ohio and have begun to erect a fort there. The French are preparing an expedition to descend upon them."

"I wish I could get away to warn them, don't you?"

"I am not so sure. Much as I mistrust the Popish motives of the French, I am not so certain that their control out here would be any worse than that of the Virginians. Thee hast observed how Captain Joncaire treats the Indians with courtesy, as equals. Contrast that with the behavior of those two Virginians at Logstown. Remember how they despised the Indians."

"Perhaps so. I'd just as soon not get into another argument about that."

Haworth seemed neither hurt nor offended by Jason's occasional outbursts against him. The Quaker accepted his growing frankness and, responding to his obvious irritation, stopped speaking so much of piety and religion. Instead he encouraged Jason to talk about his childhood and his apprenticeship with Ernst Koch and his feelings for Sallie. This show of personal interest overcame Jason's initial reticence and soon he felt easy telling about his parents and their life as squatters on Indian lands. Haworth also drew out Jason about his hopes for the future, listening with a half smile as the lad described how he felt it would be to marry Sallie and rear a family. When Jason fell into an uncommunicative mood, the Quaker would tell him about his own childhood and marriage. Jason soon came to feel that he knew as much about Philadelphia as anyone could without actually having lived there.

Except for one brief snow and a spell of windy, rainy weather, March was a mild month, just inclement enough to make them not entirely unhappy to be in their cellar room. And by the end of the month, they had become closer friends than ever before. Haworth now treated Jason as an adult, as an intelligent equal, and no longer acted as a teacher except when the lad asked for instruction.

And then late one afternoon Joncaire returned, bringing with him a company of Canadian soldiers and a score of large boats filled with military supplies. Several French officers accompanied Joncaire. Jason and Haworth met them that evening at supper.

Joncaire greeted them as though they were old friends. At first Jason thought the man was being sarcastic as he inquired after their health. But then he said teasingly to Haworth, "Ah, my Quaker friend, you have not been candid with me."

Haworth was taken aback as much as Jason by the Frenchman's cordiality. "What dost thee mean?"

206

"Your journal. Forgive me, but I take it to Le Boeuf. I do not read the English so good. They read it to me there and to my commander. Most interesting what you write. You tell me some truth, but you do not tell me your other friend is at that village. This English trader."

Jason had never seen Haworth so completely out of countenance. The Quaker sputtered as the Frenchman turned to his fellow officers and said something in French that set them laughing. One of them spoke and his reply set off a new round of laughter.

When Joncaire turned back to Haworth, the Quaker's face had turned scarlet.

"How dare thee tell them about Wecolis? And I don't care if they do consider me a prude. Rum is the work of the devil. And thee has no right to discuss the contents of my diary with them."

Joncaire raised his eyebrows and cocked his head to one side as Haworth finished his outburst.

"Mon ami, vous parlez Francais! Pourquoi ne me l'aviez-vous pas dit?"

The room was silent for a moment. Haworth stammered as much as Jason ever had. The Frenchman cut him off.

"Do not deny it. You speak French. You understand what I say."

"Well, what if I do?"

"It was naughty of you not to tell me."

He spoke slowly in French and Haworth, with a resigned expression, replied haltingly in the same language.

"The accent is not so good, but you say a Huguenot is teaching you. But you speak it. I have another reason to keep you here."

Jason stepped forward. "What do you m-mean? What has his speaking French g-got to do with l-letting us go?"

"We have business downriver. Monsieur Haworth may have heard too much of that business. It would be better for him to stay here until it is finish."

"I can't see why you don't let us go. We won't tell anyone."

"So you can go back among the Indians to look for your brother? No, my young man. When you go, we will make sure our business is finish and you go east. Not west. No more English can stay on French land. When you come here you cross Allegheny at Forks, n'est-ce pas?"

Haworth interceded. "As thee has read my diary, thee knoweth the answers."

"Then you go back east from here. Meanwhile you stay here."

"In that case, may I have my diary and writing materials?"

"Qu'avez-vous dit? Je ne peux pas vous comprendre. Parlez-moi en Français, s'il vous plaît."

With a sheepish look, Haworth replied, haltingly, "Rends-moi mon journal, s'il te plaît."

"Very well. *Thee* may have it."

PART SIX

From the Journal of Ephraim Haworth

FOURTH MONTH 1, 1754

The name of God be praised. My journal has been returned to me. This is written at Venango on the Allegheny River at the trading post built here by John Fraser, trader and blacksmith, and now occupied by a French contingent. My young friend Jason McGee and I are prisoners of the French, having been brought here forcibly by a party of Ottawa Indians.

The commander of this new French post, one Captain Philippe-Thomas de Joncaire, at first was harsh to us, suspecting us of being English agents sent out to stir up the Indians, but having read my earlier entries in this diary—without my permission, I might add—he realizes that we are what we say we are. Still, he will not let us go because the French at Le Boeuf, on the headwaters of French Creek, are preparing a considerable military force of Canadians and Indians to descend the Allegheny and destroy a fort being constructed there by the Virginians. They intend to establish their own fort there and to sweep all English-speaking people from the lands west of the Allegheny Ridge.

Captain Joncaire says he will take us with him to the Forks of the Ohio when they make their invasion. Then he intends to force us to return to the east.

Meanwhile I find myself in agreeable circumstances, or did until last night. Jason and I mingle freely with the several officers who have joined Captain Joncaire. I had not meant them to know that I have studied French, but it did slip out in an unguarded moment and the officers now enjoy my poor efforts to converse in their language. They do not openly mock my pronunciation. They only pretend to misunderstand so that I have to repeat myself awkwardly. It is an innocent amusement, I suppose. As for Captain Joncaire, a bond of understanding was developing between us until an incident which I shall relate later. From reading my diary, or, I should say, from having it read to him at Le Boeuf, he did form a good opinion of my principles. He and I have spent several evenings conversing first in French and then in English about various subjects.

Although his profession as a soldier is one which, as a member of the Society of Friends, I abhor, still I find him a gentleman in many ways, and although his religion is one which I regard as a perversion of true Christianity, I think him to be a man who honors God. Besides all that he is good company, being well educated and tolerant, and I would not be human if I were not flattered that he seems to find me so as well.

Captain Joncaire is reluctant to talk of his family, but I understand that he is married to a Seneca woman and is much respected by the Indian tribes.

He speaks frankly about French intentions in this area. They feel that all the interior of the North American continent is theirs and say that they intend to make its eastern borders secure and to expel all unauthorized whites from this area.

He shares my dislike of the roguish Pennsylvania fur traders and the greedy Virginia land speculators, although his reasons are not the same as mine. He admits with some reluctance that English trade goods are superior to French and less expensive. And the Pennsylvania traders are both more numerous and more aggressive than the French, hence the furs of this region flow east toward Philadelphia rather than north to Montreal. He particularly despises George Croghan, the Irishman whose agents and factors dominate the fur trade out here.

Captain Joncaire says that the French could have dealt with these traders by declaring a bounty on their scalps. What concerns them more are the declared intentions of the Virginians, through their Ohio Land Company, to settle English-speaking families out here. The French will go to war rather than permit this, he says.

As diplomatically as possible, I have pointed out that there are twenty-five times as many English colonists as there are French on this continent. He brushes away this argument by noting that the population of France exceeds that of England and that the French colonists enjoy certain advantages, among them their ease of water transportation and the adaptability of their Canadians to Indian life.

I told him I prayed there would not be war, but that if it came, I thought he would find the preponderance of numbers more important than he professed to think.

He smiled at this, saying, "My friend, your Quaker government lacks the will to fight for what they say, however wrongly, is their land out here. And in your reckoning of numbers you do not take into account the Indians who have been for so long cheated of lands and treated with disrespect. What if they are persuaded to join us as allies? How long do you think your squatters and those Virginia interlopers would last? For that matter, what would happen to those English settlers farther east should the Shawanese and the Delaware return in anger to their old lands?"

His insinuation that the French might instigate the Indians to take the warpath unsettled me. "Surely, sir, thee would not incite the red man to make war on women and children," I said.

He replied, "It depends on whether your people accept our rightful title to these lands and restrict yourself to those lying east of Allegheny Mountain."

Seeing that Jason grew agitated at the suggestion of possible Indian attacks on white settlements, I turned to other subjects. Captain Joncaire, perhaps regretting he had said so much, followed me into a pleasant discussion of Indian customs, something in which he has a strong interest.

Apologizing for reading my diary—for the first time, I might add—he asked me to tell him more of what I had learned from Tallema about Delaware life. He knows the Senecas and the Ottawa tribes better than the Delaware. Although he shares my respect for the Indians, he appears little concerned with their lack of Christian charity toward their enemies, or with their personal morals. In fact, he caused me to lose my equanimity by twitting me for my refusal to accept Tallema's "gift" of Wecolis to be my paramour, knowing full well that not only am I married, but that I am a man of God. I told him that if he again referred to that matter I should refuse to converse with him anymore. He begged my pardon with what I hope was sincerity, and I accepted his apology.

As for the incident to which I alluded earlier, Captain Joncaire brought back a supply of excellent Canadian wine, which he has been sharing with me and his fellow officers at our evening meals. I allow myself but one glass, as is my custom, and it has amused him to try to persuade me to have a second portion; but I refuse, of course.

Last night, when I did so again, he said, "I will not pour it over your head, you may count on that. Not with your violent young friend at hand."

Jason did not laugh at this reference to our troubles with that awful Virginian Pratt. In fact, he does not share my respect for Captain

Joncaire, still suspecting him of having sought to turn us over to the Seneca party while knowing of their bad intentions toward us. Ignoring Jason's surly manner, the captain, who had not denied himself either a second or a third glass of wine, asked the lad what had happened to the large yellow dog of whom he had read in my diary.

"He followed Mister Cadwell."

"He is not such a faithful animal after all."

Jason acted as though he had not heard this remark, which was followed with, "Ah, and this Indian maiden, this granddaughter of the chief. Was there perhaps something between you that did not meet the eye? I am a man of the world, you can tell me."

The other officers had not been able to follow this and so Joncaire spoke to them in French, commenting on what prigs and hypocrites there were among the Anglo-Saxon race. This caused much laughter and clucking of tongues around the fire.

Joncaire resumed in English. "See how red his face becomes," he said. "I have put my finger too near the truth, n'est-ce pas?"

Jason must learn to control his temper. I am ashamed to record that he took his half-filled wine cup and hurled its contents into Captain Joncaire's face. With wine running down his face and over his lapels, the captain put his hand on his sword and for a moment I thought he would draw it.

I arose, prepared to step between them, but one of the French officers, an older man, touched Joncaire's shoulder and said in French that he should not demean himself by drawing a sword on an ignorant English peasant lad. But Joncaire was furious. He called for guards and ordered them to shut Jason away in our cellar until he is ready to apologize.

I protested, saying that if he did that to Jason he should do it to me as well. Instead he sent me to an upstairs room, larger and more comfortable, one containing a chair and a table at which I may write. So ended what had been a pleasant evening.

FOURTH MONTH 2, 1754

What a lovely day, so warm that I do not need a fire. From this corner room I can see the Allegheny flowing swift and slightly muddy. More soldiers have come down French Creek, soldiers and Indians, all armed, far too many of them to fit in the stockaded space around this log house. More officers are on hand now and Captain Joncaire, whether because he is too busy with them or because of the offense Jason gave him, barely nods when I take my daily exercise. My meals are brought to me. I am no longer allowed to dine with the officers. There are so many the common room cannot hold them all at one time. They eat in shifts. The half-breed cook who brings me my meals grumbles about their appetites.

As for Jason, the half-breed tells me he still refuses to apologize to Captain Joncaire. He is a stubborn young man. It pains me to think of him alone in that prison room without me or anyone to buoy up his hopes. Perhaps in the future he will curb his temper.

I must return to the village. By now surely the braves have returned from their winter hunting and have selected a chief to replace Tallema. I must make certain that whoever he is, he will live up to Tallema's promise that I may continue my school.

Either now or very shortly, Jason's brother, Isaac, should come back to see if Awilshahuak will have him as a husband.

Christopher Cadwell most likely is on his way to Shippensburg with all the furs that his pony, Jason's mare and my horse can carry. It may be a long time before more furs can be taken east. If Christopher waits and markets his furs properly, he will get a price that will provide him with a goodly nest egg for his life with Mrs. McGinty. I bear him no ill will. He has many good qualities. He would have no way of knowing where to find us, even if he were inclined to look.

I wonder whose side the Almighty is on in this conflict over ownership of these lands drained by the Allegheny. Does He favor the English, the French or the Iroquois? Which prayers will He heed: those uttered by Protestants, Catholics or Indian nature-worshipers?

Seeing the juggernaut the French are preparing to roll down the Allegheny, I realize that the title to this area cannot long continue in doubt. I should like to see these lands reserved to the Delaware and Shawanese alone. I should like to see the French and the Virginians, yes, and the Pennsylvania traders and the Iroquois, all withdraw and allow these dispossessed tribes to dwell here in peace. A kingdom of Christianized Indians living in peace, that is my dream. I pray for peace and that I may be permitted to continue my school.

FOURTH MONTH 3, 1754

As I have time to reflect, bits and pieces of my recent conversation with Captain Joncaire keep occurring to me.

215

When first Jason and I were brought to this place, he told me with considerable scorn that a young Virginia militia officer had come to Venango in December to order the French off these lands, but I paid scant heed to the story at that time.

Captain Joncaire entertained the newly arrived French officers with a broader account of that visit. He identified the officer as one George Washington, describing him as a hardy young giant barely in his twenties and ridiculing his efforts at bluffing the French. It seems this Washington came here accompanied by a Virginia frontiersman and a French-speaking Dutchman, bearing a letter of warning from the governor of Virginia to vacate what they feel to be their territory. Joncaire said he smothered this young Virginian with hospitality, plying him with wine and treating him with meticulous courtesy. He told of Washington's clumsy effort to hide the fact that Tanacharison himself and the other Indians from Logstown accompanied him but were camped nearby, in hiding.

When this fact slipped out, Joncaire sent for the Half King and, giving him plenteous wine, upbraided him for not coming forward at once so that he could enjoy the hospitality of his staunch friends the French. He said the young Washington was much put off by this show of French gallantry toward the Indians. Joncaire said he had gone to extra lengths to placate Tanacharison because the previous commander of the French had treated the Half King with regrettable contempt at being served a similar warning from the Iroquois. That commander was in ill health and has since died and Joncaire took great care to point all this out in the process of smoothing the Indian's ruffled feathers.

He said Washington tried to deliver his message to him but that he had referred him to his new commander at Le Boeuf, one Legardeur J. de St. Pierre. So after a brief sojourn at Venango, Washington had gone on to Le Boeuf, sixty miles up French Creek, only to receive a scornful reply from St. Pierre to take back to Williamsburg. When the bedraggled young man passed back through Venango, Joncaire persuaded Tanacharison to stay and enjoy more of his hospitality, and Washington had appeared furious at the Indian's acceptance. He and his party returned south in miserable weather, with, as Joncaire put it, their tails between their legs. . . .

These French officers are a high-spirited group, and it does give them pleasure to twit me for my principles, particularly a bright young ensign named Jumonville.

Such a thing hath occurred that my mind will take some time to adjust to it.

Every day has brought more Canadians and their Indian allies down French Creek, so that now the grounds around this house are thick-covered with the tents and lodges of hundreds of men. Their boats and canoes line the river and the banks are piled with supplies. We are in the midst of a gathering army, and the commander of this horde, a veteran soldier named Contrecoeur is here now, supervising their preparation.

I enjoy walking about in this milling crowd for as long as my guard will permit, looking into the faces of the French, Indians and half-breeds, listening to the babble of their tongues and, truth to tell, being stared at by them with equal curiosity.

But to my story. This morning, as I was deep in prayer, I heard a commotion outside the stockade, with someone shouting for Captain Joncaire to present himself at the gate, but did not go to my window as I regard communication with the Father more important than idle curiosity. Later, when Jacques, the French-Huron cook, arrived with my breakfast, I asked him the cause of the hubbub and he said the soldiers had apprehended two spies, a white man and an Indian, who had been lurking about the nearby villages asking questions. He said Joncaire at that moment was interrogating them downstairs, but that this was a mere formality before having them shot.

Scarcely had I sat down to my breakfast when a guard came to say Captain Joncaire required my presence immediately and hauled me off downstairs into the common room, where a roughly dressed white man and a slender young Indian stood with hands bound before Joncaire. The white man was saying in a loud, contemptuous voice as I entered. "You scurvy French dog. I am telling you the truth—"

Joncaire, with reddened face and outthrust chin, interrupted with, "I will have you whipped and plunged into the river, drowned rather than shot if you dare speak to me like that again—"

His angry eye spotted me in midsentence. "Ah, our missionary is here. We will see what he says."

The white man's back was turned, but I knew him already from the voice and the familiar form of the shoulders.

"Christopher," I cried.

"I'll be God d—d," he said. "You *are* here. Tell this snail-eating bastard who I am. He is talking of having me and Apauko shot."

217

A thousand questions crowded my brain as I stepped forward to embrace him. The guard restrained me.

"This is my trader friend," I said. "He is the one who guided us west. He is no more a spy than I."

"He is the one who died and returned to life, I take it." Joncaire spoke French and I replied in the same language that this was so.

"If he does not curb his tongue, he will die a death from which there can be no return. I cannot suffer myself to be insulted by such a low fellow in the presence of my officers."

"He has an unfortunate habit of expressing himself too strongly," I replied. "Pray do not be offended. I will speak to him."

Before I could begin, Christopher said, "Why don't you stop that foreign gabble and tell me in white man's talk where Jason is?"

"Thee must restrain thy tongue, Christopher," I said. "This gentleman is a French officer. I implore thee to give him no further offense."

"Well, the son of a bitch has offended me enough. Now, where the h—l is Jason?"

"He is here, locked up for insulting this same Captain Joncaire."

While all this was taking place, Apauko stood straight as a hickory sapling, no emotion showing on his face. Now he spoke, in Delaware.

"Memhalamund, your angry words make trouble for us."

This caused Christopher to calm down, so that Joncaire could continue speaking to me in French. I satisfied him that Christopher was a fur trader and nothing more. He said that he would not shoot him, then, unless he insulted him or some other French officer. I started to protest and he said, "Or would you prefer that I ask our mutual Seneca friends to come and take the three of you off my hands?"

"Very well," I said. "I will do my best, but thee can see what a difficult person he is."

"Yes," Joncaire said with an edge of sarcasm. "I am surprised that a gentleman of such impeccable piety as you should associate with such a ruffian."

I ignored that remark, instead speaking rapidly in Delaware to Christopher so that Apauko could understand, telling them in a few words how we had been abducted and hurried to this place and ending with, "I don't know how thee was able to find us. Thank thee, my dear friend, for seeking us out. I thought thee would be on thy way back to Shippensburg by now."

"Don't thank me. Thank Apauko. You are lucky there has been hardly any fresh snow since you disappeared. He returned with the other braves just three days ago and he was able to track you here."

Captain Joncaire interrupted, in French. "Enough. We will keep

218

the three of you here and send you packing east, where you belong, once our expedition is complete. Your friend may forget about his horses and furs. He will be expelled with you and the red-haired hothead."

"Three?" I asked. "What about the young Indian here?"

"He is Delaware?"

"Yes."

"He may go. I trust he will return to his village straightway and tell his people of the might of their brothers the French. It may make them easier to deal with in the future. Tell him he may go."

"Apauko," I said. "This man says thee may return to thy village. Tell them I love them as I do my own children and that I will return to continue to teach them to read and write. As soon as I am free."

Before Joncaire could interfere, Christopher said, "Yes, tell them to take good care of my horses. I will be back for my furs, and tell them to keep away from my trade goods until then. Tell Menumheck and Awilshahuak not to worry. I will bring Jason back. Tell Wecolis—"

"Enough." Joncaire shouted. "Send this young brave on his way."

The guards led Apauko to the door. As he left, he put me in mind of a freshly caught fish released back into the water. He stood in the doorway, confused for a moment, then in a flash was gone.

"Why can't we go with him?" Christopher demanded. "What are you going to do with me?"

"I have a place to put scum who insult French officers."

After Christopher had been led away, I spoke up. "If thee proposes to shut him away in that dreadful little room, then please treat me in the very same way. I must suffer as do my friends."

"What an innocent fool you are. Those two are not worth your friendship. They are riffraff. Why does a gentleman of your wealth and education associate himself with such lowborn persons? You should be back in Philadelphia, adding to your family fortune. I hear that Philadelphia is a most agreeable city."

"I would prefer to be with my friends in their dark hole than in the drawing room of the finest Philadelphia mansion."

"For a time you shall be in neither place." With that, he had me returned to this room. Here I sit with a thousand questions to put to Christopher. He is a good man at heart. To think that much as he desires to hasten back east with his furs, he risked them and his life to try to rescue us.

PART SEVEN

1

Once, when they had been small boys living in the northern shadow of the Kittatinny Ridge, Jason and Isaac had trapped a half-grown fox. Abraham had wanted them to kill the animal and sell its skin, but Gerta had sided with the boys and they had been permitted to keep the fox in a cage of woven willow branches.

At first the fox had flung itself against the sides of the cage until blood flowed from its nostrils. Then it turned round and round for hours in a frenzy to regain its freedom. At last, exhausted, it had lain down, refusing water and food, until one morning the boys found it dead.

Jason later would remember how like that fox he had acted when first he was thrust back into the little cellar, alone now and no longer allowed out to exercise. Acting on Joncaire's orders, Jacques, the cook, brought him bread and water, and acting on his own, he taunted the lad in a mixture of French and English. Jason ignored the taunts. His own thoughts were torment enough, driving him to strike the door until his knuckles were bleeding and swollen. He would not apologize. He had committed no offense except to injure the pride of a French officer who had insulted him and was wrongly holding him a prisoner.

Even now Isaac might be awaiting him back at the village, eager for a reunion. Or, worse, he might have come and, not finding Jason, left for the wilderness. What might Awilshahuak have told him? What did she think? Who was looking after Logan?

Old voices spoke to him out of the darkness, and half-forgotten images swam before his eyes. Parson Elder admonished him to keep up his reading. Pratt mocked him for not seeking revenge. Goodspeed asked him why he kept the company of fools. After a time, Jason found he could will faces to appear. Again and again he could see Sallie Koch's tear-stained face turned up to him and could hear her saying, "Come back when you can provide for me. I will wait." And he could hear Awilshahuak saying, "Ktahoallel, Mocquasaka. Ktahoallel."

Suddenly a new voice sounded unbidden in his ears. "Keep your frigging hands off me, you French bastards."

Jason tried to shut it out and regain the sound of Sallie's voice, but there it was again.

"You ain't gonna stick me in that hole."

The door opened, letting in a blinding morning sun. Someone stumbled over Jason's legs and the door slammed.

"Who is in here?"

"Me. Who is that?"

"Jason. Is that you, lad?"

"Mister Cadwell!"

They fumbled in the darkness until their hands met and grasped. "Did they capture you too? Where is Logan? What . . ."

The questions bubbled from Jason's lips faster than Cadwell could answer them, until in exasperation he said, "Why don't you just shut up and let me tell you the whole story. Then I'll hear yours."

On that Sunday afternoon when the Ottawas seized Haworth and Jason, Cadwell said, he had returned from grazing the horses and hunting, and had thought it strange that his companions were not in the new school cabin. He did not grow alarmed, though, until nightfall, at which time he interrupted the mourning ceremony for Tallema to ask Woapink if he knew where they had gone.

"What about Awilshahuak?" Jason asked.

"Well you might ask about her. The truth about you two is out. If you thought she carried on about old Tallema, you should have seen her when she learned you had disappeared. She tore her garments and went into a perfect fit. Never saw a female take on like that. The other women had to give up grieving for Tallema to calm her down. She called you her husband."

"Her husband? Where did she get such an idea?"

"Did you sleep with her?"

"Not exactly. No, not sleep."

"I don't mean go to sleep, you fool. Don't split hairs with me. Did you fuck Awilshahuak?"

Jason wanted to strangle the trader. "I d-don't have to answer that."

"You just did." Cadwell laughed. "Son of a bitch. Diddled the chief's granddaughter. Didn't know you had it in you." He laughed again. "Or her. Bet she was something. Never saw a prettier little squaw. Was she a good piece?"

"L-listen n-now. You shut your filthy mouth. You don't understand."

"Ah, so that is how it is? I'm to keep silent about this delicate matter of the heart."

"What about Isaac? Did he turn up?"

"Ah, you know about that?"

"Yes. Mister Haworth told me after they brought us here. Old Tallema told him that Meskikokant is Awilshahuak's father. And that he tried to marry Isaac to her. Tallema sent Apauko to tell Isaac I was looking for him. Did he?"

"Apauko said he was not at the hunting camp, but that Meskikokant was. He told him and generally spread the word."

"Told Meskikokant? Oh, God. Not him."

"Don't worry. He'll stay clear of you. He'll be sure you want to kill him to even the score."

"Tallema thought that I wanted to kill Meskikokant too."

"Instead you frigged his daughter. I can't figure out when you had the chance."

"I warn you. Don't say another word about that." And after a long silence, "Does everyone in the village know?"

"Afraid so, including Apauko."

"Apauko? What's it to him?"

"He fancies Awilshahuak and he hates your guts that you so easily won her heart."

"Why did Apauko trouble himself to guide you here if he feels that way?"

"First, he had no choice. Menumheck ordered him to. Besides that, he'd like nothing better than to have you and your brother reunite and head east and leave Awilshahuak to him. Everyone loves that little filly, but you're the only one . . . I forgot. I'm not to mention that."

"What about Logan?"

"He sends his love. Poor dog wouldn't eat for a while. I'd have brought him with me but feared he would give us away. Awilshahuak is keeping him."

"And the other braves came back with Apauko?"

"They did that, about three days ago. And, Jason, you never saw such furs. More beaver and otter than I can carry. With the supply cut off by the troubles out here, the price should go up. I'll make a killing if I can just get you out and back to that village."

Jason chose his next words carefully and with some embarrassment. "Look, Mister Cadwell. You did a grand thing risking your life like this to come after us. You could have taken off without us. You had what you came out here for. I am grateful to you."

"Don't thank me. Thank that devil woman Menumheck."

"How is that?"

"She calls the shots in that village and she wouldn't let those braves exchange a single pelt with me until I promised the safe return of your fine red-headed self . . . and Haworth. But you in particular."

"Me. Why?"

"Because it looks as though Awilshahuak will do herself in for love of you. And the old gal has also taken quite a fancy to you. Not in quite the same way, but you should have heard her bragging about you to the braves. Telling them what a crack shot you are. And about your skill at building. She wants you back there and soon, make no mistake."

"To marry Awilshahuak? Me?"

"In Awilshahuak's mind that is done. You killed game and brought it to her, remember? She accepted it. That is a sign of betrothal. She is your squaw."

"Oh, my God. You came for that?"

"Well, it is a damned fool notion, but if I don't deliver you, they don't deliver the pelts."

"Me married to an Indian?"

"That's the way the wind is blowing."

"Look, I like Awilshahuak. But we just got carried away. I know who I shall marry. And I don't want to spend my life shivering in a cold, smoky lodge. I want a good solid stone house and my own farm or business and white children, not half-breeds."

"I know how you feel. Now let's figure a way to get away from this place so we both can have what we want."

2

That evening, as they sipped their water and nibbled on chunks of stale bread, they heard a disturbance outside and, to their amazement, recognized the voice of Haworth raised in apparent anger.

"You are naught but low French dogs."

Enraged French voices replied as the door opened and Haworth came hurtling through.

The door slammed and the bar clattered down.

"Mister Haworth. What happened?"

"Hush. Wait until the soldiers are out of earshot."

Jason lowered his voice. "You were abusing those people."

"Yes," Cadwell said. "If I didn't know better, I would have sworn you are angry. What's up?"

"All right. They are gone. No, I am not really angry. I only pretended to be. I could think of no other way to make them let me rejoin you. So I insulted Captain Joncaire, taking pains to do it in the hearing of young Jumonville and others."

"What did Joncaire do?" Cadwell asked.

"At first he acted as though he could not believe his ears. Then, in French so his companions would hear, I told him his language was a bastard offspring of Latin just as his ancestors are the bastard descendants of Roman soldiers who were scum to begin with. He exploded and told me I was an English swine dog who defiled the French language with my heretical tongue. He called me an insufferable prig and hypocrite as well, and ordered me to be thrown in here with what he called my 'low companions.' "

Cadwell was laughing even louder than Jason. When he caught his breath, he said, "My God, Ephraim, how did I ever get hooked up with such a fellow as you? How are you? I have missed you."

"And I thee, Christopher. Tell me the news from our village."

When Cadwell was done talking, he said, "So thee thinks they mean Awilshahuak to become Jason's wife?"

"She regards herself already as his wife."

"Wherever did she get that idea?"

"Our young friend is not so backward as he might seem."

"Now don't start that, Mister Cadwell. I don't want to become her husband. I just want—"

"I know. You just want to take your brother back east. But don't you see, my boy, you can't accomplish that unless you return and face them. And I can't have my furs unless you do."

Haworth joined in. "And I must return, however briefly, to be certain of my school's future."

"They've got my dog too," Jason said. "What a mess."

"That is no mess. This is the mess. How the hell are we going to get out of this shithole?"

"However we may get out," Haworth said, "it will not be through coarse speaking."

"Such as calling people low French dogs?"

"That is quite another matter. I intend ultimately to apologize to Captain Joncaire."

The young French ensign, Jumonville, came to the door two days later. With him were two soldiers carrying large bowls of stew. He addressed Haworth at length, in French. As he spoke, Jason, blinded by the outside light, had to put his hands over his eyes. The odor of the stew so tantalized him that he was tempted to charge past the officer in the doorway and seize a bowl from the soldiers. Haworth replied in French and Jumonville spoke again, gesturing toward the river as he did.

"Ask him for some of that God damned stew," Cadwell said.

Haworth put his finger to his lips and shook his head. When the ensign finished speaking, he handed each of the prisoners a bowl. The door closed and they fell to eating like starved wolves.

Cadwell scarcely paused for breath until he had finished half of his portion. Then he wiped his mouth and belched. "What did that little pipsqueak want that took so long?"

"The expedition leaves tomorrow morning. They intend to take us with them down the Allegheny. They expect to chase the Virginians away from the fort they are building and construct one of their own."

"That's a hundred miles from here. Somebody else will end up with my furs and maybe my trade goods and horses too. Damn it to hell."

"That is not the worst of it. They may keep us at the Forks for some time to work on their fort."

Jason spoke up. "D-damn them. If they keep us down there it could mean I would miss Isaac altogether. What if we just lie down and refuse to go with them?"

"There's an idea," Cadwell said. "They can't be bothered to carry three dead weights all the way to the Forks."

"My dear friends, I must disabuse you. Young Jumonville says that those Senecas are still lurking about and they know all three of us are here now. They have offered furs to Joncaire if he will turn us over to them."

"Senecas?" Cadwell asked. "What Senecas?"

Jason told him about the party that had turned up and tried to take him away.

"This is all your fault, Haworth," the trader said. "I knew this was going to haunt us. Damn you, if I had it to do over again, I would give you to those Senecas on the spot at Loyalhanning. Think of all the trouble that would have spared us, Jason."

"Aw, Mister Cadwell, don't let's go back over that. I am worried that Captain Joncaire may yet accept their offer of furs."

"I think not," Haworth said. "Not unless we make fresh trouble."

"Why not?" Jason asked. "He is angry with all three of us. I threw wine in his face. Mister Cadwell shouted at him. And even you insulted him."

"Then thee thinks thee may have acted hastily when thee cast that wine in his face?"

"Well, yes, but I'm also sorry he asked for it."

"And thee, Mister Cadwell. Dost thee regret those rude remarks uttered to the captain?"

"Hell, yes. I am sorry, particularly if I lose my furs."

"Good. Then I spoke truly to Ensign Jumonville when I told him just now that we all wished to convey our sincere apologies to the captain and beg his pardon and that we will make no further affronts to his dignity."

They finished their stew in silence. Cadwell set his bowl on the floor. "I'm glad you said it, Haworth, but let me tell you, if I had that French bastard alone in the woods, I wouldn't apologize."

3

Jason fell into a dreamless sleep until soon after midnight, when he awakened abruptly, thinking someone had whispered his name. He lay on his pile of damp straw marveling at the quiet that had fallen over the sleeping French army.

"Jason. Jason McGee. Are you in there?"

The voice, speaking in Delaware, came from the other side of the door.

"Who's out there?"

"Never mind. Come to the door."

The voice was husky. "Listen. Your guard has gone to pee in the bushes. We have little time. I will make a noise so he will go look. A panther scream. You understand?"

"Yes."

Now Cadwell had awakened. "What's going on?"

"Shh. Someone wants to help us."

The voice continued. "I will take the bar off the door. You put it back. Go straight to the river, to the end of the line of boats. A canoe is there with two paddles. Cross the river and go home. You promise?"

"I hear you."

"You promise?"

"I promise. But who are you?"

"Never mind. Just leave. Remember. When you hear the scream of a panther. And go home if you want to stay alive."

They could barely hear the sound of the bar being lifted. Frantically they awakened Haworth, Cadwell putting his hand over the Quaker's mouth as they lifted him to his feet. He recovered his wits quickly and, to Jason's relief, offered no protest. They heard the footsteps of the returning guard and then the cry of a panther and a voice shouting, "Help. Over here. Le couguar." The guard called to another and both of them ran toward the sound of the voice. In a second the three companions were outside the door, replacing the bar.

"To the river," Cadwell said.

"Go ahead and wait for me there," Jason replied. "I'll be along shortly."

Cadwell started to protest and Jason said, "Don't argue. Do as I say."

The trader seized Haworth's arm and fairly dragged him toward the river. Left behind, Jason was glad he had been shut away so long in a dark place, for his night vision was the better for it. He crept along the wall of the Fraser house to the back door, where a guard was usually posted. Evidently he, too, had gone to investigate the panther's scream.

Jason entered the kitchen. Coals smoldered in the fireplace. Jacques slept in the nook beside the chimney. Praying the boards would not creak enough to awaken him, Jason tiptoed into the hall and to the door of the bedroom where Joncaire slept. A fire burned low in that room too, its light revealing the forms of several officers sleeping on pallets. Joncaire himself lay on the bed with two other officers. Jason stood stock still, barely daring to breathe as he looked about. An officer muttered in his sleep. Another ground his teeth. There it was, leaning against the mantel, its walnut and maple stock reflecting the firelight.

Jason stepped over first one man and then another. At last his hand closed on the rifle. He hoisted the pouch and powder horns, judging from their weight that they were full, and put their straps over his shoulder, then he stepped back across the sleeping officers.

On reentering the kitchen, he scooped up a half loaf of bread and some scraps of venison from the table and packed them into his shot pouch. Outside, the guards had not yet returned to their posts. Jason could hear the two men calling out in the bushes for the person who had shouted the warning about the panther. Quickly Jason darted around the corner of the house. It seemed an eternity before he reached the riverbank and another before he picked his way along the line of boats to where Haworth and Cadwell waited.

"Here, Jason. Here, in the canoe. Where the hell have you been? Another minute and I would have left you. Get in."

They had saved the front position for him. He knelt there and Cadwell passed up a paddle.

"Whoever that was that freed us made me promise to cross the river and go home."

"You promised. I didn't. And I am steering."

"Where shall we go, then?"

"Downstream. Now shut up and start paddling. Haworth, keep flat on the bottom and don't rock this damned thing. We will be passing through a gorge the first few miles and I don't care to get dumped into this cold water."

There was just enough moon for them to discern the course of the river, but not enough to make out rocks and snags. They proceeded gingerly, not daring to paddle too fast or even to talk, lest it interfere with Cadwell's hearing as he listened for the sound of rapids. Even so, they struck against several rocks, nearly overturning once and another time making Jason think they surely must have penetrated the bark skin of the canoe. He was glad to find that his old skill at handling his dugout back on the Susquehanna returned. Picking up the rhythm, he paddled on one side only, feathering the strokes to help Cadwell keep control. His knees ached from the unaccustomed kneeling and later he thought his arms would drop off, but the fear of being recaptured by the French spurred him on.

Cadwell had said the night before that only a miracle from Haworth's God could save them. Jason wondered about the Indian who had released them. Certainly no manito could have aided them any better. What was the Delaware's motive for doing something that might have earned him death had the French caught him?

By the time dawn broke, they were a dozen miles downstream from Venango, where the banks of the river were lower and the surrounding terrain flatter. Cadwell allowed them to beach the canoe and relieve their bladders and stretch their aching legs.

"I'd give anything for a bite to eat," Cadwell said.

"Would you give up your place in the stern and let me steer?"

Jason asked and, before Cadwell could reply, drew out the bread and meat he had stolen. Despite their hunger, Cadwell would let them eat only half the food.

"You are a good provider, my lad. All we need now is old Logan and my furs and my horses."

"*Our* horses," Jason reminded him. "The mare is still mine."

By daylight, and with Jason steering, they made much better time down the river. There were still occasional rapids and Jason was glad he knew the trick of aiming for the V-shaped ripples pointing downstream and avoiding those pointing upstream. As they sped along they fell to discussing what they should do. The discussion soon deteriorated into an argument between Haworth, who wanted to stop soon and walk west, and Cadwell, who insisted that they must continue downstream for another day. "There is no decent trail to the west until we reach Kittanning. We'd either lose time or get lost if we tried walking from here."

It was Jason who raised the question of whether they should warn the Virginians at the Forks of the Ohio of the French armada set to descend upon them. He brought it up when they stopped, exhausted, at noon near the entrance of a large creek and consumed the last of the food filched from the kitchen at Venango.

"That's their lookout," Cadwell said. "I ain't risking my furs and horses to go four or five days out of my way to tell them. If they have any sense, they will be prepared. They ought to know the French mean to move against them. It was common knowledge last summer."

"What about you, Mister Haworth? You've been mighty quiet about all this."

"I have been pondering the question in my heart ever since we escaped."

"Jason and I have been too busy paddling to ponder."

Haworth ignored the gibe. "I abhor war, and I refuse to take sides in this ugly contest over land and furs between two parties who care naught for the Indians. My struggle is against sin and ignorance."

Jason frowned. "That is all well and good, but the fact remains that nigh onto a thousand French and Indians right now are on their way down this river to attack people of our race and tongue. The Virginians might stop them if they had a warning in time."

Cadwell snorted. "You can go to hell if you think I'm going to paddle clear down to the Forks. I don't want to waste a single hour getting back to the village. And Haworth has his school to look after. And have you forgotten your precious brother could be there, waiting for you?"

232

Nonetheless, Jason could not stop thinking about the Virginians as they glided down the Allegheny, past its rocky bluffs and deep-wooded shores.

Haworth seemed to have read his thoughts. "There *is* much at stake in this matter," he said after a long silence. "What we do or do not do this very day could affect the history of this region for all time."

Jason chimed in. "That is just what I have been thinking, Mister Haworth. You may not like what the Virginians want to do because you think only Indians have a right to be here, and Mister Cadwell's friends may not like them bringing in white families because it could hurt the fur trade, but I was a settler myself, remember."

"So what?" Cadwell said.

"So what if somebody had known that Meskikokant was on his way to kill my mother and little sister and what if that somebody had refused to go out of his way to warn us. Suppose he had said, 'It is none of my concern. I have important business this day,' or 'I don't give a damn, as they are only squatters and they should be taught a lesson.' "

Jason shifted his paddle to the left to ease the strain on his arms, and continued. "Besides, whether the French win or not, Mister Cadwell can get his furs and horses out in the next few weeks. He has time for that. And no matter whether the Virginia fort falls or stands, I should be able to take my brother back east. But, Mister Haworth, the future of your school may well depend on whether the Virginians are warned to prepare for the French attack. The French will bring in Catholic missions and would never permit you to have your school."

"Thee makes thy point as well as any philosopher. What are we to do?"

"I'll tell you what we are to do," Cadwell said. "We are to do nothing."

That night they halted just before dusk at a point where a swarm of passenger pigeons were roosting. Cadwell swore at their lack of a fowling piece, but Jason was able to shoot three of the birds, one at a time, with his rifle before it became too dark to see. Later, with much difficulty, they managed to start a fire and roast the pigeons, which they consumed down to the last edible morsels, including the hearts and livers. The sun and the strenuous paddling had kept them warm during the day, but now, without blankets or proper coats, they were miserably cold. Still Cadwell would not allow them to build up the fire beyond what was necessary to roast the pigeons, for fear of attracting attention. They were too weary to talk long, and too uncom-

233

fortable to sleep deeply, and so spent the chilly April night in a fitful torpor.

Cadwell had them up at the first hint of dawn. Jason offered to shoot more of the pigeons, but the trader would not hear of it.

"Right now, somewhere upstream, all them French and their Indian friends are getting up. We don't know whether they are just around the last bend or halfway back to Venango. Let's not lose our lead on them."

The river ran smoother, its calm waters divided at one point by a large island, where Cadwell let them stop so that Jason could shoot a pair of squirrels chasing each other around the trunk of a large poplar. He would not permit them to stop and cook the animals, however. At last, near dusk, and nearly fainting from fatigue, they saw ahead, on the left bank, a collection of Indian lodges set on a wide flood plain stretching gently up to a line of low hills.

"That is the mighty Delaware town of Kittanning, gentlemen," Cadwell said. "We made it."

"Praise be to God for delivering us from our enemies."

"They will give us some hot food, I expect," Jason said.

"They would, but we ain't stopping there. I'd just as soon the Indians don't know we are around. If they don't know, they can't tell the French. Pull in against the right bank down there."

He pointed to a bushy spot on the west side of the river in the shadow of a steep ridge. They found a nearby lean-to with a fire pit. Jason started a small blaze, over which they charred the squirrels, then ate them before they were well cooked inside.

4

As they sat sucking the marrow from the squirrel bones, Cadwell brought up the subject Jason had been thinking about throughout the day.

"Well, lad, have you decided what you will say to Awilshahuak when we get to the village? What will you do about her?"

"Do? Nothing. I am not married to her."

"If she was an ordinary Delaware girl, you could get by with that, but not only is she the granddaughter of a chief, she is the apple of her mother's eye, and her mother is a woman not to be meddled with."

"Don't concern yourself. It's none of your business."

"Ah, but it is. If you refuse to stay as Awilshahuak's husband, that could be as bad for me as if you did not come back at all. Menumheck would refuse to let the braves trade with me, unless I could say you got caught up in the troubles of the white men's war and you will be delayed getting back, or that we don't know where you are. Or that you are dead."

"What would I do about Isaac if I don't go back? My brother means more to me than all the furs in the world."

"We could bring him out to you, one way or another."

Haworth was indignant. "I cannot support thy deceiving my Indian friends."

"Haworth, shut up and stay out of this. Am I making sense to you, Jason?"

"Sort of. I have been dreading having to tell Awilshahuak I can't be her husband. Would you promise not to leave without Isaac?"

"If we have to hogtie him and drag him out."

"And Logan too?"

"Logan too."

Jason stared into the fire for a long while. "What if Isaac should not be there?"

"I could get Apauko to help you search. He would do that if he thought it would mean keeping Awilshahuak from you and your brother."

"How long would it take someone who knew how to handle a canoe to make it to the Forks alone?"

Cadwell grinned. "Let's see. We had a half day, or I should say a half night's, start. And they will be held back by their heavier, slower boats, all trying to keep together. Without a fat Quaker to haul, you could make it there in two days and that would be probably a full day ahead of the French, barring bad luck. The Virginians might have time to send some men upstream and lay an ambush for the French."

"That means more killing of human beings," said Haworth.

"Only of Frenchmen," Cadwell replied. "Look, Haworth, you can't have everything. Somebody is bound to get hurt. If it's the French, you have a better chance of maintaining your school. Jason is volunteering to warn the Virginians while you and I head straight to the village and our business there."

"I have not volunteered," Jason said. "I was only discussing it."

They slept better that night, in the lean-to. Again Cadwell got them up early, explaining that he wanted to get moving before the Indians across the river began stirring. Haworth and Cadwell stood staring at Jason. Finally Cadwell spoke.

"I was thinking after we turned in last night, Jason. I don't blame you for being afraid to go down that river and risk your life to save them Virginians and their forts."

"I did not say I was afraid."

"You acted like you were afraid. Excuse me if I misjudged you. Anyway, this is the place to start walking. We had better drag the canoe back in the bushes and cover it. We got a two-day walk ahead of us and I reckon Jason is anxious to get there and explain to Awilshahuak and Menumheck what he is going to do."

"Where would I meet up with you again if I went to the Forks?"

"Just cross the river at the Forks and follow the Venango trail north to where it crosses the Kittanning path and wait there. If we get there first, we'll wait for you."

"What do you think I should do, Mister Haworth?"

"I can't decide for thee, Jason. My advice would be colored by my desire that my school be preserved."

Jason would never forget those few seconds when he stood on the bank of the Allegheny River trying to decide whether to follow his friends due west to where, he felt reasonably sure, he would be reunited with Isaac, or to proceed down the river alone to warn the Virginians that they were in imminent danger of French capture. Suddenly he felt a curious hatred for his two friends as they stood gazing at him, Haworth with an earnest, expectant expression on his broad, unlined face, and Cadwell with a cynical, half-amused look. He wished they would tell him what they wanted him to do.

Just then a bird began chirping nearby and another, farther away, answered. The sound touched off a memory of that day in October 1744, a few minutes before the attack on his family, when he had lain taking his ease beside the great hickory tree overlooking the McGee cabin. He stood just so, with blank eyes and open mouth, until Cadwell said impatiently, "Well. What is it to be?"

"I have got to live with myself for the rest of my life."

"That strikes me as a safe statement," the trader said dryly.

"And I don't want to remember that it lay in my power to save some fellow Americans but that I refused to help."

"Thee is a good young man, Jason. Thee hath put the lives of others ahead of thy own self-interest. Thee will not regret it."

236

Haworth stepped forward as if to embrace Jason, but the lad avoided him. Cadwell reached for his hand, but upon Jason's refusal to shake, said, "You've got guts, lad."

Jason took up a paddle. "You can both go to hell. I wish I had never laid eyes on either of you. Your d-damned furs and y-your silly s-school aren't worth a hair on my b-brother's head, but I got to live with m-myself. You b-both are too selfish or s-scared to do what must be done."

Avoiding Haworth's pained eyes, he got into the canoe. The two men stood on the bank looking down at him. Even Cadwell appeared embarrassed.

"One thing more, Cadwell. If you don't bring my brother out to me, don't you try to b-bring any of your G-God damned furs either. I will shoot you if you try to trick me."

Haworth found his voice. "Jason, I do affirm to thee before Almighty God that we will do all in our power to bring out Isaac. I will take thy place in that canoe if thee wishes me to carry the warning to the Virginians."

"Don't be silly. Like Cadwell says, you'd drown."

"Remember, Jason," Cadwell said. "Give your message to the bloody Virginians and clear out immediately. Cross the river and follow the Venango path north to the Kittanning-Kuskusky trail and wait there. And, Jason . . ."

"Yes?"

"Don't think hard of me. You've got the rest of your life to find your brother. Haworth, too, is young enough and rich enough to build another mission someday. But I am forty-five years old, and this is my last chance. Nothing will ever be the same out here again."

5

Jason's anger at his friends persisted like the dense morning mist that hovered over the Allegheny. Whether deliberately or unconsciously, those two had manipulated him into making this detour. Haworth's offer to undertake the trip was ridiculous. He must have known the others would not permit it. And Cadwell's seemingly offhand reminder that trouble awaited Jason at the village in the form of Menumheck was a piece of guile. More than they would admit, both those bastards had wanted the Virginians to be warned, but they had trapped him into making the trip, and it wasn't fair.

As he reflected on his own motives for agreeing to go, however, Jason had to acknowledge that he was acting partly out of cowardice. If he could give the Virginians a timely warning, he would not have them on his conscience the rest of his life, and at the same time he would avoid a painful confrontation at the village. Like the morning mists, his anger dissipated with the growing strength of the April sun. Haworth and Cadwell, they weren't such a bad pair after all. They had given him a lifetime of memories. Someday he would amuse Sallie with stories of his two unusual companions, of their eccentricities and their contrariness. He would miss those two after he went back east with Isaac. He missed them now, damn their eyes.

The distance between Kittanning and the Forks was only thirty-eight miles in a straight line, but the Allegheny's southwesterly course meandered over nearly fifty. It would have been an easy overnight trip for two well-fed men in an unladen canoe. It was difficult for one who had not eaten properly in days. Even so, except for his hunger, Jason found the trip pleasant enough, being borne along on the Allegheny's brisk current, encountering few rapids. He had a good start on the slower French flotilla, and perhaps there was no reason to exhaust himself paddling.

Several times he laid his paddle across the thwarts and leaned back to stare at the sky, letting his mind drift with the canoe. He was glad he had "volunteered" after all. In his imagination he saw himself arriving at the Forks in plenty of time to tell the Virginians to close their gates and prepare to repel the French. They would proclaim him a hero. After filling his stomach with warm food and getting a good night's sleep, he would cross the Allegheny and walk along the Venango trail at his own pace while the French fleet paddled into a trap. Back east he would be known as the man who set aside his own interests to save the fort. The Ohio Land Company, of which Goodspeed had spoken, might want to express its appreciation by giving him and Sallie a land grant out here. At one blow he would wipe out the stigma of his father's shiftlessness and establish himself as a frontier hero, perhaps a mighty landowner as well.

Jason might have made better time that first day had he been better fed and had he not indulged himself so much in daydreaming. His mind wandered from Sallie to Awilshahuak. He could never tell his wife about the beautiful Indian girl whose love he had won, and even more certainly he would not reveal what had occurred between them in the forest that Sabbath afternoon. That would be a secret he would keep to himself to be remembered now and then, like a rare possession one brought out of hiding to fondle and admire. Awil-shahuak wished him to stay and be her husband, to become a brave. That was flattering. If it weren't for Sallie . . . No, it was more than that. It was Ernst Koch and Parson Elder and the Harris family, all those people back on the Susquehanna who must be shown that Jason McGee did amount to something, that he was not following in his father's footsteps as another feckless hangabout. The sound of fast water made Jason sit up reluctantly and resume paddling.

In the afternoon he saw a small bark lodge on the right bank. At first he thought he would paddle past without stopping, but then he noticed a squaw sitting before the lodge door. She was a large, moon-faced woman. After satisfying himself that no one else was near, Jason steered the canoe against the bank and greeted the woman in Delaware. She replied pleasantly without arising. Her husband was away hunting for the day, she said. Food? Yes, she had plenty and would be glad to share it with a traveler.

Jason's legs were weak, trembling so he could hardly stand. The woman gave him a bowl of maple sugar mixed with fine-ground corn meal and bear's fat, which he consumed on the spot, ladling the concoction into his mouth with his fingers. Impressed by his appetite, she held out a strip of dried venison. Yes, he could have more to take with him. Jason still had coins he had earned working around Kelly's blacksmith shop at Logstown, but the woman refused any payment. As he started to leave, she asked where he was going.

"I am on a mission."

"Who for?"

Jason was slow to reply.

"For myself, little mother."

6

The brief rest and the woman's food restored Jason's strength. And he had enough of her dried venison in his shot pouch to sustain him through the next day. Although he had been keeping his rifle loaded and ready to fire except for priming powder, thinking he would have to stop and shoot his supper, he had been dreading the chore of building a fire and cleaning the game. Now that was not necessary.

He passed several more Indian lodges that afternoon, but did not stop, continuing at a leisurely rate until near sundown, when he came to a large island lying close to the east bank of the river. He reckoned that he had covered at least half the distance to the Forks and so beached his canoe and found a mossy spot under a sycamore tree to spend the night. By piling up a bed of leaves on the moss and burrowing beneath them, Jason warded off the worst of the night chill. It occurred to him as he settled himself that this might be the last night he would spend alone as an obscure frontier lad. Tomorrow night he would be put up at the fort as a hero.

He slept later than he had intended, being awakened by a shaft of early morning sun on his face. There was little mist on the river as he got in his canoe. An owl returning from a night of hunting skimmed across the water and lit in a dead tree at the lower tip of the island.

Jason paddled the canoe out to catch the current. As he passed the dead tree, the owl called, "Who? Who?"

Jason laughed at the ludicrous sound. "I am Jason McGee. That's who."

"Who? Who?"

"I said I am Jason McGee, and don't you forget that name."

Yes, by God, everyone would know his name after this day. Haworth talked of writing a book about the Delawares. He might write one about his own experiences. Having breakfasted on the dried venison the squaw had given him and being rested after a night of sound sleep, Jason felt a great sense of well-being and pleasant anticipation. What a glorious country this was: all around him low hills just beginning to show green, all nature full of a stored-up power about to burst forth. By God, it was good to be alive.

The owl called again. "Who?"

Jason glanced over his shoulder for a final look at the bird. That is how he first saw the two canoes bearing down on him, a little over a mile upstream.

At first he could not tell whether they were French or Indian, or indeed how many men they carried; he only observed that they were shaped very much like the large elm bark canoes he had seen at Venango.

Jason put his back into his paddling, hoping to keep his lead on the two approaching craft. He refused to look over his shoulder again for a good quarter hour as he leaned forward and drew the paddle smoothly through the water, using his entire body, moving the canoe forward as fast as he could without exhausting himself.

When he did stop to look back, the two canoes had gained on

240

him. He could see why. Each of the craft carried four men, three of whom were paddling. One paddler sat in the stern and the other two amidships, side by side. The fourth man in each canoe sat near the bow, holding a musket. The distance was still too far for Jason to tell more than that they appeared to be Indians. He resumed paddling, feeling uneasier than ever. Even if he had not escaped from the French, even if he were not carrying a crucial message to the Virginians, still he would have felt apprehensive at being overtaken by so large a party. His rifle was both a means of protection against attack and an invitation to robbery. And against eight men, the best of guns would not be a sure defense. Or was he acting like an old woman, full of baseless fears?

The river curved and narrowed, forming a current that made the canoe surge ahead until he came to wider, calmer water. He could not see the two canoes for a while and almost succeeded in putting them out of his mind. When he looked again, however, there they were, charging through the narrows, and now he could discern that one of the armed men was dressed like a Frenchman and the other wore a blanket in the Indian manner.

Jason longed for a chance to rest. He had been working hard for over half an hour and still they gained on him. At this rate, they would soon overtake him. For a while he consoled himself with the thought that they wished only to pass him. Why should he assume they meant him any harm? After all, they had covered several miles since he first sighted them and they had made no hostile sign. Still, he wished he had not spent so much time drifting and woolgathering the previous day and he regretted that leisurely overnight stop on the island. Now he dared not rest, and paddled as fast as he could without displaying his panic.

He heard the first shot just in time to look back and see a plume of water fly up behind him and a puff of white smoke from the lead canoe, some five hundred yards away.

Jason's fatigue evaporated and he was frantically working away with his paddle when a second shot sounded and a spent ball skipped along the water beside the canoe.

His rifle could kill at that same range, but it would be pure luck if he could hit a man at such a distance. Besides, he did not want to lose the time it would take to fire and reload. Perhaps they were testing him to see if he was armed. Later Jason would reflect on how stupid his pursuers had been to fire while they were so far away, but that was after he discovered they were carrying smoothbore muskets. All he knew at the time was that eight men were pursuing him.

The sweat rolled into his eyes, and his arms and back ached from the exertion. What could he do? If he stopped to shoot back, they would only close the distance that much faster, and they had only to hit one target to end the game. Even if he went ashore and tried to pick them off one by one, he could hardly kill them all. He would have an even chance of escaping on foot, except for the fact that he was on the wrong side of the river. It would take him too long to work his way across the current to the east bank.

Both muskets fired again and the balls plopped into the water in front of Jason's canoe, just where the river began another bend. For a few minutes he was out of their sight, but his respite was brief, his false sense of security shattered by two shots that whistled close to his head.

He looked again and now could identify the two men in the front of the canoes. One was Jacques, the half-breed cook, and the other Kiasutha, the Seneca. They had to realize who he was. They would know the rifle was missing from Joncaire's possession, but not whether he or one of his two friends had it. At this range, if he halted, he had a fair chance of picking off one of them. Did he dare kill?

Ahead of him the river was divided by a small island, which obscured their view enough to give him time to run his canoe close to the west riverbank. It was the wrong side, but there was no other way. Two more shots sounded; one of them glanced off a large rock on the shore and the other ripped through one side of the canoe, coming out just below the waterline on the other side.

With his canoe leaking, the race was over. Jason sprang out into the water up to his knees and scrambled ashore. Now they could see that he carried a rifle, but he did not care. Standing on a large rock in their easy view, he splashed powder into the firing pan and raised the butt to his shoulder. They had stopped paddling, obviously disconcerted by the sight of a rifle leveled at them. The men with the muskets were trying to reload quickly. He caught Kiasutha in his sights and squeezed the trigger.

One of the Indians sitting amidships behind the Seneca slumped over the gunwales. Both craft headed for the shore. Jason reloaded his rifle, but seeing his targets in such furious motion, he turned and ran south, along the Allegheny, still a good fifteen miles from the Forks and on the wrong side of the river.

Jason began running out of instinct rather than design, following the rocky trail where it took him. He thought briefly of heading west into the forest, but feared he would get lost. He ran until his lungs burned and his heart felt ready to burst, and finally he had to stop. The trail was a faint one here, leading inshore from the river for a way. The well-worn trading paths such as the Venango trail lay farther inland, following higher and more level terrain. Grasping his loaded rifle, he leaned against a tree to look back down the trail and listen. Hearing and seeing nothing, he convinced himself that he had eluded them. They were afraid to follow him; they feared his rifle. That had to be it.

And then he saw two of them moving along the trail at a lope, not running full tilt as he had been doing, but covering the ground steadily while conserving strength. Jason raised his rifle and fired, then turned to run without waiting to see if he had hit anyone. He ran until he again was exhausted, ran until he remembered that his rifle was not loaded. He stopped at the top of a hill from where he had a long view of the trail through the trees, and there, with shaking hands, rammed in a fresh charge of powder, seated a ball and filled the firing pan. He had to rest. There was no one coming. Good. His shot must have discouraged them. They must realize that sooner or later he would kill one or two of them if they persisted.

Then there they came again, moving at that relentless pace, Jacques in the lead and three others behind him. Jason got the half-breed in his sights and fired. Suddenly the man was sitting down, holding his leg, and one of the Senecas was taking his musket while the others ran toward Jason, tomahawks in hands.

Jason fled, wishing desperately there were time to reload his rifle, wishing he had not fired at all. He could hear the feet of the Indians pounding after him and suddenly remembered the Indian trick of chasing game; they would follow their quarry all day, husbanding their strength while their prey spent his in foolish spurts. They were not even returning his fire, waiting no doubt until they could not miss. They had learned their lesson back on the river when they began firing too soon.

At last Jason gained enough so he could stop to reload, but he had barely filled the firing pan when he heard them moving through the trees on either side of the path, no longer exposing themselves to his view but taking no precautions against noise. Indeed, it seemed as though they wanted to advertise their approach.

He turned and began running again, now adjusting himself to their tactics by moving at a lope, saving his strength for a burst of speed if that became necessary. If only he were on the other side of the river, he could flee right into the arms of the Virginians. Or if he were not so weary, he could swim across when he came to the right spot.

A spring lay just beside the trail at the bottom of a hill, surrounded by white pines. Jason paused to drink. His legs ached and the sweat poured from him. Never had water tasted so cool and sweet. Hearing nothing, he took out a piece of dried venison and ate it. As he leaned down to drink again, the forest seemed to explode with the sound of a musket shot.

He arose and raced to the south, not daring to turn around and fire, not with them so close on his heels. He ran until he thought he would faint, and then ran some more, until he ceased to care whether they caught him or not. No torture they could inflict could be worse than this agony. He fled, no longer in fear for himself, but only because he knew that if he stopped, all chance of his becoming a hero would end.

Ahead, the path sloped up across a bald, or clearing, to a rocky crest. Jason's legs began to give out as he ran up this open hillside. As his pace faltered, two shots sounded from the woods behind him, and one of the balls passed so close he felt the breeze. It was hopeless. He could run no more. He stopped at the crest of the hill and ducked behind a boulder.

Here they came across the treeless space, foolishly strung out but still moving at that ominous gait. Jason caught the lead Indian in his sights and fired. The man's hands flew up and his body twisted so that his legs carried him forward for a moment in a kind of St. Vitus's dance. Then he was down and his two companions were falling back into the woods.

Jason took his time reloading. His breath came in agonizing gasps and his heart pounded, but at last he had the advantage. Let them fear him now. He would stay here until he had rested, and when he left, it would be at a sensible pace. There were only two of them. They would have to advance across the bald and he was sure to get one of them with his rifle. Let the other take his chance of one-to-one combat. He was tired of being chased like a rabbit. God damn these Indians.

A musket shot rang out from the trees beyond the clearing, the ball glancing off the rocks near Jason. He did not return their fire as they probably hoped he would. Let them sweat. They would not know whether he was still there and would have to gamble their lives to find out.

Jason was too intent on watching the woods to pay any attention to the path behind him or to the river at his right. And so he did not see the three Senecas who had continued to paddle downstream after he disembarked and who had now come ashore and stolen north along the path, toward the sound of the firing. He was aware momentarily of a noise behind him, but before he could turn around, the flat of a tomahawk had fallen across the back of his head.

7

When Jason came to, he was lying on his side with his hands bound behind him and his head aching. Kiasutha and four of his Senecas squatted in a circle around him, staring. Kiasutha nursed Jason's rifle. The body of the brave whom Jason had shot in the clearing had been brought to the top of the hill and was lying beside the path.

Seeing that he was awake, the Indians hauled Jason to his feet. He could barely stand, his head ached so. They made him continue standing while they jammed their dead companion into a crevice and piled stones over his body. Then Kiasutha came over and struck Jason several times on the back with the handle of his tomahawk and slapped him twice across the face. At a command from Kiasutha, one of the braves placed a rawhide noose around Jason's head and kicked him. Thus tied and utterly without hope, he followed them down the path for half a mile to where Kiasutha had left his canoe.

The five Indians talked for a while in Seneca; it appeared to Jason that they were arguing. At last Kiasutha shook his head and pointed upriver. Two of the braves got in the canoe and began paddling upstream, making their way through the calm water near the shore, where they did not have to work against the main current. Jason assumed they were being sent back to notify the French commander that they had apprehended one of the escapees before he had reached the Virginia fort with a warning.

Jason had heard many stories of how the Senecas treated prisoners and therefore was relieved at first when they did no more to him than jerk him roughly to his feet and take turns kicking him. As it turned out, being forced to walk when his head ached so and his legs were so weak was torture enough. Kiasutha led the way, carrying Jason's rifle, while the other two braves walked just behind, ready with kicks and blows when he faltered. Even so, their progress was slow and it was late afternoon before they drew even with Shannopin's Town, which lay on the east bank of the Allegheny about two miles above the Forks of the Ohio. Had he managed to elude these people, here is where Jason might have crossed the river. All that laborious paddling and frantic running had been for naught. How stupid to have thought he could thwart the will of the French. Not only had he failed in that; he had spoiled his own hopes of a quick recovery of his brother. Abraham McGee himself could not have botched things any worse.

Across the river, the cooking fires of Shannopin's Town were sending up strands of smoke. Kiasutha signaled them to halt and to remain quiet. All three Indians stood listening with cocked heads. Kiasutha lifted his face to the south and sniffed. Jason could hear or smell nothing. At another signal from Kiasutha, one of the braves followed him down the path, leaving the other to guard Jason. Jason's legs were too tired and his head hurt too much for him to care what they were up to. Were he feeling better and were his hands not bound, he might have disabled the guard and swum across the river. As it was, he was grateful just to be allowed to lie down beside the path.

His guard, holding a battered French flintlock, squatted beside him. He was an ugly, beak-nosed fellow, a little older than Jason, with only a tuft of stiff black hair atop his head. Jason looked into the man's eyes for some sign of sympathy, but they were as merciless as a snake's.

The two remained so for half an hour, until the sun had nearly gone down. When they heard a whippoorwill cry twice, the guard stood up and repeated the call. It sounded again.

He kicked Jason in the ribs and drew him to his feet with the noose. Several hundred yards beyond, the trail merged with a wider, well-worn path, and off to one side in a small clearing was a lean-to. There stood Kiasutha and the other Indians, looking down at Geoffry Goodspeed and Cicero, his black slave, who sat on the ground with their hands tied behind them.

The Virginian's horse was tethered to a nearby tree and his possessions were piled inside the lean-to. A campfire blazed nearby and a pewter plate and wine goblet rested on a rock. Apparently Goodspeed had been interrupted while eating his supper.

"McGee. They've got you too. What the hell are they up to?"

Kiasutha kicked the Virginian and motioned him to be quiet.

"You bloody savage. You don't know who you are kicking. You will pay for this."

Kiasutha drew back the hammer of Jason's rifle and put the muzzle against Goodspeed's head.

"They are coming to take the new fort. Nearly a thousand French and Indians," Jason said.

Kiasutha turned, slapped Jason and shoved him down. The blow and the fall made Jason's head feel as though it were exploding. After that the Indians bound the feet of all three captives and dragged

246

them into the lean-to, leaving them there while they feasted on the remains of Goodspeed's supper, which they washed down with his wine.

"Bastards, drinking my good Madeira. Look at them, Cicero," Goodspeed muttered. Then to Jason: "Who are they?"

"Senecas," Jason whispered. "There are hundreds more with the French on their way down the river."

"My God. This means war."

"Yes. I am sorry I did not get here in time to warn your people."

Then Goodspeed dealt Jason's morale the worst blow of the day, saying, "It is just as well. There are only fifty men at the Forks and the fort needs weeks more work. Your warning would not have made a farthing's difference."

"If I had known that sooner, I could have saved myself a great deal of grief."

"Your grief is not yet over. Whatever they do to you, show no fear. Make them think you are indifferent to them. It is the only way. You understand?"

"I think so."

"You too, Cicero?"

"Whatever you say, Massa Geoffry."

The Senecas were nearly as tired as Jason, and the wine apparently had made them sleepy. Before they retired, however, they tightened the thongs binding their prisoners and, at Kiasutha's orders, forced them to sit up, back to back, with a rope passed around their elbows so they could not lie down. In this position, it was impossible for them to do more than doze, but at least the proximity of two other bodies provided some extra warmth. They sat thus, in silence, until all three Indians were snoring. Jason, keeping his voice so low that Goodspeed barely could hear him, told of his imprisonment and escape; also of what Joncaire had said and what Haworth had overheard of French plans.

"I am alarmed that the French are so bold as to make this move. I am even more alarmed that the Senecas are helping them. The Six Nations generally favor British interests, you know. In fact, Tanacharison, who is a Seneca himself, has thrice warned the French to stay out."

"These are western Seneca. The French are closer to them. Joncaire himself is married to one of their squaws."

"I just hope this French disease does not spread to the Delaware and the Shawanese."

They dozed and awakened, to talk again.

"McGee, I have been thinking. Perhaps this French move is not so bad a thing after all. Gets the issue out in the open. It should stir the Crown or at least the Virginia government to take strong action. And if we can defeat the French and chase them back to Canada, it would be better than having this land in perpetual dispute. War will settle things. And it will be up to us Virginians to win it. You Pennsylvanians are too much infected with Quakerism to send troops. So if the Virginians kick out the French, we will be rid of their pretenses to the land, and at the same time will quash Pennsylvania claims."

"I am glad you can see any good in our situation," Jason said dryly. "I cannot."

"Ah, there is always advantage somewhere for a man of drive and intelligence. I have my eye on a dozen tracts as beautiful as any in the world. That is what I have been doing since last I saw you at Logstown. My plans may be delayed and changed, but my ultimate purpose will be more fully realized than I first thought."

Jason began to think Goodspeed was in a delirium, to be talking so confidently in such circumstances.

The Virginian continued. "I have always admired men of history such as Julius Caesar and Alexander the Great. Men of strong will and vigor. Builders of empire. Bold leaders of great armies. Yes, that's it. I must get back to Virginia and raise a body of armed men. Return and teach these French and their Indian allies a proper respect for Anglo-Saxon courage."

Jason was growing irritated at Goodspeed. The man's arrogance annoyed him as much as had Haworth's piety. When he was a small boy hanging about Harris's Ferry, Jason had watched some ruffians amuse themselves by tying together the tails of two cats and throwing the animals over a fence rail. The cats had screeched and clawed each other furiously in their torment. Then Jason had laughed. Now he could sympathize with the cats.

Jason wondered what Goodspeed would do if he asked him to shut up. But he did not. He only asked him not to lean back so hard. "You are making my back ache."

"Sorry. By the way, McGee, you were brave to try to warn our people. I am glad that Quaker has not turned you into a coward."

"That Quaker is not a coward, Mister Goodspeed."

"A fool, then."

"Maybe not a fool either."

"What do you call him, then?"

"Like yourself and the French, he has a dream for this land. And like you, he has a strong will."

248

The three Senecas slept until well past sunup. One at a time, under guard, Goodspeed, Jason and Cicero were taken to the bushes so they could urinate and to the river so they could drink.

The Indians spent much of the morning going through Goodspeed's bags and scanning the river to the north. Jason assumed they were watching for the French expedition. Near noon they freed Cicero's hands but hobbled his feet and indicated that he was to prepare a meal. The Negro skillfully made a corn pone, which they washed down with more wine. Without warning after that, Kiasutha came over and began kicking Jason, sparing Cicero and Goodspeed.

When he turned away, Goodspeed whispered, "It helps to think what you will do to them when you get a chance."

Next Kiasutha and one of his braves led Jason to the edge of the river and forced his head under repeatedly, holding him by his hair until he thought he would drown.

"Go limp when you've had enough," Goodspeed shouted. "Pretend you are drowned."

Jason immediately went limp, which seemed to alarm his tormentors, for they hastily lifted him to the bank.

Next the Senecas hauled him up to the fire and took turns thrusting brands into his face. Beyond closing his eyes, Jason would not flinch, even when his eyebrows were singed. One form of torment followed another throughout the afternoon, with a respite only to stop and consume the rest of Goodspeed's wine. At first their cruelties had been performed methodically, but now the Indians became boisterous, dancing and laughing and mocking their prisoners. Kiasutha took Goodspeed's goblet and walked about with toes widespread, on his heels, in imitation of the white man's gait. Then he urinated in the goblet and poured its contents over Jason's head. This made the other Indians laugh even more; each of them inflicted the same indignity on Goodspeed. Jason, seeing the cold light in the Virginian's eyes, cautioned him, "At least they aren't injuring you."

Their next torment was to stretch Jason on his back and force Cicero to lead the horse at a trot over his body. They became angry because the animal shied and avoided stepping on him, and for the first time they kicked and slapped Cicero, finally binding him again.

"They will pay for this a thousand times," said Goodspeed, who reeked of urine. With blistered face and no eyebrows, Jason nodded.

Kiasutha spat in his face and slapped him, but when he would not flinch, the Senecas withdrew to talk among themselves and argue into the afternoon. With his head still hurting from the blow of the tomahawk on the previous day, his back aching and his face stinging, Jason began to wish they would kill him and end the misery.

Kiasutha returned with his knife drawn and took Jason's hair in his left hand. This is how it is to die, the boy thought. But his curious feeling of relief turned to panic when the Seneca put the point of the knife against his scalp and pulled his hair excruciatingly tight. Jason closed his eyes and braced himself for the pain.

"Courage, McGee," Goodspeed said. "If you can hold out a little longer, all will be well."

Ever after, Jason would wonder whether Kiasutha had really meant to scalp him alive. It seemed that the Senecas only wanted to humiliate Goodspeed, but bore a personal grudge against Jason, not only because he had killed one of them and wounded two others, but also because of the incident of Haworth's freeing their two Catawba captives. He would never be sure, for just at that moment one of the braves shouted and pointed to the river. They all ran to the water's edge, then came back and forced Jason and Goodspeed to accompany them. In the distance Jason could see a mass of canoes and boats coming down the Allegheny. The three Indians danced about, laughing and pointing out the approaching armada to their captives.

Hurriedly they packed Goodspeed's effects on his horse and herded their captives toward the water, waving their arms to attract the attention of their comrades.

Though relieved at this diversion of their attention, Jason at the same time felt even more hopeless. It was still too far for the invaders to see them. The western sun illuminated the opposite shore, making the lodges of Shannopin's Town stand out clearly.

"The game is up," Jason said. "We are lost."

8

The crack of the rifle shot, coming from behind the lean-to, made them all start, Indians and captives alike. One of the braves dropped his musket and fell backward into the water. The next few minutes became a pandemonium. A shrill cry like that of a charging panther. A streak of buckskin garments. A knife flashing. And the frontiersman Pratt had the scalp lock of the second brave in his left hand. The knife plunged once and slashed again, and the brave was on his knees, his hands vainly trying to stanch the blood gushing from his throat.

Now Pratt and Kiasutha faced each other, each with a knife in his hand, each with an eye on the two muskets lying on the ground, neither daring to let down his guard enough to grab for the weapons.

They were dangerous adversaries: the frontiersman standing tall, thick of chest and arm; the Indian lighter-framed but just as tall, with long, smooth muscles. They moved in a circle, slowly, six feet apart, their knives extended toward each other. Pratt's face wore a strange half smile; Kiasutha's no expression at all. Their eyes—the frontiersman's yellowish hazel and the Seneca's hard brown—were fixed on each other's knives.

"Easy, Pratt," Goodspeed said softly. "He has been drinking my wine, but he is not drunk."

"What tribe is he?" Pratt asked, without breaking his sideways shuffle.

"Seneca."

"Good." And with that, he began talking softly to Kiasutha, whose face momentarily showed surprise at hearing his own language from this white devil.

Jason, still sitting with feet and hands bound, as were Goodspeed and Cicero, stared in fascination at these two killers confronting each other like a pair of steel-spurred gamecocks.

"What is he saying?"

"I expect he is commenting on our friend's ancestry. Speculating about his mother. The true identity of his father. Questioning his manhood."

Suddenly Kiasutha lunged forward and Pratt stepped aside and seized the Indian's right wrist with his left hand. But as he began his counterthrust, the Seneca made the same move. Now each held the other's right wrist with his left hand, and it became a contest of endurance.

Jason would have thought Pratt far the stronger of the two, but Kiasutha held his own. Sweat streaming from his face, the Virginian was not smiling anymore. He tried once to put his knee into Kiasutha's groin, but the Indian twisted to catch the blow on his hip and Pratt almost lost his footing.

Goodspeed, who had been watching with an air of expectant triumph, began to look worried. "Can't you finish him, Pratt?"

"Bastard is too strong," Pratt gasped.

Kiasutha forced the Virginian to retreat two steps. His knife point was only a few inches from Pratt's throat now.

"Work him this way," Goodspeed said.

Pratt retreated two more steps, and the two men were straining against each other very near to where Goodspeed and Jason sat.

251

"A little more," Goodspeed murmured.

Pratt gave way yet another step and Goodspeed lashed out with his bound feet, barely touching Kiasutha's ankles but distracting him enough so that in a flash Pratt could drop his own knife and seize the Seneca's other wrist with both his hands. With a mighty wrench he twisted the Indian's right arm, throwing all his weight into the move. Jason could hear the shoulder socket and tendons snap.

Kiasutha gasped in pain and, with his mouth open and his eyes shocked, fell to his knees, dropping his knife.

Pratt leaped back and scooped up a musket. The Seneca was on his feet in an instant and began running like a terrified animal, his right arm flapping as uselessly as a rag doll's. He was thirty yards or more away by the time Pratt could cock and aim the musket. The crash of the shot seemed only to make the Seneca go faster.

"Missed the bastard."

"Let him go," Goodspeed said. "Where have you been? I expected you back last night."

"I was delayed. But I have been out there since noon watching you."

"Since noon? Why did you wait so long? I began to give up hope."

"Mister Goodspeed, I have been on my belly working my way along. Had to wait my chance. They had two muskets, you know that. Besides, they weren't doing much to you. Just to the redhead."

Seeing Jason's face cloud at this remark, he added, "I was ready to shoot him when he seemed about to scalp you, though."

Pratt cut their bonds and they stood up. Jason was subjected to a fresh torture when the blood began flowing again into his numbed feet and hands.

"Is there time to warn the fort?" he asked.

"No. Look there," Goodspeed replied.

Scores of boats and canoes were disembarking across the river at Shannopin's Town, and more were descending the river. Their attention apparently having been drawn by Pratt's musket shot, some of the French were gazing across at them.

"There is nothing we can do. We would only get ourselves captured," Goodspeed said. "In fact, we may get captured if we stay here much longer. What will you do, McGee?"

"What I should have in the first place. Go get my brother. Nothing will stop me now."

Jason told them of the arrangement he had made with Cadwell.

"And you want the Venango path?" Pratt said. "You are practically standing on it. Follow it due north. Less than two days' walk to where the Kittanning-Kuskusky path crosses."

He told Jason the landmarks he would encounter. There was enough jerky and corn meal in the pouches of the two dead Indians to provide Jason with rations for his trip. Jason put one of their pouches, containing this food, over his shoulder and picked up his rifle and Kiasutha's blanket and kinfe.

Pratt and Goodspeed watched as he loaded his rifle.

"You don't need that gun, boy," Pratt said.

"Why not?"

"You are ugly enough to scare a bear. No eyebrows and your face scorched. You should see yourself."

Thinking how the Virginian could have stopped the Senecas before he was disfigured, he ignored the comment.

"McGee," Goodspeed said, "you have pluck. Come back out here and help us kick out the French. I will give you employment."

"I don't think I would want to work for you, Mister Goodspeed."

"Why not?"

"You might have told me you expected Pratt to save us."

"What does it matter? Besides, I did not want you to give the game away."

"Sure, McGee," Pratt said. "A glance from you at the wrong time and they would have spotted me. Besides, it is good for you to find out what they are really like. Still think they are people just like you and me?"

"So you sat and let them torture me all afternoon. What if they had been doing that to him or Cicero?"

"Cicero is just a nigger, but Mister Goodspeed is a different matter. I work for him."

"And I never will."

But he shook hands with them anyway, and then turned and began walking north along the Venango path.

9

The Jason McGee who set out north from the ford opposite Shannopin's Town late that afternoon of April 16, 1754, was very different from the Jason McGee who had left Shippensburg six and a half months earlier. And much of the change had taken place in the three days since he had said goodbye to his two friends at Kittanning.

He was weary and sore from his ordeal at the hands of the Seneca. In killing one man and wounding two more, and in witnessing the killing of another two and the maiming of a third, he had lost some of his own humanity, together with his illusion that he might halt the French invasion single-handedly. He had been treated cruelly by the Senecas and callously by the two Virginians. Never again, he vowed, would he be put in a similar situation; he would remain vigilant hereafter against any affront to his dignity or threat to his person.

He stopped after dark, found a thicket well off the trail and wrapped himself in Kiasutha's blanket to sleep. Once during the night he was awakened by the sound of a bear snuffling about in the dark, and again by a hooting contest between two owls. Too weary to remain long awake, he slept until first light, then arose and pressed north on a narrow trail that wound its way along ridge lines to a large creek. He waded across in water up to his knees, and slogged on at a steady walk. Twice he heard the approach of other people in time to conceal himself. Once it was a family of Delawares headed south, the squaw leading the way laden with possessions; another time it was a white trader and his Indian wife, with a bony horse carrying a half load of deerskins.

At first the trail was more winding than Jason had expected, but in the afternoon, after crossing three more creeks, he found the going much smoother and straighter. His dark mood began to pass as he fixed his thoughts on seeing his brother at last and on being reunited with his companions.

He spent the night again well off the trail, with his rifle at hand, loaded and primed, and Kiasutha's knife in his belt. As he lay wrapped in the Seneca's blanket, looking through the treetops at the stars, he wondered what the warrior was doing. He did not see how the man could ever use his right arm again. And he had been injured in spirit perhaps even more grievously.

He had seen Kiasutha awing a hunting camp of Delawares at Loyalhanning by displaying his Catawba prisoners and reenacting their capture. He had seen him in a cold rage upon discovering that someone had released those same prisoners. And Jason himself had confronted him in hot anger at Venango. Finally he had suffered savage treatment at his hands. But in those few seconds when the Seneca had been on his knees with his arm twisted up behind his back, Jason had pitied him. He doubted that Kiasutha ever again would play the arrogant warrior. Pratt might as well have castrated him.

The next morning Jason followed the path along a high ridge over easy ground until he came to the point where it intersected the trail connecting Kittanning and Kuskusky.

Cadwell had told him he would leave a sign of his passing. There it was on the elm tree beside the trail, freshly carved in the bark:

A lean-to stood near the elm, but although its shelter looked inviting, Jason scouted through the nearby woods until he found a large, newly fallen poplar lying across the rotten trunk of another tree. This spot was off the trail far enough so that he would be concealed but near enough for him to hear voices or hoofbeats.

He located a small spring, and after drinking from it and eating a handful of corn meal, he made himself a bed of leaves under the tree trunk and dozed. He awakened to the sound of hoofs on the trail and the jingling of harness bells. His heart leaped at the sound, but when he peered out of the bushes he saw it was only two fur traders glumly leading a string of five ponies east with empty packsaddles. He let them pass without hailing them.

In the evening when it began to grow chilly, Jason was tempted to move to the lean-to and build a fire, but he reminded himself of the fact that he was alone in a country now in armed dispute between the French and the English, and of the appeal his rifle might have for a larcenous fur trader or an Indian. So he spent the night under his log without a fire.

He remained in the locality for three more days, never roaming far from his hiding place. He became familiar with individual birds and squirrels around his lair, and after the first day they took little notice of him. Deer strayed by and stopped to gaze at him. Once a panther paused to watch with twitching tail, staring so long that Jason, growing apprehensive, drew back the hammer of his rifle. But the animal became bored and slunk away.

Oddly, Jason did not get bored. Having suffered so much from human beings in recent weeks, he was glad to be alone. People had mistreated and manipulated him for their own purposes. It was good to be here in the wilderness, quietly observing other creatures and enjoying his private thoughts. Haworth had told him Tallema's story of being banished by his family without food until he saw his vision. Jason could believe that story now, for he began to sense a spirit in all the living things about him. Each bird, each squirrel, was taking on a character of its own. He even began to feel that each of the trees around him had its own personality. Perhaps the Indians were right in the way they fitted into nature rather than trying to shape it to themselves.

Jason moved about during the day, scouting down the trail for a mile to the west to get the lay of the land. As he walked he imagined hearing the approach of Cadwell and then seeing his three horses piled high with furs. In his mind he could see the face of Haworth

255

breaking into a smile and his saying, "Well, Jason, here he is."

And there would be Isaac, a grown man. But he could not see Isaac's face. He could conjure up no mental image.

On the second day of his hermithood, Jason happened upon a half-grown bear clawing at a rotten tree trunk and whining in pain. Going closer, he could see bees darting around the animal's head. The bear would stop and swat at the bees, then return to its task.

Jason ran back to his lair for Kiasutha's blanket. Returning, he sat and laughingly watched the poor, driven bear until it had ripped away enough of the tree trunk to expose the honey. Jason gave the animal a few minutes to enjoy itself before he chased it away by throwing stones and shouting. After letting the bees calm down, he drew the blanket over his head, sneaked up to the hollow tree, thrust his hand into the mass of honeycomb, pulled out a large chunk and then, with a string of aroused bees following him, fled to where he had left his rifle.

Back at his fallen tree, he happily consumed the honey, chewing the wax until his jaws became weary and then licking his fingers much as he had seen the bear lick its paws. It occurred to Jason that he had treated the bear somewhat as he had been treated by his companions. That honey had meant much to the bear, for it to have endured many bee stings. Jason should have allowed it longer to enjoy itself.

By the middle of his third day, Jason calculated that Haworth and Cadwell would have had time to reach the village, complete their business there and be well on their way back to this spot. More than a week had passed since he had parted company with them at Kittanning. He felt strengthened in body and restored in spirit by his rest in the woods, and now he was ready to move. Enough of watching birds and squirrels and ants and beetles. Tomorrow morning he would head west to meet his brother and his friends. He would wait here no longer.

10

After reaching this decision, Jason rolled up in his blanket under the log for a nap. Easy in his mind again, once more full of hope, he fell asleep to the reassuring call of a mourning dove. Awakening in a curious state of anticipation, he lay listening to the sounds of the forest and trying to think what it was that had brought him out of his pleasant doze.

There it was again, a long way off: a man's voice singing. He sat up and cupped his hands behind his ears.

" 'And from her grave there grew a rose . . .' " He could just distinguish the words.

He stood up so quickly his head swam.

" 'And out of his a brier . . .' "

In his excitement, Jason almost left his rifle and blanket behind. He would remember that later, remember it ruefully. He ran to the trail and stopped beside the lean-to to listen.

" '. . . The red rose and the brier.' " The voice came from the west. The singing now was blocked out by the sound of a dog barking.

"Logan!" Jason began trotting down the trail. The dog barked again. And then a musket shot echoed to the west. Jason stopped and raised his rifle to return the salute, but decided he would rather surprise them. Later he would wonder whether it was by his own will or through some perverse working of fate that he lowered his rifle and began to run.

Logan's barking had become frantic now. Could it be that the dog sensed his presence? Then, as Jason loped around a bend in the trail, a hundred yards away he saw someone lying face down beside the trail. Three horses tossing their heads and shying about. The back of a huge Indian, who was holding a musket in one hand and a toma-hawk in the other. Still another Indian-like figure, clad in a blanket and his hair worn in a scalp lock, standing beside Haworth. And Logan circling the big Indian, barking madly.

The giant dropped his musket and moved with upraised tomahawk toward Haworth, who, with his hands up to protect himself, began backing away.

"Stop!" Jason shouted.

The big Indian turned and Jason saw that the end of his nose was missing.

For ten years he had dreamed of how it would have been if he had been armed with a rifle that day in October, 1744, when this same evil giant was pursuing his mother. Then he had been paralyzed, too shocked and frightened to cry out. Now he acted before he felt any emotion. He brought the rifle to his shoulder and got the huge bulk in his sights. But in the same instant that he squeezed the trigger, Meskikokant bent over to retrieve his own musket.

At the crack of Jason's rifle, Logan lunged for the other Indian, who toppled backward. Jason drew out Kiasutha's knife and shouted

257

again. Meskikokant turned and ran into the woods, with Logan in pursuit.

Without stopping to reload his rifle, Jason followed the sound of Logan's barking. He could tell that the dog was right on the Indian's heels. When he came upon them, Meskikokant had taken refuge in the lower branches of a maple tree and was reloading his musket.

Jason walked up beside Logan and raised his rifle, forgetting that it was not loaded. The dog began leaping up to lick his face. Meskikokant sat in the tree, no longer trying to load his musket.

"Drop your gun or I shoot you," Jason said.

Meskikokant stared down at him. Jason repeated it in Delaware. Still the Indian defied him.

"I will shoot you and take your scalp back. All will know the wicked Meskikokant is dead."

The musket slid to the ground.

"Climb down."

Meskikokant lowered himself from the tree. Jason was amazed at the size of the man.

"Kneel!"

The Indian acted as though he had not heard.

"I am the son of the woman you killed ten years ago. I am the brother of the little girl. I have killed you a thousand times in my dreams. It would please me to kill you now."

Just as Jason remembered that he had not reloaded his rifle, the Indian knelt. As he did, a glint of gold showed on his massive chest. Jason recognized the golden cross his mother had so loved. For the first time, the old anger surged. He circled behind the kneeling Meskikokant and smashed the butt of his rifle against the back of his skull. The Indian fell forward.

Ignoring Logan's violent greetings, Jason removed the Indian's belt and used it to bind his wrists behind his back, marveling as he did so at the length of his arms and the size of his hands. With that done, he recovered his mother's cross and placed the chain around his own neck.

Meskikokant came to in time to see Jason reload his rifle.

"You are evil," Jason said to him. "And you are stupid. My gun was not loaded. You could have killed me. I shall tell everyone what a fool you are."

Jason prodded him to his feet and, with Logan's help, forced him back toward the trail, calling out to his companions as he did.

"Jason, Jason. Over here." It was Haworth. "Quickly or you will be too late."

Now there were two men lying along the path. Cadwell was sprawled face down where Jason had seen him earlier.

Haworth was kneeling beside the other fallen figure. Jason looked down into a deep-bronzed face topped by a warrior's scalp lock, and into vividly blue eyes.

"Jason," the man was saying. "You have found me at last."

PART EIGHT

1

Long and painful minutes would pass before Jason discovered exactly what had happened between the time he heard Cadwell singing and his reunion with the wounded Isaac; before he learned that the shot from the woods was fired by the lurking Meskikokant and that it had slain Cadwell; before it dawned upon him, to his horror, that the rifle ball he had meant for Meskikokant had struck his brother.

The Quaker opened Isaac's deerskin blouse so they could examine his wound. The blood lay thick on the milky white chest and abdomen; all they could do was press Haworth's handkerchief against the puncture to stop the flow.

"Isaac. Isaac," Jason moaned.

Haworth put his coat under Isaac's head so the brothers could look into each other's faces.

Jason knelt and took Isaac's hand. "Oh, Isaac. I have searched for you so long."

"I heard."

"Are you all right? I mean, have you been all right?"

"Until this."

"You will be all right. Everything will be fine now."

Isaac made a face at his pain. "Pa is dead."

Jason could not tell whether it was a statement or a question.

"He headed west four years ago to look for you. But he died on the way."

"Sorry. And you?"

"I have been all right. I learned to be a blacksmith. I want you to go back with me. We can go in together."

"No. No. I tried . . . I wanted to tell you . . . why did you not go back when you had the chance? You brought this on me."

"Look, you are hurt, but we can leave part of the furs here and you can ride a horse."

263

"Too late."

"If you can't ride, we could build a litter and sling it between the mare and the pony. We can take it slow and easy. Can't we, Mister Haworth? Ain't that the way? Mister Cadwell won't mind leaving his furs behind."

Jason was babbling now, trying frantically to hold Isaac's attention.

"Jason," Haworth said. "Christopher is dead. He is lying over there, dead."

His words registered only dimly with Jason.

"Look, Isaac. There is a lean-to up the trail. We'll take you there and let you rest while I build a litter."

Isaac's eyes began to go cloudy.

"No, no. Too late. Can't."

"Why?"

"He will tell you," Isaac whispered, rolling his eyes toward Haworth. "He knows the whole story."

"Isaac, you have to go back. It means everything to me. I have dreamed about it for years. We can stay right here until you are well, even if it takes a year. I won't leave you out here."

"Awilshahuak. You met her."

"Yes, yes."

"You love her?"

"I love a girl in Lancaster County. I shall marry her when we get back."

Isaac's face relaxed. The lips were no longer drawn back and his breathing became easier.

"Awilshahuak . . ."

"Yes, I know who you mean."

"Jason . . ."

"Yes, Isaac. I am here."

"Mama . . ."

"Can't we do something for him?" Jason looked into the Quaker's face.

"Just comfort him, lad. He wants to say goodbye to you."

"Meskikokant . . ."

"Never mind him. I'll settle with him for what he did. Oh, Isaac, we must never be parted again. Even if it means I stay out here with you. Don't talk of saying goodbye."

Isaac's eyes were no longer focused on Jason's face.

"Ktahoallel," he murmured.

He was trying to say something else, when he coughed and the blood gushed forth bright red from his mouth, spilling over his chin and down to his bare chest. His eyes remained wide open, with dilated pupils, unseeing.

During all this, Jason had given no thought to either Cadwell or Meskikokant. The Indian had been standing near him, guarded only by Logan. Although his hands were bound behind him, his feet were free and he could have run off into the woods had he wished. Before Jason could comprehend that his brother was gone, Meskikokant dropped to his knees beside Isaac's body. He bent his head low over Isaac's face and moaned like a wounded animal.

Jason rose and took up his rifle, his first emotion one of anger at this intrusion into his own grief.

"You beast. You caused this." He made as if to strike Meskikokant.

"Jason, thee doesn't understand," Haworth was saying. "He loved Isaac. He regarded him as his son."

Jason drew back the hammer of his rifle.

"What does this savage know of love? He killed him."

He put the muzzle of his rifle against Meskikokant's forehead. The Indian stopped moaning, but remained kneeling with his eyes closed.

"I will kill you now, you murdering bastard."

"Jason! Thee must not!"

"He killed Isaac, and Mister Cadwell too. He deserves to die."

"Jason, Jason. Thee doesn't understand. He did not kill Isaac, only Christopher. It was thee who shot Isaac."

"I—I?"

"Yes. Isaac would not want thee to kill this man. He regarded him as his father. He told me so. Doth thee not see, Jason—they loved each other."

Only then did Jason give in to his grief, falling upon Isaac's body and sobbing until Haworth marveled at the volume of his tears.

2

While Jason still wept, a party of five Delawares came along the trail, headed for Kuskusky, and Haworth persuaded them to stop and help dig two shallow graves. There were five of them: two sisters, their mother and their husbands, plus a pony whose back was piled high with household goods. Fortunately they had a grubbing hoe among their effects; with that and their hands, they quickly scooped out the two holes.

Once they understood from Haworth the circumstances of his party, the young braves did not look at or speak to Meskikokant. They remained there quietly, awed by the grief being expressed by this strange white youth with the fiery red hair and singed eyebrows and by the Indian giant who had no nose.

At Haworth's nod, they lowered the bodies of Cadwell and Isaac into the graves and the Quaker leaned in to close the eyes of the two men and cover their faces with handkerchiefs.

He persuaded Jason and Meskikokant to stand quietly with heads bowed, first in silent prayer and then while he recited the Lord's Prayer. At last, in Delaware so that Meskikokant and the other Indians could understand, the Quaker prayed aloud, addressing his words to the "Great Spirit." He asked that the wrongdoings of the two dead men in this world not be held against them in the next. He prayed that their friends left behind should seek no revenge for their deaths, and that the lands on the upper Ohio should remain in peace, with Indian and white, Delaware and Iroquois, French and English, Pennsylvanian and Virginian, living there as brothers.

Neither Jason nor Meskikokant seemed to comprehend what he was saying, but the older squaw was much moved by his eloquence, for she nodded her head several times during the long prayer and nudged her daughters to be sure they attended to the words of this good man.

At last they covered the bodies and placed rocks and logs over the graves to protect them from wolves. Haworth thanked the Indians, wishing them a safe journey to their new home at Kuskusky. As they started to leave, the old squaw drew him aside.

"That one," she said. "Is that not Meskikokant?"

"It is. Dost thee know him?"

"I have heard of him."

"What dost thee know of him?"

"Skingalaw . . . he is hated. You should slay him. He is treacherous."

"Nay, nay. We shall not slay him. There has been too much killing."

Jason got control of himself enough to hobble Meskikokant's feet and lash him to a corner of the lean-to, then build a fire. After that he sat staring into the forest while Haworth prepared a warm supper. Neither Jason nor Meskikokant would eat the food. Logan, who had been dividing his attention between trying to lick Jason's face and growling at Meskikokant, happily ate their suppers for them.

Even though he was in far more comfortable circumstances than he had been for many a night, Jason did not sleep. He was racked with contending emotions. It was more than losing the last member of his family, for he dimly realized that Isaac had already been lost to him. No, his brother was to have been a trophy, the physical evidence by which he could demonstrate back east that Jason McGee was not like his father. And this huge, noseless, evil Indian was the cause of it all. He had set all Jason's woes in motion by his unprovoked attack on an innocent family ten years earlier. The slayer of his mother and sister, of Christopher Cadwell too. The man who had stolen Isaac and alienated his love, who had caused him, Jason, to kill his brother. This man now sat a few feet away, at his mercy. It would be so easy to put a rifle ball into his brain. They could dig a third grave. It still would be a simple thing to take Kiasutha's knife and . . .

But Jason was sick of blood and death. He had killed one man, shot two others. He had seen Pratt kill two and maim a third. And now two more dead. He had had enough.

Until then, Jason had been too overcome by grief for Isaac to think much about Cadwell. He had been fond of the trader, but he had never expected much from one so blatantly self-seeking. How strange that in dying, Cadwell should become his benefactor. Meskikokant brought to trial and three horseloads, six bales, of the finest furs brought to market. They would be trophy and treasure enough to win the hand of Sallie Koch. And with her he could build his own family. These were the thoughts with which Jason comforted himself during that long night beside the Kittanning-Kuskusky trail.

When it became light enough, Jason saw that Meskikokant sat staring at him and realized that the Indian had not slept either. He might have been a caged wolf, the way he sat, his massive face like a noseless mask from which dark eyes gazed without expression: no fear, no appeal for mercy, not even defiance. Acceptance: that was what Jason saw.

As they ate their cold rations that morning, he told Haworth what they would do. Wisely, Haworth did not question Jason's judgment.

"If that is what thee feels thee must do."

"This savage is a murderer. If you don't want him shot on the spot, then we must take him back to Carlisle and see him legally hanged."

"I think thee means 'brought to trial.'"

"If I thought for one minute he would not be hanged, I would execute him here and now and save ourselves the bother of marching him back over the mountains."

"Then thee would be a murderer too, Jason."

Jason stood up and looked down at the Quaker. "Mister Haworth, it will take us a good two weeks to make our way back to the Susquehanna. You are welcome to travel with me on one condition. Don't preach to me. I don't want to listen to your claptrap about mercy and loving your fellow man and all that. You understand?"

"I understand that thee is deeply distraught and with good reason. And I will keep my silence."

Jason was annoyed at the tears in the Quaker's eyes. "And you understand that I am in charge."

"Yes, Jason. Now dost thee wish to hear how we found Isaac and persuaded him to come with us? I have so much to tell thee."

"I have much to tell thee *too,* but I don't feel like talking or listening just yet. After we cross the Allegheny, perhaps."

Leaving Meskikokant lashed to the lean-to, Jason walked back down the trail to the two graves. He stood beside Isaac's for a long while, fingering his mother's cross and trying in vain to form a prayer.

"Brothers should love each other," their mother had said to them. Well, he had loved Isaac, even when they were fighting like bobcats. How different their lives might have been had they grown into maturity together.

"Goodbye, Isaac," he murmured.

He paused for a moment at the other grave.

"You too, Christopher Cadwell."

When he got back to the lean-to, Haworth was feeding a piece of jerky to Meskikokant. Jason unhobbled the giant's feet and formed the lashing into a noose. He could see the concern in Haworth's face as he put the noose over Meskikokant's head and attached the other end to the packsaddle of the horse. But wisely, the Quaker kept silent.

It took two days to reach the Allegheny River opposite Kittanning. They spent the night in the same place where the three companions had parted just eleven days earlier. So much had happened it seemed like eleven months.

Jason was armed with three guns now: his own rifle, which he kept loaded and primed; but also Meskikokant's musket, which he meant to be evidence in his murder trial, and Cadwell's old smoothbore. After a night of rest on the west bank of the river, Jason double-charged Cadwell's musket and fired it into the air to attract the attention of some Delawares working on a boat on the opposite shore. They came over and readily agreed to ferry both furs and passengers in exchange for Cadwell's old gun. Jason knew he was overpaying them, but he did not want to waste time haggling.

The Indians paddled Haworth and four bales of furs across, then came back to swim the horses over. Jason and Logan remained on the west bank, guarding Meskikokant and the rest of the furs. The Indian squatted, no longer staring at Jason, his eyes clouded with his own thoughts. Jason wondered what they were. Could he think at all? How could Isaac have looked upon this ugly, hulking human wolf as his father? Even his own people despised and feared him. And how could such a grotesque beast have fathered the delicate, beautiful Awilshahuak?

With Haworth across the river, well out of hearing, and the Delawares leading the horses to the other side, Jason could do and say what he pleased to Meskikokant. It grated on him that he had seen no sign of remorse or fear on the Indian's mutilated face. Only an inappropriate grief at the death of Isaac, and now no sign even of that. No apology for causing his death. No regret for shooting Cadwell. No word about Gerta and little Stella. How simple it would be to make him walk a few steps to the west and shoot him in the back of the head. Haworth would think the Indian had tried to run away.

After all the pain and turmoil this man had caused him, swift death would be too merciful. No, it would be better to march him in humiliation across the mountains, let him rot in a white man's jail for a while with people staring at him, put him on trial, and then see him hanged in public. Damn him for squatting there as if he did not care what he had done.

"Meskikokant," he said softly.

The Indian looked at him without answering.

"You are the husband of Menumheck?"

He nodded.

"And Awilshahuak is your daughter?"

Meskikokant only stared, but Jason felt elated that he had his attention.

"Remember Tallema?"

Again, only a stare.

"Tallema despised you. Menumheck hates you. Awilshahuak regrets that you are her father."

He let his words sink in.

"I hate your very guts. Everyone hates you."

At last Meskikokant spoke.

"Hopiquon did not hate me."

3

Kittanning was a considerable town in 1754, with several hundred Indians, mostly Delawares, living in lodges and cabins dotted over the wide flood plain that stretched from the river east to a line of gentle hills. The people of the village came out to stare at the strange sight of a tall red-haired white youth clutching a long rifle and leading a fine horse, a pony and an old mare, each laden with two packs of furs, and followed by a stocky yellow-haired white man wearing the remnants of a long black coat and a broad-brimmed hat. But strangest of all, an Indian was tied to the mare's packsaddle, walking along with his hands bound behind him and a noose around his neck. An enormous Indian with only the upper half of a nose. And he was being guarded by a large yellow dog, who growled when the Indian lagged.

Some of the older Indians recognized him as Meskikokant, the renegade who had brought shame to their people a decade before. He had slaughtered a white family back on the Susquehanna, after abandoning his wife and daughter. A bad man. Yet what a pity to see their own kind dragged along as though he were one of the white man's horses.

Jason took no notice of the gaping Indians.

Earlier, when he had turned over Cadwell's musket to the men with the boat, one of them told him what had happened at the Forks of the Ohio.

"The French came down in canoes and boats as numerous as the leaves on a tree."

"I know that. What did they do?"

"The Long Knives were building a strong house. The French made them tear it down. They say they will build another, larger one."

"Was there fighting?"

"No. My brother was there. He says the Long Knives gave up like helpless women. The French took pity on them. They told them never to come back here. They sent them home like whipped children."

So much for his thinking he had failed to prevent a massacre of his own English-speaking kind.

After waiting for a response from Jason and getting none, the

270

boatman had continued. "The French are very strong. Will the English let them stay?"

"I do not know."

"If the English cannot protect the Lenni Lenape, what can we do? Perhaps we shall have to protect ourselves. Choose our own friends and enemies. We and our brothers the Shawanese."

"What you Indians do is no concern of mine," Jason had replied.

The Indian's face had darkened. He did not like this young man's rudeness and he did not like being balked when he asked what the youth intended doing with Meskikokant. All the same, he had answered Jason's questions about the Frankstown path, which connected Kittanning with the Susquehanna. It was a longer trail than the route by which the three companions had come west. Lying to the north, it worked its way around mountains and through gaps so there were fewer steep climbs. In recent years it had become the chief path east for the fur trade.

Without a farewell or thanks, Jason had led his party east. Although the path was wide and well worn from the hoofs of packhorses and the feet of traders, they progressed slowly, partly because of their animals' heavy loads, but mainly because Jason himself was heavy in spirit. He set a slow, deliberate pace, speaking to Haworth no more than he had to and to Meskikokant not at all.

By late morning they reached a high hill lying several miles east of Kittanning and they could look back over the Allegheny Valley. Under different circumstances, Jason might have felt a sadness to be departing that beautiful country. Now he hated the land. He did not care what happened to the Delawares, the Shawanese, the fur traders, the Virginians or the French. They could tear each other apart if they wished.

In the afternoon, the trail led up a long, easy climb to a point from which they could look out to the south over miles of jumbled ridges and valleys. They descended to a creek, where they found a newly built brush shelter. There they stopped for the night. As he would every night, Jason hobbled the feet of Meskikokant and lashed him to a small tree, knowing that Haworth disapproved of this, but knowing, too, that the Quaker would not dare protest. Jason would permit him to show the Indian no kindness beyond giving him food and water. After they had unloaded the furs and tied the horses out to graze, Jason and Haworth sat in front of a fire, finishing their supper.

"Thee will tell me when thee wishes to hear about our visit at the village?"

"Tell me now."

Haworth did not waste words. He and Cadwell, he said, had made good time after they parted from Jason at Kittanning. They had reached the village via Kuskusky in three days. Isaac had come in the night before and the village was in a turmoil. Awilshahauk was in her lodge, in seclusion. All were amazed to see them.

"What about Isaac?"

"Jason, this pains me much to tell thee, but thee must know the truth. Isaac knew thee was seeking him. He was avoiding thee. He did not want to go back. He wished to marry Awilshahuak and remain out here."

"I don't believe you. What was he doing with you if that is true?"

"It is a tangled matter. Remember at Venango when Captain Joncaire released Apauko and told him to return to his village?"

"Yes."

"Apauko did not obey. He went north and located Isaac. He told him his brother was being held prisoner by the French and that they meant to execute him as a spy. He thought Isaac would free thee and then return east with thee, leaving Awilshahuak for himself."

"But I never saw Isaac before we met on the trail."

"No, but thee heard him."

Haworth waited for him to understand.

"That was Isaac at the door?"

"It was. And he took a great risk. The French might have shot him."

"But he spoke in Delaware."

"Apauko had told him thee had learned some Delaware. He wished only to save thee, not be reunited with thee. He had discarded his white name and his white ways. He had become an Indian and he wished to remain so."

"Then why did he come with you, if he had no intention of returning with me?"

"Awilshahuak thought thee was dead because Apauko told her so. Isaac knew thee was not dead but he kept silent, meaning to wait out her grief. Cadwell took Isaac aside and told him of thy great desire to see him. He would not accompany us until Christopher threatened to reveal to Awilshahuak that thee still lived. Reluctantly he agreed to come and explain his feelings to thee in person. Thy hard words back at Kittanning wounded poor Christopher and this was his way of making things right with thee."

"Isaac is dead. But I shall have my revenge. I have Meskikokant. How did he get into this?"

"The people of the village would not permit him in their midst.

I can only assume that he had been skulking about, waiting to see if Isaac won the hand of Awilshahuak, and that he stalked us, thinking we were taking his adopted white son from him."

"It does not matter. He will hang in any case."

They sat quietly, watching the fire die.

"The news is not all bad, Jason."

"Oh?"

"No. Menumheck persuaded the braves that I should be allowed to return with my wife and other teachers to continue my school."

Haworth continued prattling about his plans until Jason interrupted coldly with, "You may have a long time to wait."

Haworth made no reply.

4

The terrain became flatter the next day, so that except for an occasional creek crossing, the path was easy. How different from their outward journey was this return, Jason thought; as different as a funeral procession from a joyful excursion. Then Cadwell's swearing and singing had kept Jason and Haworth alternately amused and shocked. Now even Logan acted serious, too intent on guarding Meskikokant to bark at the wildlife.

It troubled Jason to think how Isaac had become an Indian in all but blood. He had seen it in his brother's face during those few minutes they had together on the Kittanning-Kuskusky trail. Except for the blueness of Isaac's eyes, it was the face of an Indian, and his voice had been that of a Delaware or an Ottawa struggling with English. He did not expect Haworth to understand this, but Jason hated Meskikokant more for the change he had wrought in Isaac than for the murder of Gerta and Stella. His years of daydreaming had been based on the assumption that Isaac was being kept a miserable prisoner, when actually he was living a free and happy life, thinking and acting like a savage. Jason had been the prisoner, not Isaac. He felt an anger toward Isaac too, for having caused him so much trouble, for being so faithless toward his own kind. There had been nothing to prevent Isaac's sneaking away and coming home. Yet where had his home been? Where, for that matter, was Jason's now? He had no family. There was only Sallie Koch. She had told him to return when he was a man. She would get more of a man than she ever

273

expected. She would be able to see it in his lean, hard body and in his bearing. She had said goodbye to an uncertain boy and she would be getting a real man who had shot Indians, endured torture and held his own through adversity. She would see him bring in the dreaded Meskikokant as he would lead a sheep.

They stopped for the night beside a spring, deep in the forest. After they were settled down under their blankets, Haworth tentatively opened a conversation.

"Jason, what will thee do with these furs?"

"Sell them for the best price."

"And what will thee do with the money?"

"Give half to you and keep the other half to get married on."

"I do not want half the money. It is not mine. Thee may have it all."

Jason was touched by the Quaker's generosity.

"Surely you want your horse, though."

"Yes, I should like him back."

"He is yours."

"Jason, is thee aware of how Awilshahuak loved thee?"

Jason was embarrassed. "Now, Mister Haworth, that is all in the past."

"For thee, perhaps. Not for her. Thee did not hear her mourning. It was all I could do to keep from telling her that thee was not only alive, but was waiting for us. She would have followed us. Jason, thee took cruel advantage of that sweet girl."

"What business is that of yours? Besides, the Indians don't put great store in such things. It is like sleeping or eating with them."

"It should be the business of thy conscience, then."

"Yes, and not the business of yours. Now look, Haworth, I warned you not to preach to me."

The Quaker was quiet for a while and when he spoke it was no longer in a kindly tone.

"Thee look, *Mister* McGee. I will not be told to be silent by thee. Remember that couple that tried to cheat thee at Shippensburg? Who prevented them? Who preserved the life of Christopher when he was so dreadfully sick? Hast thee forgotten who persuaded Tallema to let us remain in his village?"

"I don't see what that has to do with Awilshahuak."

"You do not love Awilshahuak. Others do."

"Like who?"

"If I had not been married and a man of God . . . Dost thee feel thee is the only one who noted her gracious beauty? When I think of that comely maiden bending over her grinding bowl . . . thee young fool, thee took her as you might some tavern bawd, and she was a princess. To think that such a pearl was cast before thee."

"I did not know you fancied her so. Besides, I did not mean for anything to happen between us. It just did. What is your complaint anyway?"

"Call this preaching if thee will, but I will say it nonetheless. Thee is offended that Meskikokant won the love of thy brother, that he turned him from a white man like thyself into an Indian. I can see it, so do not deny it. Yet consider how offended he would be if he knew thee won the love of his daughter. Apauko, too, was deeply hurt at the way thee captured her affections when he, an Indian, could not."

"That is foolish talk. Am I to worry about the feelings of every Indian?"

"How unfeeling thee has become in thinking only of thy own feelings. Listen, my young friend, even Isaac was hurt when he realized that Awilshahuak's strange grief was caused by his own brother."

"I am tired of this talk."

"Well, I am tired of thy acting as though thee alone has suffered loss and hurt. I have been patient and long-suffering with thee out of pity and because I saw in thee some signs of character. But I will tell thee now: I, too, was offended by the ease with which thee, in thy youth, became so close to one to whom I was attracted. And I am even more offended to learn that thee did not and do not care, when she will remember for the rest of her life. None of my business indeed. When will thee grow up?"

Jason saw that his mastery of his party was slipping. He had heard Haworth speak with emotion to others, but never at such length or with such force. To think that this pious married man had loved Awilshahuak and kept it so to himself.

"I apologize, Mister Haworth."

"Let us speak no more of this painful subject."

5

The next morning, as Jason unlashed Meskikokant and removed the hobbles from his feet, the Indian spoke in Delaware, taking him aback. He asked him to repeat his words.

"What you do with me?"

"I think you know what I will do with you. You will be tried in a court of law for killing my mother and sister—yes, and for murdering that trader, who was my friend."

Meskikokant made no response, allowing himself to be tied to the mare's packsaddle for yet another day of trudging east.

They climbed their first real mountain that day, laboring up a long ascent, across the broad crest and down the back slope, then up another rise to where they could see ridge after ridge arrayed to the east. The next day they climbed an even steeper mountain, so steep that Logan occasionally relaxed his vigil over Meskikokant to run up and nip at the heels of the horses. They slept beside a large spring, in a place that must have been a favorite stopover for fur traders, judging from the remains of several lean-tos and the well-trodden earth.

Since Haworth had upbraided him for his lack of concern over Awilshahuak, Jason had avoided conversation, although the Quaker obviously wanted to talk. Pleading fatigue, Jason pretended to go to sleep, but Haworth persisted.

"Jason, thee has told me so little about thy experiences getting down to the Forks of the Ohio. Surely thee would like to speak of them."

"It is something I would just as soon put out of my mind. Maybe later I will feel like talking about it."

The following day they passed through a deep forest and along a small river to a clearing at the base of a high hill. A large cabin with a porch across the front, with several outbuildings and an animal corral, was set in the clearing.

"What place is this?" Haworth asked.

"Frankstown, I should think."

There were a dozen or more horses in the corral, but seeing no one about the buildings, Jason continued past the trading post without stopping, until a loud voice called out:

"Hey there, McGee. Wait up!"

Tiny Little stood in the doorway of the cabin.

"Hey, MacDonald! Levy! Come see who is here."

The three cronies gathered around Jason, asking him questions faster than he could reply and poking about in the bales of furs and looking with awe at the giant Indian.

"Where the hell is Christopher? Left him bedded down with some squaw, I expect."

"Mister Cadwell is dead. He was shot, back on the trail between Kittanning and Kuskusky, six days ago."

"Did this Indian do it? Is that why you have him trussed up so?"

Before Jason could reply, MacDonald let out a whoop. "That's him. That's the big one that killed my friends at Pixawillany and helped eat Old Briton."

Levy chimed in. "McGee, is he not the one who killed your mother?"

"And my little sister."

"And you have got him, asshole to deadwood," Little said. "Son of a bitch."

After that, nothing Jason could do or say could get him out of stopping to talk. After they dragged him back to the post to introduce him to the proprietor, Jason relented and agreed to remain with them until the next day.

It was impossible to remain close-mouthed with these three. They wanted to know everything: the circumstances of Christopher's death, all about Tallema's village, the source of the furs, and whether he had found his brother. The questions tumbled from their lips and Jason answered them, albeit reluctantly. Whenever their questions lagged, Haworth would give them a fresh scent that sent them baying off down another trail.

"Yes; you see, we separated at Kittanning and Jason continued down the Allegheny to warn the Virginians."

"Did ye, boy?" MacDonald said. "And what happened?"

Thus did Haworth inform both himself and the three traders about the canoe chase, the pursuit along the shore, Jason's capture and release by Pratt.

"Ah, that terrible Pratt," Tiny said. "You say he broke the arm of the Seneca?"

"He twisted it so that I doubt the man will ever use it again."

"What a tale!" MacDonald smote his hands together. "Too bad such a thing was not done to the evil beast ye left tied outside."

"Why did you not shoot him on the spot, lad?" Tiny asked.

"I thought it would be too merciful."

"I see your point, but it seems a pity ye must haul him back to Carlisle or Lancaster to see justice done. These offenses took place in Indian territory. We could try him ourselves."

"Yes, and hang him here as well," said Tiny.

They all trooped back outside to stand around Meskikokant, staring at him as at a chained bear. The Indian ignored them while they swore at him in English, commenting rudely on his hideous countenance and his unusual size. "Half a head taller than me and nigh as heavy, I warrant," said Tiny.

"And ye say he ran off and left a wife and daughter?"

"Yes, and his wife was the daughter of the chief of the village where we stayed."

"I should have thought his wife would be the one to run off from one so loathsome," Tiny said, watching Meskikokant's face for some sign he understood. Seeing none, he continued, "I hope his daughter is prettier than him. Is she?"

"Beautiful."

"Oh, and did you sample a bit of this daughter, McGee?"

"Gentlemen, I pray you," Haworth said. "I fail to see any good purpose in baiting this man. He will be brought to trial for his misdeeds. It is not civilized to torment him."

Little laughed. "So our Quaker still remains tender about the Indians, after all he has seen them do."

"He would not be so tender had he seen this fellow raging about with blood on his hands at Pixawillany," said MacDonald. "Oh, how it galls me that I may not be at his trial."

"We *could* try him here," said Little, but when Haworth started to protest, he held up his hand. "I don't mean a real trial. A mock trial, but make him think it is real. You can't object to that, my Quaker friend."

"I fail to see the purpose."

"Then stand aside. He is not your prisoner," said MacDonald. "How about it, McGee? Ye would gain practice for the real trial. He knows ye intend to bring him to trial, don't he?"

"Yes."

"Then we will try him here and now, and ye can carry our verdict back to the court at Lancaster. What do you think, Levy?"

"You want him to think we really are trying him for his life?"

"That is the idea."

"Who will be the judge?"

"You can be the judge. MacDonald is a witness, so I will be the prosecutor. Stevens, the storekeeper, and his wife and them three Indians can be the jury."

"Who will defend him?"

"You are determined to go through with this charade?" Haworth asked.

"We are indeed."

"Then I shall defend him."

6

While Jason went out to bring in Meskikokant, and the storekeeper rounded up his wife and explained to the three Indians what was expected of them, Levy produced a bottle of rum. Jason was hesitant about drinking, but it was easier to take a swallow than to explain his somber emotions to these three high-spirited companions.

They drank a toast to the memory of Christopher Cadwell, all except Haworth. Even the three Indian jurymen, who had never heard of the trader, drank to his "new life in Paradise, joined at last with his dear wife and two children."

The storekeeper, his wife and the three Indians sat on a bench designated as the jury box, while Levy perched on a stool behind the store counter. The prisoner stood lashed to the center post, which supported a loft piled high with bags of flour and meal and various trade goods. With his head almost touching the loft, he looked like Samson in the house of the Philistines.

At first Jason was afraid the traders would make a joke of something in which he saw no humor, but they assumed a gravity that would have been found acceptable in a courthouse.

Levy called the court to order and announced in Delaware, so that Meskikokant could understand, the exact nature of the charges: to wit, the murder of Gerta and Stella McGee in October, 1744, of various traders and the Miami chief Old Briton at Pixawillany in 1752, and the more recent shooting of Christopher Cadwell.

"You have heard the charges," Levy said. "Your life is at stake. How do you plead?"

Haworth arose and cleared his throat. "Your Honor, the defendant pleads nolo contendere."

"What in the hell does that mean?" Tiny demanded.

"Silence in the court," Levy commanded. "That means . . ."

"That he pleads neither guilty nor innocent. It is for this court to decide."

"And so this court shall. Let us hear the charges in detail. What is your case, Mister Prosecutor?"

Tiny drew himself up with an air of great dignity as he outlined just what he intended to prove against Meskikokant, ending his speech with: "And we have a witness prepared to swear that on April 22, 1754, this same man did lie in wait beside the trail between Kittanning and Kuskusky, and with malice aforethought did deliberately shoot and kill one Christopher Cadwell."

They delayed the proceedings long enough for another round of rum. Jason, who had drunk no spirits since they had arrived at Tallema's village, found that the first drink warmed his blood and the second made his head swim. He was not sure he should have let the farce begin, but it was too late now to back out.

Tiny called Jason as his first witness. As briefly as he could, Jason told the circumstances of the murder of his mother and sister. To his surprise, he did not stutter. It occurred to him as he answered Tiny's questions that he had not stammered for many days now.

"And you observed this same Indian and his companions burn your family cabin with the bodies inside?"

"I did."

"Then what did the defendant do?"

"He killed our milk cow. Cut her throat."

"What else did he do?"

"He put the cow's rope around my brother's neck and led him away."

"Your witness," Tiny said to Haworth.

The Quaker arose and looked first at Meskikokant and then at Jason.

"When and where did thee say this took place?"

"At our family farm just north of the Kittatinny Mountain, about fifteen miles from Harris's Ferry."

"And this was in 1744. Then, as now, is that land not prohibited to white settlement?"

"Yes."

"So you were illegal squatters."

"Some called us that. We thought of ourselves as settlers."

"But then, as now, the land on which thy family settled or squatted was not within the bounds of any organized county of the province of Pennsylvania."

"What are you getting at?" Levy asked.

"Why, it seems to me that these charges should be brought before a council of the Six Nations who claim sovereignty over the territory and the Delawares who live in it. There is no precedent for these proceedings."

"The hell there ain't," Tiny bellowed. "Take the Jack Armstrong case. A Delaware murdered him down the Juniata from here a ways.

They took him off to Philadelphia and tried him. Found him guilty too."

"The court holds that it does have jurisdiction," Levy said. "Let's get on with the trial."

Next, Tiny called MacDonald to testify about the Pixawillany massacre. The Scot relished the opportunity to tell his story. He went on at such length that finally even Tiny became weary and instructed him to speak more to the point.

"And you have no doubt this defendant was the man you saw at Pixawillany?"

"Could I forget a face like that?"

MacDonald began a fresh recital, but Levy cut him off with, "That is enough. Cross examine."

Haworth began gently. "Thee has said thee observed this man participating in the alleged massacre."

"Ye heard me."

"Where exactly was thee situated when thee made these observations?"

"A friend gave me shelter."

"What sort of friend?"

"A Miami squaw, if ye must know, but I don't see what difference it makes."

"Answer the question," said Levy.

"Thee was in her tepee?"

"In her lodge."

"How could thee see? If thee was in such mortal danger thyself, I should think thee would not dare expose thyself."

"I was peering out. Through a crack between the logs."

"And through that crack thee could see an entire village and all that took place?"

"I saw enough. I saw this man raging about and bellowing like a bull. He was carrying a bloody ax."

"Carrying a bloody ax and bellowing is not an offense. Did thee see him strike, kill anyone?"

"Not actually do it, no."

"And there were others in the attack. Many others, I expect."

"Yes, there was quite a few."

"Including some Frenchmen?"

"Yes."

"Dost thee know their names?"

"I have heard that—"

"Nay, tell the court not what thee *heard*. Of thy own knowledge

281

dost thee know of others who were present at Pixawillany?"

"I heard this Meskikokant call the name of one of the others, but he was an Indian."

Before Haworth could speak again, MacDonald continued. "He called to someone named Hopiquon."

Jason felt as though he would faint. Haworth began, "Hopiquon . . . ?"

"Yes, and this Indian with broad shoulders came running up with a scalp in his hands to show Meskikokant."

Frowning, Haworth looked into Jason's face.

Tiny was on his feet again, shouting. "It is Meskikokant who is on trial. Not some other Indian. Levy, you are not running this trial right."

Levy rapped for order. "The lawyer for the defense will please keep to the point. Any other questions?"

Haworth looked at the floor for a long while and finally said softly, avoiding Jason's eyes, "So thee cannot in good conscience say that thee saw Meskikokant kill anyone?"

"Aye, but he knows he did, and I know it too."

"No more questions."

Next Levy called for witnesses to the shooting of Christopher Cadwell. Tiny had to speak Jason's name three times before he responded. Having lost all stomach for the "trial," the youth mumbled out a brief account of what he knew. Haworth began his cross examination with an apologetic air.

"Thee heard a musket shot?"

"You know I did."

"But thee did not see this man fire that shot."

"No, but you did. You told me what happened."

"I am not a witness. So thy testimony is hearsay. No further questions."

After refusing a heated demand from Tiny that he be allowed to call Haworth as a witness, Levy asked for the closing arguments.

Tiny took a long swallow of rum, and loosened his belt. For half an hour he rambled back and forth over the testimony they had heard. As he spoke, he paced about, waving his hands and pausing now and then to shake his finger in the face of Meskikokant.

MacDonald's words rang in Jason's head: *He called to someone named Hopiquon.*

Tiny ran on blithely. "What you see here is a creature too wicked to be allowed to roam the earth anymore. He murders without cause. He lies in wait and strikes without warning. He kills innocent women and children. An innocent trader. He eats human flesh. He is worse than a mad dog. Gentlemen of the jury and you, too, Mrs. Stevens, how can you not be convinced that this mad dog is guilty and guilty again of murder? How can you not pronounce him guilty, and you, Your Honor, how can you not condemn him to death?"

Vastly pleased with himself and with MacDonald's congratulations, Tiny sat down. Levy warned MacDonald that he would be found in contempt if he continued to clap his hands.

"What has the defense by way of reply?"

Haworth rose and peered slowly into the faces of each of the jury members, as if searching for a key to his best approach. Jason, grateful to the Quaker for changing his line of questioning with MacDonald at the mention of the name Hopiquon, wished desperately for him to make his closing remarks quickly and discreetly.

"You have heard my client described as a mad dog," Haworth began. "I do not condone what he did those ten years ago. I could point out that in burning the cabin he did no more than the magistrates of Lancaster County did to squatters in the same area a few months before, but I will not, nor will I speak to you of the growing anger Indians felt over these incursions on their lands. As for the murder at Pixawillany, well, the witness for the prosecution could not and did not testify that he saw the defendant murder anyone. He says only that he saw him—through a crack in a squaw's cabin wall—'bellowing like a bull' and 'carrying a bloody ax.' Unless you wish a new trial to be held on charges of disturbing the peace, I should think you might well disregard that testimony. The charge of murdering Christopher Cadwell is another matter. The witness produced by the prosecution did not see the shooting. He only heard it. And even if he had observed it with his own eyes, he would not have known the entire truth. For that matter, when he, as a frightened child, observed the first murder, that of his mother and sister, he did not know the whole truth. To get that entire truth, we must go back to the times our defendant himself was a child and even earlier."

Tiny groaned. "Your Honor, we don't want to hear all this. Why don't he speak to the point or sit down?"

Levy rapped his knuckles on the counter. "You keep quiet. Nobody broke in on you when you were speaking."

Haworth, after thanking Levy, resumed slowly in Delaware, harking back to the Lenni Lenape welcome of William Penn and to the various sales of their lands to the proprietors as well as to the treaties that had been made and broken. He spoke movingly of the peaceful ways of this great Indian tribe, and then his voice became biting.

"And how have they been repaid for putting their trust in us?"

Quickly, in a rising tone, he outlined the encroachments made by white men against the Delaware, emphasizing the so-called Walking Purchase of 1737.

"Hired professional woodsmen, mind you. And they did not walk for one full day, as the agreement specified, to set the boundaries of the purchase. No, they ran and thereby wrongfully gained twice the land the Indians meant to convey."

He went on to point out how the government of Pennsylvania, having obtained all the land owned by the Delaware, then relinquished control of the tribe to the powerful Six Nations.

"You must remember what took place at Lancaster in July of the same year of the alleged murder, for it played its role in this. Remember the great conference held in that town, with representatives of Pennsylvania, Maryland and Virginia meeting with leaders from several tribes. All were represented except for the Delaware. The Iroquois forbade them to attend. They bargained away their rights, I tell you."

He paused to study the effect he was having on the jury. The Stevenses were gazing at the floor, but the three Indian jurymen were looking square at him, as was Meskikokant. Haworth resumed in a lower, almost sorrowful voice.

"You have heard my client called a mad dog. But he was not always as you see him. Once he was a fine, strong young brave brought up to believe in the Great Spirit, full of knowledge of the proud history of his people. A mad dog has no pride. He attacks randomly. Meskikokant had done wrong, but see how much wrong had been done to him and his people. And where will they go for justice? This is a make-believe court. I almost said the wrong person is on trial."

Haworth stopped, near tears. Then, in English: "This is a foolish undertaking. I should not have engaged in it."

He sat down and, after blowing his nose, wiped his eyes on his sleeve. Jason was not sure whether he loved or hated the man.

As Levy, embarrassed at the Quaker's show of emotion, made his hesitant charge to the jury, Jason dared not reveal his own feelings lest the others learn the truth. . . . *this Indian with broad shoulders came running up with a scalp in his hands* . . . Could Isaac have done such a thing? Thank God the three traders did not know his Indian name.

Levy droned on to his conclusion. When he finished, a guttural voice spoke out, as hollow as a call from a grave.

"Wait. I wish to speak."

Everyone was startled, looking at Meskikokant with open mouths. At last Tiny responded.

"He can't speak now. The trial is over. It is up to the jury."

"I wish to speak."

Levy looked at Haworth. "Do you want your defendant to speak on his own behalf?"

"I had not thought he would testify, but as this is a moot court anyway, why not hear what he has to say?"

"This is an outrage," Tiny roared. "He keeps quiet until after the testimony and then when he can't be cross-examined, he wants to speak. You ain't going to permit this, are you, Levy?"

"I can't see the harm of it."

"Then ye are a damned fool, as I have always suspected," MacDonald shouted. "We should not have chosen a Jew to be judge. They are as bad as Quakers. They don't look at things like the rest of us."

Levy's face turned red. "That last remark removes all doubt. This prisoner shall be allowed to speak. As for you, MacDonald, I will take up this matter with you personally after these proceedings."

As soon as MacDonald and Tiny had stopped grumbling, Levy said to Meskikokant in Delaware, "Yes. What do you wish to say?"

"You say I am guilty. Guilty of what? A pack of wolves come upon your land. What do you do? You drive them away. You kill them. The white man is worse than any wolves. He bring rum and make the Indian drunk. He cheat them. He steal land. He cut down trees. He frighten the animals away. The Indian move. He try to get away from these wolves with white skins. The white man send traders to follow with foolish gifts so the Indian will kill off game for furs. The white man never get enough. He is evil. He treat the Lenni Lenape like shit. Mingo treat the Lenni Lenape like shit. They call us women. They do not let us speak for ourselves. They are white men in red skins. What do you do when wolves come to your land? You kill them all, bitches and cubs too. You drive them away. You are white wolves. You are the guilty ones. Not Meskikokant."

"I won't listen to any more of this." Tiny walked over to confront the Indian. "You shot my friend Christopher Cadwell for no reason. He treated Indians fair and square. You are a liar if you call him a wolf."

"He take away my only son. He take away—"

Haworth was on his feet now. "Let us stop this farce. It has gone too far. A real judge in a real court would not permit this."

Tiny stood facing Meskikokant, his great fists clenched. "You are guilty. Guilty of murder. Hanging is too good for you."

"The white man is guilty. He seek to destroy my people."

Meskikokant spat in Tiny's face.

Tiny drove his fist against the Indian's jaw. The blow thrust Meskikokant's head back against the post to which he was tied.

"No, no, please," Haworth said.

"Order, order in this court," Levy shouted.

Meskikokant growled like a wounded bear and threw himself forward toward Tiny as far as his bindings would permit. The braces at the top of the post groaned. He shoved his great shoulders back, snapping the pegs fastening the pillar to the loft floor.

Again he uttered a deep growl and, with his feet set back for leverage, brought every muscle into play. Tiny retreated a half step. The braces at the top of the post gave way. Meskikokant lunged forward upon Tiny and they went down in a heap, the two men and the post.

Without its support, the loft sagged and sacks of meal and sugar, bales of blankets and piles of pots avalanched onto the two giants. The others sprang out from under the loft and MacDonald began kicking Meskikokant's sides as Tiny bellowed, "Get the son of a bitch off me." Mrs. Stevens was screaming and Logan was barking.

After extricating Tiny, they left Meskikokant lying stretched out, still lashed to his post. Tiny rose and brushed the meal from his clothes.

"The bastard was trying to bite me. To hell with the trial. Let's take him out and shoot him."

"That's it," MacDonald agreed. "Let's shoot him and have done with it."

"This trial is not over," Levy said. "The jury has not returned a verdict."

"Hang the jury."

At this point, the storekeeper demanded to know who would repair the damage to his loft.

"It was *his* prisoner that done it." Levy pointed to Jason.

"This trial was not my idea," Jason said.

"He is right, Mister Little," the storekeeper said. "You ordered the fellow brought in here and tied to the post. Now he has pulled down my loft and spilled ten pounds' worth of meal and sugar onto a dirt floor. It is your responsibility."

"For Christ's name, man, you can sweep up the stuff and no one will know the difference. Sell it to the Indians. Besides, Levy is the judge. What happens in his courtroom is his responsibility."

Levy called for order. "Mister Stevens wishes to remove his property from the use of this court. And he refuses to serve on the jury. So there will not be a jury vote after all. But wait. This court will act. Jason McGee, I charge you to turn this prisoner over to the authorities in Lancaster and to inform them that I find cause why he should be tried for the aforementioned crimes of murder."

"There," Tiny shouted. "The judge rules the bastard be tried for murder. It ain't the same as the jury finding him guilty and us shooting him here and now, but under the circumstances it is the best we can do. Justice has been served. Let's celebrate Judge Levy's decision."

Tiny brought out the rum bottle. After taking the first swallow, he gave the bottle to MacDonald, who drank and held it out to Levy.

"No, thank you."

"What do you mean, 'No, thank you'? Don't tell me you are still playing judge with us."

"I will not drink with a man who insults my religion."

"How did I insult ye?"

"You said a Jew should not be a judge."

"Well, I hear enough fun poked at Scots and I niver knew ye to complain of that."

"Yes, and you fight back, I have noticed. I am not fighting you. I am just not drinking with you."

"Well, I call it most unsociable," said MacDonald.

"I do too," Tiny said. "Jew or not, you are a white man and we have always accepted you as such. Don't sulk and spoil our celebration. I thought you were a fine judge, even though you should not have let him speak after the testimony and closing arguments. Now come on, Levy. MacDonald, tell him you are sorry."

"I beg your pardon, Levy. I did not know ye were so sensitive."

"I generally am not. I have not been in a synagogue since I left Poland as a boy, but I remember what our village rabbi taught me of the history of my people. What Mister Haworth said of the plight of the Delawares put me in mind of the way the Romans drove my ancestors from their homeland and scattered them about. It is a miracle that we survive."

"I have apologized, Levy, but I will not agree with ye that you Hebrews have any special cause for self-pity. Ye forget that I was at Culloden. The English and their Lowlander friends crushed my Highland folk there. I am as much a refugee as any Jew. I was lucky to escape that bloody field."

"Was there no squaw handy to hide you there?" Tiny said. But before MacDonald could retort, he added, "Shut up, the both of you.

Here, McGee, you look down-at-the-mouth. Have a drink."

"No, thank you," Jason replied. "I don't feel like drinking anymore."

He and Haworth helped straighten up the storeroom.

"Jason, if we untied his hands, Meskikokant could, with Tiny's help, lift the end of the loft so that we could set the post back in place."

"No. We will not untie his hands until we turn him over to the authorities."

"But see, Jason. His wrists are bleeding."

"They are bleeding because he tried to break free. Let him bleed. I will hear no more. Leave him as he is."

The storekeeper recovered his good humor upon Tiny's promise that he and his companions would delay their travel for a day to repair the loft.

"That is settled, then," Tiny said. "All's well that ends well."

"Aye. I only hope this business with the French ends as well, so we can return to the west and resume our trade."

"May it end well and quickly too," Levy agreed. "I fear it will not, however."

"Now, there is no call for such gloom," Timy replied. "The Crown can't take this lying down. Surely King George will send royal troops and surely both Virginia and Pennsylvania will raise militia to assist."

"It is a long way from London to the Forks of the Ohio," Levy replied. "And a long way from Philadelphia and Williamsburg. It will take much time, and meanwhile the French will have a free hand to work on the Delawares and the Shawanese. We have seen how the Western Seneca have assisted them. No, I shall not hold my breath until we can return. I am thinking of going into another line."

"What can ye do, Levy?"

"The law. I have always had a taste for the law."

His companions laughed until Levy became offended and again they had to apologize to him, this time for mocking his legal pretensions.

After that, the more they drank, the less convivial they became, until the party ended with the three of them lying about in a stupor. Jason reflected on the contrast with their Logstown party, which had gone on until Levy and MacDonald carried Tiny out the door. Haworth covered Meskikokant with a blanket and they settled down to sleep against sacks of corn meal.

The three traders still slept the next morning when Haworth and Jason awoke. After helping free Meskikokant from his post, Haworth purchased a small box of ointment from the storekeeper and he spread the balm on the cuts on the Indian's wrists and on his face where Tiny had struck him.

"We should not have let them detain us," Jason said. "It was a waste of time. Let us stop for no one until we reach Aughwick. I reckon that lies a good three days away. There we can consult with George Croghan as to whether to take our prisoner to Carlisle or to Lancaster."

"As thee wishes. Jason . . ."

"Yes?"

"I do hope thee was not upset about what MacDonald said of the Pixawillany affair. He might have been mistaken, thee knowest."

"I do not wish to discuss that."

7

The Frankstown path wound along streams and through gorges, occasionally taking shortcuts over low ridges, but avoiding long, steep climbs. Spring had brought a profusion of flowering trees and bushes into bloom, and the meadows and stream banks danced with the blossoms of wildflowers. Haworth's occasional exclamations over the beauty of the flowers only annoyed Jason. His mind was absorbed by the revelations of his brother's involvement in the Pixawillany massacre. Not only had Isaac turned into an Indian, he had become a bad one, no better than Meskikokant. Old Tallema had been right in withholding approval of Isaac as a husband for Awilshahuak, in thinking that Meskikokant might have warped the youth in his own image. No wonder Isaac had not wanted to return to his own people. Had he lived, he would have belonged in a courtroom with Meskikokant.

East of Frankstown, the trail led them over a ridge, away from the creek and down again across a valley, through a gorge at the other end and up another ridge, where they halted for the night. The next day they descended into a wide, level valley and followed the stream once more to another gorge, so narrow that they splashed along in the water for a while to avoid the rock-strewn banks. They crossed to the right bank of the stream and followed it about three miles, until they came in sight of a log house with several horses tied outside. They ignored the greetings called out to them from the doorway, plodding along as though they were deaf. A little way beyond, the trail turned away from the stream and led up to a ridge and along its spine for several miles until at last they gained a grand view of the Juniata River.

"There she is," Jason said. "Standing Stone crossing. The way to Aughwick will be easy now. We follow the river right down through Jack's Narrows, ford her again, and march along south to Croghan's trading post. Our ordeal is nearly over."

"And his is just beginning."

"Whose?"

"Meskikokant's."

"Who gives a damn about him?"

"I do. God does."

"Speaking for God again, are you? Don't start up on that, please."

"I am starting nothing, but I do wish we could free his hands and let him bathe when we cross the river. I can't see the harm of showing him a bit of mercy."

"That would be a stupid thing to do. He is dangerous. You saw what he tried to do to Tiny."

"Jason, he is a man too. I have exchanged a few words with him since that wretched pretense of a trial. I think he may be sorry for his misdeeds. He was much affected by my words in his defense."

"I expect he was. You condoned his murdering whites."

"That is putting it rather strongly."

"I shall put something to you even stronger. Don't touch the bonds on my prisoner. Don't speak to him again. And don't talk to me about freeing his hands for even one moment. Not until we reach Aughwick."

"Jason?"

"What, Mister Haworth? On another subject, I hope."

"Yes. It is about thyself. I have seen thee change from a shy green youth last October into a strong, self-reliant man. I am pleased at thy growth. Dost thee realize that thee no longer has that unfortunate stammer?"

"I am not afraid any longer."

"Quite. I could caution thee not to let thy timidity or fear be replaced by hatred. It would grieve me to see thee become like Pratt."

"Is this your way of asking me again to show kindness to the man that murdered my family and turned my brother into a murderer?"

"Thee mistakes me. I do not seek to deter thee from thy purpose."

"Then what, pray tell, are you after?"

"I urge thee to examine thy motives. The purpose of thy turning Meskikokant over to the authorities should be to seek justice and not revenge."

"Would an Indian know the difference?"

"It is *thy* soul of which I speak, not his. Revenge turns the heart to stone. Justice has nothing to do with revenge. It examines our acts in the light of the law." Jason looked into the earnest, pleading countenance. It struck him how drawn the once placid face had become. He laughed, without humor.

"What strikes thee as funny?"

"Nothing. I was just thinking of what Christopher Cadwell would say if he were here."

"Oh?"

"Yes. He would say, 'What a load of horseshit.'"

To Jason's amazement, Haworth laughed. "I expect thee is right."

Jason smiled at his companion. "We agree on that, at least. Now let's go down and ford the river before sundown. We can camp on the other side and the horses will have plenty of time to graze."

8

They splashed across the Juniata without getting the bales of fur wet. Only Logan had to swim. On the other shore, they stopped and unloaded the horses at a lean-to. Jason hobbled the animals and let them graze on the tender young spring grass along the riverbank. Later he found Haworth talking to Meskikokant and reminded him of Jason's order not to converse with the Indian.

"He was only asking me to put more balm on his wounds."

"I'd sooner use salt. Forget that and make yourself useful. Logan and I will go see if we can shoot some pigeons if you will get busy and cut branches for the roof. It looks like rain."

Jason gave the Quaker his hatchet and set his rifle in a corner of the lean-to, taking with him the smoothbore musket with which Meskikokant had shot Cadwell.

"This will be better for fowl. Come along, Logan."

In less than half an hour, Jason had shot a small turkey, which Logan retrieved. Thinking they might spot a deer on their return, he reloaded the musket with a solid ball.

Damn the man, Jason thought as he approached the lean-to. There Haworth sat with his back against a tree in front of the fire pit, a pile of hemlock branches beside him. He knew how to weave them into a roof. And he had done nothing about firewood. If he was talking to Meskikokant again, after all the warnings . . . The man really was a fool.

He would have abandoned him west of Kittanning if he had not felt a responsibility for him—yes, and affection too, but just now irritation.

"Mister Haworth," Jason said roughly as he came up behind him. "Would it be asking too much to suggest that you get off your ass and . . ."

Jason stopped, wondering why the Quaker did not turn around. Logan began to whine.

Afraid of what he would see, Jason dropped the turkey and cocked the musket. He circled the lean-to and looked at a scene that sickened him. Haworth's legs were spread out in front of him and his hands were lying at his sides, palms up. His face and the front of his shirt and coat gleamed with blood. The hatchet Jason had left now protruded from his forehead.

Fighting back his nausea, Jason waved away a swarm of flies and lifted the hat. The naked skull lay exposed between strips of scalp on either side. Jason wheeled, musket at the ready, to face the corner of the lean-to where he had left Meskikokant lashed. The rawhide thongs that had bound the giant lay on the ground. And Jason realized with a further shock that his rifle was missing.

For a moment Jason thought he would faint. Indeed, he might have, had a voice not called out from the other bank of the river.

"Mocquasaka! Look here."

He turned, already knowing who called. There on a large rock stood Meskikokant, holding Ernst Koch's beautiful rifle in his right hand as easily as if it were a toy. Then he raised his left hand, displaying the patch of blood-streaked blond hair as a grisly trophy.

"You bastard!" Jason screamed. "Why did you do it?"

The Indian laughed. "He was stupid. Like one of your white man's cows. You are stupid. Hopiquon was smarter than you."

"I should have shot you. I will hunt you down if it takes the rest of my life."

Again that mocking laugh that brought back the recollection of the massacre.

"You are a fool, Mocquasaka. I will take your hair too."

Now the rifle was coming up to the giant shoulder. Jason first thought of running, then of flinging himself down, but instead he started to raise the musket.

He did not hear the report of the rifle, only saw the billow of white smoke across the river and felt the ball strike his upper thigh.

Once, when he worked at Ernst Koch's blacksmith shop, a horse had kicked him near the same spot. Then, as now, he had been thrown off his feet by the force, but this pain was worse. Somehow, although sitting down and near fainting, he had kept his grasp on the musket. He raised the gun and pulled the trigger, out of reflex. The kick shoved him on his back. As he tried to sit up, the pain mounted and he passed out.

PART NINE

1

It was raining. Dark had fallen. Logan curled up against Jason, whining. Jason's right thigh ached and burned as though a hot poker had been thrust clear into the bone. He moaned and Logan arose and licked his face. Through the noise of the river he could hear the horses whickering.

"Mister Haworth," he called. And then he remembered.

He was lying on his back. To keep the rain off his face, he tried to turn over. The pain made him cry aloud. *Meskikokant—he might be lurking about.*

Jason shuddered at the memory of what he had seen when he removed Haworth's hat. He reached forward until his hands felt the butt of the musket. Grasping it, he began sliding himself along on his back toward the lean-to. It seemed an eternity before he bumped into the hoofs of one of the horses, causing the animal to shy away. A few more feet and he was under shelter, lying against a bale of furs, gasping from the pain as raindrops on the dried leaves of the brush roof rasped in his ears.

Poor Haworth. Dead. Killed and scalped by the man for whom he had sought mercy. Jason wondered if the Quaker might forgive Meskikokant even for this. His home in Philadelphia, his school at Tallema's village, his beautiful young wife—what did they mean now? A blow of a hatchet and he was gone.

Jason wondered whether Haworth, despite Jason's warnings, had freed Meskikokant or whether the giant had worked his way loose. The balm the Quaker had been applying might have made it easier. Why had it been Cadwell and not Haworth whom Meskikokant had shot on the Kuskusky trail? Christopher would never have allowed the Indian to escape.

Both his companions were dead now. He had blamed them for causing him so much misfortune and it had been he who had cost them their lives. And now he feared for his own life. He could tell from the grating in his leg that the bone was cracked. Somewhere out there in the dark, Meskikokant could be hiding with the best rifle in the wilderness, while he lay helpless. Jason fumbled with the musket, but lacked the strength to draw back the hammer. The effort wearied him so that he passed out.

Birds sang. The light hurt his eyes. His clothes were wet. Logan lay awake inches away, his head between his paws. The horses had crowded under the shelter too. Jason marveled that they had not wandered away. Though his broken leg ached, he was able to pull himself up to a sitting position against a bale of furs. He looked around, but wished he had not when he recognized the legs and feet of Haworth beyond a corner of the lean-to.

Lowering his eyes, he saw that his right trouser leg was caked with blood. No wonder he was so weak. He would give anything for a drink. There was a river flowing a few dozen feet away, and he could not reach it.

Meskikokant had not returned after all. He must have thought he had killed Jason. Perhaps he was afraid of Logan; that was why he had not recrossed the river to take Jason's scalp.

How long could he lie here without food and water? If only he could make Logan understand what he needed. Jason closed his eyes so he would not see Haworth's feet. There was nothing to do but wait for death. He had seen so much dying. His mother and sister. His Seneca tormentors. Cadwell. Isaac. Haworth. And now himself. The only natural deaths had been Tallema's and the false one of Cadwell at Logstown. To think that the trader had returned from the dead only to meet death on the Kuskusky trail.

Haworth had warned Jason against seeking revenge. Now even his revenge was denied him. He would die here beside the Juniata River, surrounded by three horses and six bales of prime furs worth a small fortune. He had lost everything. Life was a bad joke. Sallie Koch would never even know what he had done. Someone else would possess her. She would bear another man's children. And when at night she lay with her arms about that man, would she remember the red-haired apprentice her father had employed for three years? Perhaps when she and her old-maid sister, Katie, visited with each other, they would reminisce about their childhood.

"You remember Jason, Katie?"

"Yes, the redhead who stuttered. You used to like to tease him."

"He was a foolish lad."

"Remember how angry Pa got when he wanted to marry you?"

"He was a sweet boy. I never told you that I promised to wait for him when he went away."

"No. You got over him?"

"Sure. It was just puppy love. I wonder what happened to him."

"Probably married a squaw."

That is what they would say, if they remembered him at all.

More likely Awilshahuak would remember him longer. With both him and Isaac gone and with Menumheck's blessing, perhaps the tribe would allow Apauko to have her after all. She would not forget, but to whom could she speak about the tall white boy who had lain with her beside the creek in the forest?

And Tiny, Levy and MacDonald. Tiny was a grand storyteller. How he would embellish the tale of what had happened at Frankstown.

"It was in late April, 1754, a few days after the French took the Virginian fort at the Forks of the Ohio. At Frank Stevens's trading post. This red-headed young fellow we had met at Logstown and this Quaker missionary came in with three horseloads of the prettiest furs you ever saw and an Indian prisoner. A giant, taller than me, fellow by the name of Meskikokant . . ."

And after he had done telling the story of the trial, someone would ask, "What happened after all that?"

"They found the Quaker and the boy dead near the Standing Stone crossing of the Juniata. The Quaker had been scalped and the boy shot to death. The Indian got clean away. And I had wanted to shoot him there at Frankstown. After giving him a fair trial, you know."

2

All that day and through the next night, Jason lay in the lean-to. The horses wandered off on their hobbled legs to graze. When morning came again, a flock of crows roosted in the trees nearby to speculate raucously about whether it would be safe to explore the carrion in the clearing. After two of them lit near Haworth's body and were promptly chased off by an indignant Logan, the flock flapped across the river to settle in another grove.

Soon two, then three and more vultures were circling over the same grove. Jason wondered how long it would be until they would have his carcass to feed upon.

When Haworth had confessed his doubts at Venango, he had said he sometimes thought that only the grave and its worms awaited man at the end. Might not he have felt an even deeper despair if he had suspected he would end up as a feast for crows and vultures?

As the day wore on, Jason lost his grasp on reality. He no longer saw the vultures and crows; nor did he hear the sound of the river. Haworth stood before him, saying: "Jason, thee must love, not hate. Love others as thy Creator loves thee."

Christopher Cadwell was there too. "McGee, you are as big a damned fool as Haworth. He was the one I feared would get us in trouble. But it was you, and your damned brother."

Pratt appeared, looking down with his sideways smile. "McGee, you were too soft. You should have killed that Indian straightway, when you had the chance."

"I couldn't. I wanted to bring him to court."

"Well, ye wouldn't take our advice, and see what it got ye." Mac-Donald's voice. "Ye were hell bent to have him tried and he has killed your Quaker do-gooder and shot ye. How did it happen?"

"Go away and let me die in peace."

"We will help you," Levy said softly. "You're in a bad way. How long have you been like this?"

"Quit asking fool questions," Tiny boomed. "The lad knows he is in a bad way."

"Don't ye think we should give the Quaker a decent burial?"

"Yes, but go through his pockets. No reason to bury good money."

Levy spoke again. "Look at those furs. Whose are they now?"

"They are my furs," Jason moaned. "Cadwell is dead. Haworth would have left them out there or given them to the Indians. He said I could have them."

"We can sort them out after we bury the Quaker and figure how to carry the lad. Do you think the dog will bite me if I touch him? McGee, call off your dog."

"Water. For God's sake, water."

"We will give you water and rum too, but tell your damned dog to stand aside."

"You are worse than the vultures. You are after my furs."

"McGee, stop babbling and open your eyes. We are your friends."

Jason did open his eyes. There stood Tiny Little, Levy and Mac-

Donald, confronted by Logan, growling and with his teeth bared. Each of the men held the reins of two pack ponies.

"I was ready to die."

"You can forget dying if you will only speak to your God damned dog."

"I thought you were a dream."

"I have been called many things," Tiny said, "but never a dream."

That was when Jason saw that the trader carried Ernst Koch's rifle and that the Scot held two scalps: one blond and the other a wiry black.

3

They had found the body of Meskikokant lying face down on the trail several hundred yards beyond the river.

Tiny explained: "The crows had been at him so we couldn't tell what killed him, but of course we knew it was him. MacDonald lifted his scalp just as a memento, you might say. We wondered what happened to you and soon as we seen the poor Quaker, and you lying here talking to yerself, we knew."

"He got free somehow while I was hunting. He shot first, from across the river. I fired after I was down. I had no idea I had hit him."

"Hit him ye did, lad. He left a trail of blood behind him. A good shot it must have been. I'm glad it was a Scots lad that ridded the world of such a monster."

They spent the rest of that day burying Haworth and making Jason more comfortable. Tiny let him drink more rum than he should that evening, then sat about with his companions while Jason told them more of what had happened. Tiny was as tender as a mother with him.

"At Aughwick we either can pull the bullet out or find someone who can. And we'll set your leg too. We dare not start you bleeding again here, though."

The next morning, while Tiny and Levy fashioned a litter out of two poles and a pair of blankets, MacDonald rounded up Jason's three horses and loaded the furs on them. They strapped the litter between two of their own horses and placed Jason gently on the contrivance.

"Lie back and enjoy the ride, McGee," Tiny said. "You are lucky it happened here. The rest of the way to Aughwick is level and easy. Except for a crossing of the river downstream, there should be no problem."

"Here," said Levy. "Haworth has a book with writing in it. Found it in his pouch. Is it worth keeping?"

"Yes," Jason said. "It was his journal. I want to keep it. What about his money?"

"Don't fret yourself about such things, lad. We found this stone in his pocket too."

"It was his charm. Let me have it. You can keep the money."

Despite Tiny's assurances, Jason found the trip an agony, with his leg throbbing at every hoofbeat. By early afternoon, when they reached the point about ten miles downstream where they were to cross the river and turn south, he was nearly delirious from the pain, grinding his teeth and begging them to stop and give him a respite from the jolting. They set the litter on the ground and an anxious Logan licked his face. Levy suggested remaining there until morning, but Tiny overruled him.

"It's only another seven miles. Let's get it over with. I'll give him more rum."

Jason heard himself screaming as the horses stumbled over the rocky ford and again when one lost its footing scrambling up the opposite bank. He almost wished he had died before the three traders found him. But the path south became smooth again and the rum did its work, so that he became easier. And late that afternoon Tiny announced, "There she is, Aughwick. By God, boys, I wish you would look. Croghan has got himself a regular city out here now."

4

The next few weeks were a blur of pain and despair in Jason's mind.

He would remember George Croghan, looking gray and sickly himself, directing his transfer from the litter to a shuck bed in the trader's own home, then a night of tormented sleeplessness, and finally the horror of suffering the rifle ball to be removed from his leg and the setting of the bone. They gave him both whiskey and laudanum, but even so, Tiny Little and MacDonald had to hold him down while Croghan and Levy probed for the bullet as he writhed and screamed, clutching the small white stone that had been Haworth's talisman. After that he endured a day and night of wild, morphine-induced dreams, awakening the next day soaked with sweat, to discover that his throbbing leg now was splinted with hickory staves. His hands ached, for he still clenched the little white stone in one fist and, in the other, the bullet they had taken from his thigh.

He became more and more feverish after that until he went out of his head again, calling for Isaac, for Gerta and, most of all, for Sallie, while the three fur traders stood about talking of what to do with him and his furs. He would remember their murmuring of death and their showing him a piece of paper concerning the furs.

Later some Indians gathered about his bed. After examining him carefully, taking a particular interest in the redness of his pubic hairs, a fat squaw went away, to return a few hours later with a pungent liquid which she forced down his burning throat, all the while speaking to him soothingly. Still later, she came with a stinking poultice for his leg. Thereafter he slept for many hours without dreaming. When he awoke, his fever had broken and his leg hurt only when he moved it. The seamed face of the squaw looked angelic to Jason as she sat watching him with eyes that could be surprised at nothing anymore.

When he heard that Jason was conscious again, Croghan came and shooed the squaw from the room.

"Well, young fellow, Wipeki has brought ye around. I don't know whether to thank her or not."

Jason looked about the bare room. "Where am I?"

"Ye are at Aughwick. Your friends left ye here, thinking ye might die. Don't ye remember me?"

"You are Mister Croghan."

"Right ye are. We met at Carlisle last October at the big powwow with the Indians. Ye wouldn't tell me much about yourself, but I well recall ye, not to mention your dog and your rifle."

"I am sorry. I had my reasons for keeping my own counsel."

"Aye, and I know those reasons now. Yer friends told me about ye and what happened to ye. Amazing story."

"Where are they? Little and the others?"

"Ah, they went their way. Back to other pursuits. I hated to let Tiny go, but I've no employment for him anymore. My fur trade is shot to hell by the French, damn their eyes. Tiny thought he might return to farming."

303

"What about my furs and my rifle?"

"They took the furs. They left the rifle with me."

"They had no right to do that."

"Ye signed a paper about the furs, so they said. And they told me I could keep the rifle in case ye did not recover."

"Then they have cheated me. Is there no one in this world I can trust?"

"At the time they left, it was doubtful ye would live. They did go to a deal of trouble to bring ye here."

"What about my horses and my dog?"

"Fat chance they had of taking your dog. He would let no one near ye. Wipeki has him tied up at her lodge. Your horses are here, eating me out of corn and fodder."

Jason was too washed out in body and spirit to care. "At least bring my dog to me."

Logan charged into the room, diving upon Jason with such enthusiasm that he could not help laughing. The dog would not budge from his side again.

Several days later, when four Indians carried Jason out into the spring sunshine, he could not believe how good it felt to lie under the trees surrounding Croghan's substantial log house, to be free of the tiresome little sickroom and free of the worst of his pain. He learned to his surprise that just the day before, Croghan had departed for the west to lend his services to an expedition of Virginians sent to retake the Forks of the Ohio.

Jason would remain at Aughwick through August and during that time he was amazed at the number of Indians who came down the Frankstown path to impose themselves upon the hospitality of George Croghan. Some were Delawares and Shawanese, but even more were Iroquois who had been dependent on the English. They milled around like children who had lost their parents, waiting for some sign that Brother Onas in Philadelphia would come to his senses and send help so they could recover their lands in the west from the French. And the longer they waited, the more disillusioned they became.

Late in July a crestfallen Croghan returned from his mission, and soon was followed by Tanacharison himself. The Half King was full of complaints against the young George Washington, whom the Virginians had sent with two companies of militiamen to dislodge the French from the Forks of the Ohio.

Washington had built a small works named Fort Necessity at Great Meadows, fifty miles southeast of the Forks, and on May 28 had ambushed a French reconnaissance party, killing the young ensign

304

Jumonville and capturing a dozen others, but, Tanacharison reported in disgust, he had surrendered his fort to a large force sent out in retaliation. That was on July 3. Tanacharison had come east in the hope of persuading the Pennsylvanians to raise a larger body of men than the Virginians had. It would take a considerable army, he reported, for the French had nearly completed a formidable fort at the Forks, complete with cannon and manned by several hundred soldiers. There could be no passage of the Ohio as long as they remained.

Throughout his illness, until he could hobble about with a crutch, Jason was tended by Wipeki and he could not have found a more attentive nurse. At last he dismissed her because not only did she insist on examining him without his trousers daily, but began to bring in other squaws, who expressed their astonishment that what Wipeki said about the young man was true: his private parts were covered with hair as red as that on his head.

Croghan gave him back his rifle, somewhat reluctantly, Jason thought. But then the wily Irishman recovered part of his loss by setting Jason up to shoot in matches against freshly arrived traders from the west.

Even before he could discard his crutch, Jason began riding Haworth's horse. His leg was still splinted and he was so weak that he had to return to his bed after the first ride. But day by day, as his strength returned, he rode farther and farther.

By August the meadows and groves around Aughwick resembled Logstown itself. Those Delawares and Shawanese who still maintained their loyalty to the English, together with their Iroquois overseers, returned in droves to the Pennsylvania outpost to wait and see how the contest for the Ohio would go.

Jason was very nearly ready to undertake the hundred-mile ride to Lancaster and a reunion with Sallie Koch, when another important visitor came to Aughwick. He was Conrad Weiser, the German pietist who had acted for years as Pennsylvania's emissary to the Iroquois. He had been at a great conference with the Six Nations at Albany in New York, and there had helped win Iroquoian permission for white settlements north of the Kittatinny Mountain and west of the Susquehanna. A stocky, middle-aged man, with a large head and kindly eyes, he talked only briefly with Jason, for he was more interested in conferring with Croghan and others about this cession of new lands than in chatting with a twenty-year-old frontier lad. The Indians with whom Jason talked were less enthusiastic than Weiser about the new expansion of white settlements.

"Mingo sell the land from under the feet of Lenni Lenape again,"

Wipeki complained with tears in her eyes. "French man say land out there belongs to them. Brother Onas say land back here belong to white man. Where we go?"

"You have been kind, Wipeki," Jason replied. "You saved my life. Would you like to have the one-eyed mare I brought back?"

Her face brightened. "Mocquasaka, you are good." And she went away to tell her family of her good fortune, all thoughts of land driven from her mind.

George Croghan took time from his conversations with Weiser, Tanacharison and others to say goodbye to Jason. He accepted the offer of Christopher Cadwell's pack pony, but with far less apparent gratitude, it seemed to Jason, than Wipeki had shown.

"I wish ye good luck, McGee. I niver thought to see ye ride out of here alive. Come back when our troubles with the French are over and I'll give ye a good job."

5

It was well after sunup on a hot morning in early September, 1754, when Jason McGee rode south out of Aughwick. Beyond Shade Gap he had a choice of continuing due south and over the mountains via Traders Gap to Shippensburg, Carlisle and Harris's Ferry, or, if he preferred an easier trail, he could follow a longer, roundabout route that avoided the mountains except for a gap now called Croghan's after the trader himself. The latter trail had become popular with men leading long, heavily laden pack trains. Thinking he should stop and inform Maud McGinty of Cadwell's fate, Jason set out with the intention of taking the first route, since it led to Shippensburg.

Except when he mounted or dismounted or walked too far, his leg would not pain him much, Jason thought. Even with a makeshift saddle, riding Haworth's horse was easy. So with Logan trotting behind and his rifle slung over his shoulder, Jason rode along like a country squire, quickly covering the ten miles to Shade Gap, where he stopped to rest, and then another ten miles to where the trail to Shippensburg turned south and the New Path north. There, as he lolled beside the trail after eating his lunch, he heard first a woman's voice in the distance, rising shrilly from the trail to the south, and then the sounds of two sets of hoofs and the lower tones of a man's replies. Long before he could make out their words, Jason recognized the louder, shriller voice as that of Mrs. Pickering, the tavernkeeper's wife in Shippensburg. He got to his feet, leaning against his horse as he waited for them to come around a bend in the southward trail.

"You promised we'd not be more than one night on the trail, Sam Pickering," she was saying. "I'll hold you to your word. I do not intend to sleep on the ground again like a common squaw."

Pickering, red-faced and sweating, was leading an ancient horse whose back was piled high with blankets, pots, pans and other belongings, while he carried a small chest on his shoulder and his wife rode a nimble-footed mule. They stopped talking at the sight of the strange-looking red-haired youth beside the trail.

"Why, bless my soul, I wish you would look there, Mrs. Pickering. Do you recognize who that is?"

"Indeed I do. It is that young rapscallion you allowed to deprive us of a valuable mare."

They stopped a few feet away.

"Mister and Mrs. Pickering," Jason said, smiling in spite of himself. "What brings you into the wilderness?"

"Haven't you heard, lad? Pennsylvania has made a treaty with the Iroquois. This land is open to settlement now."

"I would not have taken you for the settler sort."

Mrs. Pickering spoke up. "Does he think we mean to cut down trees and plant corn? Explain to him that we intend to open a public house."

"And a store," her husband added.

"Yes, a store as well. For once we are not waiting until someone gets the jump on us. We will be established when the settlers start passing through."

"Indeed we will, my pet. In time we will be as rich as John Harris himself."

"Or George Croghan."

"What about your place in Shippensburg?"

"We sold it to a newly married couple as wants to use it for a home," Pickering replied. "Offered us more than we could refuse just after we got intelligence of this Indian treaty. Had to move quick, we did, did we not, my love?"

"Quick as a fox," Mrs. Pickering said. "By the bye, the young man might remember the woman as bought our establishment. 'Twas Maud McGinty. We directed him to her the day he defrauded us of our mare."

Jason frowned. "But she was to marry Christopher Cadwell."

307

"Hah! Surely the young man knew that one was supposed to come back in the spring to claim her hand, as he already had other parts of her person. He did not, and she accepted the proposal of a horse dealer. A man with five children and considerable lands. Ask the young man what happened to the fine Mister Cadwell."

Going into as little detail as he could, Jason told them of Cadwell's death. They shook their heads at the news.

"Mrs. McGinty did well not to wait for him, then, Mister Pickering. That widower would have married another woman if she had delayed another week. He was considered quite a catch."

"Yes," her husband said. "And we might not have sold our property. What about yourself, young man? You look older. And gaunt. Wouldn't have recognized you without your dog or that rifle. Wait. . . ."

He walked around Haworth's horse, wiping his face, his eyes narrowed appraisingly.

"Is this not the fine animal that Quaker gentleman from Philadelphia brought to our place last fall?"

"It is indeed." Jason went on to explain briefly about Haworth's death.

"Both your companions dead, alas. What will you do now?"

"First return to Lancaster County and marry the girl that waits for me there. Then I shall look about for an opportunity."

"I shouldn't worry about *his* future," Mrs. Pickering said archly. "I should only worry about those innocent persons with whom he may deal."

"What does she mean?"

Before his wife could say more, Pickering spoke. "Take no offense, young sir. Mrs. Pickering feels that you dealt rather closely with us in the matter of the one-eyed mare your father left to us."

"I can speak for myself, Mister Pickering. He took advantage of our situation. He and that Quaker person. Just because we did not have receipts and such, they made it appear we had stolen that horse from his father."

Jason's amusement gave way to irritation. "I don't care to discuss that with you."

"No, I don't expect that he does. But we are used to being taken advantage of. He is not the only person who has defrauded us. One must expect such when dealing with the public."

"Enough, dear Mrs. Pickering. Enough. Water over the dam. Are you headed for Shippensburg, Master McGee?"

"I was, but now I think I'll take the other route to Harris's Ferry."

308

"Back up this valley and out over Croghan's Gap? That is miles out of your way. Not carrying a load as you are, you'd save time going out the way we have just come."

"No. I have no business in Shippensburg. Not now. And I may have on the other path."

Jason shook hands with Pickering and bowed to Mrs. Pickering, who pretended she did not see the gesture. They rode away toward Aughwick. Jason could hear Mrs. Pickering's voice even after he had mounted and turned left onto the New Path to Croghan's Gap.

6

This so-called New Path actually ran north for twenty-five miles to a break in the mountains, where it doubled back and slanted up and over a low ridge. There Jason spent the night. The next morning he proceeded leisurely across a region of level forest land much cut up by streams, through country he knew well from having roamed over it with Isaac and Abraham.

He allowed the horse to go at its own pace, several times stopping to let the animal graze or drink. He did this partly to ease the strain on his mending leg and partly out of pity for poor Logan, who was taking the heat badly.

Late in the afternoon, at Sherman's Creek, he halted to rest, and seeing Logan plunge into the rocky stream's cool water, took off his clothes and swam with the dog. He and Isaac often had gone swimming in this very spot. Just downstream was one of their favorite fishing holes. Even the trees looked like old friends.

A curious feeling came upon him as he and the dog splashed about. It was as though he had remained in this area with his parents right into manhood. He imagined what it would be like if Abraham and Gerta still lived in the cabin and were waiting there for their son to return from the west. He thought how they would admire the splendid horse and beautiful rifle.

As if in a trance, he dressed himself and rode up the long slope toward the old homesite. He turned off the path, forcing the horse through the underbrush in the fading sunlight.

There stood the chimney, its base overgrown with vines. And Gerta's beloved vegetable patch now was dotted with young pines and cedars. He looked down at the place where the cabin door had been. Up there was the knoll and the great hickory tree where he had stood watching in frozen horror. Over there was where Isaac had tried to defend himself with a mattock. And here, under his horse's hoofs, was the very place where his mother . . .

He got off the horse and limped about the clearing until he found the stones with which he and Abraham had outlined the graves. A few feet away, one corner of the lean-to had collapsed from rot, but there was still shelter enough under the other end. Tying his horse to a sapling, he built a fire in front of the ruin and heated water for sassafras tea to wash down the food packed for him by Wipeki.

Afterward he stared into the fire until he fell asleep.

He awakened to the sound of Logan's whining. The fire had died out, and there was not even a glimmer of starlight to relieve the utter blackness of the night. The dog had never made such a peculiar noise. Jason put out his hand and felt him trembling.

"Hush, Logan. It is all right."

He drifted back to sleep and slept until dawn brought another stiflingly hot day to the old clearing.

Before he mounted the horse, Jason rummaged through the underbrush again and, to his amazement, uncovered the brass pot Abraham had flung away when he heard of the death of his wife and daughter. It had turned black with tarnish. Jason balled up his blanket and put it in the pot. Then he took his hatchet and went around the clearing, slashing the trees to show that this land had been occupied.

After that, he took the pot and mounted the horse. In a little while, he and Logan were back on the New Path, climbing toward Croghan's Gap and the east. From the top of the gap he could see many miles beyond the North Valley, dotted with the clearings of the Ulster Scots, to the hills on the other side of the Susquehanna, across the land of his father's people, very nearly to that of his mother's.

Jason sat for a long while astride his horse, staring out over the familiar landscape. The last time he had come over this gap had been with his father and their old horse in October of 1744. So much had happened in the last ten years, especially in the past eleven months. To think that just a year ago he had been working for Ernst Koch and gathering his courage to speak for Sallie's hand.

Logan seemed to know they were returning to their old haunts. He started along the trail down the south slope of the Kittatinny Ridge and turned to see what detained his master. At last he barked impatiently, breaking Jason's reverie. They began their descent.

7

The Susquehanna was low enough so that Jason had no difficulty fording the great river on horseback. Out of pity for the footsore Logan, he allowed the dog to climb upon the horse's back behind him. On the eastern shore, intent on reaching the Kochs' by night, he did not pause to pay his respects to the young John Harris. Although his leg had begun to ache again, and he had not eaten since his breakfast at the old home clearing, he pushed on.

Throughout the long, hot afternoon riding down the road to Lancaster, Jason passed several immigrant parties headed in the opposite direction, with all they possessed piled on oxcarts and their own backs.

His leg hurt more than ever now, but he would not stop to eat or to rest. There would be food and rest enough for him after he reached his Sallie. He pictured himself riding into the yard of the smithy. She would be hanging out clothes for her mother and, seeing him first, would come running out to throw her arms around his neck. Once again he would smell her fresh sweetness and feel her body against his. Then he would be home.

The sun was not yet down when he came in sight of the smithy and the house. Koch's hammer was still clanging away. Nothing seemed to have changed.

A stocky German lad looked out the smithy door to see who had ridden up. He spoke to Koch and the blacksmith came to ask what the rider wanted. Jason's teeth were clenched against the pain in his leg and he was weak from having gone so long without eating, but he felt a sense of triumph to be sitting on his fine horse and thinking what short work Pratt or Kiasutha or Meskikokant would have made of this slow ox in a real fight.

"Don't you recognize me?"

The smith put his hand over his eyes to shield them from the setting sun.

"Who?"

"It is Jason. Jason McGee."

"Chason?" He came out for a closer look.

Just then Logan, who had fallen behind, limped up to greet the smith.

"So you came back, you scoundrel. You run off and take my rifle and now you come back."

Jason unslung the gun and handed it down to him.

"You can have it back. I am through with it."

"Where you been?"

"I was in the west. Looking for my brother."

"You find him?"

"Yes."

"I don't see him."

"He is dead now."

"Dead? How?"

Jason had to cling to the makeshift saddle to keep his seat. He lacked the strength to get off the horse and he did not want to ask Koch for help.

"Never mind now. The important thing I have to tell you is that I killed the Indian that murdered my mother and sister and kidnapped my brother."

"So? You killed him? With my rifle, maybe?"

"Maybe. Where is Sallie?"

"Oh, Sallie. Well . . ."

Now Maria Koch was coming out her kitchen door, but before she could cross the yard, Katie came out and ran past her mother.

"Jason. Jason," she called.

"Where is Sallie?" Jason asked Koch again.

"You don't know about Sallie, eh?"

"She is not sick, is she?"

Katie ran up to the horse and took the reins. "Jason, you are home."

"Hello, Katie. Hello, Mrs. Koch."

"Ah, Chason. How is my boy? You don't look well, son. Get down off that horse and let us see you. You are just in time for supper."

"He was asking about Sallie, Mama," Koch said. "You want to tell him?"

"There will be time for that at supper."

"What about Sallie?" Their evasions made him feel panicky. He would have to ask for help to dismount and he could not do that until he knew.

"She is fine," Mrs. Koch said.

"Then where is she? I have been riding since early this morning so I could see her before dark."

Katie put her hand on his knee. "Jason, you might as well know and have it over with. Sallie was married last Christmas."

312

"Ja," Koch said. "And she expects a child now. Before Christmas."

"But she promised."

Their faces began to blur. Sweat was streaming down his face and the pain in his leg was becoming more than he could bear.

The horse, unused to so many people pressing around him, tossed his head and stepped away from them. The slight movement unseated Jason. The last thing he could remember was sliding toward the well-trodden earth of the smithy yard.

8

At Maria's insistence, Koch and his apprentice carried Jason to the house and put him upstairs in Sallie's old bed. When Jason came to, he felt numb, as though he were paralyzed. Maria coaxed him into eating a few spoonfuls of broth, but he refused to talk to them after he found that his stutter had returned.

He lay with frozen brain throughout the night, beyond tears or even thought. He simply could not believe that Sallie had not waited.

Surely in the morning the bedroom door would open and she would appear to welcome him home. He dozed a bit and awoke to the sound of footsteps on the stairs. For a moment his heart leaped in the hope that it might be Sallie after all, but the door opened and Katie walked in with a breakfast tray.

"Jason. You are awake."

"Y-yes."

"You feel better this morning? You slept well?"

"N-no."

"Are you hungry?"

"N-no."

She stood beside his bed, her level gray eyes frowning with concern. There was just enough family resemblance to Sallie to cause him anguish.

"When did you last eat?"

"Y-yesterday morning."

"How far did you ride?"

"From the other side of Croghan's Gap. Sixty miles, I suppose."

"So far without eating. That was not so smart. And your leg is hurt."

"Y-yes. I got sh-shot."

"You want to tell me about it?"

"N-no."

"You are not being very polite, you know. What is the matter with you?"

"S-Sallie. Why did she do it?"

"Jason. I tried to tell you that Sallie was a goose. She had her heart set on marrying somebody important. A new pastor came to our church, Christian Kleinpeter. He is nearly thirty. A man of education. They fell in love and got married."

"She promised to wait."

"But she did not and now she is happily married. You can sulk for the rest of your life but you can't change that. Now eat your breakfast or I will pour hot tea over your red head."

She smiled at him and tousled his hair. Then she set the tray on the bed and went downstairs.

Jason barely had the strength to feed himself. He ate a few bites of the bread and cheese, drank half a cup of tea and, drenched with sweat, lay back exhausted. Maria came up later, and seeing his condition, called for Katie to fetch a bowl of water and cloths. Together they drew off his shirt and bathed his upper body.

"Poor Chason. You are so weak. Katie says you were shot."

"Y-yes."

"And you don't want to tell us about it?"

"N-not really."

"Then we won't bother you. You sleep now. Come, Katie."

Refreshed by the bath and comforted by their attention, he did sleep, past noon. When he awoke, Katie was standing by his bed, her arms crossed. He looked up into her determined face.

"So you are awake."

"Y-yes."

"Jason McGee, you say you got shot. Papa says you told him you found your brother but he died. Papa says you said you killed the Indian that murdered your mother. Is that right?"

"Y-yes."

"Well, I want to hear about it. And I won't go away until you tell me."

"I don't w-want to t-talk about it."

She drew up a stool and sat down. "I will sit here until you tell me."

Jason could not help smiling. It struck him that although her face was longer and plainer than Sallie's, she had a prettier mouth and better eyes.

"So that night you took Papa's rifle and left. Where did you go first?"

"Harris's Ferry."

"And what did you do there?"

"I crossed the river in a boat that used to belong to me. I spent the night in a haystack and the next day walked to Carlisle."

Thus did she draw him out slowly. As he began to talk, his stutter disappeared. Her interest flattered him and he heard himself telling her about his encounter with the Pickerings and his meeting with Haworth and Cadwell. She would let him gloss over nothing, demanding that he go into detail.

By late afternoon, he had got only so far as his sojourn at Logstown. Maria interrupted to ask Katie to help prepare supper.

"I want to hear the rest of your story, Jason. I particularly want to know more about that Quaker man."

"If you can read English, look in my saddlebag and you will find a book. He wrote down part of what we did out there."

"Good. I'll get the book." She arose. "By the bye, where did that old brass pot you were carrying come from?"

"I'll tell you later."

Having talked so long, Jason was weary again, but he no longer felt so dejected. He lay awake a long while, planning just how he would relate the rest of his story to Katie.

9

He was disappointed when Maria, rather than Katie, brought him his supper.

"You look better, Chason. The rest is doing you good."

"Where is Katie?"

"In the kitchen, reading that book you gave her."

"She was supposed to come back and talk."

"You will have plenty of time to talk. You can stay as long as you like."

"I don't want to impose on you."

"Don't you fret about that. Eat before your supper gets cold."

After eating, he lay back and stared at the ceiling, waiting for Katie's footsteps on the stairs. It was well past dark and he had nearly despaired of her coming, when he heard her quick, light tread. She entered, carrying a candle in one hand and Haworth's journal in the other.

"You read it?"

"Right through to the end. Papa got mad at me for reading by candlelight, but I could not stop. What a lovely man is your Mister Haworth. I should like to meet him. Where is he now?"

"I don't know whether I can talk about that." But at her gentle urging, he did. He talked until Koch roared up the steps for Katie to come to bed. But she was back again in the morning with his breakfast, full of questions. Maria discreetly left them alone. Now and then Katie would ask a question to clarify a point or would make him go back and explain something in more detail, but in the main she merely listened. Never before had Jason spoken so long and so frankly to another person. By evening he had grown hoarse, but he had finished his story.

She sat with her hands in her lap, looking at him as though he were a new person.

Then she stood, bent down and kissed him. "I am glad you came back, Jason."

After she had gone, he thought of the one thing he had not told her, of the thing he would never speak of to any person. The possibility that Isaac might have taken scalps at Pixawillany was a secret he would take to his grave.

Katie was kept busy in the kitchen for the rest of the evening. Jason was tired from having talked so long and yet he felt better than he had for weeks. How good it was to have a sympathetic, intelligent person to talk to, someone who knew him well and who was truly interested in what he had to say. And how dense he had been not to have perceived that Katie had appeared plain only because he had always been blinded by Sallie's surface beauty.

After supper, Ernst Koch himself came up the stairs with heavy feet. He stood in the growing dark, embarrassed and awkward until he found his voice. "Chason, Katie has been telling us what you done out there. How you found your brother and how you caught that Indian. And how you tried to save the fort. That was something, what you done. What are you going to do now?"

"I'm not sure."

"I been talking with Maria. How about you stay here and go partners with me? I don't have enough time to work on my rifles. That's what I like to do. And this boy we got now is a dummkopf."

Jason took a long while to reply. "I could never be cooped up in a blacksmith shop after what I've been through. I am thinking of going back over the mountains to a certain piece of land."

Jason fell asleep quickly after the disgruntled Koch left. Just before he dropped off, he thought how stupid he had been ever to let the scorn of this dull man sting him so. Koch's approval or disapproval meant nothing to him now. He slept deeply, purged by his long talk with Katie.

Jason awoke after midnight, suddenly aware that someone was standing by his bed. "Who's there?"

"Sh-sh. Keep quiet or Papa will hear."

Katie sat on the side of his bed. "Jason. I got to know something. I can't sleep until you tell me."

"What is it?"

"You and that Indian girl. Did you do anything?"

"What a question."

"Yes, and let's hear what an answer you got for it."

"Katie, it is none of your business. I shall not tell you anything."

"I will not go away until you tell me. Pa will find me here in the morning and there will be hell to pay."

"I am not afraid of your pa. And I don't want you to go away, at least not just yet, so that's another reason for not telling you."

"You don't want me to go?"

"I said so, didn't I?"

Fully awake now, he threw back the cover and drew her down beside him. She resisted for a moment and then relaxed and lay on her side facing him, nightgown up about her knees.

"Jason, I should not do this, but I couldn't bear it lying there awake and thinking of you in here alone and wanting to talk to you." Her voice caught. "Oh, Jason, I love you so. . . ."

She began to weep softly and Jason put his arms about her. She was taller than either Sallie or Awilshahuak, with a supple strong body and firm breasts. She put her arms about his neck and laid her face against his chest.

"Stop crying. You are getting me wet."

"I don't care. I love you, Jason."

"Thank you, Katie. Now stop crying."

"I can't stop. You got to tell me about that Indian girl. You made love to her. I know you did. Tell the truth."

"It didn't mean anything."

"I bet it meant something to her."

"I suppose it did."

She was quiet for a while after that and they lay holding each other.

"Jason, Pa said he offered you the chance to stay here and be his partner and you said you won't do it. What will you do?"

"I haven't made up my mind. If I feel up to it, I may ride into Lancaster tomorrow to see about getting a license for the land where my family used to live."

"Is that what you want to do? Go take up land?"

"I don't know what I want anymore, Katie. Everything I set out to do a year ago turned out wrong. Instead of bringing my brother back, I killed him. Instead of marrying Sallie, I got nobody."

"That is what you think."

She kissed him on the mouth, clinging to his lips, until he felt himself stirring. He pulled her atop him and she lay there kissing his face and neck until, unable to bear the tension, he rolled her over on her back.

His experience with the Logstown squaw and Awilshahuak or even Sallie had been nothing like this with Katie. He marveled first at her passion and then at his own, considering his illness.

When it was over, they lay still joined, awed by the experience and reluctant to let each other go.

"So that is what it is like. I always wondered."

"Yes, Katie."

"Nobody ever told me it was so nice."

"It is something you have to find out for yourself."

"Thank you, Jason. I only wish you loved me the way I love you. I loved you the first time I laid eyes on you standing in our kitchen while your pa and mine talked about you as if you were a colt and not a human being. It made me so mad, the way Sallie took you for granted. I used to lie in bed wishing you were two years older or I were two years younger and that it was me you loved and not Sallie."

She wept again.

"Katie, two years older or younger makes no difference."

"Then you love me a little bit?"

"I do now, yes."

And with that, they made love again, gently but joyously.

10

Jason slept until midmorning and awoke feeling strong and full of hope. Maria was surprised to see him come down to the kitchen. Katie served him breakfast at the family table, but would not look at him or speak to him. However, when Maria went outside to feed the chickens, he drew Katie onto his lap and kissed her neck.

"Oh, Katie. Was that a dream last night?"

"If it was, we both had it."

They sat murmuring and kissing each other until, at the sound of Maria's approach, she hastily got up and began clearing the table.

As Jason started to leave the kitchen, Katie said, "Here is a paper I found in your saddlebag when I put back the journal. It says something about furs."

Jason was amazed to see that it was a receipt from Levy for six bales of assorted beaver and otter pelts, dated May 7, 1754, at Aughwick.

"Does it mean anything?" she asked.

"It may mean a great deal. I'll know soon."

Leaving Logan behind, Jason rode his horse into Lancaster, and after making inquiries, found his way to the sheds of Joseph Simon's trading post.

"Why, it is McGee."

MacDonald left the group of traders with whom he had been talking. "Ye are alive, after all. Ye pulled through. We were wondering about ye."

"Where is Mister Little?"

"Oh, he went off to Philadelphia. Intends to go into a different line of work. Never wants to go west again, the great tub of guts."

"And yourself?"

"I'm thinking of offering my military services to the Virginians. I have been in war and whether the Quakers of this province realize it or not, we are at war with France."

"And Mister Levy?"

"Ah, Levy, he will do whatever will make money."

"Speaking of money, I want to see the both of you."

"What for?"

"My furs."

"Your furs. Yes. Your furs."

"McGee. You are alive." Levy was coming out of the office building. "You pulled through."

"So he did," said MacDonald. "And instead of thanking us for saving his life, what do ye think is the first thing he asks me about, the ungrateful wretch?"

"What?"

"His furs. At least, he calls them his furs."

"Furs? What furs?"

"Now come on, you two. There were six bales of furs—the finest

319

otter and beaver. You brought them to Aughwick and you took them away with you. Look, I have your receipt."

Levy laughed. "Cool down, lad. Yes, that is my receipt."

"Well, where are they?"

"They have been sold."

"You had no right to do that."

"Indeed we did. You signed them over to us."

"Where are the proceeds?"

"Simon himself is holding the money. Brought a good price, they did, nearly fifty pounds. We were holding the money until we heard whether you lived or died. If we had not taken them with us, George Croghan might have cheated you."

"Yes, we thought that this way, if ye died, at least the furs would not end up in the wrong hands."

"You sound disappointed that I lived."

"Don't say such hard things to a fellow Scot, lad. Except for our modest fees for hauling them from the Juniata and the usual commission, the money shall all be yours. Right, Levy?"

"MacDonald speaks the truth for once," Levy said.

There was more money than Jason had imagined, even after deductions for Levy and MacDonald. After turning it over to him, they led him in triumph to the two-story brick Lancaster County Courthouse, where Jason became the center of an admiring circle of officials and onlookers. First he told them of his adventures in the west informally and, thanks to his practice with Katie, succinctly. Later they had him repeat the circumstances of the deaths of Cadwell, Isaac, Haworth and Meskikokant for an official report to be forwarded to Philadelphia. And that done, they drew up a license for the land he wanted.

The meeting adjourned to a local tavern, where Jason stood everyone to a dram of whiskey. MacDonald made an elaborate toast, calling him a true Scots hero, and getting so carried away in his enthusiasm that he paid for a second round. Levy added his praises.

"There is someone else I would like to honor," said Jason, unsteady on his feet from the unaccustomed drinking.

"Who may that be?"

"To the bravest man I have ever known, Ephraim Haworth, late of Philadelphia. No, put down your mugs and stand in silence in his memory. That is the way to honor him."

He broke the silence by saying, with raised mug, "And a final toast to Christopher Cadwell, who was a better and more courageous man than any of us realized."

After wringing a promise from the justice of the peace who had taken his deposition that he would notify the family of Ephraim Haworth of his death, Jason shook hands with everyone and said goodbye.

His head reeling from so much whiskey, Jason rode back in the dusk for the Koch home, to find the family just sitting down to supper. Not realizing how drunk he was, they insisted on his joining them.

Katie looked at him curiously, wondering why he was smiling in such a silly way.

"Have you been drinking?" she whispered.

"Just a little, Katie. Only a dram or two."

Jason, who had so often sat at this same table, as shy as the German apprentice they now employed, felt like a self-confident man purged of his hates and fears and with his pocketful of money.

Too self-absorbed to notice the mood of his guest, Koch leaned across the table when they had eaten. "So you think you are too good now to be a blacksmith, Chason. Just what will you be?"

"A landowner. A husband. A father."

"A squatter like your pa, maybe?"

"Not a squatter like my pa, and certainly not a blacksmith like yourself."

"How will you buy land? And you got nobody to work it with you."

"Don't concern yourself with my problems, Mister Koch. It is none of your business."

The smith's face darkened, but before he could respond, Jason continued. "I have killed two men. I have been through misery that would have broken you down. I am no longer a stripling who can be traded for a cast-off musket and a one-eyed mare. I don't want your advice or help, thank you just the same."

Jason was sorry that he had sat at the same table with this man. Yet he did not want to humiliate Katie, and so was grateful to Maria for ending the encounter by insisting that Jason return to his bed.

"You should not have got up so soon," she said, herding him out of the presence of her glowering husband. "Back to bed with you."

Jason awoke sober and alert a few hours later, and lay listening to the sound of Koch's snoring. He could not bear the thought of remaining under that man's roof for another day. He arose, dressed and, taking his belongings, tiptoed down the hall to Katie's room. She awoke quickly to his touch.

"You want in beside me?"

"No. I want you to get dressed. Take a bag of clothes and come away with me."

"Where to?"

"Just come. You will see."

"Whatever you say, Jason."

While he went outside to saddle the horse, she filled the brass pot, which he had given her, with food. When he reentered the kitchen, Maria was standing with a candle in her hand, her long, gray-streaked hair around her shoulders. She and Katie both were crying.

"So you are going to take my Katrinka away?"

"If she wants to go."

"I will miss her, but she is right for you, Jason. I always thought so."

"I know it too now."

"What will you do?"

He told them about the money and about marking his claim to the old family site.

"You will make my Katie happy? You promise?"

"I promise."

"You don't want to stay here awhile and get married in our church?"

"By Sallie's husband? No, thank you."

"But you will not just go off and not marry."

"Like my pa and ma? Don't worry. There is a Presbyterian pastor at Paxton who taught me to read and write. He will do the job."

Jason put his arm around Mrs. Koch and kissed her. The mother and daughter embraced, weeping.

Logan, anticipating another journey, was wagging his tail, eager to get started.

The first light of dawn was appearing as they went outside. Jason lifted Katie up to the horse's back, then mounted behind her.

"Wait once," Mrs. Koch said.

She was back in a moment with the rifle Jason had carried west.

"Take it as her dowry. Ernst would want you to have it, even though his pride would not let him say so."

Jason handed it back. "Katie doesn't need a dowry. I can buy another rifle."

"Here, give it to me." Katie took the gun. "I will use it if he forgets about the pastor. Tell Pa thanks. And tell the stubborn old bull I love him."

"When will we see you again?"

"When the first baby is due, we will send for you. We won't be that far away."

Logan, already standing in the road, barked impatiently. Jason jabbed his heels in the horse's ribs, and they set off toward the west.

322